SIGN
OF THE
CROSS

Glenn Cooper chairs a media company, Lascaux Media, which produced three independent feature-length films. His debut novel, *The Library of the Dead*, became an international bestseller and was translated into thirty languages. All of his seven published books have become top-ten international bestsellers.

@GlennCooper glenncooperbooks.com

SIGN
OF THE
CROSS

GLENN
COOPER

BLACKTHORN

First published in Great Britain, the USA and Canada in 2019
by Black Thorn, an imprint of Canongate Books Ltd,
14 High Street, Edinburgh EH1 1TE

Distributed in the USA by Publishers Group West and in Canada by
Publishers Group Canada

First published in 2018 by Severn House Publishers Ltd,
Eardley House, 4 Uxbridge Street, London W8 7SY

blackthornbooks.com

1

British Library Cataloguing in Publication Data
A catalogue record for this title is available on request from the British
Library

ISBN 978 1 78689 487 8

Typeset by Palimpsest Book Production Ltd, Falkirk,
Stirlingshire, Scotland

Printed and bound in Great Britain by Clays Ltd, Elcograf S.p.A.

ONE

The relentless Jerusalem sun had baked the earth hard as stone. Despite the midday heat, the leather-skinned laborers swinging heavy picks dared not break their cadence. The lady was close by, watching their every move, listening to the musical pings of iron striking the hard concretion.

She sat, shaded by her tent, on a flattened mound of detritus overlooking the excavation. Unsmiling Roman soldiers stood guard at each corner of the open-sided enclosure. These men and their comrades, who encircled the site with a ring of steel, were no ordinary legionnaires, but an elite cohort of centurions chosen by the emperor himself. It was not as if there were specific threats against the lady's person or even a general sense of menace. In truth, most of the people of Jerusalem were supportive of her actions and appreciative of her generosity to the poor. But there was no room for a cavalier error. One malcontent with a sling could have wrought disaster. This was the emperor's mother, an empress in her own right.

Flavia Iulia Helena Augusta.

The tavern girl who was consort to an emperor, Constantius Chlorus, and birthed a greater one, whom history would come to know as Constantine the Great. The man who defied centuries of Roman tradition, sweeping aside the gods and embracing Christianity.

If Constantine did the sweeping, then Helena was the broom.

So enamored was she with this young Christian religion, that at the age of near-eighty – when most noble women in extreme dotage were being carried from room to room in comfortable Roman villas – spry Helena was making pilgrimages to distant lands in search of the relics of Christ.

Arriving in the holy city of Jerusalem with her entourage, she astonished the ordinary populace by walking among them in

their markets and churches, asking what they had learned
from their ancestors about the location of Christ's tomb and
Golgotha: the site of his crucifixion. The oral history was strong.
Three hundred years in a land so ancient and rich in storytellers
was but a grain of time. Now, two years into her expedition, the
end was in sight and Helena's success was staggering. She had
churches built on the site in Bethlehem, which she deemed to
be that of Christ's birth, and on the Mount of Olives, the place
of his ascension. These discoveries were but a trifle compared
with the enormous task at Calvary: the site most often mentioned
by locals as Jesus's burial place. Two hundred years earlier,
Emperor Hadrian had undertaken a reconstruction of Jerusalem
following the violent and destructive Jewish revolts. At Calvary,
he covered the mound with earth and erected a large temple to
Venus and it had fallen to Helena to take that building down,
block by block.

The venerated Bishop Macarius of Jerusalem was Helena's
constant companion, spiritual advisor and it was he who had
chosen the spot for excavation, once the ground was laid bare.
A team of pick and shovel men (Syrians and Greeks for the most
part) led by the foreman, an unctuous Syrian named Safar, had
soon found an old, Jewish-style rock-cut tomb. Safar helped
Macarius descend a ladder into the excavation pit and when the
old bishop returned to Helena's side he tearfully proclaimed it
to be the Savior's very tomb. Weeks later, at a nearby location,
the diggers unearthed three sets of decayed and petrified timbers.
Lifted from the pit and laid out for Helena's inspection, she and
Macarius joyfully declared them to be the crosses of Christ
and the two thieves. But which one was Christ's?

Macarius proposed a solution to the vexing problem.

Pieces of each cross were taken to the bedside of a cachectic
woman dying from tumors in her belly. Firstly, one piece of
wood was placed in her hand. Nothing happened. Likewise a
second piece had no effect. But the third piece was miraculous.
Clutching the splinter, her color went from yellow to pink and
the swelling of her belly receded. She sat up, the first time she
had been able to do so in ages and smiled.

They had found the True Cross.

Now Helena had one final quest before she could bundle up

her relics and journey back to Rome. She sent the diggers back into the pit to find the nails of the crucifixion.

'Will there be three or four?' she asked Macarius.

The bishop sat beside her in the tent. 'I cannot say, my lady. Some executioners preferred a separate spike for each ankle. Others speared both ankles with a single one.'

'I do wish they would hurry,' she said. 'I am an old woman.'

The bishop dutifully laughed. He had heard her say the same countless times.

Down in the pit and hidden from view, Safar watched his men scrape away at the earth beneath the spot where they had found the True Cross. His keen eye spotted something. He pushed the nearest man aside and continued the task with his handpick. Digging on his knees he exposed a large spike, black with oxidation. It was as long as a man's hand, quadrangular, with an intact, flat head. He was about to pull it out when his eye settled on a black dot a short distance away and soon he had exposed a second nail, this one shorter, with a broken tip. Then a man several feet away called out to him in Syrian. He had unearthed another nail and while Safar was cleaning along the shaft he noticed yet another trace of black. Soon four nails were exposed. The last one was missing half its head, apparently sheared off in its insertion or removal from the cross.

'The lady will be pleased, no?' the worker said to Safar.

'I am sure she will be most pleased,' Safar said, looking up at the pale sky. 'Her work is done. She will leave us now.'

'Will she give us coins?' the worker asked.

'She will give me a bag of coins and if you keep your mouth shut then I will give you a nice share.'

'Keep my mouth shut about what?'

'She will receive three nails only.'

'What of the fourth?'

'That one is mine,' he said, pointing to the last found, the one with the broken head. 'I have long endured laboring under the yolk of a woman.'

'She is an empress.'

'She is still a woman. This is my reward for the indignity. Besides, it is broken and she will accuse us of causing the damage. I will sell the relic. If you talk, you will die poor.'

Safar used his pick to loosen the dirt around the fourth nail, until he could pry it out. He greedily closed his fingers around it to feel its heft but he loosened his grip at once. There was a tingling sensation in his wrist, a slightly unpleasant warmth, and he quickly shoved the nail into the front pocket of his robe.

The other worker climbed from the pit and ran over to Helena's tent.

'Safar has found the nails, your majesty!' he declared.

Helena's wrinkled face lit up at the news. 'How many?' she asked, as Safar approached. 'Three or four?'

Safar gave her a gap-toothed grin. 'Three, your majesty. Only three.'

TWO

Asunción, Paraguay, 1955

He was a sensitive eleven-year old, prone to flinching when his father was beastly which only made the towering figure angrier.

'Be a man, goddamn it! Don't whimper!'

His father was like a volcano. When the pressure inside him redlined, he would erupt. Otto Schneider's isolation was so complete that there was no one on the receiving end other than his wife and son. But for every ten times his father threatened young Lambret for some real or imagined transgression, he smacked him only once. This restraint quotient of ten to one was so uncannily accurate, young Lambret would know when it was time for a bruise and steel himself. His mother couldn't bear corporal punishment, so when it was imminent she would flee the room in tears and come back when it was over to offer kisses and a piece of tea cake. And when she was the recipient of an open hand or worse, the boy would emulate her kindness and bring his mother sweets.

'I hate him.'

'He doesn't mean it, Lambret. You must love him. He's under a lot of strain. He was a general, a big man. Now he's, well, he's your father. We must understand.'

The boy wasn't enrolled in school. His father refused to allow him to learn Spanish, which he considered a degenerate language, and the fewer people who knew that the family in the modest house were German, the better. His mother had been a language teacher back home and she was the one who dealt with the world outside their garden gate. She homeschooled Lambret six days a week, five hours a day, longer if his father thought he was having it too easy. He received a steady diet of Latin and Greek along with German literature and culture. The only subject in which Otto took an interest was history. The trials and tribulations of the Aryan race were particularly important to him. The boy needed to know the truth, not Zionist propaganda and claptrap. The boy had been born in Berlin in late 1944, as the war effort was going from bad to worse. Otto had named him Lambret, meaning 'light of the land' in old German, a ridiculously optimistic gesture given the darkness descending on Deutschland. There was a photo kept locked in his father's study desk of Himmler planting a kiss on baby Lambret's cheek.

That desk was the source of endless fascination. Over their years in the house, the boy had seen his father unlock the desk drawers and examine all manner of wonderful artifacts. When he'd ask about them he was always angrily rebuffed, until the time his father finally told him that one day all the treasures in the desk would be his.

'When?'

'When I'm dead.'

'When will that be?'

'Soon enough, if the bastards have their way.'

Lambret didn't know who these bastards were but he quietly rooted for them.

Of late, when his father napped in the afternoons and his mother prepared supper, the boy began to surrender to his curiosity about the contents of the big desk and made forays into the study to look for the drawer key. It was a large room with many possible hiding places. There were hundreds of books, ashtrays, pipe racks, regimental and decorative beer steins, and bric-a-brac. It was even possible that the key was always on his father's person. But Lambret was not deterred. He would spend no more than five minutes a day on the furtive search. The consequences of being discovered rummaging in the forbidden room were too great to contemplate.

Lambret tried again. Glancing repeatedly at the pendulum clock on the study mantelpiece, so as not to lose track of time, the boy looked inside and under every beer stein although he had covered this ground before. A neighbor's dog barked. The pendulum clock chimed once for the half hour. It occurred to him that he'd never inspected the clock. Pulling a chair over, he climbed up and carefully lifted the glass-domed clock down and rested it on the desk. There was writing on the brass base: an honorific inscription to his father from his regiment and a swastika inlaid with small ruby-red stones. He raised the clock to have a look underneath and there it was! The desk key held in a leather loop.

The dog barked again.

Trembling, the boy took the key and inserted it into the keyhole in the top drawer. Turning it, he heard a satisfying clunk as the mechanism unlocked the side drawers. In the distance he heard his mother placing a heavy pot on the stove. Half his exploration time remained. He went straight for the lowest drawer on the right. The one he had long ago seen his father remove an artifact from which, to this day, fevered his imagination. Inside was a single long object wrapped in blue velvet.

It was heavy.

He sat in his father's chair, placed it on the desk and slowly unwrapped it.

It was just as he remembered.

The spearhead was two-feet long from its sharp tip to its empty socket. At its widest it was two inches across. The steel was dark, almost black. He was transfixed by its weight and embellishments. A thin sheath of beaten gold, so shiny it hurt his eyes, was wrapped around the midsection of the blade. Above the golden sheath, a thin, black spike was occupying a central cavity cut into the steel. It was held in place with four separate coils of tightly wrapped silver wire. The spear seemed the embodiment of physical strength and, as the boy cradled it in his small hands, he could almost feel its destructive power.

'What are you doing?'

Lambret almost dropped the weapon.

His father was standing at the door in his stockinged feet.

'I'm sorry,' the boy stammered.

'You know you're going to be severely punished, don't you?'

Lambret knew he was due for a beating and by rights it was going to be a bad one. But there was a disconnect. His father seemed entirely too calm for the circumstance and that unnerved the boy further.

The boy's mouth was so dry the words almost didn't come out. 'I know.'

'I heard the dog bark,' his father said absently. He stepped into the room. For a fleeting moment Lambret considered defending himself with the object in his hands. 'Do you know what it is?'

'A spear?'

'A lance, actually. The head of a Roman lance. It's a replica. Do you know what that means?'

'That it's not real?'

'It's real enough. It means it's not the original, but it's still quite special. It's a replica of the Lance of Longinus, also called the Spear of Destiny by some. Ever heard of it?'

The boy shook his head.

'Longinus was the Roman soldier who used his lance to finish off Jesus when he was on the cross. Christians say the lance is holy.'

'Is it?'

'I don't know about that, but it possesses certain powers. The real one, that is.'

Lambret was emboldened by the fluidity of the conversation. Usually, a quick volley of shouts and curses preceded a punishment. 'Where did you get it?'

'It was given to me in the last days of the war by Heinrich Himmler himself. You do know who he was, don't you?'

'Yes.'

'Himmler had the real Holy Lance but it was too valuable to show off, so he had this replica made by a famous Japanese sword maker, who came to Germany all the way from Kyoto.

At the end of the war, Himmler gave it to me for my service to the Reich. It was a proud moment.'

'Where's the real one?'

'Ah, I will have that conversation with you when you are a good deal older. I have high hopes for you, Lambret. I intend for you to live up to your name and restore light and hope to our crippled Fatherland. I believe it is your destiny to one day find . . .'

There was a short scream from the kitchen. Hearing his mother's cry, the boy dropped the spearhead onto the rug.

Otto Schneider ran to the study window and parted the curtain. A black sedan was idling at the curb.

Lambret heard heavy footsteps beating down the hall.

His father spat out the words, 'Israeli swine. It's finally happened,' and covered the distance from the window to the desk in two strides. He opened the center drawer and grabbed a small black pistol, the same Walther model that Hitler had used on himself. Lambret saw him raise the gun to his temple.

'Papa?'

'Don't look away!' his father shouted. 'I will not have you look away! This will make you into a man!'

The study door flung open and an intruder yelled, 'Don't!'

Lambret did as he was told and watched his father blow out his brains.

THREE

Abruzzo, Italy, present day

The young priest, Giovanni Berardino, awoke from his afternoon nap damp with sweat. The shutters were closed and his room was dark and uncomfortably warm despite the whirring table fan. Even the simple act of switching on his bedside lamp had become difficult. He had already taught himself how to get out of bed without using his hands by throwing his legs down with speed and using the momentum to stand. Once upright, he hesitantly inspected his gauze-wrapped wrists. They were stained through with fresh blood. Choking back tears, he gingerly placed his palms together and bowed his head in prayer.

The painful bleeding had begun a month earlier. So far, he had been able to hide it from his new parishioners in the medieval hill town of Monte Sulla, but he feared he would be found out and compelled to see a physician. Already the nuns and a few parishioners had noticed that the jovial disposition he'd displayed on his arrival had turned sour and tongues were wagging. Was he upset about something? Was he facing the self-doubts that plague many a young man in the early days of priesthood? Or was there something about his new brothers and sisters that displeased him?

The priest's house was directly across the piazza from the ancient church of Santa Croce. His small room had an en suite bathroom and there, after donning his black trousers, he slowly unwrapped the gauze. He didn't like to look at the wounds. They were deep and bloody, the diameter of a two euro coin. He applied some ointment and rewrapped them with the last of his fresh gauze. He would have to get more at the pharmacy that afternoon. The pharmacist had made a light comment about his need for so many bandages: 'Are you making a mummy, padre?' He dreaded the scrutiny but what was he to do? He couldn't ask Sister Theresa or Sister Vera to make the purchase for him.

Despite the heat, he had been forced to eschew his short-sleeved, black clerical shirts in favor of long-sleeved ones. He slipped one over his undershirt and began the slow, difficult task of buttoning it. When he was done, he flinched as he slid the plastic Roman collar into the tab on his shirt.

The vision began as suddenly and unexpectedly as always. Since the wounds had appeared, not a day had passed without at least one. This was his second since breakfast. He had come to welcome these interludes for so many reasons, one of which was the remission of pain that accompanied them. He closed his eyes tightly and let his arms fall to his sides, letting the vision wash over him, through him.

His face softened and he spoke. 'Yes, yes, yes, yes.'

At the exact same time, Irene Berardino was shopping in the city center of Francavilla al Mare some ninety kilometers to the east of Monte Sulla on the Adriatic coast.

Lugging a heavy, nylon shopping bag she traded the air-conditioned supermarket for the steamy humidity of Viale Nettuno. She began heading toward the apartment she shared with her mother, when she stopped dead in her tracks to stare at the man walking into a shop. At first she thought the abrupt temperature change was playing tricks on her mind, but it took little time to conclude her eyes weren't deceiving her.

No one else looked like her brother and this was his favorite gelato café.

He was easy to spot being over six-feet tall, roly-poly, having short black hair with a widow's peak and long retro sideburns. Then there were his feet, so large he used to be teased for them. 'What are those, shoes or rowboats?' the children used to cry. And of course, there was his clerical collar.

'Giovanni?' she shouted as the door closed behind him.

She rushed down the street and peered through the window of the shop. The owner was behind the counter scooping chocolate chip gelato into plastic cups for a mother and her two young children. She couldn't see Giovanni.

She pushed the door open and went inside.

'Excuse me?' she asked. 'Where did the priest go?'

'What priest?' the owner asked.

'The one who just came in.'

'I didn't see any priest.'

'I'm sorry,' Irene said, 'I just saw him go inside.'

The mother stared over her glasses at the young woman. 'No one came in,' she said.

'That's impossible,' Irene said. 'Is there a toilet or a back door?'

'Only behind the counter,' the owner said, becoming irritated. 'No one came in. Now, do you want a gelato or do you want to leave?'

FOUR

H is opponent was twenty-five years younger than him; a standout at the Harvard Boxing Club, where most of the members had never put on a pair of gloves before joining. The kid, a senior from Louisiana, was the exception. He'd done a couple of years of Junior Golden Gloves in high school and was the club captain.

Cal Donovan had sparred with him before but not for a while. It had been a busy year. With his heavy course load and writing and speaking commitments, Cal's gym time had suffered.

Climbing into the ring, the kid called out to him, 'Haven't seen you around lately.'

'I've been training in secret,' Cal said, pounding his gloves together.

The boxing ring had been erected under an open-air tent on the university Science Center Plaza. It was the club's annual Fight Night and curious students wandered into the tent, grabbed seats and, as the warm evening progressed, got into the hooting and hollering required of the occasion.

The club was an athletic oddity in that it drew its membership from both students and faculty, though in recent years Cal had been the only faculty member. The first time he'd boxed was during his brief stint in the army, before concluding that maybe college wasn't such a bad idea after all. Over the years he'd used the sport as a way to blow off steam but not everyone, including his young corner man, thought it was a great idea.

Joe Murphy had a fresh-off-the plane Irish accent, pure Galway.

'Look at the size of him,' he said, watching the kid dance and do a flurry of air punches. 'He's quick too. I think you should forfeit.'

'You ought to be a motivational speaker,' Cal said. 'Do something useful and smear on some Vaseline.'

'On where?'

'My eyebrows, Joe. You ever seen a fight before?'

'Not one. How's he going to get to your eyebrows through the headgear?'

'You'd be surprised.'

Murphy performed the task, climbed out of the ring and picked up a towel.

'What are you doing with that?' Cal asked.

'Getting ready to concede. A towel is the sign, is it not?'

The announcer, a Harvard athletic department trainer who served as club coach, took to the microphone.

'All right, ladies and gentlemen, this is the last fight on our card, the 178-pound heavyweight class. Wearing crimson trunks, hailing from Baton Rouge let's hear it for club captain and senior Jason 'Kid Bayou' Moran!'

There was a spirited roar from a contingent of Moran's Adams House buddies.

'And in blue trunks, most definitely our most unusual club member, hailing from Cambridge, please give it up for Calvin 'The Reaper' Donovan, professor of the history of religion and archaeology at the Harvard Divinity School! How about that for a mouthful?'

Cal didn't have a following. He received some polite applause but one woman seated a few rows back shouted, 'Way to go, Cal!'

Cal turned to her and performed a deep bow.

She was with another woman who said to her, 'You know him?'

'Oh yeah, I know him.'

The second woman pressed on, 'Know him or *know* him?'

'Both actually. We were an item a few years ago.'

'Past tense. Past tense is good. He's gorgeous. Is he unattached?'

'Far as I know but things are always fluid with Cal.'

'How old is he?'

'I don't know, about forty-five.'

'Most guys I know that age look like bowling pins. You could play those abs like a washboard. Will you introduce me?'

'On one condition.'

'What?'

'Promise you won't hate me for it later.'

After Cal and Jason were given instructions by the ref, the kid pushed his mouth guard halfway out with his tongue and said, 'I see you've got a priest in your corner. Perfect.' Then he expertly sucked the mouth guard back into place.

Cal worried that if he tried the same maneuver he'd lose the mouth guard to the mat so he only smiled and grunted. Back in his corner, Father Murphy called out to him, 'Stay away from his left and while you're at it, stay away from his right too.'

At the bell, the kid came out fast and waited for Cal to amble to the center of the ring. Here he was met with a flurry of left jabs, half of them connecting to his face. Cal's headgear absorbed the blows painlessly, but the same couldn't be said for the straight right to his jaw. He felt that one all the way down to the soles of his feet.

He backed up but the kid followed, sticking his left in Cal's face and measuring him for another right.

Cal figured it was time to stop being the kid's speed bag, so he tried a quick left-right combination, but got tangled in Jason's size-thirteen shoes and hit the mat hip first.

'It's a slip!' the ref shouted, pushing the kid away while Cal picked himself up.

'Why the hell didn't you stay down?' Murphy yelled.

It was impossible to give the priest the finger from inside a boxing glove. When the fight resumed, Cal took several more blows to the head and only managed to land one crisp uppercut as the kid was leaning in on him. It caught him in the forehead but didn't seem to slow him down. Puffing from exertion, Cal figured he'd run out the clock on the round and try not to get hit again but Jason wasn't going to let him off the hook. He kept on steamrolling, launching effective combinations to his face with his superior reach. Cal was starting to feel fuzzy-headed. He could either go down or try something else. The kid's head was too far away but his belly was in range. He went for Jason's middle and landed a solid right hook just as the bell rang.

Murphy was waiting for him in the corner with a stool, a water bottle and a spit bucket.

'To be honest, I can't bear to watch this,' he said, squirting water into Cal's mouth. 'I had no idea it would be so violent.'

'You didn't know boxing was violent?' Cal panted.

'Never thought the college variety was, I suppose.'

'Do you see that?' Cal asked, looking toward the opposite corner.

'See what?'

'He's rubbing his stomach. I think I hurt him. He felt kind of soft down there. He's probably sliding like seniors do, drinking beer and eating too much bread and pasta.'

'Would you stop referring to my diet in such a derogatory way?'

'I'm going to try something. If it doesn't work I'll need a ride over to Cambridge City Hospital.'

Murphy's clerical collar had gone askew, he adjusted it. 'I had no idea how varied my duties would be as your graduate student.'

When the bell sounded for the second round, he let the kid come to him. Cal struck a purely defensive posture: bending sharply at the waist, raising his gloves to his face and using his arms and elbows to protect his midsection. His opponent took the bait and got in close, firing a blizzard of uppercuts into Cal's gloves, trying to part them and get to his face.

Cal absorbed the blows on his gloves for a good thirty seconds, until he sensed the kid was losing steam. Then, as the young man dropped his right hand low to try to get more oomph on an uppercut, Cal pounced, sending his own right hand in a lightning roundhouse to the gut.

The kid grunted and momentarily let both hands go slack. Cal followed up with a left to the same spot and a mighty right and another left. The kid grunted again and backed away with a glassy expression so Cal didn't pursue him. Before the ref could react, out popped the kid's mouth guard, followed by his lunch.

The Adams House clan began hurling abuse at their boy and tossing crumpled program sheets into the ring.

That's when the ref jumped in and stopped the fight, raising Cal's arm in victory. Cal went over to the kid and put his arm around his drooping shoulders.

'Good fight, Jason. I'm glad you're graduating so you won't have a chance at a revenge match.'

Murphy climbed into the ring and congratulated his mentor. 'Fine job, professor. You're a credit to this exceedingly troubling sport.'

Cal gestured toward the mess at the center of the ring. 'I told you the kid was eating too much pasta.'

Cal was unwrapping his hands on a front-row seat when the two women came over.

'Very impressive, Cal.' His ex-girlfriend was an assistant professor in anthropology.

He smiled up at her. 'Hey, Cary. I got lucky.'

'That's you. One lucky guy. I'd like you to meet a friend of mine. Deborah has just joined the faculty in the chemistry department.'

'Hi!' Deborah said with a bouncy enthusiasm.

'Well, my job here is done,' Cary said, waving off. 'I'll leave you two alone.'

'Is this some kind of a setup?' Cal asked, continuing to remove his competition wraps.

'Something like that. I'm new in town. Got to be a little aggressive to meet interesting people.'

She was a bit too all-American and wholesome for his tastes but he liked her spunk. 'Well, I don't know much about the chemistry department but I can definitely give you some generic academic survival tips. Lunch tomorrow, faculty club?'

'Where's the faculty club?'

'You are a newbie, aren't you? I'll pick you up in front of the Mallinckrodt Labs at noon.'

The luncheon at the faculty club, a light-filled room of understated elegance, was buffet. When Cal and Deborah filled their plates, they returned to their table for two by a window.

The waiter offered a wine selection but she told him she didn't drink.

'I do,' Cal said, ordering a white.

'Cary told me you like to knock them back.'

'What else did she tell you?'

'That she broke off with you, not vice versa.'

'So far she's an accurate witness to history.'

'I didn't ask her too many questions,' she said. 'I prefer figuring out people for myself.'

'Admirable.'

'I did look you up, though. Just factual stuff.'

'No criminal background check?'

'You need a social security number for that.'

'And what did you unearth?'

'Nothing that would surprise you. One of the youngest tenured professors in the history of Harvard . . .'

'Fifteenth youngest, but who's counting? If I hadn't wasted two years in the army I might have been eleventh.'

'Your history of religion course is one of the most popular at the university.'

'I'm an easy grader.'

'You've got over twenty books and three hundred papers published.'

'An idle brain is the devil's workshop.'

'You're quick with the comeback.'

'Was that on my Wikipedia page?'

'No, personal observation. Why the army, if you don't mind my asking?'

'The rebellious act of an eighteen-year old. I had, shall we say, an interesting upbringing. My parents had an open marriage and, lest you think it was bohemian and sophisticated, for me it was a mess with all sorts of weirdos weaving in and out of our lives, interfering with domestic tranquility. My father was Walter Donovan, eighth youngest full professor at Harvard, mainline Boston Irish Catholic. My mother was Jewish, hailing from the Upper East Side of Manhattan. He got dibs on my last name. She got to pick my middle name, Abraham. In a rare act of compromise they chose an arch-Protestant first name, Calvin.'

'Cary told me that your initials, CAD, said it all.'

'That's not an original observation.'

'How'd you get out of the army after only two years?'

'Long story but I punched my sergeant. Should have been a dishonorable discharge but my father got our senator to do his magic. Harvard took me anyway, again, because of my father. Anyway, enough about me. Do you hang out at a lot of boxing matches?'

'It was my first one. Cary thought it would be interesting.'

'Was it?'

'I'd say so.'

She was a newly-minted assistant professor who'd done most

of her training at Penn. The end of the academic year was approaching and she was planning to use the summer to set up her lab and work on the syllabus for the first course she'd be teaching in the fall. She was a tenure-track hire with a million questions about the university tenure process. She skipped dessert; he had a heaping portion of bread pudding. When they finished their coffees he told her he had to get back to the office.

'This was fun,' she said.

He agreed.

'Are you going to be around this summer?'

'For some of it. I usually do field work but I've got a book deadline. I'll do my usual month in Rome at a minimum.'

'Sounds wonderful.' She took out a business card from her purse and wrote her number on the back. 'If you're around and want to get a drink sometime,' she said.

He slipped it into a sports coat pocket with a sly smile. 'Thought you didn't drink.'

'Cary warned me that if I started seeing you, I'd probably start.'

Divinity Hall was the oldest Harvard building outside the cloistered Harvard Yard. Built in 1826, its plain, redbrick façade was a testament to Protestant understatement. In his history of the Divinity School, George Huntston Williams had written that theological students needed to be housed apart from the undergraduates in case they drink up 'more of the spirit of the University than of the spirit of their profession.' As for Cal, it was ideally placed. He had only to skip down its granite steps and cross Divinity Avenue to enter his second home, the Peabody Museum of Archaeology and Ethnology.

His office was exceedingly tidy. Books that couldn't be accommodated on shelves were stacked vertically in precise piles on his desk and side tables. A laptop computer on his desk was open to the chapter in progress of his new book on St Thomas Aquinas, the cursor blinking at the word, God. Boxes of file cards with his research notes were arranged on the floor. Cal was meticulous in his record keeping. His note-taking techniques were a throwback to the pre-computer age of fountain pen jottings on 3X5 cards. When it was time to write a book, cards were shuffled and arranged and a chapter emerged. It was the way he'd watched his father do research and to this day he still used his father's old Montblanc pens.

Father Murphy sat across from Cal for his weekly thesis review, a good-natured grilling intended to keep the young priest on track to finish his PhD dissertation the following year. His topic was an examination of the scholarship of Pope Gregory I, one of the earliest chroniclers of St Benedict. Poring over a printout of Murphy's latest section, Cal was taking him to task on a Latin translation of one of Gregory's surviving papal letters.

'I think you're shading the meaning of this to suit your thesis,' he scolded.

'I don't think I am, actually,' Murphy said, defensively, before admitting that perhaps he was doing exactly that.

One of the department secretaries knocked on Cal's door.

'I'm in a meeting,' Cal said.

The woman seemed flustered. 'I'm sorry, professor, but it's the cardinal.'

'Which one? There are two hundred and nineteen of them.'

'Cardinal Da Silva.'

The cardinal of Boston was an old friend of Cal's and Murphy gathered his papers in awareness that he was about to be bumped. Cal looked at his desk phone. None of the lines were blinking.

'Well, we can't keep him waiting,' Cal said. 'Put his call through.'

'He's not on the phone,' she said, 'he's here. He said he's sorry to barge in but it's urgent.'

Murphy said, 'I was just leaving.'

'Don't you want to meet him?' Cal asked.

'I'll just do a quick bow on my way out. That will suffice.'

'You'll never make bishop with that attitude.'

'Not on my bucket list.'

The cardinal flew in and warmly greeted Cal with a bracing shoulder clasp. He was short and rotund. His flowing black simar and scarlet sash, formed the perfect garment to cloak his love of eating. He was crowned by a scarlet zucchetto, molded perfectly to the dome of his large bald head.

'Good of you to see me on zero notice,' he said, taking the chair, its cushion still warm from Murphy.

'Minha casa é sua casa,' Cal said. His Portuguese accent was poor but the cardinal appreciated the effort.

'Is there anything you don't know?' the cardinal cried.

'I am ignorant about more things than I care to admit,' Cal said. 'How can I help you today?'

'Well, I don't make a habit of arriving in people's offices uninvited, especially someone as busy as yourself. But I happened to be in Cambridge today and I also happened to have an urgent piece of business to discuss with you.'

Cal had first met Da Silva years earlier, when he was the bishop of the heavily Portuguese city of Fall River. They appeared on a panel debating the church's position on women and the liturgy, amiably clashed on stage and had become fast friends from that point on. Cal was at his side when he was elevated to archbishop of the Boston archdiocese and accompanied him to Rome when Da Silva received his red hat from the pope.

'What was it that brought you to our fair city?' Cal said.

'A sad occasion. A dear parishioner is in the hospital on death's door. He's from my own village in the Azores. It gave the family comfort to have me personally deliver last rights.'

'That was good of you.'

'As I was preparing to leave my office, the Holy Father telephoned. He rarely rings me directly so I knew it must be something important. It concerned you.'

Cal blinked in shock. 'Me?'

'Yes, he specifically requested your help in a delicate matter.'

'I wasn't aware he knew of me. We've never met.'

'He's quite well read, you know. An intellectually curious man.' The cardinal pushed himself from the chair and placed his index finger on a spine in the bookcase. 'This is the reason he wants you.'

The book was one of Cal's, *Holy Wounds, A History of Stigmata from the Middle Ages to the Present*.

'He's read it?' Cal asked incredulously.

'Apparently so. He sang its praises. Says he found it quite balanced and sensitive. He asked me for help contacting you and was delighted to hear that I not only knew you but that we were friends.'

'I'm flattered and I'm listening.'

'Have you heard the story of the young Italian priest who claims to have stigmata on his wrists?'

'Giovanni Berardino. Of course.'

Da Silva clapped his pudgy hands. 'See, you do know everything.'

'His case is in my wheelhouse. I've got a folder somewhere of Italian newspaper stories. If I ever update the stigmata book I'll need to do some work on him. Why is this a papal issue?'

'In the few months since his stigmata became public knowledge, pilgrims and tourists have flocked to this priest's small town. Apparently the situation has rapidly gotten completely out of hand. Ordinary parishioners can't get a seat at Mass. The local police and town officials are overwhelmed by the crowds, particularly on Sundays, and the Vatican is being bombarded by journalists who want to know the position of the Church on the matter.'

'I would have thought the Church would do what it always does in these situations – convene a Miracle Commission and punt on a comment.'

'The Holy Father feels a need for an intermediate step in such a high-profile case. A Miracles Commission might take months or years to conclude its business. He believes you have the credibility and proper historical and theological perspective to perform a rapid and discrete investigation to exclude the most obvious finding.'

'That the priest is a charlatan.'

The cardinal nodded. 'If the young man is inducing his stigmata then he will be quietly removed from his position and given help.'

'These kinds of investigations require a medical examination. I'm not a doctor.'

'A competent physician from the Consulta Medica will be provided. Are you aware of this group?'

'Sure. A group of Catholic physicians who review the medical evidence for miraculous cures, for sainthood investigations.'

'Correct. The Consulta Medica usually works in concert with the Congregation for the Causes of Saints: the office that oversees sainthood applications. For this matter, the Holy Father does not wish to use the CCS as we are not investigating a potential saint.'

He interrupted himself with a laugh. 'At least not yet. Instead we will use the body that investigated Padre Pio, the Congregation for the Doctrine of Faith, headed by Cardinal Gallegos. You would be a consultant to the CDF.'

Cal sighed. 'When does the pope want this done?'

'Your schedule permitting, as soon as possible.'

That prompted a frown. 'I'll need to ask Thomas Aquinas for permission.'

'I don't understand.'

Cal turned his laptop toward his guest. 'My unfinished book on Aquinas.'

'I see. Well, I'm sure Saint Thomas would be most anxious for you to serve the Holy Father. As for me, one of the saint's sayings comes to mind: "There is nothing on this earth more to be prized than true friendship." You are a true friend, Cal.'

'There's only one thing I'd like for my troubles.'

'And what is that?'

'I'd like to meet the pope.'

'That won't be a problem. He expects you to deliver your report in person.'

FIVE

Abruzzo, Italy

C al had been advised to arrive early to secure a seat. But when he and his traveling companion approached the church from the side street where they had parked, he realized it hadn't been early enough. The piazza was jammed with people, it was so packed that those who surrounded the central fountain were in danger of being pushed into knee-deep water. There was a police presence but most of the officers sat inside air-conditioned cars, comfortably paying scant attention to crowd control.

The white-haired man accompanying Cal was not dressed for the stifling June sun that was baking the arid hilltop. Nevertheless, he looked cool and composed in a tailored black suit and dark blue tie. Faced with the prospect of being shut out of attendance at Mass, Cal politely tried to wriggle his way through the mass of people but his companion got fed up and declared, 'This is how Romans do it.'

Umberto Tellini used his outstretched hands like the prow of an icebreaker to forge ahead, shouting that he was a doctor and needed to get through. Cal tucked in and rode Tellini's wake until they made it to the church stairs. There, progress came to a halt as the crowd became funneled by the church doors.

Tellini spotted a vexed, sweating man in a rumpled suit standing near the doors surveying the crowd. He shouted at him, 'Are you an official?'

The man gave a shrug as if to say: I am but what do you expect me to do?

'What's your position here?' Tellini yelled.

It was probably the elegant and commanding appearance of Tellini that prompted the man to give him the time of day.

'I'm the sacristan.'

'Good. I am Dr Tellini. We're here from the Vatican. We have an appointment with the priest.'

'But he's about to celebrate Mass.'

Tellini shouted back, as if stating the obvious, 'After the Mass. We require seats. We will not stand.'

'I don't mind standing,' Cal told Tellini.

'You may. I will not.'

'The Vatican, you say?' the sacristan shouted.

Tellini nodded vigorously.

The sacristan reluctantly sprung to action, stopping people from entering the church and demanding that enough space be created up the stairs for the VIPs to squeeze through.

Inside, Tellini, true to his word, made a beeline to an empty middle seat in a rear pew, while Cal staked out a place to stand on the side of the nave near the north transept. From that vantage point he drank in the cool and dark interior. It was a welcome respite from the squinting glare of the piazza. The Baroque church had been built in the sixteenth century and its claim to fame – before all this business with the new priest – was a series of canvases adorning the sanctuary. There were New Testament scenes and an Old Testament-themed fresco on the transept ceiling attributed to the workshop of Giovanni Lanfranco. Ancient, solid pews – polished by the rumps of centuries of parishioners – sat on a smooth floor of marble squares. By way of homework, Cal had read that the pipe organ was dilapidated but with donations pouring in, repairs had been commissioned.

The church became stuffed beyond its seating and standing-room capacity and Cal wondered if the fire brigade would arrive to sort out the crush. They did not. He studied the crowd and tried to draw some conclusions about its demographics. It was overwhelmingly Italian, though he picked up some English, Dutch, German and Spanish bantered about.

Near the appointed hour, the sacristan appeared at the altar with a microphone in his hand.

'Ladies and gentlemen, out of respect for the parishioners of the church, who have not been able to obtain seats for today's Mass, I ask any day-travelers with seats: please relinquish them to the local people. Please.'

Necks craned and about a dozen people, mostly foreign tourists by the look of them, stood and sheepishly moved to the packed aisles, while the sacristan pointed at parishioners standing at the rear to try to come forward. When the exercise was done he made a second announcement.

'Following the Mass, I must inform you that Padre Berardino will be unable to perform any special blessings due to an important obligation. I'm sorry but there can be no exceptions.'

He left the stage amidst loud grumblings but the congregation fell silent when the priest appeared at the rear of the processional, which was slowly making its way to the sanctuary. Cal had seen plenty of photos, but in person he was struck how boyish he was. His cheeks were full and his complexion was pink and blotchy, more like a teenager's than a grown man. His chasuble was tented by his thick middle, but the overall impression he gave was that baby fat more than adult overindulgence was responsible for his heft. But it was his hands that really struck Cal. He kept them clasped together and fixed to his chest as if they were attached to his garment. Staring straight ahead, with an immobile expression, he avoided the intense gazes of every person in the church. And ringing clear over the deeper voices of his acolytes, his almost adolescent voice soared.

Ascending the altar he was handed a censer. Cal was shocked by the agony that flickered across the priest's face as he swung the chain back and forth, sanctifying the altar with smoky incense. Others saw it too and the pews filled with whispers.

The Mass progressed routinely. The gospel reading was from Matthew and the priest's brief homily was about Christian charity. Cal found it rather uninspired but the church hadn't filled to the bursting point because of Father Berardino's oratorical skills. Some were there anticipating that the priest's holiness might flow to them, healing body or soul, giving hope. Others had come simply to tell their friends and family they had seen the bleeding priest up close. Some snuck photos with their phones and those who forgot to turn off the flash got raw stares and wagging fingers from town residents.

Anticipation grew palpable during the Eucharist. When the distribution of communion began, there was an urgent movement toward the aisles as if the wafers would be rationed. But the priest administered the sacrament to all comers and it became the longest communion Cal had ever seen. Many, returning to the pews, were tearful and the church buzzed with chatter during the ritual. One of the last to receive communion was Dr Tellini, who passed by Cal with a shrug on his way back to his seat as if to say: hey, I'm a Catholic first, examiner second.

Before the concluding rites were over, Cal and Tellini slipped out to the piazza. During the recessional, some on the aisles reached out to touch the priest's vestments as he passed. When he exited the church there was a loud cheer from the faithful and curious who had been turned away from the overcrowded Mass. The sacristan was waiting with two police officers to escort the priest the short, clogged distance to his residence, while people called out to him to deliver a blessing.

When Cal and Tellini rang the bell of the modest house, a young African nun, Sister Vera, cautiously opened the door but warmed to them when they told her they had an appointment.

'The gentlemen from the Vatican,' she said as excitedly as if the pope himself was at the threshold. 'Come in, please. Father will be down shortly. May I get you water or perhaps some orange juice?'

They sat in a sparsely decorated, threadbare parlor that seemed rooted in the 1960s. An old phonograph sat on a small table; the bookcase had ecclesiastical history books, travel volumes and fifty year-old novels. It did not seem like a young man's or even a young priest's residence. When the priest came downstairs, dressed in a fresh, long-sleeved clerical shirt and black trousers he looked tired and pale.

Cal and the doctor rose and instinctively held out hands but the priest quickly apologized.

'One of the many things that have changed for me is that it is difficult to shake another's hand. I hope you understand.' Then he caught himself and started to repeat himself in imperfect English.

Cal replied in Italian that he spoke the language.

'He more than speaks it,' Tellini said. 'He speaks it like a native.'

The priest gratefully continued in Italian. 'I understand you are American, from Harvard University.'

'That's correct.'

'And you came all this way to interview me?'

'I was asked and was pleased to come.'

Tellini scoffed. 'Asked, he said. The Holy Father himself was the one who asked.'

'The Holy Father,' the priest said, his voice trailing off. 'I have been such a bother to so many and now even the pope is inconvenienced by me.'

'I wouldn't call it an inconvenience,' Cal said. 'Your circumstances of your putative stigmata are of great interest to the Church. I'm sure you can appreciate that.'

The priest gave him a wry smile. 'Putative?'

'I'm approaching this assignment with an open mind and without any preconceived opinions,' Cal said.

'I'm sure that's a sensible approach,' the priest said. 'I'm sorry if I feel like I'm the subject of an inquisition.'

Tellini countered, 'But my dear fellow, that's exactly what this is.'

Cal wished the good doctor had remained silent during this phase of the interview. While he didn't want to insult the man, he did want to control the tone. 'I'm not sure I would characterize our role that way. I believe our remit is simply to establish the facts and tender our professional conclusions.'

'Very well. I will submit to your questions cheerfully,' the priest said, his hands resting motionless on his lap. Cal found it odd conversing with an Italian who didn't 'speak' with his hands.

'For accuracy, may I record this conversation?'

'Of course.'

Cal opened a recording app on his phone. 'May I ask you when you first noticed the wounds on your wrists?' Cal asked.

'It was four months ago in early February.'

'Do you remember the exact date?'

'The sixth of February.'

'You're sure of that.'

'Completely. One doesn't forget such things.'

'You hadn't been ordained as a priest then, am I correct?'

'I received my holy orders at the end of February.'

'From the Archbishop of L'Aquila.'

'That's correct.'

'Where were you on February sixth?'

'Dubrovnik.'

'And what were you doing there?'

'My studies at the seminary were complete and just before ordination I took a holiday with a fellow seminarian. We found we could go to Croatia cheaply.'

'Could you tell me the circumstances of the first occurrence of these wounds?'

'Circumstances?'

'Specifically, where were you when you noticed them? Who were you with? What events preceded their appearance? Those types of things.'

'I was in my hotel room a good distance from the city center. We stayed at this particular hotel since it was very inexpensive and we each had our own rooms. I awoke in the morning and noticed my wrists were tender. When I examined them I saw raw, red marks.'

'What did you do?'

'Do? I did nothing.'

'You didn't show your companion?'

'No.'

'Or seek out a doctor?'

'No.'

'Why not?'

'I thought the problem would go away on its own.'

'Why did you think that?'

'I don't know, I just did.'

'So you weren't concerned.'

'Not terribly.'

'Did you pray?'

'Yes.'

Cal watched the young man's demeanor change. He looked like he wished he hadn't given that answer. The doctor must have noticed too since he leaned forward intently.

'If you weren't concerned, why pray?' Cal asked.

'I had just awoken. It's a natural time to pray.' He didn't sound convincing.

'I see. Where were you the previous evening?' Cal asked.

'At a restaurant in the city center.'

'Did anything out of the ordinary happen that evening?'

'Nothing.'

'And earlier that day, where were you?'

There was a small but noticeable hesitation. 'We hired a car and decided to visit an old monastery in the mountains to the north of Dubrovnik. St Athanasius. Do you know it?'

'I do, though I've never been. It's seventh century, isn't it?'

The priest looked impressed.

'Tell me about that visit.'

'The monastery occupies a pretty spot on the top of a hill. The chapel is the oldest part. My friend and I spent part of an afternoon there.'

'Specifically, what did you do and see?'

'Touristic things, although given our education, we were quite well informed about the context of the monastery in Church history.'

'Was there a formal tour? Were many people there?'

'Very few visitors. Maybe a handful, I don't recall exactly. There was no tour. Before we saw the chapel, we wandered the grounds. There were only two monks left. The rest have died out and they haven't had novices in many years. We met the monks in the chapel where they were praying. One of the monks offered to show us the crypt.'

'I see. Both of you went?'

'Yes, myself and the monk.'

'I meant your friend.'

'He was a bit claustrophobic, so he didn't want to go down the small stairs.'

'Did you see anything interesting down there?'

'Yes, some graves of bishops from the Middle Ages.'

'Just that?'

Another hesitation. Cal filed it away as a poker player might do with an opponent's tell.

'Nothing more.'

'Nothing that you might consider spiritual in nature?'

'No.'

'Was that the extent of your tour?'

'Pretty much.'

'And then you left?'

'We drove back to our hotel.'

'And the next morning was the first time you saw the wounds?'

'Yes, as I said.'

'What did you do for the rest of that day?'

'We took the ferry to Italy.'

'At any time during your visit to the monastery, or any time during your trip to Croatia, did you have any, what one might call, mystical experiences?'

'I don't think so.'

Cal found the reply puzzling. 'You don't think so.'

'Yes. I mean no.'

'Do you know what a mystical experience is?'

The priest seemed offended. 'I may be young and I may be a young priest, but I surely do know the meaning.'

Cal apologized. 'I was simply surprised you weren't more definitive. Most people who claim to have mystical experiences find them life-altering.'

'I have not made any such claim.'

'True. You haven't.'

'In the days that followed, tell me what happened to your wounds.'

'They persisted and became progressively deeper, more liable to bleed. Also the pain became worse.'

'And what did you do about it?'

'Do? I bandaged my wrists and I prayed.'

'What did you pray for?'

The priest seemed perturbed by the question, as if prayer were a wholly personal matter. 'I prayed for many things. I wanted the pain to go away. I was scared I would lose the use of my hands.'

'Did you see a doctor?'

'No.'

'Why not? If you were scared about the loss of function, why didn't you anxiously seek medical advice? I would have beaten my doctor's door down.'

'I was about to receive holy orders. I was worried the bishop would delay my ordination.'

'So you kept it to yourself and you were ordained.'

He nodded.

'But you couldn't keep it a secret forever, could you?'

'Sadly, no.'

'Why do you say that?'

'I wanted to be a simple priest tending to the spiritual needs of a community. I never wanted this kind of craziness.'

'How did your secret get out?'

'After I became a priest the wounds became quite bad.'

'Can you pinpoint the date that there was a marked worsening?'

'In fact I can. It was the day of ordination.'

Cal found this interesting and decided to drill down. 'Before or after the ceremony?'

'During.'

'During?'

'I was lying prostrate before the altar, with my brother seminarians, when the pain became quite unbearable. I felt the dampness of blood seeping through my bandages. When the ceremony was complete I excused myself and went to the lavatory. I had stuffed clean bandages in my pocket just in case and I was able to re-bandage my wrists.'

'And no one noticed?'

'One of my brothers saw some blood on my palms and

expressed concern but I told him it was a minor thing. No one else saw.'

'You haven't said how your wounds became public knowledge.'

'I was assigned to take the place of a retiring priest here in Monte Sulla. I wanted to stay in Abruzzo to be close to my family so I was overjoyed. I was here for only a few weeks when the bleeding became even worse. I began to be quite weak and suffered dizzy spells. Unfortunately, I fainted during Mass one day and was taken to the hospital. I was examined and, well, the rest you know. Someone at the hospital had a big mouth and soon, everyone knew.'

Tellini spoke up. 'Your doctor, I'd like permission to talk to him and review your charts.'

'Yes, no problem,' the priest said wearily.

'Were you told you had anemia?' Tellini asked.

'Yes. They gave me a transfusion and I felt stronger.'

'Have you had further transfusions?' the doctor asked.

'Several.'

Tellini had another question. 'Were you given a diagnosis?'

'They said they found no disease in my body.'

Cal politely asked if he could finish his line of questioning and Tellini grudgingly relinquished the floor.

'I know you said you didn't have any mystical experiences in Croatia. Since then, have you had any types of visions, heard voices or had dreams that seemed unusually real?'

He answered with a headshake.

'Do you know what bilocation is?'

'I don't know the term.'

'It's where a person appears in two places at the same time. To your knowledge have you ever experienced or has anyone reported episodes of bilocation?'

'No! I don't know why you would even ask me this question.'

'It was one of the miracles attributed to Padre Pio.'

The priest became visibly upset. 'Padre Pio, Padre Pio, Padre Pio. I've had it up to here with these comparisons to him! The people have even taken to calling me Padre Gio. Can you imagine?'

'You can hardly blame people for drawing the analogy.'

Cal had written extensively about the case of Padre Pio in his book. The priest, born Francesco Forgione in 1887 in the southern Italian town of Pietrelcina, began exhibiting the five wounds of Christ shortly after he was ordained a priest. These corresponded to the crucifixion puncture-wounds of palms, feet and side. Pio also was said to have developed spiritual visions, psychic abilities and episodes of bilocation were claimed throughout his life. When word of his stigmata spread, his Capuchin Friary in the mountainous San Giovanni Rotondo became besieged with the devoted, anxious for his blessings. The Holy See was initially highly skeptical, suspecting some form of chicanery and self-promotion, and in 1921 Pope Pius XI banned Pio from conducting Mass or administering confessions. But in 1933, the tide of opinion turned and the pope reversed his bans and restored all his priestly authorities. From then, until his death in 1968 at the age of eighty-one, Pio, whose stigmata only healed on his deathbed, was venerated by the faithful who flocked to San Giovanni Rotondo in droves. In 2002 Pope John Paul II bestowed sainthood on the monk. Yet even to the present day, controversies continued to swirl about Pio, with skeptics claiming his stigmata resulted from the self-application of carbolic acid or some other caustic agent.

The young priest sounded exasperated. 'Padre Pio was a true holy man, a saint! I am a nonentity, a simple priest who has little interest in fame or notoriety.'

'You're giving a pretty fair description of how Pio saw himself too,' Cal said.

'I won't discuss Padre Pio any further. It makes me uncomfortable.'

'Tell me something,' Cal asked. 'What would you like to happen now?'

'I don't understand your question.'

'If you could choose what path your life would follow, what would that be?'

Giovanni blinked as he thought. A sign of nerves?

'I would choose for the blood to stop and the wounds to heal. I would choose to be an ordinary priest. I would choose to have you and this doctor disappear.'

Cal smiled. 'Thank you, father. I suggest we let Dr Tellini do his examination so we can leave you in peace.'

Tellini asked the young man to stand beside a reading lamp. He switched it on and adjusted the light to his liking. 'Could you please roll up your sleeves?' he asked.

The bandages were clean and white.

'When did you last change them?' Tellini asked, producing a pair of latex gloves and a packet of gauze from a trouser pocket.

'After Mass.'

The doctor asked for permission to unwrap them and he did so with a neat efficiency. Cal stood a few paces away, so as not to be intrusive, but he had to suppress a gasp when the wounds were bared.

The circular lesions on each wrist were identical. Both were raw, oozing fresh red blood, and far from superficial. In fact, after Tellini blotted the blood away, bluish, glistening fascia, the deep connective tissue layer, was visible.

'Can I see you wiggle your fingers, please?' the doctor asked.

The priest did so to a limited degree, his discomfort apparent.

'Have you had any pus, any sign of infection?'

'I don't think so.'

'Do you apply any ointments, any antibacterial agents?'

'No.'

'Have you taken antibiotic tablets?'

Again, the answer was no.

Tellini pinched his mobile phone from his breast pocket and snapped a series of photos before re-bandaging the wounds.

'Any lesions on your feet or ankles?'

'None.'

'And your flank?'

'No, just the wrists.'

'I must ask you this question directly,' the doctor said. 'Are you doing this to yourself?'

The priest sighed heavily, his chest rising and deflating like a bellows. 'I am not.'

'Do you have any strong acids or bases in your house? Any caustic agents?'

'I don't think so but you might ask the sisters.'

'Can I look around the premises?'

'I have no objection.'

The priest called for Sister Vera who came bounding in from the kitchen. He asked her to let Tellini have free reign to look around the house, including his bedroom and bathroom.

Alone, Cal and the young man sat in silence for several seconds, until the priest asked, 'Has this been satisfactory?'

'I think so, yes.'

'Am I what you expected?'

'I had no preconceptions.'

His eyes were piercing and Cal noticed for the first time they were an astonishingly deep shade of blue. 'Are you sure?'

Cal was disarmed by the question. 'Actually I was expecting not to like you.'

'Why?'

'Because I tend not to like fraudsters.'

'But you don't dislike me?'

'I find you sincere and engaging.'

'Am I not a fraudster then?'

'I have to be honest. I don't know.'

'I'm not producing the stigmata myself. That's all I can attest to.'

'I'll put that in my report.'

The priest rose to pour some water from a pitcher. He needed two hands to lift the small jug and his strain was evident. He sat down and took a small sip. 'May I ask you something?' he asked.

'Anything you like.'

'How old were you when your father died?'

The question stunned Cal into silence.

'I'm sorry,' the priest said. 'I didn't intend to make you uncomfortable.'

Cal knew what biographical info of his was available online. Obtaining details about his father was doable but it would take some digging. 'How do you know about my father?'

'I know nothing about him.'

'You didn't look me up?'

'I'm afraid I've stopped using the internet. I don't enjoy reading about myself and it's become difficult for me to use the keyboard and mouse.'

'Then how do you know he died?'

The priest's expression turned dreamy. 'I just knew. I can't explain it. If you don't wish to answer my question I understand.'

Cal was of two minds. He worried he was falling into a trap. The young man certainly would be aware of the Padre Pio's alleged psychic abilities. Despite his denials, he could have researched Cal's background. On the other hand he felt strangely compelled to open up to him.

'I was sixteen.'

'A delicate age,' the priest said. 'I myself was fourteen when my father died.'

Cal thought, *why is he telling me this*? He said, 'I'm sure it was difficult. I know it was for me.'

'My father died from an intestinal cancer. What claimed your father?'

Claimed. An interesting choice of words. 'To this day I don't know what happened. We always suspected foul play but it was never confirmed.'

The priest's eyes were sad. Though he didn't ask another question, Cal felt he was being egged on to say more.

'He was an archaeologist,' Cal said. 'He was on a dig when it happened. They said he fell into a trench and hit his head on a rock. I never believed it. He was sure-footed, like a mountain goat. I remember hiking with him on steep trails. I was an athletic kid but I couldn't keep up with his scrambling.'

The priest closed his eyes. A tear formed. 'I can picture you as a boy striving to compete with him.'

Compete. Another interesting choice of words. Cal had always strived to compete with his father's almost mythic persona, especially after his death. He had even requested the same office at the Peabody Museum that his father had occupied. He only taught a single undergraduate archaeology course, Introduction to Biblical Archaeology, but when he received students for office hours at the Peabody, he felt like his father was looking over his shoulder.

'He was larger than life,' was all Cal said.

'My father too, at least to me,' the priest said. 'He was a baker, the best in our city. He was very authoritative but also capable of great kindness. May I ask another question?'

Cal nodded numbly.

'Are you a Catholic?'

How had the priest turned the tables on him so effectively? 'I'm a hybrid. My mother's Jewish which makes me a Jew as a matter of Jewish law. My father was Catholic. I've always self-identified as Catholic. Well, actually more than that. I've been baptized and confirmed.'

'What does your mother think about this?'

The question was too personal but he answered it anyway. 'She never objected. She's not a religious person.'

'Do you attend Mass?'

'Only when I happen to be visiting a European church or cathedral. For me it's more of an academic exercise than a spiritual one.'

'When was the last time you took confession?'

The answer should have been, it's none of your business, but instead he said, 'A long time.'

'Would you like to confess now?'

'What, here?'

'If you close the doors, no one will enter.'

On the face of it, it seemed thoroughly bizarre. Here he was, a Vatican-commissioned examiner with the heart of a professional skeptic, being turned around by a baby-faced priest. Yet, unaccountably, he found himself wanting to confess, even needing to confess.

He closed the lounge doors and moved his chair to within a few feet of the priest.

'In the name of the Father, and of the Son, and of the Holy Spirit, my last confession was twenty years ago.'

It wasn't a long confession and it wasn't terribly detailed. On the spur of the moment he could hardly have been expected to produce a full and fair account of two decades of sins. So he covered the high points: the aimless womanizing, the drinking, the abandonment of faith.

There was a faint knock on one of the doors. The priest asked the nun to wait a few moments.

'I think I'm finished anyway,' Cal said. He was sweating.

The priest absolved him and gave him a light penance at which point he told Sister Vera to enter.

Tellini came in, looking puzzled that they had sequestered themselves.

'Did you find anything?' the priest asked.

'Nothing at all,' the doctor said. 'No noxious chemicals of any kind.'

Cal stood. His legs felt rubbery.

'I think we're done,' he said. 'I want to thank you for giving us your time, father. If we have any further questions, I hope we can call you.'

The priest used his elbows to push himself from his chair. 'Of course. I hope you will have a safe journey to Francavilla.'

'We didn't say we were going there,' Cal said.

'Didn't you?'

It was then the priest approached Cal and unexpectedly threw his arms around him.

The effect was immediate.

Later, Cal would liken the effect to electrocution.

A powerful jolt ran through his body, arching his back. It wasn't painful. It was an intense, somatic, trumpet-call heralding what came next.

A face.

A fleeting vision of a face with fine, delicate features, appeared but disappeared too fast to register, and with its passing, the electricity dissipated and his body relaxed. Was it male or female? Young or old? Friend or stranger? When it was gone, Cal felt a longing akin to catching a whiff of perfume from a passing beauty he might never see again.

Giovanni released Cal from the hug and when he did they both saw a trickle of blood running down both of the priest's palms. The young man quickly circled around to inspect the back of Cal's blazer.

'I'm so sorry,' he said. 'I've gotten blood on your jacket.'

SIX

Buenos Aires, 1973

T he flight attendant made the announcement first in German, then in Spanish. Lufthansa flight 433 from Munich to Buenos Aires would be landing in fifteen minutes.

The 747 banked gently, bringing the coast of Argentina into

full view. Eight men had flown together in the comfort of business class. The youngest two sat together, enjoying the rich food and the excellent wine. Although they had been warned not to get drunk, both were a little tipsy and in high spirits.

Oskar Hufnagel was thirty and this was his first time on an airplane. His seatmate was twenty-nine and was considerably more worldly and well-traveled.

'Let me have a look,' Oskar said, pushing the other man back in his seat so he too could see out the window.

'It's just a coastline,' Lambret Schneider said. He tried to sound nonchalant but he was excited. This was the first time he'd been to South America since he was a boy.

'Yes, but there's a beach,' Hufnagel said. 'Where there's a beach, there are girls.'

'We're not here to see girls,' Schneider said.

Hufnagel shook his head. 'You're sounding like Kempner more and more every day.'

Klaus Kempner, the expedition leader, was in his sixties. To call him stern would be a great understatement. He was ex-Waffen-SS, formerly one of Himmler's favorite junior officers, and a grim survivor of the Russian siege of Berlin who had simply removed his uniform in May of 1945 and melted into the chaos of post-war Germany. Schneider had never seen him smile, never heard him tell a joke. He had once asked Bruckner, another older member of the team, how many men Kempner had killed during the war and was told, 'More than all the steaks you'll ever eat.'

The seats in front of them began to rock slightly and Schneider heard low voices. He peeked through the crack between the seats and swore. The men in the next row were Orthodox Jews and they were praying.

'They're at it again,' Schneider whispered.

Hufnagel shrugged.

'Did you see their passports?'

'No, why?'

'Israelis,' Schneider spat.

'Lot of Jews there, I hear,' Hufnagel said, laughing at his own joke.

Schneider clenched his jaw and didn't release it until the

stewardess came by to remind him to put his seat forward for
landing.

At baggage claim, the eight men were met by a laconic German
driver who led them to a Mercedes van parked outside the
terminal. They were driven to a spacious, walled villa in the leafy
Belgrano district where they were each assigned bedrooms.

'Don't get too comfortable,' Kempner growled. 'This will be
the last time on the journey you will have such luxury. We meet
for supper at six p.m. sharp.'

Schneider was hoping to learn more about their mission that
evening. All the prior meetings had been woefully uninformative.

Kempner had approached him several weeks earlier. The two
had met only once before on the occasion of Schneider's gradu-
ation from the University of Mannheim, where he had studied
business. His mother had died within two years of his father's
suicide. His only family at the ceremony was the uncle and aunt
who had raised him.

When Kempner had introduced himself, Lambret's uncle
immediately pulled his wife away for a walk. He seemed to know
who this man was.

'I knew your father quite well,' Kempner had said stiffly. 'He
was a great man.'

'Thank you.'

An envelope had appeared from an inside jacket pocket and
was presented to the graduate. 'This is a gift from an organization to which your father belonged.'

'What organization?'

'It is better you don't know.'

A peek revealed a small fortune in large-denomination
Deutsche Marks.

'I can't,' the young man had said before trying unsuccessfully
to hand it back.

'You can and you will. One day you'll see me again. Then I
will tell you more.'

'When will that be?'

With nothing more than a curt nod, Kempner had taken his
leave.

Their second meeting had been no less enigmatic. Schneider
had just gotten off work at a commercial insurance company

in Koblenz when Kempner collared him in the employee parking lot.

'Do you remember me?' Kempner had asked.

'Of course I do.'

'In six weeks' time you will join me and six other men in a mission of great importance.'

'Mission? What mission?'

'I cannot say until we are on our way.'

Schneider had laughed. 'You sound like I don't have a choice.'

Kempner's square jaw hardly moved when he spoke. 'You don't,' he had said. 'It's your father's command from the grave.'

'How long will I be gone?'

'Approximately one month.'

'I don't have that much holiday time. I'll be fired.'

'Your organization will find you a better job when you return.'

'I don't belong to an organization.'

'Yes you do. You have always been a member. You just didn't know.'

'But I'm married. What will I tell my wife?'

'You will tell her nothing because you will know nothing. Feel free to make up a suitable story.'

So that night in Buenos Aires, after a typical German meal prepared by unseen kitchen staff, Schneider sat among his new colleagues and eagerly listened to Kempner's speech.

'Bruckner knows the truth of this mission but the rest of you do not,' Kempner began. 'We are here today because of the bravery of a band of German submariners, who were selected for a secret mission in the last days of the war. In the spring of 1945, Himmler and the Führer both recognized the inevitable . . . that the Reich would be defeated. Knowing this, they refused to let certain precious artifacts of the Reich fall into the hands of the enemy. Therefore, an elite force of soldiers and sailors was commissioned by Himmler to transport these items to a remote and secure fortress, which had been prepared years earlier in case it was ever needed. A U-boat, U-530, left Kiel harbor on the thirteenth day of April 1945. The code name for this mission was Valkure Zwei.'

Lambret was listening with rapt attention when he was blindsided by Kempner calling out his name.

'Schneider, you're the youngest so you'd better get used to doing the shit work. Clear the table.'

Schneider accepted the ribbing of his comrades with good humor and sped to move the plates, glasses and cutlery to the sideboard. When he was done, Kempner unrolled a map onto the table and used a thick forefinger to stab at a spot on the bottom of the world.

'Here is where we are going, gentlemen.'

Antarctica.

'This is where we will recover the greatest treasures known to man. And when we do, we will be that much closer to the dawn of a new age, a new Fatherland, a new Reich.'

SEVEN

C al closed the door on his small, charming hotel room. At the reception desk he turned in his key and asked for the bill.

'How was your stay, signore?' the owner of the Hotel Claila asked.

'Very pleasant, thank you.'

'You are American, no? Where are you from?' she asked.

'Cambridge, in Massachusetts.'

'Ah, Harvard University, no?'

'Yes, exactly.'

'I would like for my son to attend their business school one day.'

'You're not alone in that. It's a lot more practical than the divinity school where I teach.'

Outside, the sun seemed to be chasing away the morning fog. Cal paused to admire the hotel; a white-washed, nineteenth-century building. It would not have been so remarkable, had it not been one of the few buildings in the town not leveled by Allied or Nazi bombs during the Second World War. Adjusting his shoulder bag, he followed the gulls toward the sea.

The apartment was a third-floor walk-up on an unassuming

block, a little too far from the sea for a view of anything other than another unassuming block of flats. Cal accepted the offer of a cup of coffee from the matronly, sad-eyed woman who called into the kitchen, where the voice of a younger woman replied, 'Coming, mama.'

Domenica Berardino, Giovanni's mother, had asked Cal to hold his questions until her daughter came in. As he struggled through some small talk, he scanned the sitting room to get some sense of Padre Gio's boyhood. His first impression was that the family had more dignity than money. The furnishings were humble but everything was immaculate. He had every reason to believe that if he were to run a white-gloved finger over the framed pictures of Giovanni, her late husband and the pope (Domenica's trinity) that there wouldn't be a speck of dust.

He asked the woman if she'd ever been to Boston, expecting a no, but her answer surprised him. The farthest from home she had ever been was Rome and there, only twice.

'Does everyone in Boston speak Italian so well?' she asked.

He started to explain how, not so long ago, you could walk down Hanover Street in the city's North End and hear only Italian, but he stopped short when Irene Berardino emerged with a coffee tray. Irene made it abundantly clear, with a lemon-sucking pucker of her small mouth, that he wasn't entirely welcome. Despite her obvious displeasure, he found it hard not to stare back at her. She was tall and proud with classic dark looks and shoulder-scraping black hair. Her creamy, olive skin would have been less perfect with make-up.

'I'm Calvin Donovan,' he said. 'I . . .'

'I know who you are,' she said abruptly. 'Do you take sugar?'

He shook his head and took the espresso from her delicate hand.

Domenica Berardino had the distressed look of a woman who would have scolded her daughter, if they spoke a language their visitor could not understand.

Instead she said, 'Signore Donovan has come a long way. Giovanni tells me the pope himself asked him to investigate his holy wounds.'

'Don't be fooled, the Vatican wants to discredit him, mama.'

Cal sipped the coffee and said, 'I can assure you, I have approached this task with a completely open mind.'

'So, you've seen my brother,' Irene said sitting on the sofa, demurely crossing her legs and pulling down her skirt. 'Tell me what you think.'

'My interview with him was only one piece of my investigation. I have a number of interviews to conduct before I form any opinions.'

'We want to help Giovanni,' his mother said. 'We will answer your questions.'

Cal asked for their permission to take notes and began. 'When did Giovanni decide to become a priest?'

'It wasn't something he talked about when he was younger,' Domenica said. 'We went to Mass on Sundays and we were always respectful to the Church, but my husband and I weren't devout. My husband was a very busy man, a baker. Work was more important to him than religion.'

'Giovanni told me about him,' Cal said.

'He was very close to my husband. A papa's boy, for sure. Alfredo's death was very hard for him, hard for us all.'

'I understand. As I told him, I also lost my father as a boy.'

Irene squinted at him suspiciously as if suspecting he was playing them.

'It's a terrible thing for a boy,' Domenica said. 'He grew up quite lonely. He was always heavy and didn't like playing football with the boys in the neighborhood. He enjoyed reading and video games. He was such a sweet and kind child. Wasn't he, Irene?'

'He is still sweet and kind, mama. It's just that all the pain and unwanted attention is hiding his disposition.'

'He always had time for a sick animal or a lonely child,' Domenica said. 'He was a good artist too and used to draw cartoons. That's what he wanted to do. Make cartoons or become, what's it called?'

'A graphic designer,' her daughter said.

'He went to university for a year but didn't like it so he stopped and got a job.'

'What kind of job?' Cal asked.

'There was a marketing company in Pescara. They hired him to do small tasks. He thought he'd be able to become an artist for them, but when nothing happened he got frustrated and left. It was then that a school friend of his decided to go to the seminary. They talked and talked and Giovanni got interested. He decided to try it too. I didn't think he would follow through with it because, well, his mind was often changeable, but he surprised me with his devotion to the calling.'

'What was his friend's name?'

'Antonio Forcisi.'

'He's on my list.'

'He's a good boy too.'

Irene challenged him. 'Why is he on your list?'

Cal answered, 'He was in Croatia with Giovanni when the stigmata appeared. What did Giovanni tell you about the first time he developed the bleeding?'

'He hid it from us. We only found out when he was in hospital after he collapsed,' Irene said.

His mother dabbed at her eyes with a tissue. 'He told us he was frightened. He didn't understand why it was happening to him.'

'And now that he's lived with it for several months, what does he say about it?'

'You should ask *him* that,' Irene snapped.

'I did,' he replied gently. 'Now I'm asking you.'

'He accepts it,' Domenica said. 'He accepts that he has been chosen for some purpose. If he can help people find God, then his suffering is worth it.'

'I assume it's changed your lives too,' Cal said.

'I have become a stronger believer,' Domenica said. 'Yes, my faith is strong now.'

'Is it the same for you?' he asked Irene.

'I don't think that is any of your business,' she said angrily.

'Irene!' her mother gasped.

'I'm sorry, mama, but I find this interrogation inappropriate.'

Cal felt a sharp pang of guilt. He was flying without radar. Perhaps it was an inappropriate question. 'No, I'm sorry,' he said. 'You're right. Your beliefs are none of my business.'

Irene seemed taken aback by his climbdown. 'I'm glad you understand.'

'Can I ask you this; have either of you had any odd experiences in the presence of Giovanni or even in his absence?'

'I don't understand what you mean,' Domenica said.

'Any visions, anything of a spiritual or unexplained nature involving him.'

The two women looked at each other and shook their heads.

He carried on with another several minutes of questions, failing to find anything illuminating. As he was getting up to leave he asked if he might have a peek at Giovanni's boyhood room.

'It's ok,' his mother said. 'Show him, Irene.'

The small room with a narrow bed was a time capsule; a tribute to the awkward, talented teenager who used to live there. The walls were plastered with pairs of Star Wars and Star Trek film posters; one was real, the other, Giovanni's own painted version, was distinctively different in a charming way. The bookcase held a hodgepodge of novels and schoolbooks. Cal scanned the room for any trace of religious devotion or iconography. There was none, not even a bible.

'He didn't have a bible?' he asked.

'I don't think so,' Irene said. 'We have a family bible. Maybe he read it, I don't know.'

'It's just that it's hard to see the seeds of a young man who felt a calling toward the priesthood.'

She shrugged. 'We didn't see it coming either. Life is like that.'

'Were the two of you close growing up?'

'I'm only four years older but I was his protector. When he was bullied at school, they had to answer to me.'

'It must be upsetting, all of this happening to him.'

'You have no idea. I would like to help him escape but he's trapped. I hope you will tell the Vatican to cut him off from the public, for his sake.'

'I don't think they want my recommendation, just my opinion.'

'And what is your opinion now that you've spoken to me and my mother?'

'I still don't have one.'

Her voice dripped with acid. 'When you do,' she said, 'maybe the famous Harvard professor will find the time to tell the people who love Giovanni.'

When Cal was gone, the two women took the coffee cups to the kitchen.

'Why didn't you tell him you saw Giovanni walking in the town when he wasn't there?' Domenica asked.

'For the same reason you didn't tell him about what you saw, when he gave you a hug. He's a stranger. A Vatican hired gun. They don't care about Giovanni. Only we do. To be honest, I hope this man concludes he is a fraud. I hope the Vatican decides to move him from his parish and stop this freak show before it kills him.'

His mother cried, 'But we know he's not a fraud.'

'Yes, mama, we know.'

Cal thanked the bartender for his second cocktail of the night and tasted it to see if the vodka was as cold as he liked it. As darkness settled over Rome, the view from the hotel roof garden became even more beguiling and he sought out a chair near the railing. The warm night air carried the scents from the nearby restaurant kitchens and the voices of tourists and street vendors. Cal smiled at a pair of businesswomen seated nearby. They were chatting away in English and largely ignored him, allowing him to retreat into his own thoughts. A few minutes later, one of the women asked to be excused. The one who remained, an attractive brunette roughly Cal's age, finished her drink and stared over the railing for a while before speaking.

'It's lovely, isn't it?'

Since there was no one else within earshot, Cal answered, 'It certainly is.'

The view was breathtaking. The rooftop garden loomed over the dome of the Pantheon, so close it seemed one could almost reach out and touch it.

She introduced herself. She was an advertising executive from London. She asked about him but, before he could answer, the waiter passed by and she asked for another glass of wine.

'I'm buying,' Cal said. 'And get me another one of these, please.'

The waiter nodded and the woman shifted her seat to be closer.

'What are you drinking?' she asked.

'Grey Goose Martinis uncontaminated with vermouth.'

'Why don't you just call it vodka?'

'Sounds way less appealing, don't you think?'

She asked what he did and he told her he was a professor.

'I hate to sound like a snob,' she said, 'but I'm surprised that an academic is staying at a hotel like the Minerve.'

She did come off as the snob he was sure she was. But the back-to-back vodkas had taken the edge off her personality and a fresh drink had just arrived.

He sipped at it and said, 'Harvard pays well.'

It didn't pay that well. Cal's father came from serious money and Cal had been a trust fund baby. Without a family or a hankering for too many expensive toys, he enjoyed spending his money on good hotels, good restaurants and first-class travel. The Vatican had offered to reimburse him for his expenses – coach, airfare and modest accommodations – but he had declined, so he could travel in the manner to which he was accustomed.

'Well, here's to the Ivy League,' she said, raising her glass. 'What is it you teach?'

'History of religion mostly.'

She snorted, 'Well that's something I know very little about.'

'I'm not a font of knowledge about advertising.'

'Well, well,' she said, 'whatever shall we talk about?'

He took another pull at his drink and felt the alcohol soak his brain. 'I'm sure we'll figure something out.'

'Has anyone told you you're a very attractive man?' she asked.

He laughed. 'You mean today?'

'Your room or mine?' she asked, getting down to business.

'Do you have a suite?' he said.

'I don't,' she pouted.

He signed for the drinks and said, 'I do.'

The archbishop of Abruzzo, Donato Fasoli, was displaying a decidedly unpleasant attitude and Cal was trying his hardest to remain civil. At the bishop's request, their audience had been arranged at the Vatican where Fasoli had business, rather than at his archdiocese in L'Aquila. The two of them were crammed into a small office, one of many reserved for visiting bishops at the Apostolic Palace. The space was small enough that Cal could smell Fasoli's lunch on his breath.

'I wasn't consulted about this inquiry of yours and I don't support it,' the archbishop said.

'You've made that quite clear,' Cal said.

'I don't know whose idea it was to involve an outsider. This could have been handled internally.'

'I believe it was Pope Celestine's idea.'

'That seems unlikely to me. I'd venture to say that it was Da Silva's doing. He's an ambitious one, always looking to enhance the stature of our American brethren.'

Cal said, 'I don't know about that. Apparently the Holy Father liked my book on stigmata. Have you read it?'

'Is it in Italian? I get a headache when I have to read in English.'

'It's being translated. I'll send you a copy.'

'Do that,' he replied.

Cardinal Da Silva had briefed Cal on this bishop. He'd been on excellent terms with the previous pope and had been anticipating that it was only a matter of time until he was elevated. But Celestine was a bird of a different feather, a real reformer who was trying to steer the Church hard towards a very public mission of serving the poor. He was choosing new cardinals largely from South America, Asia and Africa. So Fasoli, a hardline conservative, had to watch helplessly as the sands shifted under his feet and the cherished red hat slipped from his grasp.

'So, I hear you've interviewed our bleeding priest,' the archbishop said. 'What can I add to this circus?'

'I take it you don't think his wounds are miraculous.'

'I do not. I think Giovanni Berardino is an immature young man, who probably should not have gone into our line of work. It's not easy being a priest, especially in this day and age.'

'So you think he's self-harming.'

Fasoli shrugged.

'Why do you think he's doing it?'

'Why? I'm not a psychologist but from a theological perspective, I'd say he has a fundamental weakness in his faith. He did something foolish to draw attention and he got caught up in a situation that spiraled out of control. Now he's become the great Padre Gio and he's trapped in a web of his own making. The Vatican didn't have to bring in a Harvard professor to perform an investigation. They only had to ask me.'

'Tell me, what is your opinion about Padre Pio?'

The archbishop's eyes lit up. 'Now there's a case of true

mysticism. It was right and proper that Pope John Paul II canonized him. Pio was a true holy man, there's no doubt about it. Giovanni is an overgrown boy who should be counseled out of the priesthood. I don't find him to be sufficiently serious or weighty in his theology or certain of his faith. I've reviewed his records from his seminary training. He was a marginal student. There were always doubts about his abilities and his commitment. If we weren't so desperate to get young Italians to become priests, I'm sure he wouldn't have been passed through to ordination.'

'If it were your decision alone to make, what would you do with him at this point?' Cal asked.

'I would remove him from the public eye and would stop him from taking confessions. In no time, his bleeding would cease and his wounds would heal and the hysteria would vanish. Put that in your report.'

'I'll be sure to correctly characterize your position.'

Fasoli nodded and asked, 'And what's your opinion about him?'

'I don't have one yet. I'm still gathering facts.'

'In this book of yours, what did you say about Padre Pio?'

'I presented the facts as best I could and left it to the reader to make up his or her mind.'

The archbishop looked thoroughly disgusted. 'Wishy-washy. Just like this pope. I see a world of blacks and whites. Others see rainbows and unicorns.'

Cal faked a smile and said, 'Would you like me to put that in my report to the Holy Father too?'

EIGHT

Antarctica, 1973

The McKinnon flying boat circled low over dark, choppy seas. In the cockpit, Werner Bruckner, an accomplished though aged former Luftwaffe airman, was in the co-pilot's seat beside a younger German pilot they had met at the airport.

Klaus Kempner, the expedition leader, sat behind them in the cramped cockpit working the radio, searching for a signal from an unseen, diesel motor ship.

The other six men bumped around in the passenger and cargo section, nervously peering out the windows.

'Are we really going to land in this weather?' Oskar Hufnagel asked.

'I certainly hope so,' Lambret Schneider said. 'The alternatives are not so good.'

It had already been a long day. They had departed before dawn from a crushed-stone landing strip on Tierra del Fuego, the southernmost tip of South America, and had flown for six hours before landing on a calm Weddell Sea. There they were met by a fishing trawler that refueled the McKinnon for the second leg of its journey. Six hours later, they were a scant twenty miles from the coast of the frozen continent.

Kempner called out through the open door of the cockpit, 'We have radio contact!' When the cheers faded he added, 'We should see the Marta from the starboard side momentarily.'

'There!' Hufnagel cried. 'There she is!'

The ninety-feet long craft looked tiny at first, but became somewhat more impressive as they descended for a landing.

'Brace yourselves,' Bruckner shouted. 'The waves are going to bite our ass.'

The pontoons made contact with the water with a loud thud. Hufnagel gripped the armrests so hard his hands shook and he gave his companion a look as if to say: don't tell the others I was afraid. Schneider felt the impact of successive waves transfer to his kidneys and he wondered if he was going to be spending the next day pissing blood.

The pilot throttled back and turned the plane into the fierce wind to handle the chop lest a large wave land broadside and capsize her.

'Lifejackets, gentlemen,' Kempner shouted.

As the plane heaved and groaned, no one had to be told twice.

From his window, Schneider saw a small, rigid inflatable boat approach the plane through the heavy surf. The captain opened the hatch and got a face full of spray before a line was tossed and the tender was secured to a pontoon. Before the men disembarked, jerrycans of fresh fuel were passed inside the plane for the pilot's return journey. When that was done, Kempner ordered his men onto the pontoon. One by one they held onto a strut and timed their jumps onto the rigid inflatable boat with the troughs of the waves. The last two men out of the flying boat passed the packs of gear forward until the deck of the RIB was filled.

The tender was only a sixteen-footer with limited seating and, with ten on board, two men had to sit on the tubes. One member of the expedition had to join a crewman on the precarious perch. Kempner pointed to Mattias Beckman, a rugged fellow in his forties, to give up his seat. Beckman immediately complied without a grumble, the tender was untied and engine was thrown into gear. When they were midway between the bobbing McKinnon and the Marta, they saw the pontoon boat begin to taxi and lift off into the bright sky.

None of them saw the six-feet high wave rising up, twice as tall as the others. It hit them portside, knocking Beckman into the air. When he came down again, the boat was no longer underneath him.

'Man overboard! Hang on,' the captain shouted, spinning the wheel.

'Where is he? Do you see him?' Hufnagel yelled.

'I see him! There!' Schneider shouted.

The crewman tossed a life ring toward Beckman who swam frantically until he had it in his grasp.

'Pull alongside,' Kempner coolly ordered. 'You men, there, get him in.'

Beckman had swallowed some seawater and once in the tender, he threw up a few times and hunched over breathing hard.

'All right?' Bruckner asked him.

'I'm fine,' he replied. 'Someone else can sit in the idiot seat.'

Bruckner volunteered and they resumed their passage to the Marta.

'I can't swim, you know,' Hufnagel whispered to Schneider.

His friend looked ashen. All Schneider could do was to tell him to trust his lifejacket.

Hufnagel nodded but after only a few moments of reflection he began whispering again.

'There's a girl in Munich,' he said.

'Yes?'

'She's pregnant.'

'Is that good news or bad?' Schneider said.

'She's having the baby.'

'Are you getting married?'

'Hell no. She's a looker but I don't like her.'

'I see.'

'Here's the thing. If something happens to me, I want you to promise you'll keep an eye on the kid. It'll need a father figure.'

'It?'

'I hope it's a boy. For now it's an it.'

He reached for his billfold and pulled out a picture of a very pretty girl with her phone number written on the back.

Schneider took it and said, 'Oskar, if something happens to me, I want you to promise *me* something.'

'Anything.'

'I don't want you anywhere near my wife.'

The Marta's officers were German but the crew were dark-skinned Argentinians. Schneider and his group were given a simple, hearty stew in the officer's mess. The captain, a ruddy-cheeked man in a cable-stitched woolen jumper, said nothing about their mission. Schneider assumed he had some knowledge but Kempner only shared operational details with Bruckner. It was the evening now, but Schneider still had to squint at the powerful sunlight pouring through the windows. Kempner had planned the mission for February, to take advantage of the nearly perpetual daylight and the relatively mild temperatures, although it was still bitterly cold, especially on the high seas.

Blotting up the last of his gravy with a piece of bread roll, Kempner asked his men, 'Is everyone ready?'

A resounding chorus of 'yes' rang out and Kempner pushed his chair back sharply.

'Then, let's go.'

Schneider and the others donned their heavy Antarctica gear and carried their provisions to the aft. There an olive-green Aerospatiale helicopter was tethered to the deck, its engines being warmed by electric cables. They loaded up their supplies and climbed into the cramped cabin. Again, Bruckner joined the helicopter pilot in the cockpit, a laconic German they hadn't seen at supper.

The rotors were given full power and the helicopter lifted off.

'Gentlemen,' Kempner said, 'God willing, our next stop will be the Mühlig Hofmann Mountain Range.'

There were no cheers because almost immediately, strong crosswinds buffeted the helicopter. Schneider wished he hadn't eaten so much and struggled to hold onto his stew. The chopper fought the convection currents for forty minutes, before one of the men told them to look out the left side at a gray, rubble-strewn beach, jam-packed with basking seals, penguins, cormorants and terns. The beach quickly gave way to a terrain of snow and ice.

They flew low over this barren landscape for another half an hour, when suddenly the pilot lifted the helicopter skyward and they approached a looming mountain peak. Once clear of it, he descended just as rapidly towards a small valley and soon they were touching down on a plain of glistening ice. The men piled out and helped secure the treads with ropes and ice anchors, before the pilot shut the engine down to conserve precious fuel. Strapping on his combination traction snowshoes, Schneider breathed the icy air into his lungs. Through sunglasses he marveled at the pristine, empty expanse. Kempner took their bearings and consulted a chart he had spread out over his backpack. When the map was folded again, he pointed toward a cluster of low white peaks and, leaving the pilot behind to tend to the chopper, the eight men began trekking.

'I can't believe we're almost here,' Hufnagel said.

Schneider felt his chest bursting with pride. 'Me neither.' He looked toward a sky almost as white as the valley and imagined his father looking down on him approvingly from a heavenly Valhalla.

It took them almost ninety minutes to reach the foothills of the peaks. While they rested, Kempner and Bruckner consulted the map again and seemed satisfied they were near to where they needed to be. Turning slightly eastward, they went another hundred yards. Bruckner donned a headset and began sweeping the ice with a magnetometer. After a tense several minutes, the craggy man threw his ice axe down, pulled his earphones off and declared that he had found the spot.

'Now, gentlemen,' Kempner declared, 'this is why I needed strong, young backs.'

They began pickaxing and digging in teams of two along a span of several meters. Schneider paired up with Hufnagel, alternating between the two tools until they had shifted chunks of ice to a depth of a meter.

'Halt!' Kempner ordered and he, personally, jumped into the trench to clear the surface with a shovel. 'Now you, Beckman. We're glad you're alive so you can do the next job. Sink bore holes into each corner.'

Beckman wielded the heavy, battery-powered drill and began auguring with a three-centimeter bit. When he was finished, Bruckner removed lengths of thermal tubes from a pack and dropped them in each hole.

'Dichter, now's your time to shine,' Kempner said. The explosives expert, a man of few words who sported a perpetual grin, handled the sticks of TNT as if they were as harmless as candy canes and soon had them wired up to a detonator.

'It would be best to fall back, turn away and cover your ears,' Dichter said, talking too loudly as usual. 'You don't want to be as deaf as me.'

He counted down, pulled up on the plunger and there was an almighty *BOOM*, followed by plumes of coarse and fine ice extending high into the frigid air.

Kempner scrambled back down with a shovel and began clearing the debris from one corner. He called for a crowbar and thrust it into the gaping hole. There was a satisfying sound of metal on metal.

'Ok, off your asses, men. Time to dig again. We're close enough to taste it.' It was the first time Schneider had heard him sound joyful.

It took another hour and they were all drenched in sweat, but they had found it: a large steel door, black as night, lying at a thirty-degree angle to the bottom of the trench. By the light of a torch, Schneider could see that the door was fixed to the rock below with giant bolts studding its circumference.

'Thermal liquid,' Kempner ordered and two aluminum flasks were produced. Dichter mixed them together and quickly poured several drops of liquid onto each bolt.

After a few minutes, Schneider and Hufnagel were sent down with a huge lug wrench to manhandle the loosened bolts, one by one. Collapsing with exhaustion, the two men were relieved and four others took their place with crowbars, grappling hooks and chains.

When the time came to heave against the chains, Kempner solemnly said, 'The men who sealed this cave were the gallant crew of the U-530. It will be an honor to soon breathe the air they breathed in 1945. Now *pull!*'

The steel door groaned forward and crashed onto the floor of the trench. Kempner shone his torch into the void and wasted no more time on fine words. He clamored in, followed by Bruckner and the others. The two youngest, Schneider and Hufnagel, were the last and found they had to duck down low and light their own torches to navigate a low tunnel with steel-reinforced walls. After crab walking for ten meters, they found themselves in a huge cavern that seemed to have no end. The light from their lamps bounced off large columns of ice that took on grotesque shapes, as if an army of subterranean demons guarded the chamber.

'Gentlemen,' Kempner announced, throwing his beam around the blackness, 'Welcome to Station 211. Now that we have made it this far, I can reveal the truth. The German Antarctica Expedition of 1938 and 1939 explored this region by air, land and claimed it as New Swabia. These brave men discovered this underground formation but it was later, in 1943, under the personal command of Grand Admiral Dönitz, that this cave was expanded, reinforced and secured. Why was this done? As a precaution. To create a remote and impregnable fortress for the Führer and his high officers, to give them a chance to rebuild the Reich in the event of a disaster. Well, the disaster happened. But Hitler, as we know, simply refused to flee Berlin. Station 211 was not used for this purpose. It was used as a museum.'

Kempner consulted a small, hand-drawn map, which he kept tucked in the pages of his leather journal; a precious piece of paper that had been passed down to him years earlier by the captain of U-530. He folded the map and started walking through the cavern, his men following closely behind.

'Look at the size of this place,' Hufnagel said to Schneider. 'You could hide an entire army down here.'

Schneider felt something hit his shoulder. Alarmed he shone his light up at the ceiling of the chamber and saw a fine dust of ice raining down.

'I don't like it,' he said.

'Relax,' Hufnagel said. 'There's nothing to worry about.'

'Nothing except the dynamite we used to blast our way in.'

Schneider kept track of his paces and counted to three hundred, as Kempner traversed the cavern and passed the mouths of two further tunnels before entering a third. This low tunnel was also reinforced with steel girders and jack stands. It opened into a relatively small chamber, perhaps twenty meters across, high enough for them to stand upright with ease and there, against the far wall, was a line of large bronze chests.

Kempner spoke with the reverence of a devoted man entering a grand cathedral.

'The treasures of the Reich.'

'We can't carry all these chests back to the helicopter,' Beckman said.

'We're not taking the chests,' Kempner said. 'We are here for two objects only. We leave the rest for a brighter future. Unfortunately, we have no information to tell us which chest holds these objects. You must break the locks and look inside each one, until we find a green leather box and a small leather pouch. Get to work and hurry, unless you want to stay here forever. The helicopter engines are getting cold.'

Schneider and Hufnagel paired off to start with the chest at the right-most end of the row. Falling to their knees, they inspected the heavy padlock.

'Bolt cutters would be nice,' Hufnagel said.

'Well, we don't have any,' Schneider said, retrieving a hammer and chisel from his pack. 'Fortunately, you're as strong as an ox so go for it.'

Soon the chamber echoed with the banging of metal upon metal. With a mighty hammer blow, Hufnagel's iron lock shattered but alarmingly, it began to snow. Schneider looked up and saw a mist of ice coming from the ceiling.

Without warning, chair-size chunks of ice and stone began falling immediately to Schneider's right. Hufnagel stood and looked up. Schneider didn't have time to do the same. All he could see was the terror in his friend's eyes and feel two strong hands against his chest as Hufnagel sharply pushed him to the left.

As he fell backwards, Hufnagel and half the chest disappeared under a mound of debris.

'Oskar!' Schneider cried.

The others rushed over and Kempner shone his light onto the ceiling.

'Dig the chest out and pull it away,' he ordered calmly.

'Help him!' Schneider yelled.

'Keep quiet,' the leader said, 'or the rest of the ceiling will come down.'

The men began moving debris from around the chest with their hands and trench tools.

Schneider couldn't believe they were saving the chest and not Oskar so he began pawing at the larger mound that was concealing his body.

'Stand down, Schneider,' Kempner said, but he kept digging. 'Schneider, this is a direct order.'

'I've got to try,' he protested.

'No son of Otto Schneider would ever refuse a direct order from his superior,' Kempner said. Then he added gently, 'He's gone, Lambret. We need to finish our mission.'

Schneider was in a trance as the others pulled the bronze chest free and threw the lid open on its hinges. He numbly looked inside as Bruckner leaned over and rummaged through it. He saw an obelisk, a number of plaques, bundles of documents and photos tied in ribbons, rolled up maps. Near the bottom of the chest was a small silver box inscribed with the initials, AH. Bruckner passed it to Kempner who said reverentially, 'The Führer's ashes, collected from outside the bunker.'

'Should we take them?' Bruckner asked.

Kempner shook his head. 'We leave them. They are safer here than anywhere on the planet.'

As Bruckner replaced the box, Kempner saw something and said, 'That! To the left of your hand.'

There was a simple leather pouch, the size of a change purse.

'This?' Bruckner asked, picking it up.

'*Give it to me*,' Kempner said urgently.

Kempner undid the drawstring, looked in and saw a pointy sliver of wood.

'What is it?' one of the men asked.

Kempner let them all peek inside the pouch and said, 'This, gentlemen, is a thorn from the crown of thorns that the Romans thrust onto the head of Jesus Christ.'

'Is it real?' another asked.

'Oh yes, it's real, I assure you.' He cinched up the leather pouch and turned to Schneider. 'Here, Lambret, I'm entrusting this to you. It's a precious thing. Make sure you keep the pouch closed.'

Schneider blinked away his tears, removed his gloves and carefully placed the pouch inside a zippered outer pocket of his parka.

'All right, we have seven other chests to search,' Kempner said. 'Come now. Quickly. It's a green leather box we want now.'

As the others got back to work, Schneider could only stand and stare at the mound that had become the permanent resting place of a vibrant young man. He felt inside his trouser pocket for the photo of Oskar's knocked-up girlfriend and whispered to the mound that he would take care of his child, whatever it took.

He was still staring at the mound when he heard one of the men say, 'I think I've found it.' Lambret found himself stumbling toward an open chest. There a green box, the size of a cutlery set, lay on top of a trove of gold and silver decorative pieces, small paintings on wood and canvas, and a cluster of what looked to all the world like Fabergé eggs. The leather box was emblazoned with SS lightning bolts and the initials, HLH.

Heinrich Luitpold Himmler.

Bruckner told Kempner that he should be the one to open it and the old officer fell stiffly to his knees. He undid the clasp and opened the velvet-lined box.

Schneider recognized the object immediately, for when he was a child he had held its replica in his hands on the worst day of his life.

The Lance of Longinus, the Spear of Destiny.

When Kempner's eyes filled with tears, Schneider became angry. The old soldier's eyes had stayed dry over Oskar's death, but Lambret held his tongue. Kempner told the men they could look at the lance, but only for a moment, as they had accomplished their mission and had to leave.

'But do not touch it,' Kempner ordered.

'Why?' he was asked.

'Just do as I say.'

The box passed from hand to hand, each man admiring the long, black spearhead wrapped in a sheath of glittering gold.

Schneider was the last to take the box. He had it near the chest pocket that held the pouch and thorn.

Suddenly the spear changed color, from black to glowing red.

He felt a pain in his breast and the zippered pocket over his chest began to smoke.

Kempner snatched the box away from him, as Schneider cried, 'What the hell is happening?'

NINE

Croatia, present day

He was surprisingly youthful for a man in his forties; perhaps it was his modern haircut – longish and bottle-blonde on top, shaved sides that were several shades darker – or maybe it was the impish smile he used liberally to get his way. Regardless, he was an imposing fellow whose steroidal chest and arms bulged under a thin sweater and light rain slicker.

The man entered the ancient stone building and closed the wooden door behind him. Brother Augustin, frail and aged, was alone in the chapel of St Athanasius. It was evening and the light coming through the few small windows was fading fast. The monk tired easily these days and found it difficult to sustain even simple exertion without the need to shut his eyes for a while. His younger colleague, Brother Ivan, was no spring chicken himself and had to pick up the slack by doing more of the monastery chores. Recently, they had been forced to stretch their already tight finances by hiring a local man to help with the vegetable garden and to do occasional repairs to the plumbing and electricals. Neither monk had ever learned to drive; they had entered cloistered life in their early teens. For years, a rota of village women had shopped for them.

Augustin snorted and awoke at the sound of the heavy latch catching. He looked around and sighed at the sight of a tourist. He simply wasn't feeling up to civility.

He addressed the man in Croatian but switched to English when the big shoulders shrugged.

'Don't mind me,' the monk said. 'Have a look around.'

'Very old church,' the man said with a German accent.

The old man grunted and tried to blink away his cobwebs. He had been praying before he fell asleep and tried to start again but the man interrupted.

'Is it just you here?'

'We are a very small community. Only two monks.'

'Where's the other one?'

'Fixing supper, I hope. I am sorry but I must return to prayer.'

The man came forward down the aisle. He turned, his back to the rough stone altar and faced the monk. Before he spoke he pulled out a handkerchief and honked like a goose through his bulbous nose.

'You know about this Italian priest who's called Padre Gio, right?'

Augustin's watery eyes narrowed at the question. 'I have heard something of him on the radio. Why are you asking?'

'He came here. This priest.'

'Did he?'

'Oh yes. He came here. I think you remember.'

The monk became even more irritable than his usual crusty self. 'Leave me in peace, young man,'

'Peace,' the man said with a chuckle. 'All right, but first, let me shake your hand, ok?'

The monk objected but, with a couple of long strides, the man took hold of his right hand and pulled back the robe to look at his wrist.

'Nice and smooth,' the man said. 'Let me see the other.' He grabbed his left hand and repeated the inspection. 'Also nice and smooth but silly me. I forgot to shake your hand.' He took his right hand again and began squeezing it.

'Ow! You're hurting me.'

'I'm sorry,' he said, clamping down harder. 'Would you like me to stop?'

The monk nodded in pain.

'Then talk to me about this Italian priest.'

'All right, stop.'

The man let go and the monk rubbed his throbbing hand.

'You remember him now.'

'I remember him.'

The man flashed his winning smile. 'I knew you would. Tell me what happened when he came here.'

'Happened? Nothing happened. He came as a tourist like everyone who comes here.'

'Not everyone. I'm not a tourist. But ok. He was a tourist. He had a look around, right?'

'Yes, of course.'

'You took him to a special place, I think.'

'What place?'

'The crypt. Will you take me there too?'

The monk showed his fear now. His voice cracked. 'Who are you?'

'You may call me Gerhardt and I will call you Augustin. We can be friends. Is that the way to the crypt?'

There was an iron grate at one side of the chapel.

The monk gave a weak, 'Yes.'

The man reached for the monk's hand again, but the old man pulled it into his rough cloak in the same way a tortoise pulls into its shell at danger. He used his good hand to rise by pulling against the pew in front of him. It was only when he was upright that the disparity in size between the two men became apparent. The monk seemed like a small child being led to punishment.

The grate had a lock. The big man had to inflict a bit more pain, by squeezing the old man's shoulder, to get the monk to fish a key from his tunic. There was a wall switch in the vestibule and a spiral run of stone stairs materialized in the incandescent glow. The man told the monk to go first and followed on his heels.

The crypt was only half the size of the chapel above, a low-ceilinged space with an uneven floor, its stones polished by centuries of use. Sunk into the floor were marker stones with inscriptions in Latin, showing the resting place of ancient prelates. In a shadowed nook, a small bronze urn was on a stone shelf.

'Creepy down here,' the man said. 'Show me what you showed him, Augustin.'

The monk gestured around the chamber with his good hand. 'Nothing more than what you can see for yourself,' he said.

'Why did you take him here?'

'He wanted to see it.'

'See what?'

'The crypt. He wanted to see the burials.'

'Not much to see. Stones and, underneath them, bones. There was something else.' He pointed toward the urn. 'What's that?'

'A reliquary.'

'Augustin, Augustin,' he said with a mocking tone, 'You must explain this to me. I wasn't the best student. I don't know this word.'

'A vessel to hold relics. You know what relics are, do you not?'

The large man grunted, 'Yes. What relics are inside this one?'

'Nothing. It has been empty for a very long time.'

The man went to the nook, took the urn from its stand and shook it.

'Yes, it seems empty all right but let me check.' With a quick twist of one of his paws, the top came off. He turned the urn toward the floor. Nothing came out. 'I think that maybe something was in here recently. I think you're not telling me the truth, Augustin.'

The monk looked weary and dejected. 'There was nothing inside the urn when I came to St Athanasius sixty-five years ago and there is nothing inside now.'

'Isn't it a sin to lie?' the man said taking a few steps toward the monk. 'Especially for a man of the Church.'

'It is a sin to hurt an old man.'

The man seemed amused. 'Hurt? You call shaking your hand, hurt? I can show you hurt if you don't tell me the truth. What was in the . . .?' He fought to find the word and when he did he beamed. 'Reliquary? Did you show it to the Italian priest? Did you give it to him?'

The monk's long sigh sounded like air released from a punctured tire. He remained mute.

'All right, then,' the man said. 'I think I must encourage you. I'll have to show you hurt.'

It was dark when the man was finished.

He carried the monk's limp body up the crypt stairs and into the empty chapel.

'I think you've missed your supper, Augustin. Maybe your friend looked for you. He'll have to look harder.'

Outside, the earlier rain had stopped. The air was warm and humid. The man's gait was effortless, as if the wheezing monk on his shoulder was weightless.

He had seen the wellhead on his way to the chapel, an old-fashioned rough-stone and wood structure with posts, a crossbeam and a rope bucket. He looked around and, seeing no one, he calmly put the monk onto the grass then lifted him again, this time by his ankles.

'It's time to say goodbye, Augustin,' he said. 'I apologize for the hurt. At least this will stop it.'

He dangled the old man over the well for a moment, then released him to gravity and counted off the seconds in his head. At three there was a splash. Nodding to himself he lowered the bucket fast by pulling on the rope. The hand crank spun like a propeller shaft.

'Maybe you can climb up, Augustin,' he said quietly. 'Or maybe not.'

He had parked his car in a concealed spot behind the gardening shed. As he was about to get in, he saw someone in the shadows of the doorway.

'Who are you?' Gerhardt demanded.

The fellow stumbled forward, his flat cap askew. He had a reddish beard and big gut and reeked of travarica, the local grass brandy. He labored over a response in English.

'Me? I am gardener. I am handyman. What they need, I am. They pay shit but what I can do? This is church.'

The man smiled at him and said. 'Come closer, my friend. I'd like to talk to you.'

TEN

Berlin, present day

The years had been kind.

He was seventy-one but didn't feel like a man in his eighth decade. Aside from some morning stiffness in his fingers and a lingering tennis elbow, he had little in the way of the physical or mental decline that most of his friends and business associates grumbled about. His contemporaries so irritated him with complaints about their prostates and insomnia, their thinning hair and colonoscopy preps, that he tried whenever possible, to associate himself with younger men. And younger women.

That was one reason he had recently thrown himself so enthusiastically into recruitment. By the time a young man made it into his imposing office on Potsdamer Platz, with its killer park views through the mint-green windows over the Tiergarten, they had been vetted far more thoroughly than if they had been seeking a top intelligence job at the BND. Yet, to date, none of the interviews had progressed all the way to membership. Schneider was picky.

'We need fresh blood,' Schneider had railed at his colleagues when last they gathered at his Bavarian hunting lodge for their annual conclave. 'Do you want us to become extinct?'

'We have survived by being obsessed with security,' a retired shipbuilder from Hamburg had said, slurping oysters flown in that morning from Ireland.

'And what happens when the last of us dies?' Schneider had said. 'Don't you think our responsibility to history is stronger than an obsession with protecting our own skins?'

'None of us can afford a scandal,' another had said, 'least of all you.'

That much had been true. No one had more to lose. By and large they were a successful bunch. Industrialists, politicians, high-ranking military men, even a celebrity plastic surgeon! But Lambret Schneider was the only empire builder. His merchant bank was like an octopus, with probing tentacles and clinging suckers reaching throughout German society. He and his wife, a devoted patient of that very plastic surgeon, were boldface names in glossy magazines, renowned for their good works and philanthropy. If he were ruined, his bank would surely collapse and with it, a meaningful chunk of the German economy.

'We have the skill and the resources to do this correctly,' Schneider had said. 'A few fine young men from the right families, that's all I ask for. We dinosaurs may never find our earthly Valhalla but maybe, just maybe, the next generation will.'

The men in that taxidermy-studded, drafty old hall had been a little shocked by Schneider's tilt toward fatalism. He had been the group's most consistent cheerleader during his two decades as their leader. But who could blame him for a bout of lamentation? What had they accomplished since their glory days at the bottom of the world? What pleasure could they take in year after year of nothing new to report? None of them needed yet another exclusive social club, especially one impossible to brag about to a larger circle, and one that represented an existential danger to the lives they had built.

His assistant knocked on his door. 'Herr Schneider, your two o'clock appointment, Jürgen Besemer, is here.'

From the dossier compiled on the young man, Schneider knew he was going to be on the small side, but seeing him side by side with Gerhardt Hufnagel almost made him laugh. Though diminutive, the fellow had a refined appearance with a perfect blue suit and a fresh, conservative haircut. He wished Gerhardt were more presentable. For starters, he wanted his ridiculous hairstyle gone, along with those muscle-man shirts of his that were so clingy they looked to be spray-painted to his torso. And while he was waving a magic wand, he would have given Gerhardt a fistful of additional IQ points. The man wasn't a dimwit, but he didn't hold a candle intellectually to the bankers, analysts and lawyers Schneider had always hired. But Schneider hadn't chosen to have Gerhardt in his life. He had made a solemn promise and, to his wife's perpetual disgust, he had cared for Oskar Hufnagel's son as if he were his own.

On his return from Antarctica, Schneider had found Oskar's pretty girlfriend and given her money. Gerhardt had lived with his mother until he was eighteen but Schneider had never been far away. It had never been a matter for discussion with his wife. She had been unable to give him a child. He knew for a fact that he was potent given the number of abortions he'd arranged his mistresses to get over the years. The price he forced her to pay was allowing the too loud and often uncouth Gerhardt into their lives.

'Ah, Jürgen, come in and sit,' Schneider said. 'Thank you for coming today.'

'It is my honor, Herr Schneider,' the young man said with a reverential tone.

Gerhardt continued to stand by the door and would have probably continued to do so, if Schneider hadn't wordlessly pointed to a chair.

'So, Jürgen, you know why you're here.'

'Yes, sir. I almost could not sleep last night at the prospect of meeting you.'

'Some tea?'

'No thank you, sir.'

Schneider poured himself a cup without offering any to Gerhardt. 'And what is it you know of me?' he asked.

'I know of your business career, of course. And I know you are an important man in this organization I hope to join.'

'What do you know of the organization?'

'I was told very little. Only that its members are among the finest men of Germany, all of them committed to upholding the principles of German patriotism.'

'Tell me, Jürgen, what do you know about National Socialism?'

'I was a good student. I am knowledgeable.'

'So, your knowledge was only from school?'

'No, it was more than that. My father was a National Socialist and his father was in the SS.'

'You don't sound hesitant to mention this. These days most young people would be loath to speak of a family history that includes Nazi membership.'

'I am proud of my family, sir.'

Schneider nodded approvingly. 'I know of their service. Do you share their beliefs, Jürgen?'

'Actually, I do.'

'And do you trumpet them?'

'I do not, Herr Schneider. To do so would destroy my career at my company. Living in Germany these days is like living in a foreign country.'

'I like that!' Schneider exclaimed. 'Gerhardt, isn't that apt?'

Gerhardt moodily nodded.

'I feel comfortable speaking with you about my politics,' Besemer said. 'It is quite refreshing and liberating.'

'Good, that is good. Tell me the extent of your political activities,' Schneider asked the earnest young man.

'I am like a man alone in the desert. I have no affinity for the crude tactics and antics of the neo-Nazis. They are not my peers, they are not my equals. I keep my own counsel. I read, I study, I hope.'

'And what are your thoughts of joining a group of like-minded and refined gentlemen?'

'It would be thrilling, Herr Schneider. I only hope you would trust me to join with you.'

'You wouldn't have reached my inner sanctum if we weren't sure we could trust you. So, Jürgen, would you like to hear something about us?'

Besemer nodded eagerly.

This was the first interviewee who had progressed to this point but Schneider felt confident. He said, 'As you may know, Adolf Hitler believed in a form of Christianity, Positive Christianity.'

'I recall that his first use of the term was in Article 24 of the 1920 Nazi Party Platform,' the young man offered.

Schneider seemed slightly annoyed at the interruption, but he told the fellow he was impressed with his fund of knowledge.

'Hitler was not fond of traditional forms of Christianity,' Schneider continued. 'He found it too passive. All the nonsense about miraculous birth, suffering on the cross, redemption. The Führer found other aspects of Christ's life and death far more important and inspirational. It was this positive alternative that the Reich embraced in its early days: Christ the fighter, Christ the organizer, Christ the opposer of organized Judaism. The Reich leadership understood the practical and political significance of Christianity in Germany. After all, Germany had been Christian for over a thousand years. Hitler didn't want to alienate the German people with a blanket opposition to it – at least not at first. Himmler was not so subtle a politician.'

'Yet Himmler was a master of propaganda and organization,' Besemer said.

Schneider wished the fellow would just let him speak. 'Yes, quite,' he said gruffly, glancing at Gerhardt to see if he too was getting irritated. But the big man was looking out the window, obviously bored. 'Let me keep going or I'll lose my train of thought.'

'Of course,' Besemer said, with no diminution of eagerness.

'Hitler sought to exploit the deep-seated religious traditions of the country, for sure, but he also wished to tap the glorious Aryan traditions of the Germanic peoples as a driving force of our cultural destiny. He found the perfect metaphor for both concepts embodied in a single artifact, the Holy Lance of Longinus.'

The young man's eyes lit up. 'I . . .'

He shut the young man down with a hard stare. 'Please let me speak. Longinus, as you appear to know, was the Roman centurion who used his lance to pierce the side of Christ on the cross. His poor eyesight was cured by the splash of blood and water from the wound. Longinus, it is claimed, was an Aryan descended from Germanic tribes. The lance quickly became one of the holiest of all of the Christ relics.

In the third century, it was recorded as being in the hands of another legionnaire, a chap named Mauritius. Later that century it surfaced again and began its long line of royal ownership by Emperor Herculius. His daughter Fausta married Emperor Constantine, the first Christian Roman Emperor. Constantine's mother, the Empress Helena, was a very devout woman who promoted the symbolic value of the Christ relics, to support the power of her son and the power of the Church. Constantine publicly displayed the lance during the entire First Ecumenical Council in Nicaea, where disputes raged over which texts would be included in the Christian canon.

In the sixth century, the barbarians sacked Rome and seized the relic for a time, before it was reacquired by Emperor Justinian. He used the lance as a symbol of his intent to restore the glory of the Holy Roman Empire. That symbol became somewhat tainted, when Justinian proceeded to murder tens of thousands of nonbelievers. Because of his reputation for savagery, Christians in the next century considered the lance to be an unfit symbol for Christianity and attention shifted to the Holy Grail, which became the iconic representation of the Medieval Church.

Three centuries later, Charlemagne came to possess the lance and personally carried it in all his military campaigns. By the eleventh century the wooden shaft had disappeared. Emperor Henry IV tried to insert what he thought to be a Holy Nail, one of Christ's crucifixion spikes, in the middle of the spearhead, but the job was botched and the lance split in two. It was especially a pity since the nail was clearly a fake, nothing like a first-century Roman spike. The lance was mended with a golden sleeve and silver wire and, to this day, it bears these patches along with that preposterous skinny nail in its center.

Then, in the twelfth century, the lance was known to be carried into battle by Frederick I, best known as Barbarossa for his red beard. The lance slips from his hands at the moment of his death in 1190 and is lost for two hundred years. The story commences again in the fourteenth century, when Charles IV launches a quest for the lance and the Holy Grail, but finds only the lance. He displays it in Nürnberg and there it remains for five centuries.'

Schneider paused to sip at his tea but it was cold.

'Gerhardt, ask my girl to get me some fresh tea. Ready to hear more, Jürgen?'

'Yes, sir!'

'During these five hundred years a cult of sort developed: the cult of the Holy Lance. The artifact, it was said, possessed super-natural powers. It was revered by the people.'

'Did it?' Besemer asked.

'Did it what?'

'Have supernatural powers.'

Schneider tapped a long finger against his cheek. 'Well, I don't know about that, but I do know it possessed immense cultural and symbolic power. These qualities can be a powerful tool to rally the people, when they must be rallied. When Napoleon Bonaparte invaded Nürnberg in the late eighteenth century, he was anxious to attain for himself the trappings of power, including the Holy Lance, to legitimize his desire to become a latter-day Holy Roman Emperor. Because of the importance of the lance to the German people, prior to Napoleon's arrival, the city councilors sent the lance to Vienna for safekeeping. But later, when peace came, confusion over the ownership of the lance led the imperial Habsburgs to refuse to return it to the Nürnberg. Eventually, it wound up on public display, along with other treasures of the Holy Roman Empire, at Vienna's Imperial Treasury.'

When the serving girl returned with a hot pot of tea, the young man seized the opportunity to interrupt again.

'That was where Adolf Hitler first laid eyes on it, when he was a young art student in Vienna.'

'Yes, very good, Jürgen,' Schneider said wearily. 'That was in 1909. Hitler next saw the lance in March of 1938, at the peak of his power. The night of the Anschluss, as Panzer divisions crossed into Austria, one of Hitler's handpicked men entered the museum and seized the lance and the other treasures. It was returned to Nürnberg, where it became a powerful beacon for the Reich, as a rallying cry for the Christians and for the historical imperial greatness of the nation. Well, we all know how that ended.

After the war, the Americans came looking for the treasure. Their so-called Monuments Men, led by a Germany-born American, the art historian, Major Walter Horn, found the lance and the crown jewels of the Holy Roman Empire in the basement of a primary school in Nürnberg. Eisenhower had the treasures returned to the Imperial Treasury at the Hofburg

Palace where any tourist in Vienna may view them behind bullet-proof glass.'

Besemer leaned forward and said in a conspiratorial tone, 'But some say the lance and the other artifacts found by the Americans were fakes, that the Reich hid the real ones for a future genera-tion of German patriots to find.'

Schneider pressed his lips into a forced smile. 'I have also heard these things. I don't pay attention to internet gossip. I concern myself with making our nation great again. That is why you're here. I am the leader of a group of aging patriots. By necessity, we are a secretive bunch of old farts. The symbol of our fidelity is the Holy Lance. We call ourselves, rather pomp-ously, the Knights of Longinus, because we follow in the deep footsteps of that great centurion's Aryan and Christian roots. We need new blood, Jürgen. What do you think about that?'

The young man's spine stiffened ramrod straight. If he'd been standing, Schneider imagined he'd come close to clicking his heels. 'I would be honored to join your ranks, Herr Schneider.'

'Good, good. I will present your candidacy to the other knights. Now go about your business and you'll hear from us again before too long.'

When he was gone, Schneider asked Gerhardt what he thought of the fellow.

'Seemed like a right jerk to me,' the he said.

'Too eager for your liking?'

'Way too eager. And he doesn't know when he's supposed to shut his mouth.'

'Not one of your problems, my laconic friend.'

'Laconic?'

'Never mind. I imagine that your father and myself appeared to be too eager when we were presented to the knights at Jürgen's age. I have some reservations about the fellow myself, but overall I think he'll do nicely. I plan to recommend him to the group.'

'Why didn't you tell him the spear the Americans found was a fake?'

'He's not one of us yet. He doesn't need to know about Antarctica and all the rest. Even when he's a member, we'll be cautious until he's proven himself. We'll monitor his contacts, his internet postings and if he's the slightest bit indiscreet, we'll terminate him.'

'You mean I'll terminate him.'

Schneider settled in behind his desk and reached for an unmarked folder. 'Off you go, Gerhardt. You've got work to do.'

Reaching for his fountain pen, his hand brushed the keyboard of his laptop computer, waking it from sleep mode. The last page he'd been reading, before Jürgen Besemer had arrived, lit up the screen.

It was from the website of the Harvard University Divinity School, more specifically, the faculty biography of one, Professor Calvin A. Donovan.

Schneider spent a moment looking at the photo of the smiling, dark-haired professor and snapped the laptop closed a little too hard.

ELEVEN

The train from Rome was packed. Cal had a first-class ticket, but without any empty seats he was forced to stay put and listen to a businessman across the aisle engage in a prolonged and heated negotiation on his phone. He tried to read but was too distracted; he had to resort to putting on head-phones and drowning the fellow out with a Springsteen mix.

He'd woken that morning with a naked, hung-over British woman in his bed, who thankfully had to rush off to an early meeting. Since she was in a hurry, he was able to avoid the painful morning-after ritual of breakfast and a chat, followed by the exchange of phone numbers that would never be called.

By the time the train pulled into Naples, Cal's ears were buzzing from decibel overload. Carrying a bag on each shoulder, he made his way through the crowded station toward the taxi rank.

As he passed a café, two young men in jeans and polo shirts whispered to one another and began following him. Outside, the queue for the taxis was long and Cal took his place, across from the graffiti-strewn construction fences surrounding the Piazza

Giuseppe Garibaldi. Suddenly, he felt the weight disappear from his left shoulder when one of the young men who'd been shadowing him cut the strap of his briefcase with a straight razor.

Looking up, he saw the two youths running across the piazza with his bag. It had his passport, his laptop computer, his phone and books inside. These were all replaceable. His handwritten notes on the interviews he'd conducted were not.

'Hey, you!' he shouted. 'Stop!'

But they weren't going to stop, were they? And in an instant he knew that the only way to recover his precious notebook was to take matters into his own hands. He shed his other bag – he didn't give a damn about his clothes – and took off after the thieves. His loafers were on the new side and the leather soles were a bit too frictionless for a good grip on the smooth stones of the piazza. He picked up traction following them onto the coarser pavement of Corso Novara, a crowded street off the piazza, and gained on them.

The two men had the athleticism of young footballers and they loped easily down the street. After about two hundred meters they slowed to a jog, perhaps trying to avoid drawing attention, unaware they were being pursued.

Cal, in full sprint, pumped his arms to increase his speed and weaved around parked cars and pedestrians. He was rapidly gaining on them when they heard his footfalls and, with surprised over-the-shoulder glances, they took off running again.

Cal gave scant thought to what he was going to do when he caught up. The young man with his bag was holding it in one arm and his running was less fluid than his companion's. Cal had him in his sights and bore down for the final sprint.

Ten meters, five meters, one meter.

The man shouted for his friend just as Cal got a fistful of his T-shirt. It pulled at the fellow's throat and began to rip.

People around them began to move away and shout at Cal, who seemed to be the aggressor.

'He's got my bag!' Cal shouted.

The young man shifted the bag under his left arm as if it were a rugby ball and reached into his pocket. When he wheeled around, breaking Cal's grip on his shirt, a straight razor was in his right hand.

'Hey, watch out!' a shopper called out. 'He's got a knife! Somebody call for the police.'

Cal didn't hesitate. He balled both fists and assumed a boxer's stance, then landed a lightning left jab into an angular cheek. The man yelped and lifted his right hand above his head to deliver a slashing blow with his razor. There was the briefest of openings for Cal to deliver a straight-handed right into the man's nose that crushed cartilage and paralyzed him with pain. The bag dropped onto the pavement. Cal kept his eyes on the razor and the second man who was a few meters away, looking like he couldn't decide whether to help his friend or run. Cal decided he had to deal with the weapon if he was going to get out of this unhurt. The man's nose was bleeding and he was cursing. The hand with a razor was moving again when Cal performed a maneuver short on imagination but long on effectiveness. He hit him again with another straight right, squarely on his broken nose.

That ended it. The young man hit the ground onto his knees and dropped the razor to cover his face with both palms. That's when Cal scooped up his bag and took a few steps back, keeping his eyes on the second man. The injured man's partner ran forward but before Cal had time to figure out if he'd have to keep fighting, the second man was dragging the first up by an arm and persuading him in a torrent of words to flee.

They ran off and disappeared at the first intersection, Via Firenze.

Cal heard someone calling, 'Signore, signore!' and turned around to see a pair of young women running towards him, one of them with his clothing bag.

'We saw what happened,' the other one said, drawing close. 'The police are coming.'

Breathless, Cal responded in Italian, 'Thank you. Thank you for restoring my briefly shattered faith in humanity.'

An hour later, Cal entered the church of San Domenico Maggiore, not to pray but for his appointment. It was not Cal's first visit. He considered it one of the most beautiful churches in Naples; a treasure-filled, luminous Baroque masterpiece constructed around far more ancient chapels. The young priest, who was pacing around the tenth-century chapel at the far end of the right nave, seemed to recognize Cal.

'Professor Donovan,' he said. 'I am Antonio Forcisi. Are you all right?'

Cal had called the priest to let him know he'd been mugged at the train station and would be late.

'I'm fine,' Cal smiled. 'The thief didn't do as well.'

'I am so relieved you weren't hurt. I apologize on behalf of my adopted city.'

'Don't. I love Naples. A small incident like this doesn't change my opinion.'

'Please follow me to my office,' the priest said. 'May I take one of your bags?'

'I wish the thieves had been that polite.'

Forcisi was a pale, fresh-faced youth with a wispy, blonde moustache that would have taken mere seconds to shave off. The parish offices were near the church convent. Forcisi shared a space with two other assistant priests. One of them was at a desk but left to give them privacy.

Forcisi noticed the cut shoulder strap of Cal's briefcase and asked if he could find someone to get it mended, but Cal told him not to bother and that he'd use the handle instead.

'It's usually not such a good idea to challenge these street thieves,' the priest said. 'Some of them carry guns.'

'I got lucky, I guess,' Cal said.

'So, please tell me how I can help you,' the priest said. 'Are there additional questions you need answered?'

'Sorry, I don't understand. I haven't asked any questions yet.'

'Well, not you, but the other man.'

'Who?'

'The monsignor from the Vatican who came last week.'

Cal frowned. 'I wasn't aware of this. Who was he?'

'Monsignor Leinfelder. A German, I believe. But he could have been Austrian or Swiss. I didn't really ask about that.'

'Who did he say he represented?'

'I don't know. The Vatican. A monsignor visits me from the Vatican to ask questions and, well, I don't question him. It's the same with you. You called from the Vatican and I didn't ask questions either.'

'But I told you who I was and who I was representing.'

'Yes, you were more open. I haven't been a priest very long. I respect the church authorities and know my place in the hierarchy.'

'What did he ask you about?'

'Perhaps the same things that will interest you: my friendship with Giovanni, our days in the seminary, my knowledge of his stigmata, my opinions about his condition. Are these the matters that concern you too?'

'They are.'

'Did this monsignor leave his card?'

The priest shook his head.

'I don't suppose there's a photo of him?'

Forcisi's laugh was high-pitched. 'We didn't take a selfie, if that's what you mean.' Then he turned serious. 'Are you suggesting this man wasn't who he said he was?'

'Not at all,' Cal said. 'It's probably a typical Vatican bureaucratic snafu; the right hand not knowing what the left hand is doing.'

Cal pulled out his notebook, wrote down the German priest's name and began asking questions.

'How long have I known Giovanni?' Forcisi said. 'A long time. We attended the same primary school when we were seven. We sat next to each other, we played together at recess and lived less than a kilometer from one another. We were best friends right up until we became priests together.'

'You're no longer friends?'

The priest looked pensive. He briefly looked out the window over the piazza. 'I suppose we're still friends. We talk by telephone. Not so often. It's different now. He's not the same person. All this has changed him. He's not the fun-loving Giovanni any longer. He's carrying a heavy burden.'

'Have you talked with him about this change?'

'Not directly, no. I get the sense this topic is off-limits. Everyone around him is obsessed with the stigmata. I only want to be his friend.'

'Not his confessor?'

'Heavens no! Certainly not that. He has others who can perform this service for him. You've met him, yes?'

'A few days ago,' Cal said. 'I also went to Francavilla to meet his mother and his sister.'

'How are they? I miss them.'

'I got the impression that his notoriety is a burden on them.'

'I'm sure of that. And Giovanni? How did you find him?'

'He seemed like a very nice young man swimming against a very powerful tide.'

'I think that's a good way to describe his situation.'

Cal looked up from his notes. 'What was he like at the seminary?'

'Early on, happy. Happy and casual, I would have to say. I was always worried about the decision he made to become a priest. From when I was sixteen, I really knew I wanted to go in this direction with my life. I felt the calling quite strongly. Giovanni made fun of me, not in a cruel way but a joking way. Everything for him was a joke. He was maybe a little immature, always a little behind emotionally. I think he made his choice to follow me into the seminary not so much out of a burning desire to serve Christ, but to run away from his unhappiness with the way his life was developing.'

'Wouldn't a lot of priests admit to the same if they were being honest with themselves?' Cal asked.

'For sure. We had several men leave the seminary when they came face-to-face with that self-realization.'

'But not Giovanni.'

'You know, he was different from these men, professor. He grew as a person during the process and I really think his faith got stronger along his journey. He surprised himself. He told me that. It came to him in the last year of our studies, the conviction that he had made the right choice and that he was going to be joyfully devoted to the priesthood and tending to the spiritual needs of his community. As we got close to the end of our training he was serene, optimistic.'

'And then Croatia happened.'

'Yes,' the priest sighed. 'Croatia.'

Cal clicked his pen and prepared to take detailed notes. 'I'd like you to tell me everything you remember about the day you visited the monastery.'

*   *   *

'Look, there's the chapel,' Forcisi said excitedly, rushing ahead up the dirt path.

Giovanni was a little puffed out after climbing the hill from the car park and called ahead to his friend, 'What? Are you trying to give me a heart attack? Slow down. It's not going anywhere.'

Forcisi let Giovanni catch up. 'I'm sorry,' he said. 'It's just that I'm blown away by this. Look at it! It's ancient. Seventh century, for God's sake. The Church was so young when it was built.'

It was Giovanni who lifted the latch of the weathered door. Even though it was sunny, the interior of the stone church was dim, lit by a few wall fixtures with dirty candelabra bulbs. The chapel windows were too small to naturally light the space. Forcisi nudged his friend. There were two brown-robed monks sitting beside one another on a pew facing an empty stone altar. Giovanni closed the door as gently as he could but the latch clunked and the monks glanced to the rear before turning back to the altar. The two seminarians seated themselves in a rear pew and soon were lost in prayer and meditation.

In time, the monks finished their own prayer session and rose to depart. It was Forcisi who buttonholed them with a comment in Italian and then English when, at first, they didn't respond.

'Your church is a marvel,' he said. 'We have just finished our training at a seminary in Italy and soon we will be ordained. We are inspired by the holiness and venerability of your chapel.'

Brother Augustin was wizened and bow-legged. He didn't use a cane but his gait was unsteady and shuffling. Though Brother Ivan looked hale and healthy by comparison, he too was elderly. Ivan mumbled an insincere pleasantry in English and walked on, but Augustin stopped and inspected the seated young men. Although it was Forcisi who had spoken, Augustin looked past him, his milky eyes settled on Giovanni.

'What do you know of this church?' Augustin asked.

'Me?' Giovanni said, with the demeanor of an unprepared student being called on by his teacher.

'Yes, you.'

'It was founded by the Benedictines, I think.'

'Are you coming?' Ivan asked Augustin in Croatian.

Augustin ignored him and kept his gaze on Giovanni. 'We Benedictines have been here in an unbroken chain since the year 685.'

'That's a long time,' Giovanni said.

'Suit yourself,' Ivan said, leaving.

'It's the longest continuous Benedictine community in the world, is it not?' Forcisi said, trying to get some of the old monk's attention.

Augustin pointed a bony finger. It was then that the young men saw that his wrist was wrapped in black cloth. 'What's your name?' the monk asked.

Giovanni searched Forcisi's eyes, as if asking: why is he only interested in me?

'I'm Giovanni,' he said. 'This is Antonio. We're from Francavilla al Mare. Have you heard of it?'

'Francavilla? No. I never visited Italy. I have been at this monastery for sixty-five years. Before that I never left Croatia. Did you know the church has a crypt?'

It was Forcisi who replied. 'There was no mention of a crypt in the guide book.'

'I was speaking to Giovanni,' the monk said acidly.

'Like Antonio said,' Giovanni replied, 'we didn't know there was one.'

'Would you like to see it?'

Giovanni seemed uncomfortable at the attention directed at him. He shrugged.

'Sure we would.'

'Come with me,' the monk said. 'Just you. Not your friend.'

Giovanni protested and said that he wasn't interested if both of them couldn't go, but Forcisi told him with a pout that it was all right with him.

'That's silly, Antonio,' Giovanni said in Italian. 'This old guy is creeping me out anyway.'

'Go on,' Forcisi urged. 'Take a picture and tell me about it.'

The monk led the way and Giovanni followed him to an iron grate on one side of the chapel. He turned to look at his friend as he began descending the stone stairway. Forcisi detected a look of fear on his face and almost called him back, but he held his tongue.

Giovanni was gone for no more than ten minutes.

At one point, his friend went over to the iron grate and leaned over the stairs to try to hear what was going on but he heard nothing.

He was sitting on the rear pew when the grate swung open.

Brother Augustin emerged first and shuffled toward the door, his eyes cast downward.

Giovanni followed several seconds behind with, what Forcisi could only describe as a look of gravity on his formerly carefree face.

'Gravity?' Cal asked. 'I don't know what you mean by that.'

Forcisi seemed to be searching for the best way to answer.

'He went down into that crypt an easygoing man-child, like the Giovanni I always knew. He came up like a mature man, a sober man, like someone who had instantly acquired great wisdom.'

The two friends didn't talk until they were back at the car. Giovanni had driven the rental car from Dubrovnik since he was the better driver. Forcisi saw him wince as he turned the key. When he put the car into reverse he winced again then returned it to neutral.

'Do you think you could drive?' Giovanni said.

'What's the matter? You ok?' Forcisi asked.

'I just don't feel like driving. I'm a bit tired.'

'What happened down there? I think something happened.'

'Nothing happened.'

'Tell me what you saw.'

'Nothing much,' Giovanni answered dully. 'Some gravestones in the floor. A small altar.'

'You were down there a long time for just that.'

'Was I?'

'Look, I'll drive but I'd really like you to talk to me.'

They exchanged places in the car.

Giovanni folded his arms across his chest. 'I'm just going to close my eyes for a little while. Like I said, I'm a bit tired.'

* * *

'When I asked him about visiting the crypt he told me you didn't want to go, that you were claustrophobic,' Cal said.

'That's not so. The old monk didn't invite me. Just Giovanni.'

'I see. When you got back to your hotel in Dubrovnik how did he seem?'

Forcisi was dying to use the bathroom and he rushed inside as soon as they got into their room. When he got out he saw that Giovanni had climbed into bed, fully dressed.

'You don't look so well,' he said.

'I'm a little feverish, maybe,' Giovanni said.

'There's a pharmacy nearby,' Forcisi said. 'I'll go get you some aspirin.'

'While you're there, could you get some gauze bandages too?'

'Why?'

'Down in the crypt, I cut my wrist on a bit of metal.'

'Let me have a look.'

'No!'

Forcisi was startled at the vehemence of the response.

'All right, suit yourself. I'm only trying to be helpful. Are you going to want supper tonight?'

'I only want to sleep.'

'So you didn't see his wrists?' Cal said.

'Not that day, not ever. When we returned home I didn't see him until the day we were ordained. After the ceremony, one of the new priests told me he'd seen some blood on his cassock, but Giovanni denied it when I asked him about it later.'

'And how was his behavior in that period between your return from Croatia and ordainment, his mood?'

'Honestly, I saw very little of him. Not for lack of trying. He stayed with his mother and sister and didn't want to go out. When I did come by to try to persuade him to socialize, he was without humor. He seemed like he was carrying a great weight. His family was very worried about him, but I couldn't get him out of his shell. Now I know the burden he was hiding. Then, I couldn't imagine.'

'Have you seen him since his stigmata became known?'

'He was assigned to Monte Sulla, I was sent to Naples. When I read about the stigmata I called him several times and eventually got through to him. I offered to visit but he said no. We've spoken regularly since then but it's always me who has to initiate contact. We talk as colleagues, in generalities about pastoral life. He makes it clear he doesn't wish to speak of his situation. It's sad, really. I can say we are no longer the kind of friends we used to be, when we always had a good laugh and freely confided to one another about our hopes and dreams. He's become the revered Padre Gio, but I'm still young Antonio. I pray for him every day, professor.'

Cal closed his notebook and pocketed his pen. It was a calculated gambit intended to lull the young priest into the belief that his next question was off the record.

'Do you think he's making his wrists bleed?'

Forcisi shook his head. 'I almost wish he were because then, with psychological and spiritual help, his soul might be healed. But no, as someone who was there the day his wounds developed, I'm completely certain the stigmata are real. Something happened to him in that crypt. I told the same thing to the German monsignor.'

Giovanni was kneeling in prayer in his bedroom, when Sister Theresa knocked gently on his door.

'Padre,' she said. 'There is a phone call for you, your friend Padre Antonio.'

Giovanni came downstairs and picked up the phone in the lounge. The wrap on his left wrist was already stained through with blood.

'Hello, Antonio.'

'Giovanni, how are you?' Forcisi asked.

'I am fine, fine. What news from Naples?'

'I've had another visit from a Vatican representative, an American professor.'

'Donovan,' Giovanni said. 'He saw me too.'

'I know.'

'So?'

'He was very interested in our visit to St Athanasius.'

'And what did you tell him?'

'Only what happened. He said you told him I didn't go into the crypt because I had claustrophobia.'

'I may have said something like that.'

'Why?'

'This wasn't a confession, Antonio. It was an inquisition. The Vatican doesn't need to know everything about me.'

'I've got to ask. I've always been respectful, Giovanni but I've got to ask. What happened down there?'

'It's not something I'm prepared to discuss. Don't hate me for this.'

'I don't hate you. I love you. And God loves you.'

Giovanni teared up. 'Thank you for that.' He composed himself. 'What did you think of him, of Donovan?'

'He was thorough, efficient. He's obviously an intelligent man. Very different from the German.'

'What German?'

'First the Vatican sent a German monsignor. He wasn't clever at all, a crude man, if you ask me.'

'I was spared him, I suppose.'

'What do you think the Vatican wants?'

'Honestly, I don't know,' Giovanni said. 'Whatever it is, I will be humble and obedient.'

'Of course you will. Tell me, how is your family?'

'Mother is well enough. I hear she's been baking. Irene is coming to visit today with bags of food.'

'I saw a recent picture of you,' Forcisi said. 'You look like you've lost weight.'

Finally a chuckle. 'It's the only benefit from my situation.'

The nuns, Sister Theresa and Sister Vera, looked askance at the spread that Irene was laying out on Giovanni's table, as if to say, you don't think we can cook well enough for your brother?

'Look, she made all your favorites,' Irene said, lifting the lid on the Tupperware. 'Maccheroni alla chitarra, polpette di formaggio, agnello, cacio e uova. And for dessert, parozzo Abruzzese and my only contribution, biscotti di Cocullo.'

Giovanni shook his head. 'You don't expect me to eat all that, do you?'

'What you don't eat today, you can eat tomorrow.'

'What I don't eat today,' he said looking at the nuns, 'my brothers and sisters will eat.'

'We'll leave you alone now,' Sister Vera said curtly. 'Let us know when you're ready for coffee.'

When the nuns were gone, Irene told him she thought they were jealous.

'They are protective,' he said. 'Like mother hens.'

Irene passed him a plate she'd filled for him. 'Let me channel mama: mangia, mangia.'

As he lifted his utensils she stared at his wrapped wrists.

'Yes, they're still there,' he said.

'I'm sorry.'

'It's ok. I shouldn't have been sarcastic.' He tasted the pasta. 'Tell mama her food is delicious.'

'I will. So how are you holding up?'

He sighed. 'I celebrate Mass, I take confessions, I talk to parishioners, I deliver blessings. I'm a priest. It's what priests do.'

'If you don't want to talk about the elephant in the room, then ok,' she said.

'It's tiresome,' he said.

'Maybe for you, but not for me. I'm worried about you. Mama is worried.'

'Can't you understand how tired I am of all this Padre Gio stuff?'

'Of course I can. That's why I think you should maybe take a break from the spotlight of Monte Sulla. Please think about asking your bishop to give you a leave of absence, to send you to someplace where you can rest in isolation.'

'I'm sure the Vatican is already plotting something along those lines.'

'Would it be so bad?'

He put his fork down. 'I just want to live a normal life.'

'I'm sorry, keep eating. I'm obligated to give a food report to mama.'

They continued in silence and then ventured into the safe area of small talk about their extended family.

Over slices of chocolate cake, Irene said, 'Could I ask you something?'

He held up his wrists. 'As long as it's not about these.'

'It's not. At least I don't think it is. If I'm wrong about that, please don't be angry at me.'

He granted permission.

'A while ago, I saw something I'm having trouble explaining. I was shopping on Viale Nettuno and I saw someone go into the gelateria.'

'Who was it?' he asked.

'It was you, Giovanni.'

He looked at her strangely. 'Obviously it wasn't. I can assure you I was here last week.'

'I know you were. But it's been troubling me and I had to bring it up. I didn't *think* it was you. I *knew* it was you.'

'All right, you knew it was me,' he said blankly. 'Would you kindly tell me what I said to you?'

'You didn't say anything. I followed you into the gelateria but you had disappeared.'

'Into thin air? Or into a tub of gelato?'

She looked hurt. 'Please don't make fun of me. I know what I saw.' She wiped away a tear. 'Tell me, has anyone else had the same experience that I'm describing?'

'I'm sorry I upset you,' he said. 'I can tell you in all seriousness that no one has ever told me something like this.'

She looked at her cake to avoid looking at her brother. 'I went online, Giovanni. It's called bilocation. It's an ability some people have – maybe it's a psychic ability, maybe it's a spiritual – it's an ability to appear to be in two places at the same time. Do you want to know who was supposed to do bilocation? Padre Pio.'

He said tartly, 'Well, maybe I'm getting to be like his clone. I'll have to grow a beard. He was supposed to smell like roses. Do I smell like roses?'

'Look, here I go again, stepping into a minefield but I think you know you have some powers. When she came here a few months ago, Mama told me she had a strange experience, an overwhelmingly strong vision that came into her head when you hugged her.'

'A vision of what?' he asked.

'She didn't tell you?'

'Maybe she did,' he said quietly.

'She said it was a vision of a person. She truly believes it was Christ. She said she saw his face, so close she felt she could touch it. When you stopped hugging her, the vision stopped. Is that why you won't hug me anymore, Giovanni?' she asked. 'Is that why you won't make any physical contact with me?'

He nodded and began to weep. 'It's happened to other people too. I'll almost never touch anyone anymore.'

She told him she wished she could hold him, comfort him, but he rose from the table.

'Did mama tell Calvin Donovan about this when he saw you?'

'No, she didn't say anything. Me neither. I didn't trust him,' she said. 'Why do you mention him?'

'Because he's someone with whom I made an exception. I did touch him.'

'Why?'

'I don't know,' Giovanni said. 'I felt a closeness.'

'Closer than to me?'

'Of course not. I can't explain it. It was a kind of kinship.'

She vigorously shook her head. 'Don't let your guard down with him. I don't know what the Vatican intends to do with you, but as far as I'm concerned they hired an American hitman. I didn't like Calvin Donovan and I hope I never see him again.'

TWELVE

Berlin, present day

Toward the end of a long day, Lambret Schneider wearily stared out his office window at the night sky of Berlin. His secretaries had gone and he was quite certain he wouldn't be interrupted, but still he took the precaution of locking his door. The urge to reexamine a precious document he hadn't read in years had been growing since the morning. His personal safe was located at the rear of his coat closet. He deftly spun the dial to the combination he would never forget: the day, month and year of Oskar Hufnagel's death.

On the top shelf of the safe was an A4-size envelope that he took back to his desk. When he undid the red-stringed closure, he carefully removed the gossamer sheets of onionskin paper. The single-spaced, typewritten report was faded with age.

Otto Rahn
SS-Untersturmführer
19 Oktober 1935

An den
Reichsführer-SS und Chef der Deutschen Polizei
Heinrich Himmler
Berlin SW 11
Reichsführer!

Schneider squinted at the dense, blurred words that followed. He could have sworn that the last time he had the report in his hands he'd been able to read it without glasses. He wasn't getting any younger, he supposed, as he bitterly reached inside his desk for his readers.

Time was running out. He felt consumed by a sense of urgency.

Berlin, 1935

If you saw him once you never forgot him.

He favored black: long black trench coats over finely-tailored, black three-piece suits. His ever-present, wide-brimmed, black fedora was always at a rakish tilt over deeply sunken, shadowed eyes. In public, he liked to thrust his wedge of a chin forward in a gesture of superiority. He was whippet thin, almost emaciated in appearance, and when his unbuttoned coat billowed it seemed he might be swept off his feet into the air, like some winged gremlin.

As Otto Rahn and his taller, older companion, strutted down the bustling streets, a streetcar full of evening commuters passed them by. Some of them stared down at the young man, perhaps wondering if he was someone important, as only a celebrity would conduct himself so cockily.

His recently acquired, book-lined flat was not in the best of neighborhoods. On his return from Paris, if he hadn't required so many bookcases, he could have afforded a more salubrious address, but his needs as a researcher came first. Puffing at the top of the fourth flight of stairs, his friend, a heavy smoker, gasped for breath while Rahn fiddled with both locks.

Inside, they tossed their hats onto chairs. Rahn's hair was also black, swept back and heavily pomaded. Rahn's guest slumped onto the sofa and loosened his tie knot.

'Drink?' Rahn asked, shedding his coat.

'God yes,' Huber said. He lit a cigarette. 'Brandy.'

Rahn poured generously into a pair of large snifters.

Huber admired the stemware. 'These are new. They look expensive.'

'They were,' Rahn said. 'Very. Next to my books and my pens, I consider good brandy glasses essential, wouldn't you agree?'

'You're reveling in being the dark horse, Otto,' Huber said. 'Two months ago you write to me from Paris, complaining about being as poor a church mouse and now you're living the high life in Berlin.'

Rahn smiled mischievously. 'Stay put. I want to show you something else new.'

With Rahn in the bedroom, Huber got up to pace around his friend's study, scanning the open books on his desk and peeking at his neat notes. More of his usual: caverns, Pyrenees, Cathars, Montségur.

Through the closed door he heard, 'Ready?'

'Yes! I suppose I'm as ready as I can be,' Huber called back.

Rahn emerged and Huber could only stare at him in dumbfounded shock.

Hand on hip, Rahn modeled his body-hugging, black, woolen uniform, complete with peaked military cap, high black boots and a swastika on the red armband.

'Like it?' Rahn said. 'It's my favorite color.'

Clearly, Huber was not amused. He glanced at the door as if expecting a raid.

'What the hell are you doing, Otto? Take it off. It's an offense to impersonate an officer of the SS.'

'But I'm not an officer, at least not yet.' He pointed to his collar. 'See? No insignia. I'm told in short order I'll be given the rank of Untersturmführer.'

'You're not joking, are you?'

'I'm dead serious. I'm in the SS.'

Huber fumbled for another cigarette. 'Tell me how. Tell me why.'

'I received a telegram in Paris from an unknown benefactor who said he admired my work. If I agreed to return to Berlin, he said he would telegram me a substantial sum of money. Intrigued and impoverished, I agreed. When I arrived in Berlin, I was summoned to an address to meet this benefactor. He heaped praise on my book, *Crusade against the Grail*, and offered me a research job with an unlimited budget. Do you hear me, Huber, an *unlimited budget*? There were, of course, some conditions. Joining the SS was one of them.'

'Who was this man?'

'Heinrich Himmler.'

Huber's complexion blanched. 'You made a pact with the devil,' he hissed.

'What was I supposed to do? Say no?'

'But does he know about you?'

'That I'm a homosexual? That I have some Jewish blood? I imagine so. He's the chief of police. It didn't come up. I assume I need to be discreet.'

'You? Discreet?'

Rahn laughed and moved toward the bedroom door. 'A little more discreet, maybe. So, my dear, put the cigarette out and come and help me get out of this tight uniform.'

Following his first meeting with Himmler, Rahn had not been able to stop shaking. He had tried to medicate himself with laudanum drops and a bottle of red wine but he couldn't settle his nerves. Instinctively, he had written an entry in his personal journal. Writing always calmed him.

Now, with Huber sleeping soundly in his bed, Rahn picked up his journal and re-read the old entry.

When I saw that the address I was given on Prinz Albrecht Strasse was the police headquarters, my heart fell into my stomach. I thought I was going to be arrested, that all this had been an elaborate trap to ensnare this poor little rabbit. I considered running away but I sucked up my courage and entered. I am expected, I said to the clerk. My name was on his list and he sent me to a room on the third floor. Not just any room! The door was marked, Reichsführer-SS! I'm not a political man but I follow the news. These days only a fool would put his head in the sand. I know who holds this position, for God's sake.

Himmler, a man not much larger than myself, was seated behind a huge desk. It made him appear smaller, which I'm sure was not the intended effect. He bade me to sit without rising or extending a hand. This put me even more ill at ease but then he made my anxieties disappear. Herr Rahn, he said, I have been looking forward to meeting you. He held up a copy of my Grail book and said, 'your book was recommended to me. I enjoyed it immensely. I am your secret benefactor. I hear you have found a flat in Berlin.' I am certain there is little the head of the police does not know. I made some small talk about the differences between Paris and Berlin. He appeared impatient and began quizzing me about my research.

He asked about my theory that the thirteenth-century Cathars in southern France were descended from the Druids and were closely associated with the Knights Templar. He was conversant with my arguments about the sacred geology of the Cathar's holy mountain and their enclave at Montségur, its sunrise orientations and its relationship with other holy places. He knew all about my beliefs that the Cathars had long kept the Holy Grail within their mountain fortress and that, in 1244, they made their last futile stand against Catholic crusaders. And that, before the castle fell and all Cathars were slaughtered, three Cathars slipped away with the treasure. He was fascinated with my description of exploring the grottos of the Sabarthes area south of Montségur and though he had a bookmark on that section of my book, he wanted to hear it from my mouth. I told him about the massive cavern of Lombrives with walls covered in Templar symbols side by side with Carthar emblems. He was particularly interested in my description of the engraving of a lance.

'But you did not find the Grail,' he said. 'Alas, not,' I

replied, 'but with proper funding and resources I believe I might be successful.'

He astounded me by offering to employ me as a member of his personal staff, assigned to work in the SS heritage bureau, the Ahnenerbe, which was headed by a man I did not know: an administrator named Wolfram Sievers, whom I subsequently learned was something of a bully boy despite being a serviceable musician. I would be given a generous salary, a secretary and, more importantly, a budget for travel and research. I inquired how he thought an esoteric academician like myself could be of use to the Reich.

He began by speaking vaguely about the desire he shared with the Führer to connect the aspirations of the German people to the rich Aryan heritage of the past. 'The German people,' he said, 'respect the traditions of Christianity, but these traditions had to be put into the correct Aryan framework.' Then he got more specific. He wanted me to lead the effort to scour Europe and the middle Orient to find and procure an assemblage of all the authentic, sacred relics of Christ. The German people would take pride in their ownership and appreciate the Reich for securing their safekeeping in what was likely to be a turbulent future. He was planning to house the artifacts at the SS castle at Wewelsburg in a special shrine he was going to build.

He produced a handwritten list of the relics he desired. The Holy Grail was there, of course, but also the Holy Lance, fragments of the True Cross, the Holy Shroud, the Crown of Thorns, the Sandals and Cap of Christ, the Burial Cloth, the Holy Nails.

The Grail has been my main area of scholarship, but I offered my opinion on the Shroud and the Lance. The only credible candidate for the shroud was in plain sight at Turin and the spearhead in Vienna was likely to be authentic, given its well-documented history. I had never given much thought to the other more minor relics. Himmler told me that he wasn't worried about getting his hands on the Shroud of Turin, since he was certain Mussolini would deal it away for the right price. Enigmatically, he assured me that since the lance was already in Germanic hands he wasn't concerned about that either. I wonder if the Austrians would agree!

Then he matter-of-factly mentioned that I would have to join the SS if I was to work for him. I gulped and nodded. I wasn't going to destroy the opportunity of a lifetime by telling him what I thought of his SS goons.

He concluded by asking me where I thought I would begin my quest for the relics. I thought for a moment before replying that a good place to start was the greatest library of Christian texts: the Vatican Apostolic Library.

Five months later, Otto Rahn, climbed the stairs to his Berlin flat, dropped his battered leather suitcases on the rug and flopped onto his bed in a state of utter exhaustion. How many countries had he visited, how many cities? How many notebooks had he filled with his tight scrawl?

When he finally awoke he went to his favorite café for coffee and pastries then returned to his desk to take stock of his travels. He carefully removed the items from the paper and cloth packing materials and made labels in his best calligraphy. He set up his camera and tripod over the desk and positioned his gooseneck lamp for maximum illumination. Then, one by one, he photographed each object beside a metal rule.

The smallest artifacts were the thorns. He had been amazed at just how many purported Holy Thorns were scattered throughout Europe. Rahn had joked to the SS minder assigned to travel with him, that he didn't wonder so much about which churches claimed to possess thorns from Christ's crown, but which ones did *not* make the claim. Rahn acquired them from chapels in France, Spain, Flanders, Italy, Poland and Czechoslovakia. A combination of greed and fear generally served to separate a relic from a relic holder. Rahn travelled with hard currency and made it known that he personally represented Heinrich Himmler, a man whose reputation was known throughout the continent. Impoverished dioceses could generally be persuaded to part with their relics for the right price, but if a deal was not forthcoming, Rahn would hire local thugs to break into a church in the middle of the night and steal what could not be bought. Of course, all of the currency, threats and thievery in the world couldn't separate famous relics from places like: Notre Dame in Paris, the Basilica of the Holy Cross in Jerusalem, St Peter's in the Vatican or the Cathedrals of Monza or Milan.

He laid out each of his fourteen thorns, handling them with tweezers because of their delicacy. He had acquired only the species that his botany consultants had told him were typical of the thorny shrubs found in and near Jerusalem. European thorns were obvious fakes. The smallest spike Rahn possessed was two centimeters, the longest, five. When each was photographed and repacked, he began dealing with the even larger assemblage of petrified pieces of wood, all claimed to be fragments of Christ's cross. These ranged from pinky-nail-sized chunks to pieces as long as a hand.

Five fragments of cloth were next, each stored in its own airmail envelope. Some were allegedly from Christ's burial cloth, others from his burial cap. Most were the size of postage stamps and he also handled these with tweezers, because of their gossamer frailty. Finally, there were three small pieces of leather, said to be the remains of Christ's sandals.

The dogs that did not bark that day were those relics Rahn had failed to find or failed to acquire. The Holy Grail, the object of his own decades-long quest, remained an enigma. He would mount another prolonged expedition to the Cathar caves and labyrinthine caverns of southern France as soon as he was able. Famed relics of Holy Nails and the True Cross were on public display in the great churches of Europe and Jerusalem. Rahn made a catalogue of these for Himmler's review, but that was as far as he could go. Besides the Holy Lance relic at the Imperial Treasury in Vienna, another famous candidate for the Spear of Longinus was at the Vatican. And finally, Rahn had failed to visit Turin, as the shroud was, at least to him, unobtainable.

When he was done with the artifacts, Rahn began to review his notebooks.

Volume I chronicled his research at the Vatican Library, where he had presented his credentials as an expert in the crusade by the Medieval Church against the Cathars. The chief archivist was aware of Rahn's book and eagerly produced a copy for his signature. From then on, Rahn had access to all manner of manuscripts, books and papal edicts. During his fortnight of daily attendance at the library, he had spent most of his time doing Grail research, particularly on his pet theory of a Grail-Templar-Cathar connection. But he had uncovered one particularly intriguing nugget of information, which was on a wholly different topic that he would highlight in his report to Himmler and Wolfram Sievers, his boss at the Ahnenerbe. It had come from an old Greek manuscript with the library accession code, VAT. GR. 1001 and it had left him perplexed but excited.

The next seven notebook volumes concerned the particulars of his relic hunts throughout Europe. He eagerly opened Volume VIII, the notebook that covered the week he had spent in Yerevan. His findings would factor prominently in his report to Himmler and Wolfram Sievers.

When at the Vatican Library, Rahn had requested archival copies of the works of Eusebius of Caesarea – a Roman historian who died in the mid-fourth century – and the book, *Ecclesiastical History*, written by Theodoret, a fifth-century Cypriot. The library had a copy of the original text in which Theodoret wrote about Empress Helena, the first collector of the relics of Christ. The empress had gone so far as to commission her own excavations in Palestine, to locate the tomb of Jesus and the site of his crucifixion. According to Theodoret, Helena discovered the True Cross and the Holy Nails. Rahn had read this about the nails:

> *The mother of the emperor, on learning the accomplishment of her desire, gave orders that a portion of the nails should be inserted in the royal helmet, in order that the head of her son might be preserved from the darts of his enemies. The other portion of the nails she ordered to be formed into the bridle of his horse, not only to ensure the safety of the emperor, but also to fulfill an ancient prophecy; for long before Zechariah, the prophet, had predicted that there shall be upon the bridles of the horses Holiness unto the Lord Almighty.*

Rahn had hoped that the Eusebius would provide more details about what might have happened to Helena's nails. Eusebius had authored numerous texts on early Church history, but what had specifically interested Rahn was his *Life of Constantine*: a nearly contemporaneous account of the first Christian Emperor.

After reading the *Life of Constantine* in Latin, Rahn had been disappointed at the lack of specificity concerning Helena's Jerusalem discoveries. In discussing the book with the Vatican librarian, Rahn had learned that Eusebius, of Greek descent, had written his books in his native language, not Latin. The Latin versions of *Life of Constantine* were sixth century or later. There were no known copies of the book in the original Greek.

'Pity,' Rahn had said.

'Why is that?' the librarian had asked.

'In my experience, there are occasionally important textual differences between original manuscripts and their subsequent translations.'

'I could not agree more,' the librarian had said. 'I don't know if it would make any contribution to your scholarship, but I do know that the Latin translations of *Constantine* were based on very early Armenian translations of the lost Greek manuscripts.'

'And where might these be?' Rahn had asked.

'They are housed in Church archives in Armenia. In Yerevan.'

Rahn's reception in Armenia had been frosty; the relationship between Hitler's Germany and Stalin's Soviet Union was teetering on the brink of collapse. But he had opened the doors of the archives of the Armenian Apostolic Church the way he had opened doors in other cities: by first opening his satchel of Reichsmarks. His money had also secured the services of a young translator who sat at his side for a week, working through a pair of Armenian texts: one, a seemingly complete version of all four books of the *Life of Constantine*, the other, an earlier but clearly fragmentary version containing only Book One and parts of Book Two.

Rahn started with the complete manuscript, comparing the Armenian version to the Latin version he'd read at the Vatican. With some minor exceptions, the texts closely matched. Then, on a whim, he decided to repeat the exercise with the earlier, partial manuscript and there he discovered something of considerable interest.

In Book One, Chapter XXXVII, the completed Armenian manuscript had this to say of Emperor Constantine's defeat of Maxentius's army in Italy:

Constantine, however, filled with compassion on account of all these miseries, began to arm himself with all warlike preparation against the tyranny. Assuming therefore the Supreme God as his patron, invoking His Christ to be his preserver and aid, and setting the victorious trophy, the salutary symbol, in front of his soldiers and bodyguard, he marched with his whole forces, trying to obtain again for the Romans the freedom they had inherited from their ancestors.

And whereas, Maxentius, trusting more in his magic arts than in the affection of his subjects, dared not even advance outside the city gates, but had guarded every place and district and city subject to his tyranny, with large bodies of soldiers. The emperor, confiding in the help of God, advanced against the first and second and third divisions of the tyrant's forces, defeated them all with ease at the first assault and made his way into the very interior of Italy.

Yet in Book One, Chapter XXXVII of the earlier, fragmentary, Armenian manuscript, the second paragraph of the chapter had a slightly different second paragraph:

*And whereas, Maxentius, trusting more in his magic arts than in the affection of his subjects, dared not even advance outside the city gates, but had guarded every place and district and city subject to his tyranny, with large bodies of soldiers. The emperor, confiding in the help of God, advanced against the first and second and third divisions of the tyrant's forces, **the Holy Lance glowing like fire whenever it touched his bridle**, and defeated them all with ease at the first assault, and made his way into the very interior of Italy.*

When Rahn reread his journal entry for that day of discovery his skin prickled with the same excitement. He hadn't been able to celebrate in Yerevan, what with his joyless SS minder watching his every movement, but now he was back home and he knew how to party in Berlin.

* * *

There was a sharp, persistent knocking at his door. Rahn staggered to the door in his dressing gown in the grasp of a crushing hangover.

'What?' he asked through the closed door.

'Herr Rahn, please open the door.'

'Who is it?'

'The door, if you please.'

There were two SS officers. He recognized neither. The ranking man was a young major with a face of stone.

'Might we have a word?' the major said after giving his name.

'*You* might but I cannot until I've had a coffee,' Rahn croaked.

They waited in his sitting room until he returned with his Moka pot, a new Italian invention Rahn had taken on his travels.

'Care for some?' he asked the officers.

They waved him off. Rahn blinked in gratitude as the black coffee passed his lips.

'Now, what can I do for you?'

'We received a disturbing report last night about you,' the major said.

'Did you?'

'You were observed by someone known to us at the Eldorado Cabaret in Nollendorfplatz.'

Rahn stiffened and had another sip of coffee. 'So?'

'You are aware that it is a bar for homosexuals,' the major said.

'I hadn't noticed.'

'Beyond your attendance, our source reported that you were highly intoxicated and behaving in an overt manner.'

'Overt?'

'You were seen to go into one of the rooms at the rear of the establishment. This is where the homosexual activities occur.'

Rahn drank the rest of the coffee in a series of gulps. 'What is it you want from me?'

'To inform you what you already know, that homosexual activity is illegal and under the Law for the Protection of German Blood and German Honor such activity is punishable by death.'

'Are you here to arrest me?'

'We are not the Gestapo. If the intent was to arrest you, they would be here this morning.'

'Then what?'

'It seems you are, to a certain extent, immune from prosecution given the work you perform for the Ahnenerbe. You may consider this a warning. A stern warning. Similar behavior in the future cannot and will not be ignored or tolerated.'

Rahn exhaled deeply. All he could do was nod when the officers stood.

'I hope you realize how lucky you are,' the other officer said, speaking for the first time.

When they were gone, Rahn sat at his typewriter to begin his report. As he arched his fingers to begin he realized that his hands were still shaking.

When he entered Himmler's office, the chief of police was drumming his fingers on Rahn's report of 19 October lying on his desk.

'Sit down, Rahn,' Himmler ordered so sternly that he was scared the episode at the Eldorado had not been forgiven after all.

He watched as Himmler picked up the report, flipped to the third page and then put it down again.

'Interesting account of your travels,' Himmler said. 'Some profound disappointments, especially with respect to the Grail, tempered, perhaps, by some intriguing new findings.'

If Himmler's dour demeanor was the result of failing to locate the Grail, rather than his being caught *in flagrante delicto,* then Rahn was highly relieved.

'Yes, indeed,' he said, 'I would have loved to present you the Grail on a velvet cushion but I feel certain I might yet succeed in the future.'

'We shall see,' Himmler said. 'No candidates for Holy Nails, then?'

'No, Herr Himmler, I was unable to obtain any nails as all of them are quite famous and lavishly displayed within churches in Paris, Jerusalem, Vatican City and several shrines throughout Italy. There was no chance of quietly purchasing such notable artifacts.'

'Fine, fine. Before we get to the more interesting matters, let's have a look at the rather mundane assemblage of artifacts you *were* able to harvest.'

Rahn laid out the thorns and all the bits of wood, cloth and leather on the conference table. Himmler inspected them from afar and reiterated his disappointment.

'What makes you think any of these items are authentic?' he asked.

'I make no claim as to authenticity,' Rahn said. 'It is notoriously difficult to trace the provenance of a thorn or a piece of cloth. If I were to find the Grail within the Pyrenees, I would be quite confident of its provenance given my research into the mythology of the region. Likewise, given extensive writings concerning the Lance of Longinus, I would be willing to assert that the lance in Vienna is the True Lance or that the Shroud of Turin is the true shroud, provided we could exclude medieval fakery.'

'And the nails?'

'It would also be difficult to confirm their authenticity. As I noted in my report, there is evidence from Theodoret's *Ecclesiastical History* that the nails were fashioned into Constantine's bridle and helmet, but linking the text to specific artifacts in specific cathedrals is problematic.'

Himmler mumbled, 'Disappointing,' several times as he thumbed through Rahn's report.

Rahn could only watch him and hope that the police chief's disappointment didn't lead straight to the Eldorado and Rahn's doom. Then Rahn's gloom lifted when Himmler smiled.

'Now this, this, is interesting,' Himmler said.

'Which topic are you referring to?' Rahn asked.

'The Armenian business. What is your explanation for the disparity between the two texts?'

'Presumably, both of the early-centuries' translators had access to Eusebius's original Greek texts and worked independently, perhaps separated in time by a hundred years or more. There were multiple discrepancies between the earlier, partial text and the later, complete one. These differences went beyond the passage I highlighted in my report. It may be that the first translator was more skillful, possessing a better command of Greek. Alternatively, the underlying Greek manuscripts might have differed, reflecting the copying errors or omissions of a scribe.'

'And why is it that the texts we have today in Latin, English, German, what have you, are all missing this key phrase: "the Holy Lance glowing like fire whenever it touched his bridle"?'

'I can only assume that in the absence of a surviving Greek original, the completed Armenian translation was the one used for subsequent Latin translations. Probably, the earlier, fragmentary Armenian manuscript was not consulted because it was woefully incomplete and thus, what it contained was lost to time.'

'Until you found it, Herr Rahn.'

Rahn's chest swelled with pride.

'Thank you, sir!'

'But what does it mean: "the lance glowed like fire"?'

'I'm afraid I don't know,' Rahn confessed.

'No theory?'

'Perhaps it was a metaphor.'

'Perhaps,' Himmler said, pensively. 'I took the opportunity to telephone one of our physicists, Werner Heisenberg, in Leipzig. I asked him for his views on this. He was dismissive that the interaction between two metals could cause one to glow. I asked about the phenomenon of radioactivity as a cause but he brushed this off. He did volunteer to study one or both metals if I could provide them.'

'Can we take possession of the lance in Vienna?' Rahn asked.

'Not at this time, I'm afraid. But I suggest to you an exciting alternative explanation to the physical ones that Heisenberg seems to reject: what if there is a supernatural explanation? What if the true relics of Christ are imbued with a supernatural power that transcends the scientific and rational? And, if true, what if the Fatherland could harness this power to vanquish our enemies?'

As Himmler talked, Rahn watched the small man's eyes grow wilder. Rahn chose his next words carefully. 'That is indeed a fascinating theory! I compliment you. But I wonder how it can be tested?'

'Do you? Isn't it obvious?' Himmler asked. 'You will travel to Vienna immediately, Herr Rahn. You will take this motley collection of relics with you. I hesitate to attempt to secure permission from the Austrian foreign minister, Berger-Waldenegg, to allow you to handle the Holy Lance. He will be suspicious of our intentions with respect to this and other Imperial Treasures. One day, we will come to possess the lance, but it will not be today. You will have to use your ingenuity to conduct a test. If any of your relics cause the lance to glow like fire, then you will have proof of their authenticity and I will have something new and powerful to present to the Führer.'

Words like, ludicrous and preposterous rolled through Rahn's mind but the word that he uttered was, 'Brilliant!'

'Now as to this other item of interest in your report. It concerns the other book you found in the Vatican,' Himmler said. 'Before you return from Vienna, I want you to go to Italy. I want you to see this Italian monk who claims to have the stigmata of Christ. I want you to interrogate Padre Pio.'

Berlin, present day

Schneider carefully placed the onionskin pages into their envelope and returned it to his safe. He was no fan of homosexuals. He supposed there were some, perhaps many of them, inside his bank but he didn't want to know about it. In his view, Rahn had been foolish and had gotten what he deserved. In 1937, after repeated warnings about his openly homosexual activities, Himmler finally refused to look the other way. The Gestapo delivered the ultimatum to Rahn: either do the honorable thing or face deportation to a concentration camp with his fellow deviants. Rahn, a dedicated trekker, took control of his own fate. He made his last trip to the Tyrolean Mountains where, on a frigid March morning, he went for a hike without a coat. He was found some days later, frozen solid. Despite his loathing of Rahn's lifestyle, whenever Schneider read Rahn's report to Himmler he found himself saddened at his demise. After all, without Otto Rahn, the Knights of Longinus would only be a bunch of old men getting together to drink and complain about the rotten state of current affairs.

Two fingers of his right hand slipped in between the buttons of his dress shirt and probed the special scar on his chest, which he'd had since his expedition to Antarctica. It was a slender, heaped-up ridge of tissue, three-centimeters long where a thorn had gotten hot as a fireplace poker and burned through the pocket of his parka.

He silently thanked Rahn as he often did. Because of him, Schneider and his friends were more than a band of foolish old men. They were potent patriots who had a real shot at changing the world.

THIRTEEN

Cal's attempts to communicate with the monastery of St Athanasius were unsuccessful. They had no telephone and his email, sent to the address on the St Athanasius website, was answered by a webmaster at a Croatian web-hosting company who said he had no way of contacting the monks.

Cal felt strongly that his report on Padre Gio would be incomplete without interviewing the Croatian monks, so he booked a flight and traveled to Dubrovnik directly from Naples. At the airport he picked up his hired Peugeot and navigated the three-hour drive to the Dinaric Alps with his phone.

At the turnoff to the monastery, Cal corkscrewed up the long, narrow road to the mountaintop sanctuary. At the car park he got out, stretched and breathed in the cool, late-afternoon air. There was but one other vehicle parked there, a school minivan.

The ancient stone chapel occupied the highest point on the mountain. He headed up the dirt path past some low outbuildings and sheds and a rambling, ramshackle stone cottage where he presumed the monks lived. The party of school children was coming toward him from the chapel, running and laughing as if the school bell had rung the end of the day. Two adults lagged behind and when they passed, Cal asked them what they thought of the place.

One of the women replied in fair English, 'Very old church. Very nice. Very holy.'

'Were the monks there?' he asked.

'No monks. Church is empty.'

Cal headed toward the cottage but before he got there he spied a solitary figure working a plot of land with a garden hoe. When he got closer he saw the man was wearing the brown tunic of a monk.

'Hello, there,' Cal called out in English.

The monk looked up then continued hoeing.

Cal came closer and shifted to Italian.

The monk shot him an irritated glance and replied in English with a pronounced Croatian accent.

'Can you not see I am working?'

Cal said he was sorry to bother him but that he was there on official business from the Vatican.

'I have never been to the Vatican,' the monk said, shifting a heavy clod of soil.

'Are you Brother Augustin?' Cal asked.

'I am not. I am Brother Ivan.'

'He's the one I needed to see. Is he here?'

'He is not. He is over there.' The monk pointed in the direction of the chapel.

'I was told there was no one in the church.'

'He is not in the church. He is in the graveyard near the church.'

Cal showed his surprise. 'When did he die?'

'Recently.'

'How did he die?'

'He had an accident. He fell down the well, drawing water.'

'I'm very sorry to hear that. Perhaps I could trouble you with some questions. I've just flown here from Italy. There was no way to contact you by phone.'

'What do you wish to know?'

'I want to talk about the day two seminary students from Italy came to visit the monastery. One of them, Giovanni Berardino, was shown the crypt by Brother Augustin.'

'How long ago was this?'

'February, I believe.'

'We have many visitors from Italy and elsewhere. I cannot remember them.'

'I see. Maybe you've heard about this young Italian who is now a priest. People are calling him Padre Gio.'

'How would I hear about an Italian priest?' Ivan asked.

'He's been in the news a lot.'

The reply was gruff. 'We receive little news here.' The monk began working again and Cal thought he might ignore him but suddenly he turned and asked, 'Why is he making news?'

'Because he's developed the stigmata of Christ.'

Minutes later, Cal was drinking a cup of herbal tea at Brother

Ivan's kitchen table and commiserating with a sad, lonely old man.

'It is sobering to know that one is the last in a long line of monks that reaches back to the early days of our faith.'

'When was the last time you had a novice at the monastery?' Cal asked.

'At least twenty years. He seemed like he had a good soul but he did not last long. We have no heat in the winter other than our wood fires and there is no hot water unless we boil it. We use electricity sparingly. It is a hard life unless one can take comfort in prayer, meditation and hard work. When Augustin and I were younger we did all the gardening and repairs ourselves. We had cows and chickens. Augustin made a passable apple and elderberry wine and I could brew beer, not that we ever overindulged. We were self-sufficient. When we became old men we needed help. Women from the village bring milk and eggs and cheese. And meat for Augustin. I do not eat meat. We have a handyman we pay with the donations we receive from visitors and pilgrims. He fixes what is broken and helps with the vegetable garden. When it snows he plows and shovels.' Ivan rubbed at his scraggly beard. 'I always knew the day would come that I would be alone. You see, Augustin was older and in poor health.'

'Was it you who found his body?' Cal asked.

'No, it was Jan, the handyman. He had not been in the well for very long. When the firemen retrieved him and laid him out on the grass he looked serene, as if asleep. I can show you his grave if you want.'

Cal had talked with the monk long enough to think that he might now entertain questions about Giovanni's visit.

'Forgive me, but you do remember the Italian seminary students, don't you?'

Ivan nodded apologetically. 'It has been a long time since I told a lie.'

'I understand.'

'You see we told no one.'

'Told no one what?' Cal asked.

'How did the Vatican know that Brother Augustin also had the stigmata of Christ?'

Cal held his breath for several seconds before he said, 'I'm

not sure the Vatican or I knew about this. The present investigation concerns the young priest, Giovanni.'

The monk turned pensive. 'I wonder if I've betrayed a
confidence.'

'Betrayed whom?'

'Augustin, of course. The monks of St Athanasius have always
been cloistered. We do not turn pilgrims away but we do not
take our spiritual sustenance from the outside world. We are
private in our faith and none was more private than Augustin.
The fact of his stigmata was a matter between him and God. It
did not involve anyone else, not even me, his brother, even though
often I bore witness to his suffering. Yes, he suffered greatly for
his faith.'

'How long? How long did he suffer?'

'Since he was a young man until months before his death.'

'Where were his stigmata?'

'His wrists. Only his wrists.'

'Not ankles, not his right side.'

'No, only the wrists. They were always painful, always weeping
blood. He had to eat liver and red meat to restore his blood.'

'Do you know the circumstances of precisely when he developed stigmata?'

'I know he did not have them when he came here as a novice.
He developed them at St Athanasius in the secret tradition of the
monastery.'

Cal almost dropped his pen. 'I'm sorry, what did you just say?
A tradition?'

Ivan rose to refill the kettle. 'More tea? If you do not like
chamomile I have green tea.'

Cal said only a quick yes, not wanting to sidetrack this critical
moment with a discussion about tea. The monk stayed silent,
waiting for the whistle of the kettle.

When he rejoined Cal at the kitchen table he said, 'It is over
now. With the passing of Augustin the tradition has ended. There
is nothing more to protect. We did not want the outside world
to know about our miracle. It would have changed our way of
life and violated our spiritual mission. The tradition has passed
from monk to monk, generation to generation in an unbroken
chain extending, we believe, to the earliest days of the monastery.

Only a single monk at a time had the stigmata. When he grew very old or became ill, it was for him to choose a young monk to pass along the miracle.'

'How did he do it?' Cal asked.

Ivan looked at Cal's writing hand and asked with a pained expression, 'Must you write this down?'

He pocketed his pen. 'I'll stop. Please, go on.'

'I only know this,' the monk said. 'When the time came, a young monk was invited to join the old monk in the chapel. No one else was present. The two men descended into the crypt. What happened there, I do not know. It was not my place to ask and Augustin never talked of this. Yet he told me later that night – the day the seminarians arrived – that he decided on the spot to act.'

'Why then?'

'I believe he sensed his mortality.'

'Why didn't he pass the tradition to you?'

'I am old and it was clear there would be no one to succeed me. Augustin cried that night, joyful tears that his ordeal was over, bitter tears that the miraculous chain of St Athanasius had ended with him.'

'Tell me what you mean about his ordeal being over?'

'That very night his stigmata began to heal and within days his skin was smooth. He bled no more and suffered no more.'

'Why do you think he chose Giovanni and not the other young man, Antonio?'

The monk grasped Cal's forearm. 'Augustin held onto me the way I am holding onto you when he told me this: he saw something spiritual in the young man, some quality of holiness and piety that led him to decide as he did.'

'And he told you nothing of what transpired in the crypt.'

'Nothing.'

'Were you in the chapel when it happened? Did you see Giovanni afterwards?'

'I was here in the cottage. Nor did I see the young man depart. Augustin and I never spoke of it again and I did not know what happened to him until this day. How is he bearing his burden, this Giovanni?'

'I believe it's hard for him.'

The monk nodded knowingly. 'I suppose you will wish to see the crypt now.'

Dusk darkened the mountain as Cal began his return journey to Dubrovnik. As he drove he thought about the crypt. In his line of work, visiting churches and crypts was about as common as a kid visiting a toy store and these at St Athanasius were remarkable only for their antiquity. The crypt itself was small and dank. It had a smooth stone floor embedded with a dozen or so marker stones of medieval bishops and a few esteemed abbots, from a time when the population of the monastery was large enough to support a hierarchy. The stone walls were bare, with no evidence of early plasterwork or frescoes. The only embellishment was a nook, with a shelf carved into the wall located directly beneath the church altar. And on that shelf was a simple bronze reliquary. He had asked about the urn and Ivan had replied that he had long known it was there but had never known if it held anything. It was not his place to ask, the monk had said. Cal had gotten permission to inspect it. There were no inscriptions. He had shaken it gently before removing the lid.

It began to rain and Cal clicked on the wipers.

An empty reliquary in a seventh-century church.

With a long tradition of miracles.

A veritable stigmata factory.

He grumbled a few choice words. The front that was bringing rain to the mountain blotted out the last good light of the evening and the slick mountain switchback road was going to be that much more challenging. He slowed and used his brights but the rain began to pelt down and he found the low beams less refractive.

The rearview mirror seemed to explode with light.

He instinctively squinted hard to deal with the pain of someone's high beams reflecting directly into his dilated pupils.

'Son-of-a-bitch!' he shouted.

He pumped his brakes a few times as a signal to the jackass on his tail that he didn't appreciate the light show.

The reply was a jolt that snapped his skull against the headrest.

The sound of the rear bumper caving in and the taillights shattering drowned out his curse. The car rocketed forward and the flimsy guardrail was coming up fast, filling his windshield. He hit the brakes hard and cut the wheel to the left.

If there were a choice, he'd rather hit the mountain than fly off it.

The Peugeot was a new model with good brakes and a tight suspension. He was able to get the car under control and slow it to a crawl.

The crash must have knocked out the headlights of the vehicle behind him because he didn't see the next hit coming.

Again, his neck snapped back and again, the trunk of his Peugeot crumpled. The car lurched forward and glanced the rocky face of the mountain, deforming the front bumper. The impact was oblique enough that his airbag didn't deploy.

'Mother . . .'

He didn't have time to finish. The attacker – and yes, he had to conclude this was no accident – was fixed to what was left of his rear bumper, pushing him toward the guardrail.

In a panic, Cal depressed the clutch and rode his brakes for all they were worth but the other vehicle, probably a truck, had more mass and was edging him closer and closer to the abyss.

His options flashed through his mind.

He could jump out of the car – but that would leave him even more vulnerable to tons of metal bearing down on him.

He could throw the Peugeot into reverse.

Or he could—

He chose the third option and popped the car into second gear and hit the accelerator hard.

Free from the truck, he swerved away from the looming guardrail and began throttling down the unlit mountain road. The rain lashing his windshield and the narrow, winding road were aiding his attacker.

I'm not going to get out of this, he thought, gripping the wheel so tightly it felt the tendons in his hands would snap.

The pavement in front of him needed his full attention but he couldn't help sneaking glances in the rearview mirror. He knew the truck was still there but without lights he couldn't see it. He could be hit again any second and if it happened, he didn't know if he'd be able to maintain control at his rate of speed.

His tires squealed at a sharp bend in the road. He had to slow

down or he'd wind up self-destructing and, when he did, he saw
a point of orange in the mirror.

The truck was closer than he thought and the driver was
smoking a cigarette.

He accelerated again and fought the G-forces as he rounded
the curves.

He struggled to gauge how far it was to the base of the mountain and the turnoff to the village.

It was too far, too damned far.

He was blinded again.

Headlights coming fast.

Another car coming up the mountain.

The driver of that car should have hugged the mountain, but
he lost control when he saw the speeding Peugeot and crossed
the midline.

A second from impact, Cal twisted his steering wheel wildly
to the left.

He saw a wall of black rock, then a mirage, the fleeting vision
of the same delicate face he had seen when Giovanni had put
his arms around him. It was there no longer than the interval
between two heartbeats and then there was nothing.

A gold crucifix.

It seemed to be floating in front of his face, floating over a
sea of black and red.

Then, far away, he heard his name.

First soft, then louder.

'Professor Donovan. Professor Donovan!'

He moved his neck up and down. His head hurt. He lifted an
arm and found his wrist was stiff, fixed to a board.

Another voice, a woman's, told him not to move.

The crucifix moved away and Cal saw that it was around the
neck of a man with a black cassock and a priest's collar.

'Professor Donovan. I am Monsignor Ozren Atlan, the Bishop
of Dubrovnik.'

'Where am I?'

The woman came into focus. 'This is Dr Lukic. You had an
accident. This is Makarska Hospital.'

'My head.'

'You had concussion. Nothing is broken, no organs are damaged. You are fortunate man.'

Cal turned his head toward the bishop. 'You're not here to give me last rites?'

'Hardly,' the bishop said with a smile. 'The police found your briefcase in your car. There were letters from the Vatican. They made inquiries. Cardinal Lauriat called me and I came. The pope himself is praying for your recovery.'

In an instant he remembered what happened.

'It wasn't an accident.'

'I spoke to the police investigator,' the bishop said gently. 'Unfortunately, two men died. One was driving up the mountain, one was driving down. The man driving down was Jan Jusic who was the workman at the monastery of St Athanasius where you visited. The monk, Brother Ivan was consulted. He too is praying for you. Jusic was driving behind you on the way to the village for drinking. He was a big drinker. His truck hit the other car then fell off the mountain. Police found a bottle of brandy, travarica, in his truck. They believe he caused the accident because he was drunk.'

'It wasn't an accident,' Cal repeated. 'He hit me deliberately and tried to push me off the road.'

'Police will want to speak with you,' the doctor said, 'but we have blood alcohol test from lab. He was intoxicated.'

'My papers!' Cal suddenly said.

The bishop bent over and held up his shoulder bag. 'Your papers are safe, professor. Now you must rest.'

It was his discharge day.

Dr Lukic wanted him to stay a day or two longer but he insisted he was feeling fine. The police interviews had been frustrating. The officers had dutifully recorded his version of the accident, but they had made it abundantly clear that their conclusion would be that Jusic was driving drunk and recklessly on the rain-slicked mountain road. Perhaps, they suggested, Cal's concussion had altered his perception of the events of that night.

Once his head had stopped hurting, he used his imposed bedrest to work on his report. He was keen to complete his assignment and get back to Cambridge. When the time was right he'd have to update his stigmata book with the curious case of Padre Gio. But the time was far from right.

Thinking about his book suddenly triggered a memory of a small, seemingly inconsequential item he'd come across years earlier doing research. It was something he'd seen, a footnote in a card-catalogue at the Vatican Library. What was it again? Wasn't it something about a nail? He strained to remember but couldn't. Perhaps his concussion was clouding his brain. He knew he'd have it written down somewhere in his files back in Cambridge and he made a mental note to check it out upon his return.

A priest in Makarska had been tasked with driving him back to Dubrovnik, but before he left the hospital he decided to take the opportunity to fill in a few details for his report. Maybe he'd been wrong. Maybe the monastery handyman had been an out-of-control drunk after all. With the passage of these days he'd become less certain of his first impressions. But perhaps he'd been right. And if he was and his car crash hadn't been an 'accident', then maybe the other 'accident' on that mountain, Brother Augustin's, needed to be rethought. With the help of Bishop Atlan, he secured an interview with the chief pathologist at the hospital and while his priest-driver waited for him, he took the elevator to the basement morgue.

The pathologist, an ill-tempered lady with two nicotine-stained fingers, pulled out the autopsy file and told Cal she could give him only a few minutes.

'Brother Augustin was taken directly here from the monastery?'

She scowled. 'Where else would he go?'

'What was the cause of his death?'

'Head trauma, broken neck, drowning. The things that happen to a man who falls down a well.'

'Did you examine his wrists?'

'I examine all of him. This is my job.'

'And?'

'And what?'

'How did his wrists appear?'

Irritated, she glanced at her notes. 'Wrists were normal.'

'No ulceration of the skin? No signs of healed wounds?'

'Normal.'

'All right. Were there any other injuries?'

'He fell down deep well. There were other fractures of course. Left shoulder and clavicle, three ribs, two phalanges right hand.'

'I'm sorry,' he asked. 'What are phalanges?'

She pointed at her smoking hand. 'Finger bones. Pinky and pointer.'

'How do you break these two bones in a fall like that?'

She got up, snatching a pack of cigarettes and lighter from her desk drawer. It looked like she had an appointment to keep with the designated smoking area behind the hospital.

'These fractures were inconsistent. Looked like crush injury, kind you could get when someone squeezes hand too tight.'

She was half out the door, telling him his time was up.

In the hall, he had time for one last question before she bounded up the stairs.

'How did that injury fit in with your view that this was an accident?'

'Life is messy. So is death. Nothing is perfect. Monk slipped and fell down well.'

FOURTEEN

Since the first days of his pontificate, Pope Celestine had chosen to live and work in humble accommodations. Cardinal Lauriat had not.

The offices of the Vatican secretary of state were in the Apostolic Palace and sumptuous with enormous draped windows, gleaming parquet floors, crystal chandeliers, gold-leaf tables with marble tops and priceless Renaissance paintings.

An Italian monsignor, one of the cardinal secretary's aides, ushered Cal in. Cardinal Pascal Lauriat rose from his elaborately carved desk to greet him. He was a compact man with a small, graying goatee and thin moustache, who had spent the last two decades within the Vatican. Although he was fluent in six languages and mostly spoke Italian these days, he spoke English with the strong accent of his home city of Strasbourg.

'Professor Donovan, we were so concerned for your welfare,' Lauriat said, begging Cal to sit in a plush armchair.

Cal thanked him for the kind attention bestowed on him by Church officials in Croatia.

'We feel personally responsible for your welfare,' the cardinal said. 'After all, you are on a mission for the pontiff. We can only thank the Lord that you were not more seriously injured. How are you recovering?'

'Back to normal, I've got a thick skull.'

'Of course you do. I think you are an amateur boxer, no?'

A chuckle. 'You've done your homework.'

Cal agreed to a coffee and the monsignor went scurrying off to oblige him.

Lauriat leaned in and lowered his voice, as if to create a certain aura of intimacy. 'I wanted to have a word with you in private before I invite in Cardinal Gallegos and Dr Tellini. I have read your report to the Holy Father. He shared it with me. I admit it greatly surprised me.'

'I'm sure it did. It surprised me too,' Cal said. 'I approached this assignment with a determination to be open-minded and unbiased and my conclusions are my attempt at objectivity.'

The cardinal said 'yes' three times, tapping his armrest for emphasis with each utterance. 'I understand completely. Yet despite this laudable attitude I am sure your internal compass told you that you would likely conclude that this young priest was a fraud. Perhaps not a malicious one, but a fraud nonetheless.'

'That's true.'

Lauriat had a leather-bound folder bearing the seal of the Vatican City State. He opened it and Cal could see that his report now bore a bold personal note from the pope, presumably to Lauriat.

'But your report took us by surprise,' the cardinal said. 'What are we to do with it?' In a display of kinetic energy, he began to tap the toe of his polished black shoe on the fine, oriental rug.

Cal had a few moments to decide how to respond, because the coffee had arrived on a silver platter. The monsignor poured two cups, gave a small bow and left them alone again.

'I wouldn't presume to advise you on what your official conclusions should be,' Cal said. 'I think of the Vatican as a highly complex clock. I don't have insights into the internal mechanism. I'm only able to tell the time.'

'Well said, professor. Yes, this is a complex matter and the Holy See is a complex organization with many competing interests. We agonize enough over the declaration of miracles for those who are dead. Imagine our contortions for those who are living.'

'I expect there's a certain reluctance about facilitating a cult of personality around Giovanni.'

The cardinal opened his hands, as if to say: of course. 'Look at the crowds that flock to his little church. If this report became known . . .'

'You're not going to see a leak coming from me,' Cal said a little defensively.

'Heavens!' the cardinal exclaimed. 'It was not my intent to admonish you. We have great faith in your discretion. I was making the point to explain to you why we were not sharing it with the Congregation for the Doctrine of Faith or the Consulta Medica. That is why I wanted these moments with you.'

Cal shook his head and smiled. 'I thought I was retained as a consultant to the CDF.'

'You were but now you are not. Your work is for the Holy Father's eyes only and for anyone else with whom he chooses to share it. He has chosen to share it with me alone.'

'What do you intend to tell Cardinal Gallegos?'

'That because of your unfortunate accident you must return to America to convalesce. Your report has not yet been written and for expediency I have instructed you to deliver an oral summary of your findings today.'

As an historian well-versed in the byzantine world of the Vatican, nothing about the Holy See surprised him. But he was blind-sided by this.

He said in measured tones, 'And what would you like my oral opinion to include, or rather not to include?'

Lauriat's toe tapping accelerated and seemingly unable to channel his pent-up energy, he rose and began to pace around the conversation area, leaving Cal to follow him with his eyes.

'Well, Tellini was present with you in Monte Sulla, so your conversations with the priest are well known. These may be summarized.'

'He wasn't there for all of it.'

'Yes, the priest persuaded you to take confession. I do not see how this is relevant. You may omit it.'

'He also established quite a strong psychological connection.'

'The business of both of you losing your fathers at an early age. You may omit that too.'

'What about my interviews with Giovanni's mother and sister and with Father Forcisi?'

'These may be included, with the exception of the inconsistency between the two accounts on why Forcisi did not accompany Giovanni into the crypt.'

'I see. And I suppose you don't want me to talk about my provocative findings at St Athanasius.'

'It goes without saying. You may speak of the accident, however. They will surely ask.'

'Except that I don't think it was an accident. Nor am I convinced that Brother Augustin's death was an accident.'

'Surely this is speculation on your part, professor? You may omit that as well.'

Cal could only shake his head. 'We have a word in English for what you want me to do with my report: it's whitewash. Do you know it?'

Lauriat sat down. 'In French it is à blanchir. I am afraid this is precisely what I am asking. However, you may know that the Holy Father has read your non-whitewashed report in full. So, you may be comforted in that respect.'

The cardinal picked up the closest phone and instructed his aide to summon the others.

'There was one thing I didn't put into my report,' Cal said.

'Oh yes?'

He described the visual hallucination he'd had when Giovanni put his arms around him. The face.

The cardinal listened and told him he understood the omission. 'It does seem somewhat subjective and prejudicial,' he said. 'You did an excellent job, professor. The Holy Father appreciates the effort. He told me to pass along his admiration and blessings. I do know that the original intention was for you to meet with him upon completion of your report. That will not be possible at this time but perhaps we can accommodate an audience when next you are in Italy. It is clear you believe there is more than meets the eye with our Giovanni. Miracles do happen, of this I am certain. Perhaps we are witnessing one with our own eyes.'

'What do you think the Congregation's official report will conclude?' Cal said with a tinge of sharpness, polite but reproachful.

'It is reasonable to imagine that it will be inconclusive.'

'And Giovanni? What will happen to him?'

'He might come to conclude that a cloistered life is best-suited to the expression of his faith.'

There was a knock on the door.

'Please wait,' the cardinal called out in Italian.

'One last question. What do you think was in the crypt?'

Cal shrugged. 'I have no idea.'

Dr Tellini seemed altogether warmer than Cal had remembered. Perhaps it was his bedside manner kicking into gear; perhaps it was because he was in the presence of the cardinal secretary. In any event, he was solicitous, expressing great concern over Cal's concussion. Cardinal Gallegos, the head of the Congregation for the Doctrine of Faith, was more aloof, a dry-as-a-bone Spaniard and former archbishop of Madrid who betrayed not a lick of emotion.

'I'm fine, really,' Cal told Tellini. 'It's behind me.'

Cardinal Lauriat laid out his expectations. 'I am aware that an ad hoc committee of the Congregation for the Doctrine of Faith will meet soon to hear the report of the Consulta Medica, chaired by Dr Tellini and the report of Professor Donovan. Given the professor's car accident I have decided to accept his verbal report so he can quickly return to his home and convalesce, free from the burdens of further assignment.'

Tellini furrowed his brow but Gallegos's face was immobile. Cal knew the one he'd rather play in poker.

'So today,' Lauriat said, 'I would ask you to hear his impressions of Giovanni Berardino and accept his comments as his full and final assessment of the case. You may, of course, take notes, Ramon.'

Gallegos nodded and opened his thin briefcase to remove a legal pad and pen.

'Professor,' Lauriat said, 'you have the floor.'

Cal was a skillful university lecturer and academic presenter who could master an audience by dint of preparation and oratorical skills. But he wasn't an actor. His presentations were fact-based and to the best of his abilities, truthful and scholarly. What he had been told to do today was to perform an act of sorts, to dissemble, to omit, to outright lie. And he had to do it spontaneously.

In what seemed to him like an overly long pause – but was really only a few seconds – he went through a mental decision tree. The terms of his assignment had been clear enough. His report was for Pope Celestine's eyes; how it was used beyond that was none of Cal's business. He had relinquished rights to publish the material without the prior written permission of the Vatican. If he were to disobey the secretary of state, he would not only betray the cardinal but also the pope, whom he presumed was calling the shots on the Padre Gio case. The nature of his academic research required regular access to the Vatican Secret Archives, the Vatican Library and other ecclesiastical libraries throughout Europe and if were cut off, his future work would suffer. Finally, he had to accept this: the world of Vatican politics was not his world. It was theirs. And who was he to say with hand on heart, with absolute conviction, that this man, this priest, Giovanni, was somehow truly touched by a miracle?

He began, the way he had begun his written report to the pope, with a set of statements about historical precedents. He told them that Giovanni Berardino had to be placed into the context of the five hundred documented stigmatics throughout the ages.

The lineage stretched back to St Francis of Assisi. In the thirteenth century, on a spiritual retreat in the mountains, St Francis experienced a stupefying and dazzling vision of Christ and then erupted in bloody wounds, as nails mystically pierced his hands and feet, and a lance pierced his side.

In the fourteenth century, St Catherine of Siena exhibited the wounds of the stigmata during a visit to Pisa. The wounds disappeared after Catherine prayed to Christ that he remove them, so she would not be a subject of sensationalism but on her death bed the wounds reappeared.

In the nineteenth century, the German mystic and prophet,

Anne Catherine Emmerich, developed the five stigmata and defied doctors who tried to prove her a fraud.

In the twentieth century, another German, the renowned mystic, Therese Neumann, developed the bloody marks of the Passion, including scourge and circular head wounds, every Thursday and Friday for thirty-six years. All told she experienced the entire Passion mystery almost a thousand times.

And then, of course, there was Padre Pio of Pietrelcina, the longest-suffering stigmatic in the history of the Church, whose stigmata lasted for fifty years. Bleeding wounds on his palms, feet and flank first appeared while he was hearing confessions in 1918 and persisted until a few days before his death in 1968. Besides the stigmata, there were other manifestations of Pio's holiness. The blood flowing from his wounds was said to smell of perfume or flowers, the so-called odor of sanctity. Then there were the reports of his power to heal the sick, his prophecies, bilocation and levitation, and an ability to survive for long periods, weeks at a time, without sleep or nourishment.

Throughout his life the Church mounted periodic investigations of his stigmata including medical evaluations. Initially, the official attitude was that of skepticism. There was a suspicion that he was self-harming and in the 1920s he was banned from saying Mass and giving confessions. The Vatican had discussions about moving him to a convent in northern Italy, but there were fears of riots at San Giovanni Rotondo and he was left in place. Over the years, the Vatican softened its stance and he was gradually rehabilitated, though the Church was noncommittal on the miraculous nature of his wounds for decades. The tide definitively turned in the 1960s when Pope Paul VI dismissed all suggestions of his lack of sanctity. In 1947 the young Polish priest, Karol Józef Wojtyła, visited Padre Pio and took confession with him. Years later, as pope, he would remember what Pio had told him that day; a prophesy that he would ascend to the highest post within the Church and it was John Paul II who canonized Padre Pio in 2002.

'So, let me turn to Giovanni Berardino,' Cal said, 'a young man who, in many ways, is a typical case among the assemblage of known stigmatics and who embodies all the challenges of validation that an investigative team might encounter. These investigations generally take place against a background of high emotions and require a rigorous approach to fact gathering, observation and medical evaluation. My role has been limited to interviews with the priest himself, family members, friends and colleagues. Because he claimed to first experience stigmata the day after his visit to a church in Croatia, I visited that site and interviewed its only remaining monk. If it weren't for my close encounter with the side of a mountain, I would have returned to Rome earlier.'

After polite laughter, he continued. As he talked, he censored himself and, with each omission, he thought he detected a pleasant curling of Cardinal Lauriat's lips. He offered no mention of the dueling versions of why Antonio Forcisi didn't accompany Giovanni into the crypt, nothing of the history of stigmatics at St Athanasius or Brother Augustin's assertion of Giovanni's worthiness as a successor, and nothing about the mystical vision Cal had experienced when the young man touched him or his belief that his car crash had been no accident.

It was time to give his conclusion and this is what he said, 'I found him to be an affable and pious young priest who seemed sincere and without guile. His aspirations don't seem to go beyond remaining in his parish and tending to his community. He's no publicity hound. That said, I'm not a psychiatrist and therefore I'm not qualified to spot subtle forms of psychopathology. Interviews with friends and family added little to the overall fact pattern. St Athanasius is a special church because of its great antiquity but it offered no clues to the genesis of his stigmata. I look forward to hearing Dr Tellini's medical opinion, but overall, I would have to say that from my point of view, the nature of his stigmata is inconclusive. I certainly could not exclude the possibility of malicious fraud or subconscious self-harming for some psychological secondary gain.'

The moment he stopped talking he began to marinate in guilt.

Cardinal Gallegos nodded and said, 'Inconclusive. I see. Tellini, tell us your opinion.'

The doctor referred to a draft of his medical report as he spoke. He began by describing the location of the wounds on his wrists.

'I would have to say that the anatomy of the wrist is

better-suited for crucifixion than the palms since the weight of
the body can be better sustained. Stigmata of the palms, is, in
my view, a red flag for fabrication, as the sufferer may be
influenced by popular depictions rather than the true Roman
practice. As I have learned from the professor, stigmata confined
to the upper extremities and sparing the lower extremities are
historically unusual. Berardino's lesions are moderately deep,
extending through the dermal layers into the subcutaneous
tissue. There is irritation and spasm of tendons and this inter-
feres with some function, but there is no destruction of the
tendons. There was some dried blood at the margin of the ulcer-
ations but mostly I saw oozing, fresh blood. There were no signs
of acute or chronic infection.'

Gallegos asked, 'Is that not unusual for someone who has had
these for several months?'

'Perhaps, although it may be a testament to fastidious wound
care,' Tellini said. 'He does have ample supplies of sterile bandages and gauze. The x-rays of his wrists show no involvement
of underlying bones. His blood tests reveal that he has no issues
with his clotting mechanisms and only a mild anemia, with values
just below the lower limit of normal for a man of his age. However,
his local doctor has administered periodic blood transfusions. As
to his psychological state, I am not a psychiatrist but I am not
a novice at assessing the emotional condition of my patients. I
found him to be somewhat immature and a bit guarded in his
answers, as if he had something he wished to hide. I conducted
a search of his living quarters for acids, bases or any type of
dermal corrosives and found none. However, this was a cursory
search, not a forensic one. I could have easily missed a well-
disguised hiding place. My conclusion is in concert with the
professor's. I find the nature of his stigmata inconclusive although
my clear bias is that Giovanni Berardino is inducing these stigmata
with the periodic application of some unknown substance.'

The secretary of state looked around the circle with a satisfied expression and asked, 'Tell me, doctor, what additional
investigations you would recommend to settle this matter more
definitively?'

'I would say that he ought to be removed from Monte Sulla
and placed in some new location where he would not have access

to any irritating substances. There he would be closely observed. If the stigmata healed then the matter would be settled.'

'This is surely a maneuver that the Congregation for the Doctrine of Faith might recommend,' Gallegos said.

'Do you agree, professor?' Lauriat asked.

Cal was no longer thinking about the bleeding priest. He was thinking about getting on a plane and returning to Cambridge to lose himself in his Thomas Aquinas book. He was done with Vatican politics.

'I'm sorry, could you ask that again?'

Lauriat seemed to give him a pass, perhaps charitably attributing his inattention to his concussion. 'Of course, professor,' he said before repeating Tellini's suggestion.

'I think that's an excellent idea,' Cal said. 'I'd be interested to hear how the case resolves itself in the future.'

FIFTEEN

Vienna, 1935

No structure in a city that prided itself in celebrating its wealth was as imposing as the Hofburg Palace. Built in the fourteenth century and expanded in every century since, it stood as a sprawling testament to the wealth and power of the Austro-Hungarian Empire.

A solitary figure dressed in a black trench coat, with a black fedora, made his way across the sunny Heldenplatz, tramping over the long shadow cast by the soaring statue of Archduke Charles. At the Swiss Courtyard, the oldest part of the palace, he climbed a single flight of marble stairs and entered the Imperial Treasury.

It was late in the afternoon and the guard informed him that he had a scant half-hour for his tour before the five p.m. closing time, then asked if he needed directions to a specific gallery.

'No thank you,' Otto Rahn said. 'I know precisely where I am going.'

'I need to check your bag.'

'Why is that?' Rahn sniffed.

'We had an anarchist not too long ago with a hammer. He was going to break something valuable.'

'I am no anarchist and have no hammer.'

'It is required.'

His leather satchel contained several notebooks, a set of fountain pens and four leather pouches that were of no interest to the guard. He was waved on.

He had only recently made the trek to the museum and knew exactly where he needed to be. Passing quickly through galleries filled with priceless paintings and sculptures, he entered a room with a central glass case holding the fabled crown, orb and scepter of the Holy Roman Empire. These treasures were of little interest for Rahn but there was an elderly guard milling near the imperial regalia so Rahn slowed down, pausing as a typical tourist to study the bejeweled crown.

The next room held the object he was looking for. As he entered it, he held his breath, hoping, given the lateness in the day, that there would be no guards and few, if any visitors. He was rewarded on both scores. He waited for a man and a woman, Dutch, by the sound of them, to leave before he strode up to one of the cabinets.

There were three objects on display.

In the middle was the Imperial Cross, a wooden crucifix made in 1030 that was covered in gold and precious gems.

To the right was a smaller crucifix, fashioned in the thirteenth century around a fragment of wood, claimed to be a piece of the True Cross.

To the left, resting on a velvet wedge, was the Holy Lance, its gold sleeve shining more brightly than any golden object in the room.

Rahn checked the room again and felt within his bag for one of the leather pouches. Inside of it was an envelope with all the three leather relics he had collected throughout Europe, each one a putative scrap from Christ's sandals.

His test he planned was simple enough. With a pair of tweezers, he would gently press a relic against display-case glass at the closest point to the lance.

Then he would see if anything happened to the lance, whether, to use Eusebius's phrase, it 'glowed like fire.'

He held the first piece of leather in place.

Nothing happened, but how long should he wait?

Let's be scientific, he thought. *Five seconds for each object.*

Before positioning a new relic, he looked behind him for the guard but the coast remained clear.

None of the leather pieces caused any changes to the lance.

The next pouch contained the cloth relics, remnants perhaps of Christ's burial cap and cloth, each in its own envelope.

It took a couple of minutes to cycle through them, and again, there was no effect.

The third pouch had the wooden remnants; all supposed relics of Christ's cross. He glanced at the smaller crucifix inside the display case and thought, either it's a fake or this entire exercise is a bloody waste of time!

While he was positioning the first piece of wood, he heard a gruff voice.

'Here, you!'

Rahn palmed the relic and turned around, his shoulder bag swinging with his body and brushing the case.

The elderly guard said, 'Watch your bag. We don't want to scratch the glass, do we?'

'Certainly not,' Rahn said. 'You startled me.'

'We're closing in fifteen minutes, did you know?'

'Of course. I'll be making my way out soon enough.'

The guard muttered, 'See that you do,' and returned to the other chamber.

A few minutes later, the wooden pieces screened, Rahn fished out the last pouch that held a metal box.

He looked at his watch. The guard would be back soon.

'Waste of time,' he muttered, plucking out the first of fourteen thorns from its paper envelope. But there were no shortcuts to the experiment and he was a thorough man. The thorn was slightly curved and delicate so he couldn't press it against the glass too hard.

Again, there was nothing.

Number two, he thought, *positioning the second thorn.*

Nothing.

'Number three,' he said in a whisper.

The pain was immediate and he suppressed a yelp.

He felt it before he noticed what had happened.

The hot tweezers and the thorn were lying on the wooden floor, where he'd dropped them. The thorn and tweezers were dimming like cooling embers that had escaped from a hot fire. There was a burn on his index finger and thumb where he had grasped the tweezers.

Rahn immediately looked to the lance and gulped. The black iron of the lance was red and glowing and wisps of smoke rose from the velvet wedge.

'It glows like fire,' he whispered. The words came out too loud and he turned to make sure he was still alone.

He gingerly picked up the tweezers, now cooler to the touch, and used it to pinch the fallen thorn. He slid it into its envelope, noting its provenance, a church in France.

The lance had returned to its normal black color.

Hesitantly he repeated the process with the fourth thorn but nothing happened.

The clock edged closer to five o'clock as he cycled through almost all the remaining thorns, none of them eliciting an effect.

The fourteenth and last remained, a thorn from a monastery in Spain. Hurriedly he pressed it against the glass.

It happened again.

As his flesh burned, the thorn – now a red-hot needle – and the orange tweezers fell at his feet and the lance lit the case with its glow.

It was five minutes to five and Rahn, despite his burnt fingers, giddily strode past the elderly guard in the next room, tipping his black fedora.

So Himmler's crazy theory had been right.

Rahn judged the information he possessed too sensitive to share via telegram or even the telephone. Who knew whether a nosy operator or the Austrian secret police might be listening? So he embarked on the next phase of his mission without communicating explicitly with Berlin. He sent only a wire to Himmler with the cryptic message: *Vienna: Eusebius Confirmed. Seeking Further.*

He had come to Austria without an SS minder, so as not to arouse the suspicions of the Reich's jittery Austrian neighbors. Now, holed up in his hotel room, he pondered his next moves while gazing at the presumed pair of True Thorns and obsessively rubbing at the burn marks on his fingers.

He didn't wish to revisit every Christ relic site in Europe and the Orient. He'd been lucky with the thorns but had come up empty with the cloth, leather and wood relics. He consulted his notebooks and thought long and hard.

Nails.

He decided to concentrate on the nails. Some of them had a provenance, harking back to the Emperor Constantine and the Empress Helena. He would return to the sites that possessed the Holy Nail reliquaries he had visited on his earlier trip. If he happened to be close to a site with other famous Christ relics, the Turin Shroud, for example, or churches with alleged True Cross relics, he would visit them too.

He charted the most efficient train route to cover the stops. Over the following fortnight, he carried his shoulder satchel into churches and shrines throughout Europe.

His *modus operandi* was always the same. He would enter a shrine at a time when there were the fewest visitors then take out one of his True Thorns and press it against the glass of the reliquary case, as close as possible to the nail relic.

In Rome, the Basilica of the Holy Cross in Jerusalem, had a nail, one of the three Empress Helena was said to have found in the Holy Land and carried back to Rome. Tradition had it that the other two were sent to her son in Constantinople. One of them was allegedly purchased from the imperial treasury of the city by an Italian trader in the Middle Ages. Then bequeathed to the Santa Maria della Scala Hospital in Siena where it was on display in a gold and crystal reliquary. The fate of the purported third Holy Nail was more difficult to determine. According to lore, it was divided into smaller fragments, perhaps used by Helena as talismans to protect Emperor Constantine in battle. One fragment might have been worked into the emperor's helmet, another into his bridle. The helmet was supposedly in Monza Cathedral in Italy. There were said to be two candidates for the bridle, one in Carpentras, France that was destroyed during the French Revolution, the other in the Milan Cathedral.

There were other Holy Nail relics, of course, and Rahn did not dare ignore any of them. In Germany, there were relics in Trier, Essen and Cologne. In France, there was the reliquary of the Holy Nail in Paris at the Notre-Dame Cathedral and another in Toul. Poland had a Holy Nail relic shown within a jeweled monstrance at Wawel Castle.

His disappointments began when he tested the Holy Nails with the best provenance to Empress Helena. At Monza and Siena, the thorns remained cool. He had the highest of hopes for the bridle relic in Milan because of Eusebius's reference. But sadly, neither the thorns nor the bridle glowed.

Before leaving Italy, he journeyed to San Giovanni Rotondo in Foggia to pay his obligatory visit to the young stigmatic, Padre Pio, and following that brief but interesting diversion, with notes in hand, he resumed his travels and headed to France. Germany was next and, when he found nothing illuminating, he made his way to his last stop, Wawel Castle on a bend of the Vistula River in Kraków, home to a highly decorative nail reliquary. Repeating his timeworn routine, neither the thorns nor the nail threw off color or heat.

Rahn glumly returned the thorns to their metal box and stared at the reliquary.

A man addressed him in Polish.

Rahn turned to see that a young fellow with a museum badge on his lapel was addressing him.

Rahn replied, 'Sorry, German.'

The man smiled and continued in German. 'I was saying that it is marvelous, is it not?'

'Yes, quite.'

'I am a guide here,' the man said. 'This is our most popular exhibit.'

'Do historians believe this is really a True Nail?' Rahn asked.

'Who is to know about these things?' the man said. 'Perhaps yes, perhaps no. Well, that's the official line. I think it's not a true relic.'

Rahn didn't know why he lingered to chat. Perhaps it was because he was travel-weary, perhaps because the man was quite dashing and handsome and he was lonely.

'I'm a scholar from Berlin,' Rahn said. 'I've been on a mission to catalogue all of the known Christ relics throughout Europe.'

'Only Holy Nails?' the man asked.

'No, all of them, but I'm especially interested in nails.'

'An interest of mine, as well,' the man said, beaming. 'I'm studying for my degree in history, the history of the Church, in particular. My thesis work involves holy relics. I work here as a guide to make some money.'

Rahn thought he detected a spark of sexual chemistry and was emboldened to ask,

'When you're finished with work, could I buy you a drink? I would love to pick your brain.'

They started in a café at the city center, continued over supper at Rahn's hotel and then repaired to Rahn's bed, where they paused only to make love before resuming their equally passionate discussion of relics.

Glistening with sweat the man asked, 'So, you've been to all the usual places in Italy, France, Germany and Poland. I'll bet you haven't been to Romania.'

'You're right about that,' Rahn said, breathing hard and reaching for a cigarette.

'It's not so well known, but a small church in the town of Cluj-Napoca has a fragment of iron thought to be from Helena's third nail. I've never seen it but if you intend your paper to be thorough, you might add the place to your itinerary.'

'I might do just that,' Rahn said, 'although I'm enjoying Kraków more than I anticipated.' He offered the young man a puff of his cigarette. 'I suppose it would do little harm to linger here a day or two longer.'

Rahn was whisked into Himmler's office the moment he presented himself to his staff. Himmler had been conducting a meeting with party officials and, as they were unceremoniously being shown the door, they must have wondered about the identity of the small man with a black fedora.

Himmler refused to engage in small talk. He furiously waved Rahn's telegram and said, 'I haven't received a single communiqué from you since this obtuse wire from Vienna. As far as I knew, you'd fallen off the face of the earth. Where the hell have you been?' Rahn's serene expression and insouciant attitude seemed to fan Himmler's flames.

He casually dipped into his satchel while saying, 'I have traveled throughout Europe, Herr Himmler. I have seen great cities and middling towns, magnificent cathedrals and humble churches. There are only two venues that will be of interest to you, Vienna and Cluj-Napoca in northwest Romania. Great interest.'

'Out with it, Rahn,' Himmler hissed. 'I haven't got all day.'

Rahn theatrically placed the two thorns on Himmler's desk, told him the story of his time at the Imperial Treasury, and showed him the scars on his fingers.

'I am confident in my conclusion that both these thorns were present in the actual crown of thorns thrust onto Christ's head by the Romans on his day of execution.'

Himmler refused to touch them, even with Rahn's tweezers.

'Now you will understand why I didn't dare to communicate with you directly,' Rahn concluded.

Himmler's eyes were burning as brightly as the thorns had that day in Vienna.

'Where did you go after Austria?' he asked.

Rahn laid out a map he'd prepared with all the sites visited and the relics tested.

'Alas, all the most famous relics I tested were negative and I must conclude they are fakes,' he said.

Himmler was impatient. 'Romania! What about Romania?'

'A source in Poland told me of a church said to have a relic, a piece of one of the three nails that Empress Helena discovered in Jerusalem. This particular church and this relic were unknown to me. To my knowledge, there are no recorded mentions of the Romanian site in any reference materials on Holy Relics. Nevertheless, I decided to extend my journey and venture to Romania. I felt there was nothing to lose. The church of St James is an unassuming church in a quiet sector of the city. When I visited, there were no visitors and no worshippers. I circled the interior of the church twice without finding the relic and eventually knocked on the rectory door. The rector was a genial fellow who was happy to show me what I had come to see. I understood why I had missed it. There was a plain urn in a chapel nook that had no labels or inscriptions. He explained to me that no one really believed that the object in the urn was a relic of any importance, certainly not a piece of a True Nail. Its provenance was lost to time. It had simply always been there. He showed it to me. It was no more than a fleck of iron sitting on a wad of cotton. Just then, a parishioner entered and engaged the man in conversation, allowing me the opportunity to test the iron with a thorn. Look.'

Rahn held up the thumb and forefinger of his left hand. Both were scarred.

'What did you do?' Himmler asked.

'When the rector returned, I told him I was a collector of relics and even though this piece of iron was a nonentity it interested me and I would pay for it. Well, he took me on a tour of the church, showing me the state of disrepair. The roof leaked, there was damp, the windowsills had rot. So I made him an offer, a generous offer of hard currency.'

'And? And?'

'And here it is!' Rahn said, opening a small box.

Himmler squinted over his wire-rimmed spectacles and had to remove them and pick up a magnifying glass to have a good look.

'It's tiny,' he said.

'Tiny but important. Please observe.'

Rahn had come prepared. He used his tweezers to lift the iron fleck from the box and place it on the Himmler's desk, on the obverse of a silver five Reichsmark coin, specifically on the inscribed steeple of the Potsdam Church. With a pair of insulated tongs – he had learned his lesson – he picked up one of the thorns and held it over the coin.

Immediately the thorn changed color from brown, to orange, to fiery red and so did the iron fleck. When he moved the tongs away, the natural colors returned.

Himmler was awestruck. 'May I try?'

Himmler repeated the experiment then went quiet. He rose, paced and sat again.

'This is astonishing, Rahn. You've done well.'

'Thank you!' Rahn said, his chest swelling.

'I will need to inform the Führer but not yet. I need a more dramatic demonstration. You will return to Vienna immediately. Here is what I want you to do.'

Rahn listened to his orders and protested. 'Clearly, Herr Himmler, I cannot do this by dint of stealth or subterfuge.'

'I realize that,' Himmler said. 'I will contact the Austrian foreign minister, Egon Berger-Waldenegg, and introduce you as an official newsreel journalist for the Reich. I will tell him that this kind of cultural outreach will demonstrate that the German and Austrian peoples have common interests that transcend our political differences. It will be a gesture of our peaceful intentions. He is not a strong man. He's an optimist. I think he'll go for the bait.'

He told Rahn to be prepared to receive further instructions, but when Rahn saluted and turned to leave Himmler told him there was one more item to discuss.

'You haven't told me about the Italian monk, Padre Pio?'

'Yes, of course,' Rahn said. 'Our contacts in Mussolini's government were able to secure an audience in Foggia. My time was brief but I came away with a distinct point of view on the matter. I do not believe the monk is a genuine stigmatic. Therefore I would say that any further inquiry with respect to the Greek book I discovered at the Vatican Library, the one I referred to in my report by the code, VAT. GR. 1001, is not warranted.'

'Could you be mistaken?' Himmler asked.

'Perhaps,' Rahn said, 'but even if I am wrong, the monk vehemently denied any relevant exposures as described in the book. I consider the case of Padre Pio to be closed.'

Rahn could hardly believe that he was holding the Holy Lance in his hands. It felt heavy and powerful. The director of the museum, Herr Mueller, had insisted he wear cotton gloves before handling it. Had Mueller not been hovering like a mother hen, he might have been emboldened to remove the gloves to feel the sharp Roman steel against his bare skin.

They were in a museum storeroom, behind the Imperial Treasury curator's office, preparing for the newsreel shot. Rahn was posing as the presenter. He had brought a camera operator and a lighting man from Berlin. Rahn gently placed the lance on its red velvet wedge on a plain worktable. With a flick of a switch, it was bathed in the strong incandescence of the lighting rig.

'If you could stand just here, Herr Mueller,' Rahn said, 'I will conduct an interview and we will capture it on film.'

'What will you ask?' Mueller asked.

'Typical questions about the artifact. However, your precise answers do not matter. We will add a soundtrack later, with your approval, of course.'

'And this will be shown throughout Germany?'

'Indeed it will.'

With the lance as a backdrop, Rahn went through the motions of an interview with Mueller until the cameraman said he was satisfied.

'Is that all?' Mueller asked.

'Yes, this was quite satisfactory,' Rahn said. 'We shan't keep you longer, Herr Mueller. You must be a busy man. We will pack our equipment and leave.'

Mueller checked his watch. 'It's time for lunch. You and your men must join me in my private dining room.'

Rahn politely tried to get out of it. All he wanted to do was film a demonstration for Adolf Hitler, a powerful demonstration of the lance glowing in the presence of the thorn and the nail fragment he had brought with him. Then he would leave.

But Mueller was like a hungry dog with a bone. He insisted and Rahn had to capitulate.

'Very kind of you. Very well,' he said, 'can we leave the lance here while we dine? We will need to film some close-ups before we are done.'

'Fine, fine,' Mueller said. 'We will keep the door locked. The curator will keep an eye on things.'

Rahn went for his satchel but Mueller assured him with a laugh that if the lance was safe, his bag too would be safe.

Some thirty minutes later the curator unlocked the door and entered the storeroom to look for a box of artifacts he wished to catalogue. The lance was where they had left it. But he clucked disapprovingly when he saw that Rahn's satchel was sitting on top of the specimen box he needed. He picked it up and looked around for a new place to put it. There was a bit of room on the worktable beside the Holy Lance. When he placed it there it touched the tip of the relic.

Rahn was placing a forkful of roast pork in his mouth when he heard the blast and felt the shudder of the explosion.

Mueller sprang up, throwing his napkin aside and went to the hall where museum workers were running in the direction of the blast.

Rahn and his men followed along and as he hurried toward the curator's office he knew in his heart what must have happened.

The curator's office was blackened with smoke and strewn with rubble. The door to the storeroom was blown out. Rahn stumbled through the office and into the storeroom. There he found Mueller sobbing in the corner, standing over the curator's bloody, severed head. Rahn tried to maintain his composure but it was difficult. He was unaccustomed to carnage and destruction but knew he would have to make an accurate report of what had happened. The storeroom windows and most of the exterior wall were obliterated. The camera and lighting gear were twisted and wrecked. His satchel was nowhere to be seen. The wooden table upon which the lance had rested was a smoldering pile of sticks and splinters.

And there in the rubble was a glint of gold.

Rahn still had the gloves in his pocket. He put them on, reached down and hesitantly lifted it. It was still hot. He approached the director.

'Herr Mueller, the lance is safe.'

Another museum worker pointed toward the fractured radiator separated from the broken wall and shouted, 'Gas!'

Clutching the Holy Lance, Mueller ran out of the room with the others following on his heels.

'So they thought it was a gas explosion?' Himmler asked Rahn.

Rahn had left the Imperial Treasury only hours earlier, having proceeded with haste to the airport in Vienna for a flight to Berlin.

'That was their conclusion, yes.'

'But we know the truth,' Himmler said.

'We do.'

'The thorn was lost in the blast?' Himmler asked.

'It was. The nail fragment too.'

Himmler held up the box with the second thorn. 'So this is the only true relic we know of.'

'That and the lance.'

'The lance isn't ours, yet. One day it will be.'

'I don't doubt you, Herr Himmler,' Rahn said.

'When we do come to possess it, I also want, no, I *demand* we also possess a Holy Nail. Not merely a tiny piece of a nail, but a whole relic. Imagine the deadly power of combining a Holy Thorn and the Holy Lance and a Holy Nail! Then we'll have something that can do far more than blow up a few rooms in a museum, Rahn. We'll have something the world can only imagine.'

Rahn nodded grimly.

'You, Rahn, you will have no other tasks within the Ahnenerbe than finding me a True Nail. Forget about the Grail. Forget about all else. Succeed and you will prosper. Fail and your well-known peccadillos will be the death of you.'

Rahn licked his dry lips, bowed slightly, and left Himmler alone.

The small man immediately went to his side table and removed the cover from his typewriter. He inserted a sheet of paper and began to type.

Heinrich Himmler
Reichsführer-SS und Chef der Deutschen Polizei
7 Dezember 1935

An den
Adolf Hitler
Führer und Reichskanzler

Mein Führer!

We, at the Deutsches Ahnenerbe, have made a discovery of great importance concerning the extraordinary power of certain historical artifacts associated with the crucifixion of Jesus Christ. In short, it may be possible to create a weapon of unimaginable power that the Reich might use to change the course of human events. In this report I shall endeavor to describe our findings along with a proposed plan of action.

SIXTEEN

Cambridge, Massachusetts

C al unlocked the door to his office at Divinity Hall, opened the blinds to let sunlight in, and deposited a box of mail on his table. He scanned the desk and credenza; his Aquinas papers and books were where he had left them in precise piles and stacks.

'Miss me, St Thomas?' he asked the inanimate objects, settling happily onto a chair armed with a letter opener.

Before long, Father Murphy went past the open door and did a theatrical double take. 'As I live and breathe,' he exclaimed. 'The professor returneth.'

'I was afraid if I was gone any longer your idleness would have turned to sloth,' Cal said. 'Come on in.'

'You're confusing me with your other students. I've been a lean, mean, thesis machine.'

'What do you have to show me?'

'Chapter eight. Complete and uncensored.'

'Shoot it to me and stop by at three.'

'Don't you want to get your bearings first?'

'What I want is to get back in the saddle and blot out unpleasant memories of the Vatican.'

Murphy returned in the afternoon and plunked himself down across from Cal who was reading the last page of his new chapter.

'What do you think?' the priest asked.

'It's what I expect from you, Joe. Excellent scholarship, original insights, good writing.'

'Only good?'

'Well, more than good for someone with English as a second language.'

'Watch it,' Murphy cracked, 'or I'll send chapter nine in Gaelic.'

'I do want to drill down on your passage from Gregory's *Dialogues*, book two, chapter four, paragraph . . .'

'Paragraph two, I expect you're driving at,' Murphy said, 'where Benedict says, "Do you not see who it is that draws this monk from his prayers?"'

'Bingo. The text clearly says that he's speaking to both the abbot, Pompeianus, and the monk, Maurus. But you seem pretty sure he's aiming the question at Maurus.'

'Let me explain.'

They spent a while dissecting the passage until Cal was satisfied that Murphy was on the right path.

Collecting his papers, Murphy asked, 'So how was your trip?'

Cal rocked back in his chair. 'Did I ever tell you how much I hate the Vatican?'

'Actually, Cal, I believe I'm the one who has precious little time for all the pomp and politics. Until now you've struck me as a person who's been rather smitten by the place.'

'Well, stick a fork in me.'

'I take it you didn't have your audience with the Holy Father. If you had I expect you'd be more upbeat.'

'I was asked to take a rain check. But that wasn't the worst of it.'

Murphy rolled his eyes. 'All right then, professor, unburden yourself to the somewhat rusty Irish priest.'

Cal didn't need to be asked twice.

'It was a difficult couple of weeks.'

'Was the stigmatic not cooperative?'

'To a point, he was guarded but I found ways to get the goods on him.'

'So you unmasked the fraud.'

'If only it were that simple.'

'My, my, you didn't conclude the fellow's been touched by a miracle, did you?'

'You don't believe in miracles?'

'I couldn't very well be a practicing Catholic, let alone a priest if I didn't,' Murphy said. 'But I'm also a practicing skeptic. There's too much self-deception and outright deception in the world today. I'd say my baseline supposition about a newly minted priest who starts bleeding from the wrists is that the pressures of life have gotten the better of him. A cry for help and all that.'

'That was my baseline too.'

'But now you're in the miracle camp?'

Cal shook his head. 'I don't know where I'm at. Can I talk to you in confidence?'

'Of course,' Murphy said with an obvious turn to seriousness.

Cal didn't hold anything back. Who else was he going to be able to talk to? He spoke about Giovanni's preternatural ability to divine Cal's paternal loss, the jolting vision he'd had when the young priest touched him, the curious lineage of stigmatics at St Athanasius and its crypt, the accident on the mountain that he suspected was no accident, and being forced to deliver an alternative version of his official report. His account was cathartic. Murphy may have sensed that letting him unburden his heart was beneficial because he didn't interrupt his outpour with questions.

When he was done, Cal smiled at him and said, 'Well, that's it. Some story, huh?'

'Indeed it is. If you weren't who you are, I might take some of it with a mighty grain of salt. But you're a full professor at the Harvard Divinity School. That makes you a sober judge. Unless . . .'

'Unless what?'

'All those blows to the head from your boxing match scrambled the gray matter.'

'Yeah, maybe. The concussion didn't help.'

'You really think that fellow intentionally ran you off the road?'

'I did at the time, but now I'm not so sure to be honest.'

'Well, you certainly had quite the time of it.'

'The thing that's gotten to me isn't the factual basis of the case. As academics, we've got an obligation to do the best research we can and then give the evidence we've uncovered enough breathing room to speak for itself. It's the decision by the powers-that-be in the Vatican to cover up the facts that rankles.'

'And why do you suppose they've taken that decision? I would have thought that a credible miracle every now and again would water the tree of faith.'

Cal couldn't help himself. He decided to turn Murphy's decision into a teachable moment.

'Why do you think they've done it?' he asked.

'I imagine they're concerned about a cult of personality. I had a romp around the web about your Padre Gio. He's already a pretty big deal, at least in Italy. Give it any kind of Vatican validation during his lifetime and the situation could get severely out of control. A real loaves and fishes miracle would be red meat to the faithful and that might have the effect of drowning out all the other initiatives and priorities of the Holy See.'

Cal got a phone call from the department secretary, who asked him to come by to see the dean of the divinity school. Murphy got up to leave but Cal stopped him.

'Did I ever tell you were wise beyond your tender age, Joe?'

'First time, professor.'

'You know you'd make a damned good parish priest if you ever changed your mind. That or a corner man for a boxer.'

'I've told you before,' Murphy said with a laugh, 'this Jesuit isn't enough of a people person to tend a flock. It's academics for me.'

'Students are people too.'

'Are they now? In that case I feel I've been promoted from beast of burden.'

No sooner had his jet lag dissipated that Cal found himself calling Deborah at the chemistry department to ask for a date. It wasn't as if he'd spent a great deal of time thinking about her, but his dance card was empty and he fancied a twirl around the floor.

They met at the Queen's Head, the pub in the basement of Harvard's Memorial Hall, and got a booth. When she ordered a sparkling water he reminded her of her promise to start drinking. She stood pat. The bar didn't serve liquor so he got a beer.

'How're you settling into your job?' he asked.

'It's been kind of crazy,' she said. 'Setting up my lab, pulling together course materials for September, figuring out how things work in the department. Then, out of the blue, I got asked by my old professor at Stanford to contribute a chapter to a book.'

'When it rains it pours. But it's all good stuff.'

As they talked he was getting decidedly mixed vibes from her. She wasn't nearly as vivacious and engaged as she'd been before his trip.

'How was Italy?' she asked.

'Veni, vidi, vici,' he said.

'I'm sorry?'

At first he thought she was joking but she looked dead serious. Rather than openly lamenting the death of classical education in America he said, 'Latin. Julius Caesar. I came, I saw, I conquered.'

'I took Spanish,' she said, taking a sip of water. 'So it went well?'

'Well enough. Got my business done at the Vatican.'

'Did you see the pope?' she asked.

'I was supposed to but he stiffed me.'

'I was joking,' she said.

'I wasn't. He really did stiff me.'

She looked around the pub in a distracted way and squeezed the lemon into her drink.

'Are you, ok?' he asked. 'I'm kind of getting the impression you don't really want to be here.'

'Am I that obvious?'

'What's up?'

'I met someone last week.'

He smiled at his realization that he wasn't at all disappointed. He hadn't really thought she was his type and that was before he found out she didn't know her Julius Caesar.

'Congratulations. Who's the lucky guy?'

'Well, this is what's been worrying me. He's a grad student even though he's older than me.'

'In your department?'

She nodded.

'Hmmm. In your supervisory chain?'

'No. Different area altogether.'

'Then relax, you're ok. University policy is that faculty members can't have affairs with undergrads. Period. You also can't have sex with grad students you supervise, evaluate, or grade. Otherwise, have at it. But even though you're in the clear, I'd recommend discretion. You're new on the block and your chairman, from what I know of him, is old school. That is if you're still interested in getting tenure one day.'

'Oh God, yes, I'm desperate for tenure. I probably shouldn't ask but has this ever happened to you?'

'No comment,' he said with a wink.

'You're not mad at me, are you?' she asked. 'I haven't made enough friends to lose any yet.'

'Of course not.' He raised his glass. 'Here's to friends.'

He only wished she'd told him before he tidied his house, put out fresh towels and made his bed.

Cal lived on Lowell Street, one of those leafy roads within walking distance of the university favored by senior faculty members. The house was a renovated Victorian on a tiny lot with only enough of a backyard for a small patio and a barbecue. He'd bought it when he was awarded his tenured professorship with money from his trust fund. Now, years later, the value of property in the neighborhood had gone through the roof and he was sitting pretty in, what amounted to, a lavish bachelor pad with enough room for all the books, maps and *objet d'art* he could hope to accumulate.

Dropping his keys into a replica of a bronze Coptic bowl, he trundled up to the bedroom and selected a book from his bedside stand. He'd recently undertaken a re-reading of Joseph Campbell's *The Masks of Gods* series and in the morning he'd wake up to Campbell beside him, not the chemist. But he was still fatigued from his trip and he didn't read all that many pages before surrendering to sleep.

It happened at precisely 11:05 p.m. according to his clock radio.

He'd only been asleep for thirty minutes or so and in his confused state he wasn't sure if he was dreaming, since what he saw had a profoundly dreamlike quality.

He didn't know what had awakened him. The room was completely silent except for the whooshing blades of the ceiling fan.

A scene seemed to be playing out in the space between his bed and bathroom, where a nice Baluchi carpet lay on the floorboards. It was as if a silent 3D movie was being projected into the space, a movie so hyper-realistic that Cal instantly sat up and spouted a profanity.

He was about to fling off his covers and defend himself against the intruder when his brain processed who he saw.

Giovanni Berardino.

In pale blue pajamas.

The tubby young man looked terrified and he appeared to be struggling against unseen hands pulling at him.

Suddenly he turned ninety degrees and seemed to look straight into Cal's eyes. He mouthed something. Twice.

Cal strained to lip-read.

Then a black sack appeared over his head and *poof*, the performance piece ended. Once again, the bedroom was Cal's and Cal's alone.

He rose and walked the space that Giovanni had just occupied. Breathing hard from the shock of it, he sat back down on the bed and tried to make some sense of what he'd seen.

He replayed the silent mouthing but the phrase didn't yield to deciphering.

In English.

'Not English, Italian!' Cal said out loud.

Then he got it.

It wasn't a phrase at all, but a multisyllabic word.

Aiutatemi! Aiutatemi!

Help me! Help me!

At the exact same time, Irene Berardino was awoken by a strange sensation in her bedroom in Francavilla. At 5:05 a.m. it would be twenty minutes until sunrise and pinkish light leaked around her curtains. Later, she would be unsure about what had interrupted her sleep, yet she was certain there had been no sound.

But the vision of her brother in his pajamas near the foot of her bed so shocked her that she cried out, alerting her mother across the hall to her distress.

Giovanni looked terrified and seemed to be resisting some unseen forces tugging him in one direction.

Then he wheeled around and mouthed something at her. Again later, she would liken the experience to watching television with the sound turned off.

She knew it was irrational. She knew he wasn't really there. But she still called out to him.

'Giovanni!'

It was as if someone had suddenly twisted a volume knob.
It was so loud it scared her and made her cry.
Help me! Help me!

Cal tried to go back to sleep but his hallucination had been so vivid and troubling that he lay awake until 2:30 a.m. then gave up the ghost and got up to make a coffee. There was a six-hour time difference with Italy and at 3 a.m., a polite-enough hour for a call, he rang the number for Giovanni's parish house in Monte Sulla.

A woman picked up; she sounded rushed and troubled in her greeting.

Cal spoke to her in Italian. 'Hello, this is Calvin Donovan. I visited you recently on behalf of the Vatican.'

'Yes, yes, Professor Donovan, this is Sister Vera.' She sounded out of breath.

'I wonder if I might have a word with Father Berardino.'

'Oh, my Lord, my Lord!' she cried. 'Padre Gio is gone, professor. He's gone! Some men came and took him this morning. They wore masks. The police are here! We do not know what to do. What are we to do?'

SEVENTEEN

C al had never tried to raise a Vatican secretary of state on the phone and it proved to be a difficult task. The first time he called he identified himself and asked for Cardinal Lauriat only to be told that the prelate was unavailable.

'When will he be available?' he asked.

A monsignor replied that it was difficult to say.

'I do need to speak with him today. Could you please tell him that Calvin Donovan called? Here's my mobile number.'

He tried again an hour later, also to no avail.

Finally on the third try he ratcheted up the pressure.

'Look, I'm sorry, but you've got to tell the cardinal that it's imperative I speak to him. It concerns the priest, Giovanni Berardino. Is your office aware that he's been kidnapped?'

'I am sorry, did you say kidnapped?' the monsignor asked.

'Yes, early this morning.'

'Could you please hold the line?'

Now the secretary of state was on the phone in a flash and Cal had to conclude he'd been in his office all along, ducking his calls.

'Professor, I trust your journey home was smooth?' Lauriat said.

'I'm fine but Giovanni Berardino isn't.'

'I have heard nothing of this alleged abduction. What is the source of your information?'

'I called him this morning. One of the nuns told me what happened.'

'Why did you happen to call this morning?'

Cal lied. This was no time to talk about mystical experiences. 'I had a follow-up question for him.'

'An amazing coincidence, I would say,' the cardinal said, 'especially since your job is done. In any event I have not been notified at this time.'

Cal was incensed. The cardinal was more concerned about why he'd reached out to Giovanni than the abduction itself.

'I expect these things take time to work up through your organization,' he said. 'I've been following Twitter and Reuters – Italy. There doesn't seem to have been anything released by the local authorities yet but this is going to be big news. You'll be deluged by the press soon.'

'Well, thank you for your concern. I will see if anyone in Abruzzo has made the Vatican aware of the situation. I can assure you that the Italians have competent law enforcement authorities to handle this type of situation. If there has clearly been an abduction and a criminal organization demands a ransom, then the Vatican will have to consider its position. As to public statements, the Vatican press office is quite adept.'

'Why do you think this is the work of a criminal group?'

'Who else would take a priest, especially one with such a high profile? But you are correct, I should not speculate.' He sounded impatient now. 'Professor, I do thank you for giving me an early notice on the matter. Do tell us when you will be returning to Italy.'

'I'm getting on a plane tonight.'

'But why? Surely not because of this situation.'

It was a question he felt he couldn't answer truthfully. He couldn't tell him that the young priest had reached across the ocean to personally beg for help. He couldn't tell him that he had a strange feeling that he was somehow personally involved in the drama.

'I'm not sure I know why,' was what the only way he wanted to respond. 'But I feel I need to help in any way I can.'

'Help whom? With all due respect, professor, the Vatican has the internal resources to deal with this.'

'Help Giovanni, of course.'

The tone turned sharp. 'You are a private citizen, professor, and you are certainly free to do what you want. But please be aware that your work on this matter has ended and you do not, in any way, represent the Vatican going forward.'

On the way to the airport, Cal stopped at his office to chase up the footnote he had made a mental note to find, whilst recovering in the Croatian hospital. It was somewhere in the research he had done for his stigmata book six years ago; a footnote in the Vatican library's digital card catalogue, something about a Holy Nail. But for the life of him he still couldn't recall the exact details.

He'd forgotten how many boxes of note cards he'd accumulated in the course of the project and, with the file boxes laid out before him, he strategized on how to search through a few thousand cards. Then it dawned on him. Whatever the reference, he hadn't included it in the book because it was either inconsequential or oblique to the subject matter. There was only one file box stuffed with cards that were unused in the manuscript. Even so, there were hundreds of unsorted cards and with an eye on the clock and an approaching boarding time, he began rapidly flipping through them.

Twenty minutes into the exercise he found it.

At the time it had been a curious discovery. Even after reviewing his notes he couldn't quite recall why he had sought out the early manuscript of the book with the accession code of VAT. GR. 1001, indicating it was from the *Vaticanus graecus*, or Vatican Greek collection. Its digital file in the

Vatican Library catalogue had several footnotes, including one that Cal had recorded onto his own index card: *includes 17th cent. Nicolò Alamanni production marginalia and possibly a transcription of the author's original marginalia regarding nail relic and wounds of Christ.* The card had been stickered to indicate that the book was temporarily unavailable so Cal was unlikely to have ever retrieved it. He was unsure what to make of it but he slipped the index card into his bag, tidied his office and headed out the door.

He was on Storrow Drive when the nausea hit.

It came on without warning in a powerful spasm. He tightened his grip on the steering wheel and fought the urge to throw up. The unpleasant feeling dissipated but then returned again with a vengeance. He gagged but kept control of his stomach and waited in dread for the next wave that failed to materialize. He wondered if he'd picked up food poisoning or some damn bug and carried on toward the airport.

Irene sat alone in her brother's ransacked room, staring at his unmade bed and blue pajamas, the very ones she had seen in her vision. Like Cal, she had found out about Giovanni's abduction when she called to speak with him several hours after her early-morning awakening. She had hastily arranged for her aunt to stay with her mother and had driven at speed from Francavilla to Monte Sulla, arriving as the Polizia Locale were wrapping up their inspection of the parish house and their interviews with the rectory staff. She had willingly submitted to police interrogation, but soon had become angered by some of the questions and alarmed by the scatter-shot nature of their inquiries. It seemed to her that the police were grasping at straws.

What was Giovanni's recent state of mind? They had asked. Had he spoken about receiving threats? Was he depressed, suicidal? We know he's a priest, but did he have a girlfriend? A boyfriend? Was it possible he might have staged his own abduction? Had the family been contacted with ransom demands? Who does he know outside the country?

She had reached her breaking point and had cried, 'Why do you ask me these stupid questions? Who does he know outside Italy? Why ask me that?'

The inspectors had replied that his passport was missing. The nuns had done an inventory of his room on their behalf; they had often seen his passport in a dresser drawer and it was no longer there.

'Is anything else missing?' she had demanded.

All his clerical clothes are accounted for, she was told, but some ordinary clothes were nowhere to be found.

'Why aren't you looking for him?' she had asked angrily. 'Sisters Vera and Theresa told me they saw two men with masks dragging him into a white van. Why aren't you looking for the van? Why waste time with me?'

We already found the van, an inspector had said, only two kilometres from the church in a quiet lane with no security cameras nearby. It had been stolen the day before from a town close to Monte Sulla. The kidnappers, if that's what they were, had probably switched cars. And they regretted to add that there was blood in the back of the van.

'Of course there was blood!' she had yelled at them. 'He's Padre Gio, if you've already forgotten.'

Now, after casting her eyes around his bedroom at the finger-print powder dusting multiple surfaces, she picked up his pajama top. It had been a recent birthday present from their mother along with a dozen pair of same-color socks so he wouldn't have to worry about mismatched ones. What a mama's boy he was.

She began to cry but the tears didn't last long.

Suddenly she was seized by a powerful surge of nausea and vertigo that caused her to drop the pajamas onto the floor and gasp. She was hit again and again and just when she thought she would surely have to vomit, the nausea stopped and her equilibrium returned.

Sister Theresa must have heard her crying out and came running in.

'Are you all right, Irene?' she asked.

'No, I'm not all right,' she said. 'I want my brother back.'

Giovanni began to breathe easier. The summer squall had passed and the ocean had become calmer.

One of the men, the smaller of the two, had removed his hood when Giovanni began to get violently ill from seasickness. They didn't want him to choke on his vomit. The man spoke to him in English although when they talked among themselves it was in German.

'Where are we?' Giovanni had asked, sitting up on the bunk and looking around the dark cabin.

'On the water,' the man had said. 'Can't you tell?'

He'd been shackled with two pairs of handcuffs, one on his ankles, one, painfully, on his wrists.

'Could you open the curtains, please?' he asked.

'No.'

'Where are you taking me?'

'You don't need to know.' The man had bad breath; it wasn't making Giovanni's nausea any better.

'Why did you take me? I'm only a poor priest. I have no money.'

'Stop asking questions.' Then this thin man with ropey arm muscles had gotten angry. 'Hey, you're getting blood all over my handcuffs.'

The captor had climbed the short run of stairs and opened the door to the deck, bathing the room in gray light. He had left for a short while before returning with a first-aid kit. Without saying anything more, he had bandaged the priests bleeding wrists with a roll of gauze before leaving him alone in the dark again.

Now, with the sea becalmed and his nausea gone, Giovanni was able to think more clearly. He didn't know much about boats but judging from the way it had tossed around, this one didn't seem very large, certainly no more than fifteen meters. He didn't know from which coast they had disembarked. When he had been thrown in the van outside his house, they had kept the hood over his head and it had remained there when he was transferred to another vehicle. After a road journey of a few hours, still hooded, he had been marched down a gravel path to a chorus of sea gulls, followed by the clopping sound of shoes on a wooden dock. It must have been a private dock because the men had made no attempt to hide him from view. Surely, the sight of a hooded man frog-marched past boaters at a marina would have triggered some alarm. So now, he had no way of telling if they were heading east into the Adriatic or west into the Mediterranean.

Above his head, he heard the muffled voices of the men on deck and then the door slid open. Both of them came into the cabin, turned on a dome light and sat on the bunk across from him.

The big man was wearing a skin-tight black T-shirt and khaki trousers. He had the physique of a body builder and huge pink hands that looked like cooked hams. Nothing about him seemed delicate. His coarse features and bulbous nose, his gravelly voice, his bleached hair with buzzed sides – all of them were the epitome of crudeness. He was the kind of man who had always scared Giovanni. Before he'd become a priest, if he had seen these two fellows walking toward him on a dark night, he would have crossed the street.

'Are you hungry?' Gerhardt asked him.

Giovanni shook his head. 'Why did you take me? Are you going to ask my church for money? We are a poor order.'

The answer made him tremble.

'We don't want money, Giovanni,' Gerhardt said. 'We want information.'

'What kind of information would I have to interest men like you?'

The smaller man took offense. 'What do you mean, men like you? You think you're better than us?'

Gerhardt told his companion to shut up.

'We want you to tell us how you got your wounds,' Gerhardt said.

The priest stared at him in mute disbelief causing Gerhardt to say it again.

'My stigmata?' Giovanni finally said. 'Is that what you're asking about?'

'Yes, very good, you've figured out what I am asking,' Gerhardt said sarcastically.

'But surely you must realize that I don't know how I came to have these wounds. Christ must have had a plan for me.'

The other man snorted, 'I wonder if we're part of that plan?'

Gerhardt glowered at him and said, 'Why don't you go topside and make sure the autopilot is still on.'

'Of course it's on.'

'Go on!' he shouted.

The man slunk away like a whipped dog and made a show of slamming the sliding door against its jamb.

Giovanni's head was cast down and Gerhardt told him to look at him. 'I know you went to the St Athanasius church. I know you followed Brother Augustin into the crypt. I know you began to bleed the next day. What I want to know is this: what was in the crypt?'

A look of abject terror twisted Giovanni's face. 'Who are you?' he croaked.

'Never mind who I am. What was in the crypt?'

'Nothing. There was nothing.'

'There was a spike, wasn't there?' Gerhardt said. 'A spike, a big nail, yes?'

The priest said nothing.

Gerhardt had a small clutch bag he'd brought into the cabin. He unzipped it, took out an object wrapped in a cloth and made a show of slowly unwrapping it.

Giovanni stared at the spearhead.

'A bit more light,' Gerhardt said, sliding back a curtain over his bunk. Bright sunlight caught the golden sleeve around the middle of the spearhead and bounced into the priest's dilated pupils making him wince. 'Do you know what this is?'

Giovanni shook his head.

'It goes by many names. The Spear of Destiny. The Lance of Longinus. The Holy Lance. It is the head of the spear that was stuck into Christ's side when he was up on his cross.'

Giovanni's mouth was dry. His tongue seemed thick and useless. His voice didn't seem like his own anymore. 'Is it real?'

'You tell me. Here, put your hands out and take it. You tell me if it's real.'

Giovanni took it in his manacled hands and inspected the heavy black and gold artifact.

'Well, is it real?'

'No,' the priest said quietly. 'It's not real.'

'How do you know?'

'I just do.'

'Well, you are completely correct,' Gerhardt said, smiling for the first time, showing a row of perfectly white teeth. 'It's a replica. An excellent one but a fake. But you're not a fake, are you, Giovanni? You're genuine. Something made you bleed and it's not something you're putting on your skin. So I'm asking you again: what was in the crypt? Was it a nail?'

When there was no response, Gerhardt, took the lance from him and tested its point against his palm.

'It's quite sharp,' he said.

Then with the quickness of a cat he grabbed Giovanni's right hand and pulled it toward him. The handcuffs pulled his left hand along. There was a dot of blood staining the gauze on his right wrist and Gerhardt used it as his bullseye, thrusting the tip of the lance into it while keeping a tight grip on the hand.

The only reason he stopped was that Giovanni's screams were hurting his ears.

It seemed like the priest was going to pass out. His eyelids fluttered. Gerhardt took a water bottle and dumped it over his head.

When Giovanni opened his eyes again he found himself staring directly at the big man's bulging left biceps. The bottom half of a tattoo was poking out from under the sleeve of his T-shirt and Giovanni was still staring at it when the questions were repeated and the black steel entered his raw wound again.

The captain of the Boston to Rome Alitalia flight announced they were at cruising altitude and turned off the seatbelt signs. A business class stewardess who had been shamelessly smiling at Cal from the moment he'd boarded, came over to his aisle seat and asked if he'd like his drink refreshed.

He smiled back and lifted the glass for her.

'Vodka and ice,' she said. 'A double?'

'You're not trying to get me drunk, are you?' he answered in Italian.

'I would never do that, Dr Donovan. Are you a medical doctor? In case we have a sickness on board?'

'I'm not that kind of a doctor. I teach religion.'

'So I'll get you if we have a religious emergency.'

'I make house calls,' he said.

As she disappeared behind the galley curtain the pain hit him and hit him hard.

His right wrist felt like it was going to explode.

He gritted his teeth, clamped his eyes closed and had to use every bit of his will to keep silent.

Then, against the backdrop of his closed eyelids, he saw something, a curious image, and a minute later, when the pain had disappeared and his breathing returned to normal, he opened his notebook and furiously drew a sketch of what he'd seen.

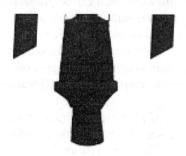

The flight attendant returned with his drink and reached over his lap to place it on a napkin.

'So, you're an artist too,' she said, looking at his notebook. 'What is it?'

He reached for the drink and said, 'I have absolutely no idea.'

EIGHTEEN

The Boston flight touched down at noon local time and while the plane was taxiing Cal turned his phone on to check his Twitter feed.

And there it was.

News of the kidnapping of Padre Gio was all over the Italian and international press.

There were photos of his church, his residence, screenshots of the white getaway van taken from a security camera across the piazza.

The internet wailed collectively: who would do such a thing? Islamic terrorists? A criminal gang? Anarchists? Anticlericals?

Someone from the young priest's earlier life seeking revenge for something he had done?

There were no reports of a ransom demand. The police had no credible leads. The priest's family was in seclusion.

Waiting in line at passport control, he read the response from the Vatican press office: *The Holy Father is aware of the unfortunate incident involving Padre Giovanni Berardino and is praying for his safe return.*

What was it that Cardinal Lauriat had said?

'With all due respect, professor, the Vatican has the internal resources to deal with this.'

Prayer, he thought. *That's their resource?*

Before collecting his rental car he searched his contacts for the number he wanted. The phone rang through to voicemail but he persisted, calling the number three times in rapid fire and on the fourth try a woman picked up.

He identified himself and politely asked whether Irene Berardino was available.

'This is Irene. Why are you calling, professor?'

'I'm concerned about your brother. I wanted to know if there was anything I can do to help.'

Her frostiness was more than obvious. 'You've done enough, I think. We're fine.'

'I'm in Rome, actually. I was wondering if I could come see you.'

'We are not taking visitors, thank you.'

He didn't want to play the card but he felt he had no choice. 'I saw something.'

The pause lasted several beats; he wondered if she'd hung up. 'What do you mean?' she asked.

He let the words tumble out. 'I can't explain it. I had just arrived back to the States. I hadn't been asleep long and I suddenly woke up. That's when it happened. I saw Giovanni in my room. It wasn't a dream. I swear he was there. He looked right at me and said something that I couldn't hear, but I'm pretty sure it was, 'Help me.''

She didn't end the conversation, she didn't tell him he was crazy, she didn't laugh.

She asked a question. 'What was he wearing?'

'Blue pajamas.'

'Come at once, professor. I will be waiting for you.'

About three hours later, Cal arrived at the Francavilla flat Irene shared with her mother. Irene let him in and in the sitting room he saw a red-eyed Domenica Berardino slumped in the same chair she'd occupied since the abduction a day earlier. She started to get up to greet him but her sister told her to sit. Carla Taglianetti was quite a bit younger than Domenica, a handsome woman who worked as a tax assessor for the city. Her son, Federico, a six-year-old boy was also there, playing on the carpet with a set of toy cars he'd retrieved from Giovanni's old room.

Cal introduced himself and asked if there had been any news.

'Nothing, nothing!' Carla said.

Cal was about to say something soothing but Domenica asked plaintively, 'Tell me, why did they take my boy?'

'I'm afraid I don't know. What have the police told you?'

Carla said contemptuously, 'They know nothing or they tell us nothing. Either way we're in the dark. Irene tells me you were sent by the Vatican to investigate Giovanni's stigmata. What did you conclude?'

'Can we offer the man a drink first?' Irene said.

'I'm fine, thanks,' he said.

Carla sharply asked again, 'So what did you conclude?'

He apologized. 'The Vatican had me sign a confidentiality agreement. I don't have permission to talk about it.'

That got her boiling mad. 'You came into my sister's house and grilled them with questions and now you don't have the courtesy to tell us what you thought about Giovanni?'

'The Vatican doesn't like him,' Domenica shouted. 'They think he's a faker. Our Giovanni is stealing the spotlight from all the powerful men with their red hats and smug faces. I wouldn't be surprised if they're behind this.'

It came out involuntarily. He shouldn't have said it but after he did he wasn't sorry. 'I don't think he's a faker,' he said.

Domenica began to cry. The boy looked up from his game and Irene rushed over and knelt by her mother.

'Mama.'

'It's what I've always said,' Domenica sobbed. 'He's been

touched by holiness. The Lord will look after him in his time of need.'

Irene patted her hand, stood and asked Cal if they might talk in her brother's room.

When the door was shut she said, 'Thank you for saying that. Was it the truth?'

'I don't know if one can ever know the truth in cases like this, but it's what I believe.'

She wearily sat on Giovanni's bed and he pulled out the desk chair so he wouldn't be looming over her.

'I saw him too,' she said.

She told him what she had seen in her bedroom across the hall. It matched his sighting to the letter except for her ability to hear his cry for help.

Cal asked her if something similar had ever happened before. Although she previously denied having visions involving Giovanni, now she opened up and told him everything: the episode of bilocation she'd witnessed, her mother's claim to have seen the face of Christ when her son hugged her.

He hung on every word and when it was his turn to speak he didn't hold back either. He spoke about the two visions he'd had of a Christ-like face, once when Giovanni embraced him, the second during his car accident in Croatia.

And after watching her face melt in wonder, he said, 'There's more. Something happened to me on my flight last night.'

She pointed to her slim right wrist. 'Was it a pain, here?'

'My God, it was,' he said.

'Mine was so bad, mama heard and came running. I told her I was having a nightmare.'

'Yeah, it hurt like hell.'

'And did you see something?' she asked.

He reached into his bag and took out his notebook to show her the drawing he'd made.

'I saw this.'

Without uttering a word she got up, left him alone and went across the hall. She returned from her room with a piece of paper and unfolded it.

He placed the two drawings, hers in pencil, his in pen, side by side on her brother's desk.

'They're identical,' he whispered. 'What in heaven's name is going on?'

'Don't you see?' she said. 'Giovanni is calling out to us. He wants our help. We're feeling what he feels, we're seeing what he sees.'

'I understand your connection, Irene. You're his sister. But why me? I'm a stranger.'

'He told me he felt a closeness to you, a kinship he said.'

'There's more I have to tell you,' he said urgently. 'Things I uncovered during my investigation.'

'I thought it was confidential.'

He finally made her smile. 'Screw the confidentiality.'

The doorbell rang and Domenica called for Irene. Cal left the bedroom with her. There were two men in the sitting room, one in civilian clothes, and the other in the black Valentino-designed uniform of a Carabinieri officer. The civilian, a tall man with broad shoulders and sympathetic eyes, was a lawyer, the mayor of Francavilla, who greeted Irene, her mother and sister with warm hugs, and patted young Federico on his head.

Seeing Cal, he said, 'I'm sorry, you have company. I should have called.'

Irene introduced Cal as a friend of the family, a professor from America, and the mayor told him he wished they were meeting under better circumstances.

Then, turning to the family the mayor said, 'I told you I would try to pull some strings. I would like to introduce Lieutenant Colonel Tommaso Cecchi from the Carabinieri's Raggruppamento Operativo Speciale.

Cecchi, an athletic man in his fifties, removed his cap and shook hands all around.

Cecchi said, 'As the mayor says, he pulled his string and I was on the other end of it.'

'He's come all the way from Rome,' the mayor said, 'from the headquarters of the ROS. I went to law school with the brother of a Carabiniere and well, he did the rest.'

'Not an ordinary Carabiniere,' Cecchi said. 'Very high up, a general.'

'Thank you. Thank you for coming in our hour of need,' Domenica said.

'Let's hope we can help,' Cecchi said.

Carla dragged her son into the kitchen while she made coffee and Irene spoke for the family.

'We haven't really gotten any detailed information from the local police in Monte Sulla,' she said.

'I made some calls, of course,' the lieutenant colonel said. 'Due to the high profile nature of your brother's case and the interest of the Vatican authorities, the Polizia Locale have already been largely pushed aside by the Polizia di Stato, who seem to be mounting a credible effort. The Carabinieri do not wish to get into a jurisdictional dispute, but my unit is happy to keep our fingers on the pulse of the investigation and intervene should our special capabilities become needed.'

'What are those capabilities?' Irene asked.

'The ROS is, as its name implies, a special operations group with assets and capabilities to deal with terrorist threats and incidents, kidnappings, organized crime. Since we are a member of the armed forces we also have excellent cross-border relationships and capabilities.'

'You mean he could be outside of Italy?' Irene asked.

'Today, I have no information about his case. Tomorrow I will know more, the day after, more still. I beg you to let me dig into the facts. The next time we talk I will be better prepared to answer your questions.'

'Thank you from the bottom of my heart,' Domenica said to the mayor and the colonel. 'I just want my boy back.'

Cecchi took his espresso standing up and asked Cal, 'So, professor, what brings you to Italy?'

'I came when I heard what happened to Giovanni. I'm here to help in any way I can.'

'You've known the family long?'

He knew his answer would raise eyebrows. 'Only two weeks.'

Cecchi's curious expression seemed to demand an explanation.

'I was asked by the Vatican to help in an inquiry into Giovanni's stigmata.'

'You are a medical professor?'

He shook his head. 'Professor of religion.'

'And what did you conclude?'

'As I told the family, I'm not authorized to divulge anything about the investigation.'

Cecchi's frown said it all. 'Not even to the Carabinieri?'

'If the Vatican gives me a waiver I'd be willing to talk with you about it.'

'So, you've just met the Berardino family, you return to the United States and turn around and come back to help them. I find this admirable and unusual at the same time.'

Cal and Irene traded glances. He knew what she was thinking. If they were ever going to describe their psychic experiences, this would be a time to pull the officer aside. But Cal knew how that story would end – with dismissiveness and ridicule.

Irene must have come to the same conclusion because she said, 'Professor Donovan is a sympathetic man, lieutenant colonel. Even though we have only known him a short while, he has demonstrated he is a friend of Giovanni's and a friend of ours. Wouldn't the world be a better place if there were more people like him?'

A small smile flickered across Cecchi's face. He handed his cup and saucer to Irene and said, 'Indeed it would. So, professor, at this point, lacking significant information about the kidnapping, I have no opinion whether the priest's stigmata might have played some role in the case. If, in the course of my investigation, I feel the necessity of requesting this waiver you spoke of, whom, may I ask, within the Vatican commissioned your work? I need to know whom to call.'

Cecchi blinked in astonishment at Cal's answer.

'Pope Celestine. I believe his number is in the Holy See directory.'

The man loitering across the street from the Berardino's apartment block casually snapped some photos, while pretending to be reading the screen of his mobile phone. He attached them to a text message and sent them to the anonymous number he'd been given.

In Berlin, Lambret Schneider's second phone pinged. He found a string of photos of a man leaving an apartment building and walking to his own lodgings attached to a blank text.

'Professor Donovan,' Schneider said out loud. 'What are you doing back in Italy?'

NINETEEN

C al was back in his rental car retracing the route to Rome, only this time he wasn't alone. Irene was beside him in the passenger seat.

Her decision to come with him was sealed during a walk along the beach. Weaving their way through the crowd of beach-goers, lounge chairs and umbrellas, they had tried to figure out some kind of plan of action.

'I see you thought that bringing up our collective visions was a bad idea,' he had said.

'A terrible idea. You read my mind?'

'It was obvious.'

'We would have no credibility if we told these things to the police. This guy, Cecchi, would have gone back to Rome and we would never hear from him again. He'd tell everyone that the missing priest's sister and this American must have escaped from the insane asylum.'

'Perhaps we have,' he had said.

'What should we do?' she had said. 'Honestly, I can't imagine what two civilians can accomplish in what is basically a police matter.'

'We've got something the police don't have. Somehow your brother is communicating with us. We just need to listen.'

The crowd had thinned the further they walked away from the pier. With the tide coming in and the water lapping at their shoes, he had turned to her and made this proposal.

'Let's work together. Come with me to Rome. I know where I want to go first.'

'I don't know how I can be of help.'

'Giovanni is calling out to us. I've got a feeling in my gut that if we're together we'll be able to hear him better.'

'That doesn't sound very scientific.'

He had laughed. 'Maybe that's because I'm only a social scientist.'

'I'm only a little better,' she said. 'I'm a science teacher.'

'At what level?'

'Liceo. Like your high school.' She had paused. 'Look, I have nowhere to stay in Rome.'

'They have hotels there,' he had said lightly.

She hadn't taken well to the remark. 'Yes, thank you for this revelation, but a school teacher can't afford to stay in hotels in Rome in the high season.'

'I'll pay. And I'm sorry I was flippant. I assure you, it's my only flaw.'

'Apology accepted,' she had said. 'Two rooms.'

'Deal.'

It was early evening, but they still had several hours of daylight and the traffic was light. Domenica had insisted on packing a bag of food and drink for the trip and Irene offered him a sandwich stuffed with leftover beef.

He took a bite and said, 'Your mother's a good cook.'

'Like all Italian mothers.'

'Surely a myth.'

'Maybe, but if I'm ever a mother the tradition ends.' She turned serious. 'I think you've got more to tell me. Maybe a lot more.'

It was the invitation he needed. To hell with confidentiality. He had to . . . he wanted to tell her everything. It had been lonely and frustrating keeping his own counsel.

It came out in a linear way, just as he'd experienced it, beginning with his interview with her brother and his sense that Giovanni hadn't been forthcoming about his experience at St Athanasius. Then he talked about his meeting in Naples with Giovanni's friend and fellow priest, Antonio, who gave a different version about the invitation from Brother Augustin to visit the crypt. But what really shocked Irene was what he told her about his time in Croatia.

The revelation that there had been a lineage of stigmatics at St Athanasius stretching back into time unnerved her and she became visibly upset when Cal suggested that Brother Augustin's subsequent death might not have been accidental.

'What do you think was in the crypt?' she asked.

'The only person who knows is your brother.'

But it was Cal's description of almost being forced off the mountain by the monastery groundskeeper that sent her into a panic.

'Do you really believe this man tried to kill you?'

'I may be the only one who believes it, but yes, I do.'

'But why would he do it?'

'Maybe he thought I found out something I wasn't supposed to know. Actually, I should have said, '*they* thought,' because from everything the Croatian police told me, the guy was a simple local man, very unsophisticated, not into anything much more exotic than gardening and drinking.'

She repeated the word, *they*, and said, 'Then we have to imagine that there could be some kind of conspiracy. First they try to kill you for what you may know, then they take Giovanni.' Her lower lip began to tremble. 'Maybe they'll torture him. Maybe they'll kill him,' she said dully.

He didn't try to give her false hope. He had come to the same conclusion.

'There's something else. I didn't see a linkage at the time but it's harder to think it's a coincidence now that Giovanni's been taken. I was mugged at the Naples train station by a couple of thugs who stole my briefcase.'

'Were you hurt?'

'I wasn't. They were. I tend not to take these things lying down. Anyway, I got my bag back but I've been thinking that maybe *they* were trying another way to find out what I knew.'

'Jesus,' she whispered.

'What I can't figure out for the life of me is this: what could have been kept in that poor, old monastery that was worth committing kidnapping or murder.'

'You still haven't told me what we're going to be doing in Rome?'

'What I do best. We're going to a library.'

At the reception desk of the Grand Hotel de la Minerve, Cal was warmly welcomed back by the evening manager.

'We weren't expecting you back so soon, professor.'

'The allure of your roof garden was too great.'

'I have two beautiful rooms for you. Shall I make you and Signorina Berardino a reservation for dinner?'

Irene was at his side, a bit star-struck at the elegance of the place.

Cal told her he was dog-tired and would probably get some room service before crashing. 'But you go. There's a great view of the Pantheon up there. Or get room service. Order anything you like.'

'I'll be fine,' she said, holding up Domenica's bag of food. 'There's enough here to feed half of Rome.'

The next morning, Cal kept his car in the hotel garage and he and Irene got a taxi to the Vatican. On the way, both of them confided that their nights had been uneventful, with no 'visitations' by Giovanni. But Irene was troubled by their absence.

She stared out the window at all the carefree tourists and said, 'At least maybe it's a sign he's alive.'

Even though it was early, it was a bright summer day and the tourists were already flocking to St Peter's Square. Their first stop was a small Vatican office just inside the Porta Angelica. Cal had called ahead to arrange a new visitor's pass for Irene and to renew his own long-standing credentials.

Badges in hand, he led her up the Via di Porta Angelica to the Via Sant Anna.

'When was the last time you visited the Vatican?' he asked her.

'I have to confess. It's been a long time. A school trip probably. You must come all the time.'

'Home away from home.'

At the Belvedere Courtyard, they made their way to the dun-colored façade of the stone wing that connected the long arms that were the Vatican Palace.

'Here we are,' Cal said. 'The Vatican Apostolic Library, or as we research nerds call it, the Vat.'

Inside, they had to undergo a bag search. The guard went through the papers in Cal's briefcase and then turned to Irene's bag, holding up a painted, plastic statuette.

'The Virgin Mary, Our Lady of Lourdes,' she said sheepishly. 'It was a gift from Giovanni. I took it with me from Francavilla for luck and maybe a little comfort.'

The guard handed it back.

'Bringing it to the Vatican is a bit like bringing coals to Newcastle,' Cal said.

At the reception desk, Cal presented their passes and asked if Monsignor Pandolfi was available.

When Guido Pandolfi came down from his office he greeted Cal with a warm embrace.

'Professor! Cal! It's so good to see you. We weren't expecting you until later in the summer.'

'I apologize for the surprise visit. Guido, this is a friend of mine, Irene Berardino. Irene, the monsignor is the vice prefect of the library.'

'Have you been here before, signorina?' he asked.

'First visit.'

'Well it's a very special and unique library, of course, and Professor Donovan is one of our most esteemed academic researchers. We have almost two million printed books, ten thousand parchment books, one hundred thousand manuscripts, many, many ancient coins and medals, and all manner of fine art. There are some fifty-two kilometers of book shelving, much of it subterranean. It is one of the great treasures of the world. Tell me, Cal, how may we assist you today?'

Cal showed him the index card he had brought with him from Cambridge.

'Ah, VAT. GR. 1001,' Pandolfi said. 'One of my favorites.'

'Get many requests for it?' Cal asked.

'You'd be surprised. Please follow me through to the reading room and I'll get it for you.'

They found seats at one of the simple wooden tables in the barrel-vaulted, frescoed reading room. The long chamber was almost empty – it was on the early side for most academics that preferred to fortify themselves in the cafés first – so they didn't have to whisper all that softly.

'What is this book you requested?' Irene asked.

'It's by a sixth-century Byzantine writer, Procopius of Caesarea, who's been called the last major historian of the ancient western world. One of his books, *The Secret History*, is a fly-on-the-wall account of the Emperor Justinian, actually a really racy and scandalous account where Procopius dished the dirt on Justinian and his wife, Theodora. This is the earliest known edition of the book, probably copied out by a fourteenth-century scribe. It had been known since the sixth century that Procopius wrote the book but it was lost to time. Historians searched for a copy for centuries but it turns out that the Vatican Library had it all along, filed away under another name. A Vatican Librarian, an Italian named Alamanni, discovered it in the seventeenth century and had it published, removing the most scandalous bits.'

She had been listening with evidently mounting impatience. 'What does this have to do with Giovanni?'

He held up his index card. 'Maybe nothing, maybe this.'

She read his notation: *includes 17th cent. Nicolò Alamanni production marginalia and possibly a transcription of the author's original marginalia regarding nail relic and wounds of Christ.*

'I'm sorry,' she said. 'I don't understand the relevance.'

'Look, it's a very thin lead, I'll admit, but when I saw it I started making some connections. One: the monastery at St Athanasius is one of the oldest in Europe, it's seventh century, maybe even earlier. Two: According to the only surviving monk, Brother Ivan, there's been a long line of secret stigmatics there. Three: Giovanni began having stigmata after visiting the crypt. Four: what's typically kept in crypts? Burials and relics. Five . . .'

'I see that you're either very creative or very crazy.'

He bowed his head at the half-compliment. 'Could be both.'

'Are you suggesting there could have been an important relic in the crypt? One of the Holy Nails of Christ?'

'The thought crossed my mind.'

'But how could a relic cause stigmata? And why would some people commit terrible crimes because of it?'

'Like I said, it's a thin reed of a theory.' He searched the reading room for Pandolfi. 'Why's he taking so long?' he asked.

Minutes turned into tens of minutes.

When Pandolfi finally appeared it was patently obvious that something was wrong.

The monsignor began speaking with his hands before any words came out. 'Professor, a great calamity I'm afraid. The book. It's gone.'

Cal understood the gravity but Irene asked innocently, 'Did someone check it out?'

Cal answered for Pandolfi. 'There's only one person on God's green earth who's allowed to check out a book from the Vat and that's the pope.'

'And the Holy Father isn't to blame, I assure you,' the librarian said. 'Here's what I've discovered. Our digital files indicate the book was last requested three weeks ago by a researcher from Belgium, a reputable scholar. It was returned to the shelves when he was done with his work. So it has disappeared within this time period.'

'What's your protocol?' Cal asked.

'We must close the library immediately and enlist all our staff to do a search in case it was misfiled. There are some other tasks we must also perform on the personnel side. Cal, please give me your mobile phone number and I will call you later in the day. Until then, please say nothing, whisper nothing, tweet nothing of this matter.'

Guido Pandolfi hastily arranged a meeting later that afternoon. He arrived at the office of the Cardinal Librarian in the Apostolic Palace the same time as the other two men. One was his immediate superior, the prefect of the Vatican Library, who was a Dutch archbishop, and the other was a member of the Vatican Gendarmerie, the deputy inspector general, Colonel Emilio Celestino.

The Cardinal Librarian, Cardinal Vittorio Pessoa, a scowling, portly man stuffed behind his ornate desk, dispensed with pleasantries. He was the man who answered to the pope and the Procopius book was one of the truly priceless treasures of the collection.

'Tell me what you know,' he demanded, wagging his finger at Pandolfi.

'We know the book was in the library three weeks ago when a well-respected academic requested it. It was logged out and logged back in two hours later. One of my most trusted librarians was the one who handled the transaction and she assures me she replaced it in its proper shelf in one of the new, climate-controlled rooms.'

'You believe her?' the cardinal asked.

'I do, Your Eminence. However, suspicion immediately fell upon another librarian, a young man named Flavio Costa, who has been with us for only four years. He abruptly resigned two weeks ago in a most unsatisfactory manner, giving essentially no notice and a vague explanation of his actions.'

The cardinal looked dyspeptic. 'Do you think he stole it?'

'I suspect so.'

'But surely it's not an easy matter to walk off with one of our manuscripts,' the Dutch prefect said. 'The book, like all our volumes, will have had an RFID computer chip that would have set off an alarm. Furthermore, all employees are subject to a physical search when they leave the library.'

Pandolfi nodded. 'Our librarians know where the chips are located and how to remove and destroy them. As to the security searches, let me ask Colonel Celestino to address this.'

Celestino, a youthful man in a smart civilian suit, said, 'We went through the duty rosters for the day that Costa resigned and identified the guard who was responsible for employee searches. At first he denied any irregularities but we had evidence to the contrary. The security camera at the employee checkpoint showed him waving Costa through that evening.'

The cardinal's mouth dropped open. 'What?'

'With persistent questioning the guard admitted his complicity,' Celestino said. 'He was paid one thousand euros by Costa to let him pass without a bag check. He is now under arrest.'

'And what of Costa?' the prefect asked.

'He's not answering his mobile or home telephone,' Celestino said. 'Working with the Roman police we have a search warrant for his flat. I personally intend to exercise this warrant now.'

Celestino accompanied a trio of municipal Roman policemen to Costa's apartment building in the San Lorenzo neighborhood of Rome. It was an area heavily populated with students, the kind of place where a poorly paid junior librarian might afford a studio flat.

As they were about to enter the building, a young man with facial piercings leaned out a first-floor window and called out, 'It's about time you guys stopped ignoring us.'

'What are you talking about?' one of the policemen said.

'We've been complaining about the smell on the third floor for a week.'

*   *   *

When Monsignor Pandolfi rang Cal in the late afternoon to see if he was available to talk in person, Cal suggested they meet over dinner at Gigetto's in the Jewish quarter, explaining he had a serious craving for fried artichokes.

Cal and Irene arrived before him and were into their second glass of wine before the priest arrived, out of breath and apologetic.

'This has surely been the strangest day I have ever experienced,' he said, accepting a pour of Pinot Grigio.

'Did you find it?' Irene asked.

'Unfortunately no, but we know what happened to it, up to a point.' He glanced at the other diners on the terrace and dropped his voice. 'One of our young staff librarians stole the book and abruptly resigned. He must have been paid a great deal of money, because he gave a library security guard one thousand euros to look the other way.'

'Do you know where he is?' Cal asked.

'We do. Unfortunately we cannot ask him any questions. We found him in his flat this afternoon. He'd been shot more than one week ago. Murdered. The book was not there.'

'My God,' Irene gasped.

Cal thought she looked faint and filled her water glass. He could see a panic attack coming on.

'Are you unwell, signorina?' Pandolfi asked.

'I'll be fine,' she said unconvincingly. 'It's awful.'

'Yes, an awful affair,' the priest agreed.

'Do you have any idea who's behind this?'

'The Roman police and our Vatican Gendarmerie are investigating but no, unfortunately not. Professor, may I ask why you wished to see the book today?'

Cal wondered if the vice prefect was suspicious about the timing. 'It's for one of my research projects on the seventeenth-century Church.'

'The text of *The Secret History* is widely available. I myself own several editions.'

'It's not the text I'm after. It's the marginalia in Latin and Greek on VAT. GR. 1001.'

'Ah, the marginalia, I see. Most were made by the librarian, Nicolò Alamanni, to aid him in the preparation of the first printed version of the book.'

'That's what I'm interested in, an insight into the Church attitudes and official censorship.'

'Well, Procopius held very little back in his description of vice and sexuality in Justinian's court,' Pandolfi said.

'Exactly,' Cal agreed, hoping that Pandolfi was unaware of the other marginalia. 'So it's a major tragedy that the book's been stolen and a minor tragedy for me that my research is stymied. I tried to see the book once before, years ago when I was doing another research project. It was unavailable then, so my luck with Procopius is pretty bad.'

'When exactly did you previously request it?'

Cal pulled out his mobile phone, searched his calendar and found the exact date he'd been at the library.

Pandolfi tapped his forehead with his finger a while and declared, 'You know, I'm quite sure we were in the midst of a photography project. The Cardinal Librarian at the time decided to grant an Italian publisher of art and photography books, the right to produce a book that was called, *Treasures of the Vatican Library*.'

'I know the book. I own a copy,' Cal said.

'The photographer hired by the publisher set up his equipment in our restoration laboratory and the book was probably there during the period you requested it. I'm quite sure that only the title page of *The Secret History* was ultimately published but I'm also quite sure that many of its pages were photographed.'

Cal leaned forward expectantly. 'Do you have those photos, Guido?'

'I'm sorry, Cal, but I don't.' As Cal was deflating with disappointment, Pandolfi added, 'But the publisher might.'

TWENTY

The offices of Edizione Penta were located near the Piazza Navona in an elegant townhouse that originally had belonged to the publisher's great grandfather. Monsignor Pandolfi had called on Cal's behalf. When Cal and Irene arrived the next morning for their appointment, Laura Penta, the company chairman, met them.

'We are very pleased to meet you, Professor Donovan,' she told him in the reception hall. 'I Googled you this morning and I see what an eminent authority you are. We will try to help.'

Cal thanked her, mentioned he owned several of the publisher's lavishly produced art and architecture books and introduced Irene.

'Berardino,' Penta said, thinking for a moment. 'That's the name of the missing stigmatic priest, isn't it?'

Cal hoped that Irene would answer vaguely but she didn't.

'I'm his sister.'

'My heavens!' the publisher said. 'I'm so sorry! What a horrible time for you. Does your appointment today have anything to do with this?'

Cal quickly answered, 'It's a complete coincidence. Irene is assisting me with my research and she thought she would carry on, to help keep her mind off the situation. The police have the family's full confidence.'

Irene pursed her lips then said, 'Yes, full confidence.'

'Well, come with me to our boardroom. We have all the prints from the *Treasures of the Vatican Library* book in boxes. That's the good news, as one says. The bad news is that, five years ago, we temporarily ran out of photographic file boxes. We urgently needed some for a new project so we robbed Peter to pay Paul. All the photos from the Vatican Library book were transferred to larger boxes, without respect for their organization. At least we retained them. We're bursting at the seams but I can't bear to throw out work we've paid for.'

Cal blanched when he saw the conference table. It was piled high with unlabeled, large cardboard boxes filled with developed photos and contact sheets.

'Yes, it's a big job,' Penta said. 'Fortunately there are two of you. There's a coffee machine and mineral water. If you need anything, my assistant is just down the hall.'

Cal opened a box at random. It was stacked to the lid with color photos. He placed the top one on the table for both of them to see, a page of parchment with Latin calligraphy. He turned it over to see if there was any label on the back. There wasn't.

'This is a problem,' he said.

'Why?' she asked.

'If they're all like this, it's going to require me to read a few lines of each to see if it's from *The Secret History*. We're not going to be able to split the workload.'

'The book is in Greek, right? I know the difference between Latin and Greek so I can sort the photos for you. And if I see any writings in margins, well, so much the better.'

Cal gave her a thumbs up. 'Smart,' he said. 'Very smart. Let's get going.'

The room was sweltering hot.

Giovanni lay on a narrow bed, the sweat streaming down his face. There was a ceiling fan but it was operating at a low speed and it moved almost no air. The two windows were open but the shutters were nailed shut. The bright sunlight cast the pattern of the shutter slats onto the peeling paint of the opposite wall. He'd been told that calling for help was useless – the house was isolated – but if he disobeyed, he'd be beaten. The only other furniture was a flimsy chair and an empty bureau. There was a ceramic jug for his urine and a few plastic bottles of warm water, with labels removed. If he needed the toilet, he had to ring a bell and the smaller man would come with a blindfold to take him along a corridor to the WC.

The journey by boat had ended the night before and when they docked, his hood had been replaced and he was blindly marched a short distance to a car. There a third man greeted the other two in German. The car journey had lasted well over an hour. When he was removed from the vehicle he had heard crickets, so he had assumed he was in the countryside. His shoes had crunched on gravel and then he was inside. When his hood had been removed he was in this bedroom.

The key turned in the lock and the large man entered with two thin sandwiches on a paper plate. Apparently, Giovanni's room wasn't the only one that was hot, because the man was shirtless, his bronze skin glistening with sweat. The priest stared at him for a moment then looked away self-consciously. The only times he had ever seen such a massive chest was at the cinema in action movies.

'Eat this,' Gerhardt said.

Giovanni held up his hands. The wounds on his wrists had bled through, soaking his bandages and his bedsheets were streaked with blood.

'May I have fresh bandages?' he asked.

'We have no gauze,' Gerhardt said. 'I'll bring strips of linen later.'

He watched while Giovanni hungrily consumed the sandwiches.

When Giovanni had taken his last bite of bread and cheese he said, 'It's time to tell me what you found inside the crypt.'

'I can only repeat what I told you before. There was nothing.'

'I gave you food. I was nice to you.'

'Kidnapping me isn't nice. Hurting me isn't nice.'

'I'll give you until tonight to think. I'll come back when it's dark and I'll hurt you worse than before. You'll tell me what the monk gave you in the crypt. It was a spike, I think. You'll tell me where it is. Until you do, you won't get any more food. You're fat. You can last a long time. And no more trips to the toilet. You'll use the floor.'

Gerhardt turned to pick up the ceramic jug and purposely spilled the urine on the tiles. When he did, Giovanni got a good look at his huge left biceps and the rest of the tattoo he'd seen on the boat.

'Four down, sixteen to go.'

Cal replaced the lid on the box, lifted it off the table and placed it on the floor beside the other three they'd searched.

'At this rate, we're going to be here tomorrow too,' Irene said, stretching her arms over her head.

She was already partway through the next box, sorting photos into piles based on the language of the text: Latin, Greek, other. He initially checked her work to make sure no photos of Greek texts got into the Latin pile, but after a while he was satisfied that she was making the correct assignments.

He was reaching for the pile of Greek photos from the fifth box when he suddenly stopped and stared at the wall.

Except he wasn't seeing the wall.

He was seeing something else, a black and tan image.

His breathing quickened and his pulse raced.

Finally, his blinking seemed to wipe the image away and he

looked over at Irene, about to talk when he noticed that she too was blinking, with a bewildered expression on her face.

'I just saw something,' she said.

'So did I.'

'I'm going to draw it,' she said urgently. 'Give me a pen, please.'

He got two pens and two pieces of loose paper from his bag and they both began to sketch.

When they were done they slid their drawings across the table to one another.

They were identical.

They had to take a walk around the Piazza Navona to clear their agitation.

Amidst the multilingual chatter of tourists and the sound of flowing water from Bernini's Fountain of Four Rivers, they tried to make sense of their latest message.

'You're a hell of a lot better of an artist than me,' he said, looking at the two sketches, one in each hand.

'But they are the same, that's clear,' she said. 'It's some kind of Nazi symbol, isn't it?'

Cal agreed. 'Those are definitely the SS lightning bolts.'

'And in between them?' she asked. 'Some kind of spear?'

'You don't recognize it?' Cal asked.

'Should I?'

'It's not just any spear. It's the Holy Lance.'

He told her its history: how it was cleaved in the eleventh

century by an artisan trying to insert what had been thought to
be a Holy Nail into the relic and patched with a sleeve of gold,
how it was seized by the Nazis in the Anschluss and how it was
returned to Vienna by the Allies after the war.

'But where would Giovanni see this kind of symbol?' she
asked. 'A painting, a poster, a book?'

'No clue,' Cal said. 'I'm sure I've never seen it before. If I
had I'd remember. What I can't figure out is why he only saw
the bottom half of the symbol first.'

'It made an impression on him,' she said. 'First the bottom
part, then the whole of it. We're not seeing everything he sees,
that's for sure, so I can only think we're seeing the things that
are most important, maybe the ones that are causing the most
stress. And I have to tell you, Cal, as upsetting as it is to receive
these – I don't know – transmissions, I'm thanking God because
it tells me he's alive.'

They made nearly a full circuit of the piazza in silence. Outside
the Church of Sant'Agnese in Agone, a little boy lost control of
his rubber ball and his father ran after it. Cal stopped it with his
shoe and tossed it to the young man. When he caught it, Cal
noticed a tattoo of a compass on his right arm, bisected and
half-obscured by his T-shirt sleeve.

'Thanks,' the man said.

'You're welcome,' Cal muttered. As the man withdrew he
whispered to Irene, 'Look at his right arm.'

'Yes, so what?' she said.

'Look at what his sleeve is half-covering.'

'Christ almighty,' she said. 'Giovanni's been looking at someone's tattoo.'

They returned to the Penta boardroom and threw themselves into
sorting through more boxes of photos. While they worked they
talked about what to do with their new information.

'Maybe we should show our drawing to Cecchi,' Irene said.

'And tell him what, that we're getting psychic messages from
your brother?'

'It's the truth.'

'I don't think he'll take it as actionable intelligence, do you?'

She thought about it and said, 'For sure he'll say we're crazy.'

'Let's try to get more data before we risk blowing our credibility. Here's what I'll do. When we get back to the hotel I'll go online and see if I can find an image match to the insignia of some SS unit during the war or afterwards. If we come up with something, maybe we can figure out a way to bring it to Cecchi's attention, without invoking mysticism.' Then he picked up a stack of photos and said, 'Come on, only twelve boxes to go.'

By the time they had to leave the Penta offices for the evening, they had found not a single one of *The Secret History* photos. There were still five unopened boxes so they arranged to return in the morning to finish the job.

They walked back to the hotel in dazzling sunshine and immediately went to Cal's room where he got out his laptop and Irene first called her mother in Francavilla and then Sister Vera in Monte Sulla to see if there was any news from the police. When she was done she asked Cal if she could turn on the TV news.

The coverage of the search for Giovanni was relentless but unrevealing. A local police spokesman only confirmed that there had been no investigative leads and that the Carabinieri ROS unit had been consulted. To expand their thin reportage, the camera crew camping out in Monte Sulla had to resort to interviewing people on the street to elicit all too predictable expressions of concern for the welfare of their priest.

'Anything?' she asked, clicking off the TV.

'Nothing yet.' Cal said. 'Lots of spears, lots of SS lightning bolts, nothing that combines them. Help yourself to a beer, wine, something stronger, from the minibar.'

'I don't really like alcohol but I'll have a juice if you don't mind.'

'Sure. You know, you're the second woman I've met in a month who doesn't drink.'

'You find that unusual?' she asked.

'In my experience, yes. It's probably a sample bias. I don't tend to gravitate to teetotalers.'

'Sorry to disappoint.'

'Didn't mean it that way. It's more of an indictment of me. Does your dislike of alcohol extend to handling it?'

'Of course not.'

'Then could you pour all the little vodka bottles in there into a glass?'

She made a face and had a look. 'There are three of them.'

'That's a disappointment but three will have to do for now.'

She handed him a half-full tumbler.

'I hope your liver doesn't fail before we find Giovanni.'

He wasn't sure she was joking.

After a while he cursed his screen and pulled out his mobile phone to take a picture of his drawing of the spear.

'What are you doing?' she asked.

'I've got a phone app for a reverse image finder. You compare a target image to the Google image database. Worth a shot.'

In under a minute he was groaning. 'Nothing. Not even close,' he said. 'Want to get a bite to eat?'

'No,' she said. 'I'm tired. Maybe I'll get a salad from room service and go to sleep early.'

He showed her to the door. 'Have a good rest. Meet you in the lobby same time tomorrow.'

Irene's room was on the fourth floor overlooking the small, bustling piazza behind the Pantheon. She had turned in early with the windows open, but she awoke just before nine at night because of the noise. She closed the windows, climbed back into bed and soon drifted back to sleep, but minutes later she began to gasp for air.

She sat bolt upright, her heart beating out of her chest, fighting for her breath.

'What in God's name is happening?' she sputtered.

The small man was holding a thrashing Giovanni down on his bed while Gerhardt poured water over the towel covering the priest's face.

'Where is it?' Gerhardt demanded. 'Tell me where it is.'

He pulled away the towel and allowed Giovanni to sit up, choking and coughing and frothing at the mouth and nose.

'It's unpleasant, yes?' Gerhardt said. 'I will do it again and again and again until you talk to me. Be reasonable. It's so easy to tell me what I want to know. Will you?'

'Go to hell,' Giovanni rasped.

'Such language from a man of the cloth. Let's go for another swim, shall we?'

Irene ran up the hotel stairwell in her nightdress and robe, coughing all the way. Outside Cal's door she could hear that he too was coughing. Clad only in jogging shorts he responded to her urgent banging. They stared at each other's florid complexions for a moment before he pulled her into the room.

'You too?' he asked.

'It was awful. I was choking,' she sobbed. 'What are they doing to Giovanni?'

He sat her down and poured her some water but she seemed to instinctively fear it.

'They probably want something from him,' he said. 'They're trying to get him to talk.'

'We've got to help him.'

'I know.'

'I'm scared to go back to my room,' she said.

He had two beds and pulled back the cover on the unused one.

'You can stay here,' he said. 'I've been told I don't snore.'

In the morning, Irene awoke before Cal and tiptoed back to her own room to dress. In the hallway a maid saw her leaving in her robe and heading to the stairwell. Irene cast her eyes downward and blushed. Cal met her later in the lobby and on the way to Edizione Penta they stopped at a café for a coffee.

'Did you sleep ok?' he asked.

'Not very. You?' she said sheepishly.

'Not very.'

Two hours later, they were in the Penta boardroom on the second-to-last box with hope fading.

'This box has quite a few photos of Greek manuscripts,' Irene said, interrupting a long silence.

Cal got up to look over her shoulder and snatched one out of her hand.

'This is it,' he said triumphantly. 'VAT. GR. 1001. Procopius. Keep going. It's the right box.'

Cal was proficient at Medieval Greek calligraphy and he scanned the photographed plates quickly. Every other page or so had marginalia, mostly the Latin scribblings of the librarian, Alamanni, who primarily seemed to be concerned with omitting the pornographic references to the Empress Theodora, a woman whom Procopius clearly detested.

Irene could tell from the appearance of the calligraphy which ones were from *The Secret History*. She announced that there were only five photos left in the series.

'They didn't photograph every single page,' Cal mumbled. 'We need to get lucky.'

And then they did.

The very next photo caused Cal to emphatically strike the table with his fist.

'Yes!'

She came over to sit next to him and he pointed to the passage that had him so excited.

'It's here,' he said. 'Book Seventeen. Procopius is writing about the crimes of Empress Theodora. Here's the passage:

> *When she confined him in Egypt, after he had suffered such humiliations as I have previously described, she was not even then satisfied with the man's punishment, but never ceased hunting for false witnesses against him. Four years later, she was able to find two members of the Green party who had taken part in the insurrection at Cyzicus, and who were said to have shared in the assault upon the bishop.*

See here? Next to the word, bishop, this is the marginalia in Greek that could be a fourteenth-century transcription of a note Procopius might have added to the original edition.

> *Eusebius, bishop of Cyzicus, who showed the wounds of Christ when he held in his hands the holy nail of Empress Helena.*

'Giovanni,' she whispered. 'My poor, poor Giovanni. They're torturing him to find the relic. But why do they want it so badly?'

Cal shook his head and said, 'I wish we knew.'

TWENTY-ONE

They found a quiet restaurant and sat at a rear table, a copy of the marginalia photo lying next to the plate of bread.

'What should we do now?' she asked.

He told her about an idea he'd had while sleepless in the middle of the night. Someone he knew might be able to help with the identification of the SS symbol. Before they'd left for the publisher that morning, he'd placed a call and he was waiting for a response.

'I was also thinking in the middle of the night,' she said.

'I thought you were sleeping,' he said.

'I thought you were sleeping too.'

'I wish you would have said something,' he said. 'I wanted to talk.'

'I'm not in the habit of spending the night in the room of a stranger,' she said. 'I suppose I don't know how to conduct myself.'

He broke a bread stick. 'How can you consider a guy you're sharing visions with a stranger?'

She laughed. 'An excellent point.'

'So what were you thinking about?'

The waiter came to take their order and when he left she answered.

'I'm not a scientist, Cal, I'm a science teacher. I teach young people a basic science curriculum: biology, chemistry, physics. To be sure, I know many things about a variety of scientific topics, but my knowledge is not deep enough to understand highly technical subjects, particularly in the realm of physics.'

'Why physics?'

'When I saw Giovanni walking down the street in Francavilla – at the same time I knew he was in Monte Sulla – I did some research on bilocation and I found that Padre Pio was also said to bilocate. I didn't spend a lot of time on it but there were some things I read that caught my attention. There were articles proposing that bilocation and other psychic phenomena could be explained using principles of quantum mechanics. Have you ever heard of something called entanglement?'

'I've been more than a little entangled a few times in life.'

She rolled her eyes. 'This is clearly not what I'm talking about.'

'Then no. What is it?'

'I could try to explain but I might not do it justice. I know someone who is better qualified to answer questions and help us decide if we can find an explanation for what's been happening to Giovanni and us.'

'You think it's worth our time?'

'Seeking knowledge is always worthwhile, don't you think?'

Cal had been to the Sapienza University of Rome before but always to visit the department of history, culture and religion. He never imagined he'd have a reason to set foot in the physics department.

Irene had been a student at the university for two years at a point in her life when she wanted to be a research biologist. But her aspirations had bumped against her conscience and she decided to abandon the university and return to Francavilla to be attentive to her lonely and morose mother. A career as a science teacher in Abruzzo would have to suffice. During her time at the university she had taken a physics course with Professor Enzo Calipari. When she called he hadn't remembered her of course – there had been so many students over the years – but he responded to her phone call with a gracious and immediate invitation.

Calipari was bald with a head shaped like a bullet and the wiry body of a cycling enthusiast. As it happened, he had done a post-doc in theoretical physics at Harvard many years earlier and Cal quickly established that they had a few faculty acquaintances in common.

He apologized for the crammed quarters of his office and took a few minutes to complain about the way professors were treated in Italy. Once he moved his bicycle into the hall, there was room for the three of them to sit.

'I apologize for not recalling you, Signorina Berardino,' he said.

'How could you?' she said. 'I was a student who sat in the middle of the lecture hall and never asked questions.'

'I have to say, when you called this morning, I was intrigued by your question and after I searched your name and discovered your connection to Padre Gio, I'm even more intrigued. Of course, I'm aware of what happened to your brother and I sympathize with your plight.'

'Thank you. It's been a difficult time.'

'But you've come to learn about quantum entanglement,' the physicist said, 'and I'm happy to serve as your humble guide.'

'It's probably a crazy notion that my brother's situation is related to quantum physics but it never hurts to talk.'

'So true, so true,' Calipari said. 'We talk for a living. Now, a little background. Quantum entanglement is much talked about lately, but it isn't a new principle. It derives from the equations at the center of classical physics and quantum mechanics. It concerns the behavior of subatomic particles, such as electrons or photons that have interacted in the past and then moved apart.

If two quantum particles are *entangled*, they become, in effect, two parts of a single unit. What happens to one entangled particle happens to the other, no matter how far apart they are. Let's say there were two particles, electrons perhaps, which were once near each other and are now separated. And maybe that separation isn't a micron or a meter, but maybe it's a light year, maybe it's across the entire universe.

Furthermore, let's imagine that these two particles have a combined spin of zero: one spins clockwise and the other spins counterclockwise. If you were to influence one particle, say by measuring its spin to be clockwise, then quantum entanglement says that its partner should instantaneously spin counterclockwise, no matter how far away the second particle has traveled. And I mean *instantly*. Even if it's across the galaxy, the far-off twin will be set spinning in the opposite direction, faster than light could have traveled between them.'

Cal piped up that, as a layman, he was having trouble wrapping his head around the concept.

'Well, Cal, you're not alone. In fact you're in excellent company. Seventy years ago Albert Einstein famously said that if the equations of quantum theory predicted such nonsense, so much the worse for quantum theory. He called the idea of entanglement, "spooky actions at a distance."'

'I thought Einstein was never wrong,' Cal said.

'*Almost* never wrong,' the physicist said. 'This was one of his rare mistakes.'

Irene politely interjected, 'But Einstein also said that nothing could go faster than the speed of light.'

'Well, he certainly wasn't wrong about that; he proved that information can't travel faster than the speed of light. But in 1964, the Irish physicist, John Bell, proved mathematically that quantum theory *requires* entanglement and that particles can still affect each other instantly even when they are far apart. It speaks to the fundamental weirdness of the principle that Einstein could be simultaneously wrong and correct about never exceeding the speed of light.

I'm a theoretical physicist. The only thing I do with my hands professionally is write on a whiteboard. But my colleagues around the world, who are experimentalists, have devised some fantastic experiments lately to absolutely prove that quantum entanglement is a real phenomenon. And it's not just for pairs of particles. For example, a recent paper describes the experimental entanglement of three thousand atoms with a single photon. And another experiment confirmed entanglement when photons were separated by over one hundred kilometers. This is real, my friends.'

'Three thousand atoms isn't a lot,' Irene said. 'What about larger things?'

'Ok! How about something as massive as black holes? Einstein showed that two black holes could be connected through far reaches of space by so-called wormholes. Now, it seems that this connectivity may be a manifestation of entanglement, a quantum form of communication between vast objects separated by space and even time. Quantum entanglement – the 'spooky action at a distance' that so troubled Einstein – could be creating the spatial connectivity that sews space together.'

Cal watched Irene take a deep breath and hesitate before posing her next question. When it came out, she had an apologetic tone as if she was embarrassing herself in front of an esteemed scientist. 'May I ask this: do you think human minds can become entangled?' she asked.

'So, signorina, I knew this question was coming and I have to say that, as far as experimental physics is concerned, the field of quantum entanglement is too young to do more than speculate. But isn't the mind just a collection of subatomic particles arranged into a complex biological structure? In theory, I would say that minds could absolutely be entangled. Certainly, researchers into extrasensory perception or PSI, as they call it, have invoked entanglement to explain premonitions, shared experiences between twins who are separated by distance, those types of things. I take it from our phone call earlier that you've had some experiences related to your missing brother.'

She nodded. 'We both have. Cal and I.'

'May I ask what they were?'

Cal answered with another question. 'We would love to share them with you, but can we have an assurance that you'll keep this conversation private?'

Calipari clapped his hands in delight. 'Of course! This is the very first time that I, as a physicist, have been sworn to confidentiality. Consider me your physics confessor.' He abruptly wiped the pleasure from his face. 'I'm sorry, signorina. Your brother is a priest. I don't wish to make light of his precarious circumstances.'

Irene assured him she took no offense and told him about the bilocations, the visions, their shared experiences of pain and breathlessness that seemed to emanate from Giovanni.

Calipari squirmed in his chair. 'Look, I don't know what I can tell you. As far as I can see, you are sober, credible observers, not a couple of new-age seekers. One could certainly say that both of you seem to have some sort of psychic connection to your brother. But to invoke quantum entanglement? This can be no more than an hypothesis that cannot be proven. The question I would pose to you is why Giovanni Berardino? What makes him this rare individual who is capable of making these kinds of connections, entangled or otherwise? And are his famous stigmata related in your way of thinking or are they a red herring?'

Cal asked Irene if he could take a stab at answering and she willingly agreed.

'We think everything – his stigmata, the bilocation, the

connectivity – all trace back to something Giovanni was exposed to,' Cal said.

'And what might that be?' the physicist asked.

'One of the venerated relics of Christ.'

Calipari looked out the window at a grassy area where students were enjoying the summer day. 'Look, I'm not a particularly religious man but I'm not an atheist. I know there is much I don't know. Atheism implies a certainty I simply don't possess. But if I can accept the possibility that this miraculous phenomenon of Christ's resurrection actually happened, then I can also accept that a physical object – one that was in contact with Christ – might be the trigger for a most dramatic demonstration of quantum entanglement, rippling across time and space. One that includes a man in the twenty-first century developing the same wounds of crucifixion that a man in the first century suffered.'

Giovanni had been enjoying the sublime respite of one of his visions. It had taken him away from the hot, fetid room and interrupted the constant ache of his stigmata. The familiar face he saw was so kind, so loving that he wished it was to be the last image he ever saw. He didn't want to go back.

But then Gerhardt unlocked the door, announcing, 'It's disgusting in here. How can you stand the smell?' and the vision ended as suddenly as a soap bubble bursts.

The priest was lying on his blood-crusted bed, dirty and dazed. He turned his face to the wall.

'This can all end,' Gerhardt said, pressing a wash cloth to his nose. 'All you need to do is unburden yourself of this secret of yours. What are you even protecting? A piece of iron? What does it matter who possesses it? Why are you the better custodian than me?'

Giovanni whispered something.

'What did you say?'

He turned his head toward his tormentor. 'I said, I made a promise.'

'To whom? To the old monk, Augustin? Did I tell you he's dead?'

'Dead?'

'Yes, quite dead. I killed him, you know. He wouldn't talk.

Of course I can't kill you because if you go, the secret goes with you. So I have to keep you alive. But that doesn't mean you'll enjoy your life. I will keep hurting you until you talk to me. Today I have a choice to make. Do I make pain or do I give you the water board? Maybe you can help me with my choice. Which one should we do?'

'Please, leave me alone.'

'I can't do that. My colleagues grow impatient.'

'Just tell me why these people want it?'

Gerhardt pulled up the chair and sat on it back-to-front, folding his arms over the back and resting his head on his hands.

'This is good. This is the first time you've acknowledged 'it."

'I'm very hungry.'

'I'm sure you are. We have excellent food in the kitchen. Chicken, steak, roasted potatoes. I'm not such a good cook but my friend has a talent. All you need to do is talk.'

'Please.'

Gerhardt stood and overturned the chair with a kick. 'I thought we were making nice progress. But I see you're stubborn. I'll be back soon with my friend. My decision is made. The solution was so simple. First we'll do the water board and then we'll make the pain. The very best of both worlds.'

Giovanni looked at the ceiling and mouthed a few words.

'I can't hear you.'

'I'll tell you what you want to know if you promise me something.'

'What would you like me to promise?'

'That you won't hurt my family.'

Schneider was in a meeting of the supervisory board of his bank when his little-used second mobile phone began to vibrate in his jacket.

He excused himself and went across the hall of the executive suite to the privacy of his office.

'Yes, Gerhardt, what news?'

'I know where it is.'

'I see. Where?'

'Francavilla. It's where he's from.'

'I want you to go there. I won't trust the job to a contractor.'

'I'll need some local men. I don't speak Italian.'

'I'll arrange it.'

'His mother and sister live there. He doesn't want them hurt.'

'I'm sure he doesn't. If they're at home when you come calling we can't have them talking to the police.'

'I understand.'

'Is he still alive?'

'He's alive.'

'Keep him that way,' Schneider said. 'We're not finished with him, not by a long shot.'

TWENTY-TWO

'Now what?' Irene asked.

They had wrapped up their meeting at the University of Rome and could think of nothing better to do, than find a sun-splashed bench on one of the college greens where they watched a carefree game of Frisbee. The disk floated over a student's head and landed at their feet. Cal tossed it back hard. It sailed over the grass with laser-like accuracy, earning him a few 'Bravos.'

'If Giovanni was given a nail relic in Croatia he must have hidden it somewhere,' he said. 'Whoever took him tore up his room in Monte Sulla looking for it. We've got to assume they didn't find it. We've got to figure out where he hid it, why he hid it and why they want it.'

'It would be worth a great deal of money. Isn't that enough of a reason?' she said.

'There's easier ways to get money. You rob a museum, you rob a bank. You don't kidnap a priest for his relic.'

'Maybe it has something to do with this entanglement,' she said.

'Who knows?' He unfolded his drawing of the lance and SS bolts. 'But this has got to be important.'

His phone rang and when he saw the caller ID his face brightened.

'Klaus, hello! I was just thinking about you. Thanks for getting back to me.'

Two hours later, their travel arrangements to Munich in place, they checked out of their hotel and climbed into Cal's rental car. They were half way to the Fiumicino Airport when his phone rang. This time it was a number he didn't recognize.

Irene watched the puzzled look on his face as he listened to the caller.

'When?' he asked. He listened again and registered a look of surprise before ending the call with, 'Yes, of course.'

'What is it?' Irene asked.

'We're going to have to get a later flight,' he said.

'Why?'

'The pope wants to see me.'

Pope Celestine IV had a nickname that secretly amused him: Pope Buddha. It had nothing to do with his philosophy and everything to do with his Buddha-like figure. With one, continuous penstroke, starting with his high forehead, flowing to his prominent nose and fleshy lips and ending with his balloon of a belly, an artist could perfectly capture his physical essence. His religious essence had always been somewhat harder to capture.

Few who knew him as the Archbishop of Genoa or the Secretary of State and Cardinal Camerlengo of the Holy Roman Church could have guessed at the pope he would become. He had always been seen to be an archly political cardinal, a master of the Curia game, attuned to the sensibilities of the previous pontificate. His predecessor had been a traditionalist who relished all the pomp and formality the Vatican could muster. The Holy See, if left to its own devices, was naturally labyrinthine, brimming with opaque fiefdoms and intense political wrangling. Pope Clement XV, it was wryly said, had presided over the most byzantine Vatican since the Byzantine Empire. And as the secretary of state, Cardinal Aspromonte, had been the pope's right-hand man, implementing the conservative and doctrinaire policies that were the hallmark of Clement's reign. The conclave that had chosen Aspromonte to become the next pope had most certainly believed they had chosen a man who would give the Vatican a decade or so of, in essence, a continuation of Clement's firm and traditional grasp of the Church apparatus.

It was perhaps only the few old-timers who had known Aspromonte as a fledgling, starry-eyed Genovese priest, who had an inkling that the rotund cardinal with an impish smile had been hiding his true colors during his ascent to the College of Cardinals and beyond. As soon as he slipped on the Ring of the Fisherman, he began to chart a new papacy, one that reflected the simmering idealism of his youth.

'The Church is difficult to change,' he had said in an interview for *America*, a weekly Catholic magazine, 'in the same way that a big ship is difficult to steer. But if a dangerous storm is in the way, the ship must change course or it will flounder. The storm in our way is poverty, hopelessness, the erosion of faith. The pope is the captain of our ship. Through humility, love and a devotion to social justice, I want to steer the church, little by little, into calmer waters where the poor are treated with the dignity that God surely requires.'

The Vatican hierarchy knew to buckle their seatbelts when Celestine refused to move into the papal apartment (opting instead for the Domus Sanctae Marthae guest house), when he sold his fleet of limousines and when he closed the Vatican Radio transmission center and converted it to a hostel for Rome's poor. And to his brethren who elected him pope, he told those who had the temerity to ask him to his face, 'I haven't changed my spots, I merely covered them so I could faithfully serve Pope Clement in his mission. Perhaps I was able to subtly influence his attitudes and soften some of his positions. Now I am pope and I expect you to serve my mission faithfully. You may also try to influence me. We shall see if you are able.'

The pope was waiting for Cal in the small room at the guesthouse that he used for conducting official business. It wasn't any larger than Cal's own office and, with the exception of a special ergonomic chair for the pope's bad back, the furniture was more modest than a Harvard professor's. Celestine rose from this chair to greet him. His face was overly fleshy, as if a sculptor had used way too much clay for effect, and his eyes seemed to dance with excitement and mirth. Unlike the previous pontiff, who reached deeply into the papal closet of vestments and regalia to emphasize the tradition rites of the Church, this pope preferred to wear a simple white cassock and sensible shoes.

'Professor Donovan,' he said in English, extending a plump hand. 'We finally meet.'

'Your Holiness,' Cal said in Italian. 'It's a great honor for me.'

'Ah, perfect Italian. This is easier for me. Sit, sit. Coffee? Tea? Water? I have everything right here, even a mini-fridge, and now I have the coffee machine with the capsules. I am quite self-sufficient.'

'I'll take a coffee if only to tell my friends the pope made it for me.'

Celestine bellowed with laughter and inserted a pod. He mentioned he wasn't supposed to have any so late in the day but he was going to give into temptation.

'It is as much temptation as a pope is permitted,' he said. 'Now, let me issue an apology. I should have seen you when you sent me your report. I was persuaded by Cardinal Lauriat to perform finesse like a bridge player and avoid any controversy and your report was quite controversial. This was a mistake but I don't blame him. When I had his job I gave similar advice countless times.'

'May I ask you something?' Cal said.

'Of course, anything. You take sugar? Milk?'

'Black, thank you. Why did you want a formal investigation at this time? It struck me as rather odd. Padre Giovanni hasn't even had stigmata a full year.'

The pope added milk and a generous spoonful of sugar to his cup. 'I'll answer your question with a question – my friends the rabbis like to do this. Was it not your impression that the Vatican wished to suppress this priest, to chop the feet out from under him, to eliminate the cult of personality that was forming around him?'

'Yes, it was. And not just me. His friends and family leapt to that conclusion. I think he did too.'

'Well, that was the official thinking promulgated by my friends in the Apostolic Palace. But it wasn't mine. You see, I find that I can think more clearly in this quiet corner of the Vatican away from the entrenched interests of the Curia. When you try to live a humble life you tend to have humble thoughts. And what can confer greater humility than opening your heart to the possibility of miracles? Miracles, after all, do not come from man. They come from God. We do not control them, we merely experience them with awe and gratitude. I do not fear miracles, I welcome them. Without miracles, religion is just philosophy. If this young man, Padre Gio, truly bears the stigmata of Christ then I am overjoyed. A miracle such as this would not overshadow the Vatican or the papacy; it would strengthen our institutions and our faith.'

'But I imagine the Church would not be well served if he was found to be a fraud.'

'Yes, indeed, professor. My brother cardinals have vigorously voiced this concern. They expected the investigation to reveal a disturbed young priest who was self-harming and deliberately or subconsciously deluding his parish. But that was not your conclusion.'

'It was not.'

'In my reading of history, the Church badly bungled the investigation of Padre Pio. As you, yourself, documented in your book, Pius XI first had him scrutinized in the nineteen twenties and found him to be suspect. The great Franciscan friar and physician, Agostino Gemelli, labeled Pio as a self-mutilating psychopath who probably kept his wounds open with carbolic acid. Some of Pio's writings describing his mystical experiences were copied verbatim from the letters of the nineteenth-century stigmatic, Gemma Galgani. Pope John XXIII was not a believer. Privately he called him a straw idol. Yet, his successor, Paul VI dismissed all accusations against Pio and John Paul II, as you know, declared him venerable and the rest is history. Now, he is Saint Pio of Pietrelcina. He has become one of the world's most popular of all our saints. There are more than three thousand prayer groups dedicated to him around the world with three million members. More Italian Catholics pray to Padre Pio for intercession than to any other figure. This is impressive, no?'

Cal agreed.

'But in your book, you are rather noncommittal.'

'Since I never met the man, all I could do as an academic was deal with the historical record, present all the glorious ambiguities and allow the reader to draw his or her own personal conclusions.'

'But you met Giovanni Berardino.'

'I did.'

'And you believe he is genuine.'

'I do.'

The pope spread his arms expansively and even though their chairs were a meter apart, Cal felt as though he was being embraced.

'And there we have it,' Celestine said. 'This is why, when I heard you had returned to Italy, that I decided I must speak to you in person. When I seek the opinion of Lauriat or Gallegos they speak to me in eloquent circles. With them I need a map to find my way to the truth. Before I was pope, I was quite good at talking a lot without saying anything. Frankly, this was required of me when I was in the secretariat of state. But now I cannot seem to train these old dogs of mine to do new tricks. Professor, I want you to give me what I believe you Americans call 'straight talk.' My dear friend, Cardinal Da Silva, recommended you highly. I've read your book. I've read your report. Now we have this puzzling and traumatic kidnapping, I need to know, more than ever, what we are dealing with.'

It was an offer Cal couldn't refuse. The pope wanted things unfiltered and he was going to oblige.

'I don't know how to say this other than just to say it,' he began, 'but I'm of the opinion that Giovanni Berardino is a living and breathing, thoroughly astonishing miracle man.'

The pope showed his surprise. 'You seemed to be leaning this way in your report but here, today, you're sounding quite definitive. Were you holding back in your report or have new facts emerged?'

'Some of both but mostly new facts, Holy Father. Many new facts.'

He didn't leave anything out. He was speaking to the spiritual leader of over a billion people, a man with a direct line of succession to Peter the Apostle. And as a Catholic himself, albeit a somewhat lapsed one, he felt the weight of the moment. First he told Celestine what he'd omitted from his report. He described the vision he'd had when Giovanni embraced him, his suspicion that a monk at St Athanasius had been murdered and his belief that something present in the crypt of the ancient church played a role in the development of the stigmata. Then he talked about his car accident, regretting the melodramatic sentence, 'I think someone wanted me dead,' as soon as he'd said it.

'Terrible, terrible,' the pontiff said. 'This is all so troubling. There is more?'

'Much more.'

He studied the shifting expression on the pope's face as he laid out the rest of his cards. Bilocation, vivid, multisensory visions, evidence, as far as Cal and Irene were concerned, that Giovanni was communicating with them. He showed him Irene's sketch of the Holy Lance tattoo and heard him mumble, 'Nazi SS insignia? What can this mean?' Then he showed him the photo from the page of *The Secret History*.

'So this is what you think this priest saw in the crypt?' Celestine asked.

'Can I prove it? No. Do I believe it? Yes. Look, I know that, by definition, Church doctrine holds that miracles require no explanation other than divine intercession. But there's an interface between mysticism and science that personally I find intriguing. Have you ever heard of quantum entanglement?'

The pope had not, but five minutes later, he thanked Cal for the lesson.

'I do find this modern physics to be quite fascinating from what of it I can understand,' Celestine said. 'Very few theology students have a mind capable of delving deeply into all this mathematics, all these complex equations. But I must tell you, I do not believe one has to invoke a certain interface between science and faith. I believe that all of science, all that we know about the physical world, all we will learn about the physical world in the future, is a manifestation of divine creation. God has given us this glorious universe of matter and energy. If this quantum entanglement is real, as you suggest it may be, if Padre Gio has stigmata from his contact with a relic that had contact with Jesus Christ, then it doesn't matter what name you put on it, miracle or science. It is marvelous. It is awesome. It is divine. Tell me, professor, what will you do now?'

'I'm going to try to find Giovanni.'

'I hope you do. The young priest is in trouble and if a good man such as yourself and a good woman such as his sister can help him then I give you my blessings.'

'Thank you.'

'But before you go, tell me one thing. Why are you devoting yourself to him? Why did you return to Italy, perhaps to your peril?'

Cal thought for a few moments before he simply said, 'Because he touched me.'

The pope nodded his large head and extended his hands. 'Professor, I understand completely.'

TWENTY-THREE

They were waiting at the baggage carousel at Munich airport for Irene's old-fashioned suitcase, the kind without wheels and too large for the overhead bins.

She apologized for the delay. 'I'm not much of a traveler,' she admitted.

'Not a problem. We've got nothing on for tonight beside checking into our hotel and finding a place for dinner.'

'Can you tell me how you know this man we're seeing tomorrow?'

'Klaus Langer was on a panel with me a few years ago at an academic conference in Paris. The subject was the Cathars. I know a fair bit about their history. He's an expert on Nazis and neo-Nazis and their links to Cathar mysticism.'

The bag appeared. He lifted it off the carousel and carried it outside. Once they were in a taxi to the city center she admitted she didn't know the first thing about the Cathars.

'They were a twelfth-century Christian sect from the Languedoc region of southern France. On the fringes of mainstream Christian thought, they were a group of dissident pacifists who believed that an evil deity had created the material world and a good God all the invisible rest. Since the evil God created all visible matter, including the human body, they thought our bodies were tainted with sin. They believed that human spirits were the genderless manifestation of angels trapped within the physical creation of

the evil God. They thought that they were cursed to be reincar-
nated until the Cathar faithful achieved salvation, through a rather
complex purification ritual.

Their clergy were known as Perfecti. They came from all walks
of life – aristocrats, merchants, peasants – you name it. Women
could also become Perfects.'

'Ahead of their time,' she said.

'Perfects also had to be celibate and vegetarians. As you can
imagine, the sect was condemned by the Church as heretical.'

'I'm not surprised.'

'Pope Innocent III tried to end Catharism by sending mission-
aries to Languedoc and persuading the local authorities to act
against them. When Cathar assassins killed a particularly hated
papal legate, Peter of Castelnau, the pope had the ideal pretext
to launch a crusade against them. A papal army marched in and
indiscriminately slaughtered twenty thousand men, women and
children, many Cathars, many not. His order was, 'Kill them all,
God will know his own.'

'How awful. But what do they have to do with Nazis?'

'The Nazis had some natural affinities to Catharism. They both
viewed Jews with contempt. In the case of the Cathars, they
believed that the God of Israel (who was the God of the Old
Testament and therefore of the Jews) was the same as their evil
God who created the material world. A Nazi academic and
member of the SS named Otto Rahn was obsessed with the
Cathars. Klaus Langer's the Rahn expert. Pretty much everything
I know about him, which isn't a lot, I learned from Langer's talk.

Rahn was sort of a Holy Grail nut and a Cathar nut rolled into
one. He was convinced there was a factual basis to Wolfram von
Eschenbach's narrative poem about the Grail, *Parzival* and that
the poem was based on long-forgotten Cathar ballads. Basically,
he thought that the Cathars had been in possession of the Grail
and whoever possessed it or came into contact with it would
have eternal life. He roamed around the Languedoc area and the
old Cathar fortress of Montségur, looking for the Grail – unsuccessfully I would add. He also visited a lot of other places in
Europe and Iceland, looking for other relics for Himmler and
Hitler who were said to subscribe to beliefs about the actual

power – or at least the psychological power – of possessing the relics most-associated with Christ.

We know the Nazis wanted the Grail but never got it. We know they wanted the Holy Lance and were able to get it from the Austrians who had it for centuries. Anyway, since the war, there's been a cottage industry of conspiracy theories connecting the Nazis to the Cathars. The most common is that Hitler, Himmler and other high-ranking Nazis were part of a neo-Cathar pagan secret society and that these secret societies exist today. That's where Langer comes in. He's got the world's most complete database on neo-Nazis and their iconography.'

The taxi was pulling into the hotel forecourt. 'And you think he can identify the tattoo?' she asked.

'He didn't make any promises but he told me he'd try to help us.'

Over dinner at a fish restaurant off the Königsplatz, Irene wanted to know if she could ask Cal a question that had been weighing on her.

'Shoot,' he said.

'Why did you come back?'

'You know why. Giovanni reached out in a way we don't completely understand and asked for my help. The same as he asked you.'

'Yes, but people ask others for help all the time and often we don't choose to respond. Giovanni is little more than a stranger to you. You met him once, for how long?'

'Less than an hour.'

'Less than an hour. And yet you immediately flew to Italy. What is it you hope to get out of this? Are you going to write a book about him? Give lectures? Are you planning to monetize the experience?'

At first he was angry, but it melted away when he saw the corner of her mouth twitching. She was holding in a lot of pain.

'Let me be honest with you,' he said. 'I felt a connection to him, a deep connection, actually. He's not a classically wise man in any way, shape or form. He's very young, a little awkward, not very sure of himself, but I still felt he had this enormous wisdom. Do you know what I mean?'

She swallowed hard and nodded.

'He sensed things about my background and my faith that rattled me at the time. He knew my father died when I was young and what he meant to me.'

'Ours too. When we were young.'

'He told me. He knew I had an almost unconscious, pent-up desire to give confession and after he took it, I felt pretty damned good. And when he put his arms around me – I can only say it was electric – not only because of the vision it produced, but because it took me back.'

She almost whispered her question. 'To where?'

He swallowed. 'To when I was a boy and my father hugged me.'

He wiped at his eyes with his napkin and apologized.

'Don't,' she said. 'You shouldn't be embarrassed.'

He smiled. 'I mean I'm twice his age but there was this kind of role reversal. Do you know what I mean?'

'Yes.'

'Was he always like that?'

'Not at all. He was always quite immature, even at the seminary. Only afterwards, when the stigmata began, did he develop this quality you describe. He went from little brother to big brother to father in a very fast way.'

'Anyway, that's why I came back. I lost my father a long time ago. I didn't want to lose Giovanni. Does that make sense?'

'It does.'

'Do you believe me?'

She reached across the table to touch his hand. 'I do.'

Domenica Berardino was rinsing the pans in her sink and placing them in her dishwasher while her sister, Carla, cleared the dinner table and young Federico watched television.

When the door buzzer went off, Carla asked through the door who was there. The reply of 'Police' was delivered with an odd accent but she opened the door anyway.

Gerhardt Hufnagel stepped over the threshold, crowding her backwards toward the lounge. Two other men followed him in and quietly closed the door. The intruders wore leather driving gloves.

'Who are you?' Carla demanded.

'You should be calm,' Gerhardt said in English, pointing menacingly at her son.

Carla didn't speak the language. 'What?'

'Tell her what I said,' Gerhardt told one of the Italians, a skittish fellow with a prominent scar on his cheek.

'He said, stay calm. For the sake of the boy.'

Domenica appeared from the kitchen and asked her sister who these men were.

Scarface said, 'We don't want to hurt you, but we will if you scream or call out. Which one is the priest's mother?'

She eyed the telephone. 'I'm his mother. What do you want?'

'Are you going to be good? If we have to get rough, she'll get hurt first, then the kid. Understand?'

Domenica nodded fearfully and said she did. Gerhardt dispatched the other Italian, a stocky man with hooded, brooding eyes, to search the flat. He soon came back and gave the all clear.

'Ok. This guy's going to ask questions and I'm going to translate,' Scarface said. 'Both of you, on the sofa.'

Gerhardt stood over them and crossed his powerful arms. 'Where is the Madonna?' he asked.

Domenica looked too bewildered to answer so her sister replied defiantly. 'Go to the church. They'll have one.'

'Don't be a smart-ass,' Scarface said. Gerhardt reacted stonily to his translation and Scarface translated his silence into Italian. 'You don't realize the trouble you're in. Your statue. Your Madonna.'

'Why are we in trouble, mama?' Federico asked.

His mother told him the men were just joking but Domenica was chewing on her lip. 'Why do you want it?' she asked.

'This is the last time I will permit you to ask *me* a question,' Gerhardt said.

'We have two of them,' Domenica said. 'I'm sorry but I really must ask a question. Which one do you want?'

'Tell me where both are.'

'There's one in my room, on my bureau. Down the hall straight ahead. My daughter has one too. It's the room across the hall from my son's.'

Gerhardt sent the stocky man to look for them. From the lounge they heard him tossing things about. He came back with hers, a ceramic statuette, but announced that the other one wasn't there.

Gerhardt took Domenica's and threw it over his shoulder. It shattered on the floor. 'I want the other one.'

Domenica said that if it wasn't in Irene's room she didn't know where it was.

Gerhardt ordered the men to search everywhere, precipitating an exercise lacking in delicacy. At first the little boy thought all the toppling and rummaging was funny, but when he saw his mother and aunt fighting back tears he began to cry.

'Keep him quiet,' Gerhardt said. 'If you don't I'll shut him up.'

Carla held the boy close and buried his face in her blouse.

Before long, the flat was turned upside down.

'For the last time,' Gerhardt said. 'Where is it?'

'Honestly, I don't know,' Domenica said. 'Maybe my daughter took it with her.'

'Where did she go?'

'To Rome.'

'Why?'

'To try to find her brother. He's missing.'

Gerhardt sneered and looked like he was going to say something but didn't. 'Did she go alone?'

'She went with an American professor.'

The sneer melted. 'Donovan?'

'Yes, how did you know?'

'Where in Rome?'

'I don't know. She hasn't called today. Yesterday she was in a hotel.'

'Which one?'

'I didn't ask.'

'Call her now. Ask her if she has it. Don't cause suspicion. My friend with the beautiful scar, he'll be listening.' He pointed toward Carla. 'If you alert your daughter in any way I'll cut her throat. Find out which hotel she's at. Do a good job and you'll all be ok.'

Irene's mobile rang while Cal was paying the restaurant check.

'Mama, I was going to call you when I got back to the hotel. Is everything all right? Have the police called about Giovanni?'

'Yes, everything is fine. I've heard nothing from the police. I was worried about you.'

'You sound a bit strange,' Irene said. 'Are you sure you haven't had any news.'

'Nothing. It's just the stress.'

'Have you been eating?'

'Yes, Carla and Federico came for dinner. They're going to stay the night. I was wondering, did you take your Our Lady of Lourdes statue with you?'

'I should have told you. Yes. It's silly but it seemed like a good idea.'

'I was just looking for it.'

There was a pause while Domenica read a scribbled note in Italian, dictated by Gerhardt.

The note said: *Which hotel?*

Irene filled in the pause herself. 'Professor Donovan and I found some interesting things, mama. Nothing that helps find Giovanni but we think it's important information. Believe it or not, the professor had an audience with the pope today. He said he is praying for Giovanni's safe return.'

'That's wonderful, wonderful.'

'We flew to Germany this afternoon. We're in Munich to see another professor. I'll be sure to call you tomorrow to let you know how we got on.'

Scarface pointed to the note again. When Domenica hesitated again, Gerhardt pulled a folding knife from his pocket and moved behind the sofa to stare down at the boy's head.

'Mama? Are you still there?'

'Yes, I'm here. Which hotel are you staying at?'

'The Weisses Schloss. Why do you want to know?'

'No reason. Just in case.'

'Ok, mama, I've got to go. I love you.'

'I love you too.'

When Irene hung up Cal said, 'What's up? You look worried. Any news?'

'My mother sounded strange.'

'It's probably the stress.'

'She said the same thing.'

* * *

Gerhardt went into Giovanni's trashed room and called Schneider.

'Do you have it?' Schneider asked.

'It's not here. The priest's sister took it with her.'

'Where is she?'

'She's in Munich.'

'Why Munich?'

'I don't know. Believe it or not, she's with Donovan.'

'I heard he was back.'

'Why didn't you tell me?'

'You didn't need to know. Now you do.'

'Do you have her location?'

'Yes.'

'Handle it personally, Gerhardt. Can you trust the Italians to take care of the mother?'

'Her sister is here too. With her boy.'

'Shit. Can they take care of all three of them?'

'They're not geniuses but they're competent enough for the job.'

'Gerhardt?'

'Yes?'

'I'm not happy that Donovan is nosing around again. Make sure you finish him this time.'

Scarface and his accomplice amused themselves by watching an old American movie on television while the boy, covered by a blanket, slept on the carpet and Domenica and Carla nodded off in their armchairs. Gerhardt had left hours earlier, after drilling them on the plan. Their orders were to wait until two a.m. before taking the women and boy out the rear service entrance of the apartment building, near where their van was parked. They would drive to the furnished flat they had rented in the outskirts of Rome, arriving before dawn. They would keep the women and child under wraps until they were contacted. They would make no mistakes, or else.

They were still an hour away from their departure time and Scarface said he was hungry.

The other man was absorbed in the movie and ignored him.

'Get me something to eat,' Scarface said.

There was still no response.

He threw a coaster from the coffee table and hit the other guy square in the face.

'What?'

'I was talking to you. See what she's got in the refrigerator.'

The man swore and got up with his moodiness on full display.

'And keep your goddamn gloves on.'

He returned with a Tupperware full of leftover pasta, a couple of plates and forks. They ate hungrily and polished the food off in no time. Time passed and while the credits of the movie were rolling, the brooding man farted and announced he was going to the toilet.

He did his business and reached for the toilet paper roll.

'How am I supposed to do this with gloves?' he mumbled.

When he finished up, Scarface was on his feet in the lounge, on his mobile.

'That was the German,' he said. 'He was making sure we were going to leave now.'

'He doesn't trust us. The man should have some faith.'

Scarface nudged Domenica to wake her up. 'I trust him to kill us if we screw this up.'

TWENTY-FOUR

Klaus Langer was fairly close in age to Cal but he seemed very much younger. He was blonde and pudgy, with a perpetually mischievous look as if he were constantly wrestling with amusing thoughts. Cal and Irene met him bright and early at the Faculty of Social Sciences at The Ludwig Maximilian University of Munich. He was waiting with a spread of pastries.

'Welcome to the LMU! It's wonderful to see you again, Cal, and to meet you, Irene. I am sorry to hear about your brother's troubles. This must be quite distressing.'

Irene was persuaded to take a sweet bun. He and Cal got each other caught up with their current research projects. Langer proudly revealed that he had recently been appointed to a federal commission on neo-Nazi crimes against Muslim immigrants to Germany.

'You'd think these vermin would die out but like cockroaches they seem to be quite hardy,' Langer said. 'Now, tell me about this SS symbol you're trying to identify.'

They showed him Irene's version of the tattoo. He studied it and screwed up his face in thought.

'There are so many of these kinds of things I've seen over the years. They're variations on the same themes. Daggers, SS bolts, eagles, what have you. This one is more unique for sure, because of the lance and yes – I agree with what you said over the phone – this is certainly meant to represent the Holy Lance. As a symbol, it would be something I'd expect to see in the Nazi period, not during our post-war neo-Nazi eras. It had a potent meaning for the likes of Himmler and Hitler, but I don't think the young thugs of modern Germany would know what it was if they tripped over it. You're sure it's modern?'

'We believe so,' Cal said.

Langer waited, perhaps to see if Cal would be more forth-coming, but when he wasn't the fellow carried on with his thoughts.

'Of course, it's hard to speak of the rather bizarre fascination of the Third Reich with Holy Relics without turning to our old friend, Otto Rahn.'

'I was telling Irene about him.'

'And the Cathars,' she added.

Langer giggled, 'Well, we can thank the Cathars for my intro-duction to Cal. So you know that Rahn got mixed up with Himmler's cultural anthropology section, the Ahnenerbe, and was given rather lavish funding to do fieldwork at Cathar sites and elsewhere, looking for the Holy Grail and other early Christian artifacts.'

'I didn't think that Rahn had anything to do with the Holy Lance,' Cal said. 'That was hiding in plain sight in Vienna. All Hitler had to do was pick it up when he invaded Austria.'

'Yes, that's so. I don't know if Rahn had any direct involve-ment with that affair. But I do think there's evidence that he was meant to be assisting Himmler with assembling all the known

Holy Relics and displaying them in Himmler's SS fortress in Wewelsburg. To what end, we don't know, but likely for propaganda purposes. You know, to rally the SS acolytes. Well, let me start you off in my archive. You can both work through archival material chronologically, starting with the Third Reich. Or one of you can begin with the earlier material and the other with the emergence of neo-Nazis in the 1970s.'

Langer's archive room was down the hall near the departmental library. He apologized for its archaic nature – it was a wall of metal filing cabinets stuffed with papers – an anachronism in a digital world. Only a long-overdue grant from the German federal government or the EU would provide digitalization funds to fix it.

'The material is mostly photographic in nature,' Langer said, 'but I've got quite a few drawings, propaganda advertisements and graphic design pieces. If it's got anything to do with Nazi and neo-Nazi symbolism, I've collected it. It's a wonder I've been able to stay so cheerful.'

Irene seemed startled by the number of cabinets. 'You don't seem old enough to have accumulated all of this,' she said.

He giggled again. 'Well, I inherited the Nazi-era material from my old professor at LMU who's retired. All the neo-Nazi stuff is mine. So have a look at it. I hope you won't be too fazed by this kind of manual searching.'

Cal assured him they'd be fine. 'It's only the second time this week we've done something like this.'

Giovanni was having a better day.

With Gerhardt gone, his sole guard, who had let on that his name was Martin, had relaxed the harsh conditions of his captivity. It seemed he wasn't as sadistic as his boss.

He moved Giovanni to another bedroom up a flight of stairs, this had an en suite and clean sheets on the bed. Martin provided him with gauze for his wrists and, as for food, he received what the fellow had prepared for himself. Best of all, with a hesitant push, Giovanni was able to open the window shutters and revealed something marvelous; a long, elevated view over verdant hayfields, a hilly village and a sparkling azure bay. The window even opened halfway, allowing a cooling breeze to enter the bedchamber. When he stuck his head out he understood why he'd been allowed this glimpse of freedom. There was a sheer drop, well over ten meters onto a stone patio and there were no visible neighboring properties. He might try calling for help but it was doubtful anyone would respond and he'd probably lose his marvelous privileges.

He unscrewed the top of a bottle of water while turning his face to catch the wind. It was then he realized that his captor hadn't bothered to remove the plastic film with its label. Font Vella. Spanish. He put it all together – the long journey by boat, the bay views – he was somewhere on the vast eastern coast of Spain.

He began to fret about the transparencies. The Germans hadn't bothered to hide their faces. And now the one called Martin was allowing him a glimpse of the geography. Didn't this mean that they had no fear of being identified? Wasn't the conclusion then obvious; they had no intention of letting him live?

His thoughts turned darkly to his family.

He was ashamed of his cowardice. He'd succumbed to the terror of near drowning and pain and had exposed his mother and sister to danger. The sadist had promised they wouldn't be hurt, but how could a man like this be trusted? He'd been weak and his weakness might have terrible consequences. Should he punish himself for his betrayal to his loved ones? Should he take his own life? It would be impossible to squeeze his big body through the half-open window, but he might be able to shatter the wood with a chair and hurl himself out. But suicide was a mortal sin and besides, he doubted he could go through with it.

Why had this terrible fate befallen him?

He had only wanted to be a humble priest.

Why had God delivered him to the St Athanasius monastery on that day? Why had he been chosen by the old monk to go down into that crypt?

Suddenly he understood that the answer lay in the question. God had chosen him. That was all he needed to know. He wasn't meant to understand God's plans. He wasn't meant to understand why his family had been drawn into it. And he wasn't meant to understand why he'd become connected to Jesus Christ in the most tangible way: by suffering and bleeding.

He put the bottle of water onto the windowsill and took a series of lung-filling breaths. A bee buzzed passed the window. Butterflies danced in the meadow. A faint strain of amplified music drifted up from the village.

He smiled.

He needed to suspend his worldly worries and surrender himself to Christ. The Lord would attend to his needs on this green Earth or in Heaven. The Lord would take care of his family.

He'd been chosen.

He gazed out the window, a happier man.

Cal and Irene were back in their groove, flipping through files. It was faster work than sorting photos of Greek and Latin calligraphy in the Vatican Library. It only took a fraction of a second to check a document to see if it matched their lance and bolt image and they were able to move through the filing cabinet drawers quickly.

An hour into it, Cal, started into his second file cabinet and moaned, 'God, I hate Nazis.'

'Me too,' Irene said. 'If I never . . .'

She stopped in midsentence and blankly stared into space as if suffering from an absence seizure.

Cal didn't notice that she had drifted off, because he too was no longer seeing the filing cabinet in front of him. He was seeing something else entirely. And his mood had, in an instant, been transformed from irritability to something very different.

They snapped out of it simultaneously.

She looked at him. 'Did you?' she asked.

He knew the exact meaning of her vague question. 'Yes.'

'I need to draw it,' she said urgently.

He'd just seen a sheet of unlined paper separating two photos in the filing cabinet. He snatched it and gave it to her.

'I won't bother,' he said. 'You're the better artist.'

She rummaged through her purse and found a lead pencil.

When she was done she showed it to him.

Nothing amazed him anymore. 'That's what I saw too,' he said.

It was a view out a window, a water bottle in the foreground with a Font Vella label, a hillside village and a crescent-shaped bay in the distance.

'It's what Giovanni is seeing,' she said.

Cal sat down. 'It gave me a feeling of tranquility,' Cal said.

'Yes,' she said. 'It was a kind of happiness. Thank God for that.'

It was almost noon when Irene found it.

The file folder was labeled: *Rally at Nürnberg, 1979/R. Kranz.*

It was a file of photojournalism, a collection of several dozen black-and-white photos shot at a neo-Nazi skinhead rally.

Cal looked up when Irene called his name quietly but urgently. She was holding one of the photos.

In it, a bare-chested young man was caught in frozen motion, shouting, his mouth twisted in rage. And on his arm was the tattoo of the Holy Lance and the SS bolts. On the border of the photo there was a pencil scrawl in German: Knights of Longinus.

They found Langer in his office.

'Ready for lunch?' he asked brightly.

'Look at this,' Cal said.

Langer inspected the photo, front and back, and looked at the folder it came from.

'I don't remember this particular shot but I recall its acquisition in the early 1990s. I was a young pup, a graduate student just getting into the field. This Kranz fellow came to the department to see my professor, but he was away on holiday or something like that. He had to settle for me. He was a collector of Nazi material, a pastime I had always found creepy and distasteful, until I became a collector myself – an academic collector I hasten to add. However, Kranz assured me he was no sympathizer. I've come to know him a little over the years, though he's a difficult man to really know. He lost members of his family to the Nazis and his collection, he said, was intended to bear witness.'

'Jewish?' Cal asked.

'Actually not. Catholic. The Nazis persecuted Roman Catholics with quite some fervor, you know. If I recall, this man's uncle was a priest who perished in Dachau. He brought this folder of photos he'd acquired from the estate of the photographer who attended this particular skinhead rally. He was trying to find out the identity of one of the speakers.' Langer went through the file and pulled out a shot of a man standing on a wooden box with a bullhorn near his mouth. 'This fellow.'

'Who was he?'

'I didn't know but I agreed to dig into it. When I eventually found out, the name meant nothing to me. Just one more bigot in a long line of them.'

'Why did he want the man's name?' Irene asked.

'I'm not even sure I ever knew. Kranz is quite the obsessive. He collects, he documents and he's reclusive. Extremely reclusive. In return for helping him, I asked if I could make copies of the photos for the departmental archive. He reluctantly agreed. This script, Knights of Longinus, is my handwriting. Apparently I copied it from the original notation of the photographer. Presumably he asked the young man something about himself or perhaps the distinctive tattoo and made a note.'

'Do you know who they are?'

'I'd forgotten about this folder entirely. I used one of the photos as a plate in an early book of mine, but I'm quite sure I've never come across a group called the Knights of Longinus again. Clearly it refers to the lance. It's intriguing, but I haven't got any more information about it.'

'Do you think Kranz might have anything to say about it?' Cal asked.

'Perhaps. Hard to know. Here's the thing about him. He became more withdrawn and reclusive the older he got. Over the years I've run into non-academic collectors, who've told me that Kranz has pulled together one of the pre-eminent archives of Nazi memorabilia and ephemera. I've tried to play on our old acquaintance to see what he's got, but he kept putting me off and I gave up some years ago. He hasn't any heirs that I know of. When he passes I hope I can get the university to buy the archive from his estate.'

'Where's he living?' Cal asked.

'A suburb of Munich. Not far.'

'I want to talk to him.'

'I can call him, I suppose. There's no harm in trying but I doubt you'll have much luck. Why don't you get it out of your system now so we can get lunch? I'm extremely hungry.'

The three of them sat around Langer's speakerphone listening to Langer talk in German to the man who picked up the line. Cal read German but his comprehension and spoken word left

much to be desired. He could tell that Langer was trying hard
to get Kranz to be receptive and finally got him to reluctantly
agree, to talk to Cal on the phone.

'Richard, you speak English, yes?'

The reply was stiff. 'I am able to converse in English.'

Cal tried his best. He told him about his background, that
he was in Munich with a colleague doing research and that he
wondered if they could come and see him about a group called
the Knights of Longinus. He described finding a photo of a man
with the distinctive tattoo in the photo archive he had contributed
to the LMU.

The reply was short and simple. 'This is not possible.'

'Have you ever heard of this group?'

'I am sorry, professor, but I am a busy man. I cannot entertain
your requests. Now if you will excuse me . . .'

Irene leaned toward the speakerphone. In English she said,
'Please, Herr Kranz, this is Irene Berardino. I understand you
are a Catholic.'

'Whatever does this have to do with anything?'

'Have you heard of the Italian priest with stigmata, the one
who they call Padre Gio?'

'The one who has gone missing. Yes.'

'He's my brother. We think he's in grave danger. There may
only be the slightest chance that visiting you might help save his
life, but I would be eternally grateful for the opportunity.'

There was an uncomfortably long silence on the line before
Kranz said, 'Then you must come at once.'

Kranz's villa was in Alt-Bogenhausen in the northeastern quarter
of Munich. It was invisible from the road, hidden by an iron gate
and mature plantings. The taxi waited while Irene, clearly the
persuasive one, buzzed Kranz from the intercom in the stanchion.
When Kranz opened the gate they let the taxi go and walked up
the long drive. The nineteenth-century mansion house had a
white-plaster façade, a tile roof and tiers of fancy balconies.

Cal whistled. 'Not too shabby.'

'Langer said he lives alone,' she said sadly. 'In such a huge
house.'

They rang the bell and waited.

'You're the one he responds to,' Cal said. 'You do the talking.'

Kranz was dwarfed by the massive front door. He was well into his eighties, hunched with scoliosis and needing a cane. His wispy white hair was plastered onto a bright pink scalp with a shiny pomade. He must have shaved for the occasion because there were a few red dots of the tissue paper he'd forgotten to remove. His elegant woolen suit was too large for him – apparently he had been more robust when younger. It was also too warm for the summer day and he was beaded with sweat.

He greeted Irene warmly and gave Cal scant attention. Cal was fine with that and let her take the lead.

The house was a masterpiece of carved wood paneling and marble floors. He took them through a series of art-filled rooms to a two-story library showcasing a magnificent collection of leather-bound historical and natural history books.

Kranz had them sit and apologized awkwardly that he wasn't much good at entertaining guests and wouldn't be offering refreshments.

'I do not trust servants although I have a woman who cleans. And a groundskeeper, of course. I live on my own. I drink instant coffee and subsist mainly on toast and jam.'

'It's a very beautiful house,' Irene said, seemingly uncomfortable at his unusual candor.

'It was my father's. He made his fortune in pharmaceuticals. As his sole heir, I have spent it on collectibles. My siblings were older. They did not survive the war. Is it just you and your brother?' he asked.

'Yes, only the two of us. We're quite close.'

'I did not love my siblings. I do not know why, but I did not. Also I did not love my parents and I suspect they did not love me. My affection was reserved for my uncle, Hans, who, like your brother, was a priest. We had a bond. The Nazis killed him. I was heartbroken. I am to this day heartbroken.'

'I'm so sorry,' Irene said, shedding a tear.

Cal wondered whether her sorrow was for the old man, for her brother, or both – not that it mattered the least.

Kranz took his pocket square and gave it to her. 'It has never been used. You may keep it.'

She composed herself and said, 'You're very kind and we appreciate you helping us. We're desperate to find Giovanni.'

'His stigmata, are they real?'

'Yes, we believe so,' she said.

'There are too few miracles in our world,' he said, his voice trailing off. 'There were none when my uncle was taken to Dachau and murdered. There were none when the Nazis butchered millions. My collection would be misinterpreted by most. They would say I have a prurient or perverse motive or that I am a glorifier. This is not the case. I collect to bear witness to what the Nazis did. When I die I will make a bequeathment. If Herr Professor Langer does not irritate me too much his university will likely receive it. I have hinted at this before. Show me the picture of what interests you.'

Cal produced Irene's sketch and Kranz's own photo of the tattooed skinhead.

'The Knights of Longinus, yes,' he said.

Cal had to speak. 'You've heard of them?'

Kranz snapped back, 'From this photograph that is labeled so. I remember it, of course. I remember every item I have collected. It is the only reference to this group in my archive. However, I have a letter, a rare letter that I acquired at great expense from the wife of a dead Nazi general, a bastard who was on Himmler's staff. The horrid woman knew it was valuable and knew I would pay. The letter was an oddity. I paid.'

Cal waited for the old man to elaborate but he seemed lost in thought, seething at the memory of the Nazi's wife.

'What was in the letter?' Irene asked gently.

'Himmler is writing to Hitler about the Holy Lance and other relics of the crucifixion of Christ. He notes some fantastical claims made by a curious figure named Otto Rahn.'

'We know who Rahn is,' Irene said, openly showing her excitement.

'He must have been a fantasist or a lunatic. The claims he made!'

Cal was jumping out of his skin and was about to open his mouth when Irene shot him down with her eyes and asked deferentially, 'Might it be possible to see the letter?'

He used his cane to rise and went to a large desk. He had

apparently already retrieved it from his archive and had placed it in a folder.

'It is very fragile. It is a carbon copy on onionskin. Please come here and read it flat on the desk. Do you read German?'

'I'm afraid not,' she said.

Cal said, 'I do.'

Kranz seemed disappointed that Irene had to take a subsidiary role to the American but the two of them sat together and talked about her brother while Cal studied the brittle letter, its type so faded and indistinct that he worried the onionskin might disintegrate before his eyes.

> *Heinrich Himmler*
> *Reichsführer-SS und Chef der Deutschen Polizei*
> *7 Dezember 1935*
>
> *An den*
> *Adolf Hitler*
> *Führer und Reichskanzler*
>
> *Mein Führer!*
>
> *We, at the Deutsches Ahnenerbe, have made a discovery of great importance concerning the extraordinary power of certain historical artifacts associated with the crucifixion of Jesus Christ. In short, it may be possible to create a weapon of unimaginable power that the Reich might use to change the course of human events. In this report I shall endeavor to describe our findings along with a proposed plan of action.*

Cal read it carefully, aware of the growing lump in his throat. By the time he got to the last paragraph, his legs had liquefied and he had to pull out the desk chair and sit to make it to Himmler's signature.

> *And so, my Führer, you can readily appreciate the import-ance of Herr Rahn's findings. While we in the Ahnenerbe have taken a keen interest in obtaining the so-called Holy Relics of Christendom for their obvious propaganda value,*

we had no inkling that they would have a highly important practical use. Rahn has rather mystical tendencies but, given the evidence he has brought forward, we must be inclined to pay his views careful attention. He speculates that the three artifacts – the Lance of Longinus, the thorns that composed the crown of thorns and the crucifixion nails – possess a special power, because they all pierced the flesh of Jesus Christ, who only a short time later would undergo the transformation of resurrection. Clearly, if this tenet of Christian belief is to be believed, then supernatural forces were manifest. Now, almost two thousand years after the crucifixion, when these three relics are placed in proximity to one another they seem to unleash a powerful force, the release of a massive burst of destructive energy. A wing of the Imperial Treasury in Vienna was destroyed when only a tiny fragment of a nail was placed beside a thorn and the lance. Imagine for a moment what destructive powers might be summoned if an entire nail were employed. Would the destruction claim an entire district? A city? A country? Would the Reich not be the most potent power on earth if we possessed such a weapon? This is what I propose: we have the second thorn stored safely in a vault in Berlin. The lance is still in Vienna and when the time is right, we must seize it and secure it. I will provide Rahn with the resources he requires and dispatch him on a quest to find more of these thorn relics, if more exist, and one or more of the nails. Nothing should be more important to the Reich than obtaining a Holy Nail of Christ.

Cal rubbed his eyes and turned his head toward Irene and Kranz.

Irene must have read the shock on his face because there was fear in her voice when she asked, 'Cal, what is it?'

'I know why they took Giovanni,' he said.

'Whom do you believe took him?' Kranz asked.

'I don't know who they are but I'd wager that they call themselves the Knights of Longinus.'

'Do you actually believe the nonsense in the letter?' Kranz asked.

'I'm afraid I do.'

'Overactive American imagination, if you ask me,' Kranz said.

Cal ignored the comment and asked, 'Can I make a copy?'

'I do not have a copier machine and you may not remove it from this house.'

'May I take a photo of it?'

Kranz immediately denied the request.

Irene asked Cal, 'Will it help find Giovanni?'

'It could.'

'Please, Herr Kranz. You were only a boy when your uncle was taken. There was nothing you could do to save him. Please help me save my brother.'

They were outside the gate of Kranz's mansion waiting for the taxi.

'The photos came out well?' Irene asked.

He took out his mobile and showed her one. The typeface was smudgy but legible.

'Well enough,' he said.

'What now?'

He pulled something from his shoulder bag. It was the business card of Lieutenant Colonel Cecchi. 'Time to see if the Carabinieri are worth their salt.'

At the same moment, they saw the taxi coming they heard a muffled ringtone from Irene's purse. She answered and shot Cal a puzzled glance.

'Yes, Lieutenant Colonel Cecchi, I was just this moment talking about you with Professor Donovan.'

She listened some more and cried, 'Oh my God! Please don't tell me this. Not mama!'

TWENTY-FIVE

A s the taxi took them back to their hotel, Cal got the gist of what had happened by listening to Irene's end of the call. She was crying, emotional, demanding to know what was being done to find her mother, her aunt, her nephew. He could tell she wasn't getting any answers.

'Let me talk to him,' he said, when it was clear the conversation was nearing its frustrating end. When he took the phone from her, she turned away and slumped against the taxi window.

'Lieutenant Colonel, this is Calvin Donovan. I need to tell you about certain information we've uncovered that might help your investigation. You might find some of it difficult to believe but I'd like you to listen objectively.'

Cecchi replied. 'I am happy to listen to you, professor. There is nothing simple or straightforward about these matters.'

Cal asked Cecchi to hold on for a moment and, while continuing in Italian, he asked the driver whether he understood what he was saying. The German kept his eyes on the road and didn't seem to realize that Cal was talking to him.

'All right,' Cal said to Cecchi. 'Here's what we know.'

He opened his kimono, laying it all out. Everything. Cecchi remained so silent that Cal had to ask periodically whether he was still on the line. What was he doing during? Taking notes? Checking emails? Playing Minesweeper?

Cal had nearly finished by the time the taxi arrived at the hotel. Irene got out and stood on the sidewalk in a terrible state. She was no longer crying but her eyes didn't seem to be focusing. Cal paid the driver and while bringing his phone call to a close, he ushered Irene into the lobby with an arm around her waist.

'That's it,' Cal said to Cecchi. 'I know it's a lot to swallow.'

Cal heard the officer loudly exhale. It wasn't a sympathetic sound.

'I'm a police officer,' he began. 'I deal in motive, opportunity, intelligence, witness statements, crime-scene evidence. You're asking me to take seriously something quite different. What you're describing is more in the realm of spiritualism or the supernatural. You want me to believe that Giovanni Berardino is somewhere in coastal Spain because you had a hallucination about a water bottle with Spanish writing. You want me to believe that some unknown group has kidnapped him because they want a Holy Relic that has the power to destroy. I really don't know how to properly respond.'

'Look, I understand and fully expected your skepticism. But I have to ask you: now that you've conducted your own evaluation of the circumstances of Giovanni's abduction and now that the other family members have been taken – have you developed a coherent theory? Has there been a ransom demand? Has any group issued a political or religious tract? Why has this priest and his family been targeted?'

The connection was so clear he could hear the officer swallow.

'To be perfectly honest, professor, I have no operational theory. The case is not behaving like a criminal one with a profit motive and it does not have the hallmarks of a terrorist kidnapping for financial gain or political aims.'

'Then listen to me. Please. What do you have to lose?'

'Only my reputation.'

'Just look at the evidence we've gathered. Meet with us in person.'

'When are you returning to Italy?'

'Tomorrow morning. We're flying to Rome.'

'Then come to my offices when you arrive. I'll try to keep an open mind. That's the best I can offer.'

Cal was reluctant to leave Irene on her own but she wanted to go to her room and told him she would skip dinner. Her doctor had given her a prescription for tranquilizers when Giovanni was kidnapped but she hadn't taken any. Tonight she would.

'Diazepam and the hotel bible. That's all I want tonight,' she said.

Cal spent the evening reviewing the disparate pieces of information they had uncovered. He tried to get into the head of a policeman and organize a presentation that would spur Cecchi into some kind of action. And while he was doing this, he was setting up and knocking down the little mini-fridge liquor bottles as if they were bowling pins.

At one a.m. the phone rang. Irene had been in a tranquilized sleep. She fumbled for the receiver and answered.

'Madam, it is the front desk. I am sorry to bother you so late but we have a plumbing leak in the room above you and need to make an emergency inspection. May we send a technician?'

'To my room?'

'Yes.'

Her voice was slurred. 'How long will it take?'

'Not long, I assure you. Only a quick check is required.'

Cal was dreaming and in the dream, his grad student, Joe Murphy, was telling him in his thick brogue to answer the goddamn phone. He was surprised when he awoke to find the receiver in his hand and Irene speaking to him.

'Cal, it's Irene. Could you come to my room?'

He squinted at the clock on the cable box.

'Are you ok?'

'Yes, I'm ok but I need to talk to you.'

'You don't sound ok. Has anything happened?'

'No, but I think we need to talk.'

Swinging his feet over the bed he said, 'I'll be right down.'

He pulled on some clothes and stuck his bare feet into his shoes before hopping on the elevator. Her door was open a crack as if she'd wanted him to come right in. Still, he knocked.

'Irene?'

When there was no reply he gently pushed the door open and took a few steps inside.

'Irene? You ok?'

Gerhardt stepped into view with a pistol in his gloved hand. He put a finger to his lips. The *shhhh* that came out was like hissing steam.

'Close the door,' he said. 'Quietly.'

Cal had been a little drunk. The sight of a hulking man with a gun sobered him up fast. He called for Irene again.

She sounded far away. 'I'm here.'

Gerhardt motioned for Cal to come forward and as he did, the German backed into the room.

Irene was sitting on the bed in her nightgown with plastic ties around her ankles and wrists.

'Who are you? What do you want?' Cal angrily asked.

'Professor Donovan,' Gerhardt said, gesturing with the suppressor screwed onto the barrel of his gun. 'Sit down just there.'

'You know me?' he asked.

'We know who you are.'

Cal locked eyes on Irene, silently ordering her to keep looking at him, to stay courageous. He sat on the desk chair that had been pulled out for his arrival, leaning forward on the balls of his feet, ready to take on this guy if he saw an opening.

'Who's us?' Cal said, without looking at the man.

Gerhardt didn't answer so Cal answered for him.

'I'm guessing you call yourself the Knights of Longinus, right?'

Cal turned his head to see the man's expression. There was little in the way of a reaction, although Cal thought he detected a flicker of amusement.

'Got one of those tattoos? The one with the lance and the SS shit?'

Gerhardt reached into a pocket and tossed long plastic ties onto Cal's lap.

'Your ankles first, to the chair legs. Tight. Then your wrists to the chair arms. Loose at first. Make one tight with your opposite hand then the other tight with your teeth.'

'Could you repeat that? I'm only a Harvard professor.'

Gerhardt pointed the gun at Irene.

'I'll do it,' Cal said. 'No sense of humor. Noted.'

When he had bound himself to the chair, Gerhardt holstered the gun inside his jacket and picked up Irene's Our Lady of Lourdes statuette standing on the desk.

Cal watched him inspect it and use his fingernail to wiggle out a plastic plug at its base. He looked inside then shook it hard until a piece of cloth was visible. He pinched at it and pulled. A sausage-shaped wad came out. Then with a flourish befitting a magician doing a reveal, Gerhardt unrolled the cloth and something dropped into his outstretched, gloved palm.

An iron spike.

A Holy Nail.

'You see?' Gerhardt said. 'It doesn't look like much but I understand it is quite important.'

It was black as night and was missing half of its flat head.

'My God! Giovanni hid it there,' Irene said. 'We had it with us all the time.'

'Jesus,' Cal whispered.

Irene began to cry. 'He wouldn't tell me where Giovanni is, or mama, Aunt Carla, Federico.'

'You've got what you want,' Cal told the man. 'You don't need hostages anymore.'

'You are telling me my business?' Gerhardt asked.

'I'm just stating the obvious. Take the nail and get the hell out of here.'

'I will leave soon.'

Gerhardt had a small workman's bag, the kind used to carry hand tools. He put the relic into a pocket on the inside of the bag and removed the other contents, a curious mixture of items: candles, candleholders, neckties and a very large bottle of vodka.

He began placing candles around the room, lighting them and turning off the lights.

'For a nice mood,' Gerhardt said.

'What are you doing, pal?' Cal asked.

'I want you to relax,' he replied, unscrewing the top of the bottle. 'I want you to have something to drink. Then I will go.'

'I don't want to drink,' Irene said.

'No, I insist,' Gerhardt said, approaching her with the bottle.

As he got close to her lips, Cal tried to stand but attached to the chair, it fell over on its side.

'Stop it!' Cal yelled from the floor.

'Quiet now,' Gerhardt warned. 'I assure you if you shout again, I will hurt her quite badly. Will you stay quiet?'

Cal seethed, 'Yes.'

'Good.'

Gerhardt pressed the bottle to Irene's unwilling lips and told her to drink.

'I don't like it. I won't drink it.'

'Would you like me to shoot him in the head? I will, you know. It will make no sound but it will make a big mess. Will you drink?'

She nodded. He put the bottle an inch into her mouth and began pouring.

She gulped and swallowed, then gagged. He stepped back to give her time to compose herself.

'More,' he said, bringing the bottle into play again.

As Cal struggled against his ties, Gerhardt repeated the cycle – pour, swallow, gag, wait – until Irene's neck was too limp to hold her head up straight and she was no longer talking.

'She gets drunk quite easily,' Gerhardt said. 'An inexpensive date, I think.'

He put the bottle down and righted Cal's chair with surprisingly little effort.

'Your turn. I think you need one, am I right?'

He put the bottle to Cal's lips and poured. Cal swallowed easily. It wasn't a brand he would have ever bought and it wasn't cold, but it was vodka, mother's milk. He got several swigs and then several more.

'We'll let that soak in a little,' Gerhardt said, moving to his tool bag and then the bed.

He used a wire cutter to snap Irene's plastic ties and while Cal watched in horror, he ripped and removed her nightgown from her limp body and laid her out naked.

'I'll kill you!' Cal shouted. 'You fucking bastard. I'll kill you.'

'If you don't shut your mouth you'll watch me screwing her. That I can promise. Ok?'

Cal gritted his teeth.

'Time to drink some more,' Gerhardt said, waving the vodka bottle.

The liquor flooded his system and fogged his brain. Fighting the booze was a switch. Usually he welcomed the feeling of having his senses dulled. It was his way of unwinding, shutting down, dampening unpleasant groundswells. Tonight he was fighting like hell. He kept looking at Irene, unconscious and vulnerable, at the candles, at the neckties. He didn't know what the brute had in mind but this wasn't going to end well.

'You're still awake,' Gerhardt said. 'More vodka. Open your mouth.'

Everything was getting fuzzy and distorted. He had to try, had to try, try, try, try . . .

When Cal's head fell forward and his chin rested on his heaving chest, Gerhardt slapped his cheeks.

'You asleep? Wake up. Wake up now. No? Ok, good.'

Gerhardt began to work quickly and efficiently. His first order of business was to snip Cal's plastic ties and lift him onto the bed, laying him on his back beside Irene. Then he stripped off all his clothes, flinging them around the room. Next came the neckties. He tied them around Cal's wrists and ankles and secured them to the headboard and legs of the bed. The nearly-empty vodka bottle was pressed against their fingertips and left on the bed. Lifting his phone, then re-pocketing it, he seemed to resist the temptation to snap a photo of the spread-eagled tableau he'd created. Next he set about arranging the candles around the room and lighting them. When that was done he wagged his finger at the sprinkler head over the bed and climbed up, finding footing in the midst of their naked bodies. With a technique he'd learned from an online video, he unscrewed the sprinkler heat seal and used a specialized tool to tighten the pressure valve. An investigation would certainly question the inoperative sprinkler head, but would likely conclude that its installation was faulty.

Finally, he took one of the candles and held it to the curtains until the fabric caught. With flames climbing he picked up his tool bag, pulled a workmen's cap over his distinctive haircut and with a final smile at his handiwork, left a do not disturb sign on the door.

From a great distance Cal heard coughing.

It was coming from far away, maybe from another room, maybe from down a long hall.

Would the guy just shut up? I'm trying to sleep here. Some people are assholes . . .

The guy started making more noise beyond coughing. A galloping noise, or was it whooshing? How was he doing that?

His eyes were stinging and watering. Got to wipe them, wipe them good.

He tried. Tried again.

What was stopping him? Were some jerks holding his hands down? His old college roommates had pulled a stunt like that once. Were they in on this? Maybe he should open his eyes and see what was up.

Cal's eyelids snapped open.

One wall and half the ceiling were ablaze and smoke was filling the room. He tried to get up but his hands and feet were bound with neckties.

Then he remembered.

She was lying next to him. He tried to nudge her with his knee. 'Irene! Irene! Wake up!'

She was out cold.

He called for help a couple of times.

Pulling at his ties proved futile. He arched his neck to look at the bed board. The neckties were knotted around heavy bed board slats.

He balled up his right fist and delivered a punch behind his head, striking a slat.

The pain was instantaneous but he hit the wood again.

Harder, goddamn it. Harder!

He felt the blood streaming down his palm.

The flames were spreading fast and it was getting hot. No one was coming.

He punched harder, another time. Two more times. Three.

There was a cracking sound. He didn't know if it was his knuckles or the slat. He pulled like crazy at the silk tie and his hand came free.

He had tugged so hard on the other ties that the knots were small and tight and he couldn't get them undone. With panic setting in, he saw the vodka bottle, grabbed it by the neck and smashed it hard against the nightstand. He had the knife he needed.

On his feet, he scooped Irene in his arms and made it out into the hall where he began yelling 'Fire!' at the top of his lungs.

TWENTY-SIX

Lieutenant Colonel Cecchi swept into his office, located off the Piazza del Popolo in Rome, apologizing profusely for keeping them waiting.

It was the evening of the day after the hotel blaze. Their lungs were irritated from the smoke and Cal's right hand was heavily bandaged from the pounding. They had both been treated and released from a Munich hospital and had spent much of the day in interviews with the police. They were tired, they were upset, but mostly they were angry.

'It was necessary to speak with the authorities in Munich,' Cecchi explained. 'They only just called me back. I'm sure you can understand.'

'Did they confirm what we told you?' Cal asked.

'Yes, in every detail. Unfortunately, the hotel personnel cannot explain how a non-guest was able to get onto the premises. Perhaps it was via the service areas. Perhaps someone was bribed. The security cameras identified a man fitting your description but his face was covered. There were many different fingerprints in the room, but as you said, he was wearing gloves. Clearly, if you hadn't awoken in time, professor, your deaths would have been linked to a sex game and heavy drinking.'

'The guy didn't realize what he was dealing with,' Cal said.

'And what was that?' Cecchi asked.

'A guy who can handle a bottle of vodka without spending the entire night in a coma.'

Cecchi squinted at him but Irene laughed a little. 'It seems my knight in shining armor is a heavy drinker.'

'I have to tell you,' Cecchi said, 'that this unfortunate incident of yours has made me more inclined to accept your evidence with that open mind I spoke of. I am ready for you to show me what you think you have.'

The men were assembling for drinks in the paneled great room of Lambret Schneider's grand hunting lodge. Amidst the taxidermy, oil paintings and a veritable forest of carved pine, they picked at canapés and drank champagne. They had been summoned to the outskirts of the Bavarian National Forest at short notice and they were keen for an explanation, though none of them had been inclined to push Schneider for details before he was ready.

Some, though not all, of the eleven men present had met the new fellow, Jürgen Besemer, and Schneider took him around for introductions.

An old, jowly man in a black, crested blazer and ascot, stuck out his hand, or rather angled it down, since he was a giant and Besemer was quite small.

'Saw your particulars, young man. Very impressive.'

'Thank you, sir.'

'First meeting then.'

'Yes sir. I'm very happy to be involved.'

'He's polite, Lambret, I'll give him that.'

Schneider clapped Besemer on the back and remarked that he certainly was, but that if politeness were a prerequisite for membership then their ranks would be thinner.

'Where's our Gerhardt then?' the old man said. 'Haven't seen him.'

'He's away, on the field of battle, Milo,' Schneider said enigmatically. 'All will be revealed. Ah, there's Kurt. Now we can begin.'

Schneider had everyone gather around as he stood with a champagne flute under an exceptionally large wild boar's head.

'Gentlemen, let us please raise our glasses to toast the Knights of Longinus, our comrades who have departed, our glorious past and our auspicious future.'

A collective '*Prost!*' rang out.

'Now sit, please. Some of you are so old you won't last another five minutes on your feet.' Like a good toastmaster, he let the laughter die down before continuing. 'I know you're all curious about this rather imperial summons of mine. Though most of you are retired gentlemen, a few, myself included, remain gainfully employed and for you to drop everything and come down here is a great show of loyalty. Thank you. If it weren't important I wouldn't have made the demand. Our new member, Jürgen, will not know our tradition, but we begin each of our increasingly irregular meetings with a show and tell, as the schoolteachers call it. And so . . .'

He went for an ornate silver box on a side table, lifted the lid and held up the box so everyone could see the black and gold relic.

'My knights, I present to you the Spear of Longinus.'

Besemer stared, his mouth agape.

After a round of applause, one old man piped up with a chuckle, 'How do we know that one's not a fake?' It was a running joke of theirs.

Schneider laughed and said, 'I assure you, this is the True Lance, the one that you, Archie, and you, Theo, and you, Milo, found with me on that frigid Antarctic day in 1973. Come here, Jürgen. Come closer for a good look. But only look, don't touch or you'll be stung.'

The young man stared down at the box.

'When Jürgen came to see me for his interview he revealed himself to be a young man who was well-versed in the history of the Reich. He told me it was his understanding that the lance found by the Americans at Nürnberg might have been a fake and that the Reich hid the real one for a future generation of German patriots to find. You said that, didn't you?'

Besemer nodded.

'Clever lad,' one of them called out.

'Clever indeed,' Schneider said. 'Yes, this is precisely what happened, Jürgen. The true lance *was* originally held in Vienna. When it was seized from the Austrians and taken to Himmler, he had two perfect replicas made. One was found by the Americans in Nürnberg after the war and returned to the Austrian government. That is the one now on display for the fat tourists in baseball hats who visit the Imperial Treasury. Himmler gave the second replica to my father who was one of his key aides. I keep it as a personal treasure. This one, the real one, was dispatched by Himmler to a secret base in Antarctica, along with other artifacts of the Reich, when it appeared we were going to lose the war. Some of these men and myself successfully recovered it during our secret expedition of 1973 but sustained a heavy loss – Gerhardt Hufnagel's father and my dear friend, Oskar, perished.'

Schneider reclaimed the lance from Besemer. There was a smaller silver box on another table. He opened that one too, revealing a tiny relic, a single, slender thorn.

'And this is a True Thorn which, two thousand years ago, was part of the jujube tree that was fashioned into Christ's crown of thorns.'

Besemer held up his hand as if he were a polite student.

'How do you know it is an actual thorn from the crown?'

'To answer this let me show you something. Then I will pour more champagne to keep everyone quiet while I tell Jürgen the story of a remarkable man named Otto Rahn.'

Schneider put on a pair of leather gloves and took the small silver box over to the larger one. When the two boxes were within a meter of one another something happened that made Besemer gasp and the other men smile knowingly.

The thorn and the lance both began to glow.

* * *

Cecchi put his glasses back on to reinspect the last pieces of evidence, the cellphone photo of the faded Himmler letter and Irene's drawing of Giovanni's windowsill. When he removed them he seemed bewildered.

'Quantum entanglement. This is a not a concept I've encountered in law enforcement.'

'It was a new one for me too,' Cal said.

'I can only imagine what my superior officer will say when he reads this in my report.'

'I appreciate your support,' Cal said. 'If we hadn't personally experienced these things I'm sure we'd be skeptical as hell.'

Cecchi held up Irene's drawing. 'And you truly believe that this sketch is a faithful reproduction of what your brother was seeing from his place of captivity?'

'I do,' Irene said. 'I'd never even heard of this Font Vella water.'

Cal nodded. 'Me neither and I saw it too.'

'And you have no idea where this might be?' the officer asked. 'This is not a place you recognize from family holidays.'

'I've never even been to Spain,' she said.

'It's certainly a Spanish brand,' Cecchi said, 'but someone could have brought it with them from Spain. He could be in Italy, Greece, anywhere coastal.'

'But chances are, it *is* in Spain,' Cal said. 'Who brings bottled water for a hostage from another country?'

Cecchi shrugged.

'We've told you everything we know,' Irene said. 'What are you going to do to find my family?'

'What am I going to do?' the officer repeated, looking at the ceiling for divine inspiration perhaps. 'I'll be honest. I don't know. I say this as it pertains to your brother. As for your mother, aunt and nephew, well, there's been a development in the investigation.'

She nearly leapt from her chair. 'What? What development?'

'I'm afraid I can't compromise the investigation at this delicate stage.'

'Please,' she begged.

'I'll only say that it's a potential lead based on forensics. I'm going to have to leave it at that but believe me, I'll contact you as soon as I am able.'

*   *   *

Although Schneider's lecture was intended for Besemer, the other men listened attentively to a story they knew by heart.

'Let me show you something, Jürgen,' Schneider said, reaching for a folder on a side table.

He handed him the letter from Himmler to Hitler describing the potential power of combining the three piercing relics of Christ and the imperative of finding the missing relic of the trio, a Holy Nail.

Besemer paused a few times to look at the men watching him and Schneider told him to take his time. When the young man was done he handed the document back with a look of dazed zeal.

'Yes, it's quite amazing, isn't it?' Schneider said. 'It's kept this room of old men going for all these years, never giving up the hope that one day we might find the nail, never giving up hope that we might be the instruments of a Fourth Reich.'

'And?' Besemer said.

'And what?'

'For God's sake, what of the nail?' Besemer asked, causing some of the old men to cluck.

Schneider grinned. 'He's an eager one, is he not?' he said. 'Eagerness is good. Recall what I told you about the scribble in the book by Procopius that Rahn discovered – the bishop who developed the wounds of Christ after handling a nail relic. I wanted to be absolutely sure that this manuscript of *The Secret History*, VAT. GR. 1001, was what Rahn claimed it to be. That's why I went to great lengths to have it stolen from the Vatican Library. Have a look.'

The old vellum manuscript was on the table next to the lance. Schneider pointed to the bookmarked marginalia and translated the Greek for Besemer.

'"*Eusebius, bishop of Cyzicus, who showed the wounds of Christ when he held in his hands the holy nail of Empress Helena.*" Do you understand what this means, Jürgen?'

'Yes, I think so.'

'That is why we have taken a great interest in the case of the Italian priest with stigmata,' Schneider said. 'Do you know of it?'

'It's been in the news. Of course,' Besemer said. 'He's the one who was kidnapped last week.'

'Whom do you think kidnapped him?' Schneider asked with a broad smile.

The young man's eyes danced. 'You? I mean, us?'

Schneider nodded with delight and the old men laughed heartily. 'Our Gerhardt's been a busy chap, that I can tell you.'

Milo interrupted the merriment with a question. 'So tell us, Lambret, has anything come of it?'

Schneider put his gloves on again and reached into his breast pocket.

'Only this.'

Besemer sprang up and the old men struggled to their feet and gathered around for a better look.

Schneider's voice rose. 'Gentlemen, I give you a Holy Nail.'

More than one reached out to touch it.

'Careful!' Schneider warned. 'Or you'll get a nasty surprise. The priest was given the relic when he visited a monastery in Croatia. An old monk there told him that non-believers in Christ weren't affected but true believers developed bleeding stigmata. I admit I touched it out of curiosity and developed some definite pain in my wrist which I find curious.' He laughed. 'Perhaps I'm not the complete atheist I've claimed to be.'

'Give it here,' one of the old men shouted. 'I'm not worried in the least!'

'Ah, but you should be worried about handling it,' Schneider said. 'We must be very careful. There was an almighty explosion in Rahn's day when a speck of metal from a holy nail came in contact with the other two relics. One slip up and, well, we wouldn't want to lose Bavaria, would we?'

Schneider pocketed the relic and removed his gloves.

'So you see, gentlemen, this is why I summoned you here. Finally, we are in a position to launch a mission we could only dream about these long years. If it is successful, we all may live to see the dawn of the Fourth Reich, the rebirth of the true Fatherland that our mothers, our fathers, our comrades died for. And gentlemen, I used the word live. We are not crazy people who strap on suicide vests. We are civilized men, we are thinking men. Someone else will die so we might live to experience a glorious future.'

*   *   *

The view from Giovanni's window was disappearing as night fell. All that was left were the distant lights of the hillside village. Downstairs, it had been quiet all day but now he heard arguing through the door. One of the voices was from the blonde fiend who mercifully had been gone for a couple of days.

The voices grew louder and the door was unbolted. When Martin and Gerhardt came in, Gerhardt pointed toward the open window and reprimanded Martin furiously in German.

'What the hell were you thinking? You bring him upstairs and then you open the goddamn window?'

'It's a long drop to the stones,' Martin protested. 'Escape is impossible.'

'But he could kill himself, you idiot. You know what would happen if he killed himself?'

'What?'

'First, you'd be dead.'

'How?'

'Because I'd kill you. Then I'd be killed. Now close the window and screw them shut. Now.'

To Giovanni's despair, Martin closed the windows and went looking for tools.

'Did you find it?' Giovanni asked in English.

'The statue wasn't at your mother's flat,' Gerhardt said. 'Your sister had it.'

'Where was she?'

'In Munich. With the American professor.'

'Donovan?'

'That's right.'

The priest shook off his confusion. 'Why were they in Munich?'

'Nice place to visit.'

He had so many questions but he asked the most important one first. 'So you've got it?'

'We do.'

'You didn't hurt Irene.'

'She's fine.'

'And you didn't hurt my mother.'

'She's fine too.'

'You'll release me now?'

'Not yet.'

'Why?'

'I need you to speak to someone.'

Gerhardt took out his mobile and made a call.

'It's me. Can you talk to him now?'

He handed the phone to Giovanni who said a tentative hello.

'Greetings, father,' Schneider said. He was talking from a hall near a dining room. Giovanni could hear the clatter and chatter of men eating. 'I must apologize for all the trouble we've put you through. I assure you it was necessary.'

'Who is this?'

'Someone who desperately wanted your Holy Nail.'

'How did you know I had it?'

'By following a very long, very incomplete trail of breadcrumbs.'

'You've got the nail but this man told me he won't release me.'

'I need you to do one small additional task for us. Then you will go free.'

'What task?'

'You'll need to take a journey to a destination that we shall reveal in due time. Once there you'll need to do something quite mundane, trivial really.'

'I don't wish to cooperate with you in any way,' Giovanni moaned. 'I've been subjected to torture. You've surely frightened my family. Release me or kill me. At this point I don't care which.'

'Such nonsense from a priest, a rational man of God. What we ask of you is completely benign. You might even enjoy it.'

'No! I won't help you.'

'I see. Could you please give the phone back to my colleague?'

Gerhardt listened to Schneider for a few moments and told him he'd ring him back. Then he opened the photo app on his phone, called Giovanni over with a crooked finger and played a file.

It was a video recorded in a furnished room Giovanni didn't recognize. The camera panned to the right and what he saw made him sag to the floor in despair.

His mother, aunt and nephew – all terrified – were standing against a lime-green wall next to a smugly smiling Gerhardt.

Gerhardt asked, 'What do you say I call my boss back?'

TWENTY-SEVEN

Colonel Juan Garrido of the Spanish Civil Guard took his videoconference speaker off its mute setting to speak again to Lieutenant Colonel Cecchi, who was conferenced in from Rome. Garrido had been offline conferring with aides at the Guard's command center in Madrid and with additional personnel in Barcelona. While they talked, Cecchi had been watching the muted split-screen view of both Spanish sites.

They had settled on English as a common language for the call and Garrido now said, 'In the interest of cooperation, my men and I would really appreciate more transparency on how you obtained this drawing.'

'As I told you,' Cecchi said, 'that is an operational detail involving the abduction of the priest, Giovanni Berardino, which I am not at liberty to divulge.' He delivered the lie he had settled upon, 'It involves a confidential informant who is in an extremely delicate situation.' He couldn't very well have said, trust me, it involves something I don't understand or even believe in, something called quantum entanglement.

Clearly exasperated, Garrido said, 'So why don't you ask your confidential informant where he or she was when they made the picture?'

'I wish it were that easy, Colonel. One day perhaps I will be able to share my dilemma with you but unfortunately, not today. So, all I can do is ask for your trust and understanding. I need an answer to our question of whether it was possible to match the drawing with a known location on the Spanish coast.'

'A coastline that is five thousand kilometers in length,' Garrido said.

Cecchi sighed. 'I won't be terribly surprised if your answer is, 'we cannot help the Carabinieri.''

'We do strive to cooperate with our fellow carabiniers,' Garrido said, 'which is why I passed your drawing to my command staffs in all our coastal regions. As it happens, our Catalan colleagues in Girona were able to provide some insights. That is why I have included Comandante Tomau Caral from Barcelona in the telecon. Comandante, please . . .'

Caral held up his copy of Irene's drawing in one hand and said, 'Actually, this is quite a classic view from our coastal region of Costa Brava. There's really no doubt. I am certain the window depicted is overlooking the town of Begur.'

Cecchi leaned forward in surprise. 'I see. And this Font Vella water, is it a common brand?'

'It is sold everywhere,' Caral said.

'If I were to send you a Red Notice via Interpol, could you narrow the possible properties for which you might obtain a search warrant to a practical number?'

'If your confidential informant is a good artist, that shouldn't be a problem,' Caral said. 'I've already made a check on satellite imagery. There are really only a handful of houses with enough elevation to give this viewing angle of the town and the bay.'

A squadron of Civil Patrol vehicles climbed the steep road up the foothills of the Pyrenees and pulled into the gravel drive of a canary-yellow cottage. A woman was tending a vegetable garden and she leaned on her hoe when Comandante Caral emerged from a Santana light utility military vehicle.

'What do you want?' the woman asked suspiciously.

'We wish to search your house.'

'What for?'

He brushed off the question and said, 'We have a warrant. It will take only a few minutes and we'll be off. Is anyone inside?'

'Just my husband. Go ahead and make a lot of noise. He needs to get off his ass and help me out here.'

When they were done, Caral said to his first sergeant, 'The view from the kitchen was close but we need a taller house or one higher up the mountain.'

Before leaving he asked the owner about the other dwellings on the road.

'Holiday rentals,' she said contemptuously. 'Foreigners. Our kind are getting priced out of living in our own province.'

The next house was almost two hundred meters to the northeast at a higher elevation. It was plastered a brilliant white and was more substantial than the previous one, with a full first and a small second story. There were no cars outside. Caral knocked on the door. After hearing nothing he sent two men to the rear and ordered that an entry-level window be forced. Soon an officer was wiggling through into the kitchen. He went around and opened the front door for the comandante.

'Hello?' Caral called out from the front hallway. 'Police on a warrant.'

The lounge was a mess of pizza boxes, dirty plates and crushed cans. Cigarette butts filled ashtrays and water-filled plastic cups. The room smelled of stale tobacco and beer.

'Search everywhere but don't touch anything,' Caral said, sending men up the stairs.

Before long he was summoned to the first floor where one of his men was already snapping pictures with his phone.

Caral's nose twitched from the smell of urine filling a paint bucket. The room was quite dark. A single floor lamp had a low-wattage bulb and the window shutters were closed. The bed was unmade and caked with dried blood.

He went to the window, withdrew a handkerchief and pressed his cloth-wrapped hand against the shutters. They didn't budge and he saw why; they were crudely screwed to the sills and window frames.

There were another two bedrooms and two bathrooms on the level. In the communal bathroom the vanity top and sink were smeared with blood.

From the hall came, 'Comandante!'

There was a single room at the top of the stairs, a small, light-filled en suite bedroom. Caral was immediately drawn to the window that overlooked the rear of the house with a sweeping view of the town of Begur and the bay. He took his copy of Irene's drawing and calmly held it up, comparing the perspective and the details. Then he looked down at the floor. There were empty plastic bottles of Font Vella water at his feet.

He pocketed the drawing, took a photo from the window and sent it via a text.

His phone rang almost immediately.

'Cecchi's confidential informant had it right, Colonel Garrido,'

Caral said. 'Giovanni Berardino was held here, in a rental, there's little doubt. But it looks like he's long gone.'

Cecchi got the call from Garrido. He listened, thanked the colonel for his cooperation and immediately rang Irene.

'You and Professor Donovan were absolutely right,' he said. 'Your brother was in Spain, one hundred kilometers north of Barcelona. The Spanish police found the house where he was held. Unfortunately, he was no longer there but there are many new leads for us to pursue. I don't pretend to understand how you and your brother are communicating but I cannot deny that it's happening.'

'What about my mother?'

'Patience, please. I'll call again soon.'

Cecchi slid his mobile into his jacket. He was in the gritty Testaccio neighborhood of Rome, where he and a squad of Carabinieri had rolled up in their Land Rovers and parked outside a pharmacy, blocking all but motorcycle traffic along the narrow street. As car horns began to blare and drivers argued with the officers who stayed with the vehicles, Cecchi and several men rushed up the stairs to one of the flats above the pharmacy.

A man in a wife-beater T-shirt was looking out the window of the second-floor flat to see what was causing the commotion when he heard a banging.

'Police. Open the door!'

'What do you want?' he called out and, when the demand was repeated, he unlocked it to find a short-barreled assault rifle aimed at his chest.

'What the hell?'

'Hands on top of your head,' an officer ordered. 'Now.'

Cecchi followed the armed men inside. The man backed into his sitting room with his arms up. Over the clattering of an off-kilter table fan, he demanded to know what was going on.

'Gianni Crestani?' Cecchi asked.

'That's my brother. I'm Mario.'

'Is he here?'

'No.'

'Where is he?'

'How the fuck should I know?'

Cecchi took the cigarette dangling from the guy's lips and stubbed it out on the rug.

The flat was tiny and it took no time to search it. An officer came from the bedroom with a small bag of marijuana buds.

'That's not mine,' the man shouted. 'You planted it.'

Cecchi rolled his eyes. 'A lieutenant colonel of the ROS raids a flea trap to plant a twenty-euro bag of weed on an insignificant thug. Tell me another one.'

Another officer came from the kitchenette with a small stack of mail.

Mario Crestani was patted down for weapons. The identity card in his wallet confirmed his name. Cecchi told him to sit down and sorted through the letters. One was from a bank. Cecchi opened it, had a quick look and put it in his jacket pocket.

'Isn't it illegal to open a guy's mail?' the man asked.

Cecchi ignored him. 'I'll ask you again, where's your brother?'

'And I'll tell you again. I don't have a clue.'

'This is his flat.'

'Yeah, so what? I'm staying here.'

'When did you see him last?'

'A week ago.'

'Where?'

'Here.'

'Where was he going?'

'He didn't say.'

'You got a record, smart guy?'

'Maybe.'

'Been to jail?'

'Maybe.'

'You're an idiot, you know that?' Cecchi said. 'It won't take me five minutes to know more about you than your whore of a mother. I looked up Gianni already. Know what I found? He's done time. Four stretches. Know what I know? He's looking at least twenty years for his latest adventure.'

'Yeah? What do you think he's done?'

'He'll be lucky if it only goes as far as kidnapping.'

Cecchi had become Cal and Irene's personal protector in Rome. He refused to let them check into a hotel where they'd have to present their identification to a front desk. He didn't know how they'd been found in Munich, but he refused to take any chances. He offered them the keys to a private flat on the Via Veneto the Carabinieri used for visiting VIPs from foreign law enforcement agencies.

The smoke from the hotel fire had destroyed Irene's clothes so their first order of business was shopping. Her frugality made her balk at using the boutiques along the Via Veneto but Cal whipped out his American Express card and insisted, arguing that they were too tired to go tramping around for bargains.

The saleswoman must have thought her customers odd or at least dysfunctional. Cal, the putative husband or boyfriend with a bandaged hand, slumped on a banquette in a semi-stupor, who paid little attention to the items Irene was trying on, and Irene, who monosyllabically accepted anything that fit without regard to the saleswoman's input.

Arriving back to the flat they found a note from Cecchi's secretary with two bags of groceries. Cal put on some coffee but fell asleep on the sofa before it brewed. When he briefly awoke an hour later, he found a comforter over him and heard Irene softly breathing from the darkened bedroom.

When Cal properly woke up; it was to the smell of simmering sauce. A glance at his watch confused him at first. It was almost midnight; he'd slept for hours. Irene was in the kitchen wearing her new jeans and top, turning their provisions into a meal.

'Smells good,' he said, startling her.

'I didn't want to wake you.'

'It's a lot of food for one person.'

She tried to smile. 'I'm quite a big eater.'

There was some red wine in a kitchen rack. He pulled out a bottle and searched the drawers for a corkscrew.

'Want some?' he asked.

'I'll never drink again,' she said. 'How can you?'

He tried the pinot noir. 'I might have to go easy on vodka for a few days.'

He watched her sorrowful eyes as she performed the small task of draining the pasta.

'I wish there was something I could do,' he said.

He knew she understood he was talking about her wretchedness, not dinner.

'I didn't think it could become more awful,' she finally said.

He didn't say anything; he wanted to let her talk.

She steadied herself against the counter. 'I mean, Jesus, Cal, here I am, wracked with worry about Giovanni, then crushed with anxiety about mama and auntie and Federico, and then Munich happens.'

He mumbled, 'I know . . .'

Her lip trembled. 'This horrible humiliation, being stripped naked by a monster, a man who was probably responsible for our family tragedy, and then . . .'

He knew what she was thinking.

'Look, just so you know, I had a woman bring me the sheets from her room before I carried you downstairs.'

'Cal,' she said, exasperated, 'I'm talking about you. *You* saw me. You're probably used to a different kind of woman, more modern, but for me, it's a mortification, an indignity.'

'Look, I know it was a horrible experience. I'm so very sorry it happened to you. You're the last person in the world who deserved it. But please believe me it's not something that's a big deal for me. It doesn't change the way I feel about you and besides . . .'

'Besides what?'

He looked away for fear of embarrassing her more. 'You're a very beautiful woman.'

Her face melted into a puddle of tears.

'I'm sorry,' he said. 'Maybe this wasn't the right time to say something like that.'

'Damn it, Cal, don't you see?' she cried.

He didn't see. He felt helpless and useless.

'I'm attracted to you. I've never met a man like you before and I don't know what to do.'

He smiled weakly. 'I'm attracted to you too. Next steps aren't all that complicated for a couple of unattached people.'

'But I am attached, don't you see?' she said. 'With my family who are in so much danger – maybe they're hurt, maybe they're – I can't even say the word . . . I can't even think about romance. And if these thoughts even creep into my head, they need to be flushed away. Do you understand?'

He did. He understood completely.

Did he want her right now? Yes.

Was he going to do anything about it? Not a chance.

TWENTY-EIGHT

He was dressed in new, typical-tourist clothes: khaki slacks, trainers and a ball cap. Given the scorching heat of the midsummer day, the only garment that didn't quite fit the look was the long-sleeved shirt that still bore the sharp creases from its plastic packaging. His small carry-on case, also purchased earlier in the day, had new pairs of socks and underwear, a couple of shirts and some travel-size Spanish toiletries. He exited the car without exchanging words with the two men who had driven him to the Barcelona-El Prat Airport and made his way to the Iberia ticket counter.

'I have a reservation,' he said.

'Your name, sir?'

He hesitated long enough for the agent to look up from her terminal and peer at him over her spectacles.

'Hugo Egger,' he said.

'Passport, please.'

He slid the Swiss passport over the counter.

She checked the photo, entered the passport number and said, 'Thank you, Mr Egger.' When she handed it back to him she noticed something on the heel of his hand and frowned. 'Did you know you're bleeding, sir?' She paused.

'What is the purpose of your visit, Mr Egger?'

As the passport control officer looked Giovanni up and down the priest felt his skin prickle. He'd been careful to re-bandage his wrists with fresh gauze in the lavatory shortly before landing, so he wouldn't bleed all over the desk. But did the officer spot his false passport? Did he suspect something? Gerhardt had told him that the security at Ben Gurion Airport was tough, especially for young men traveling alone.

'I'm a tourist.'

'What are you planning on seeing?'

'Biblical sites mostly.'

'This is your first time to Israel?'

He said it was.

'Do you consider yourself a biblical tourist?'

'Yes, exactly.'

'Are you a Christian?'

'I am, yes.'

'What kind?'

'Catholic. I'm a Catholic.'

'And what is your profession?'

Again, he'd been prepped. 'I work in a toy store. I sell toys.'

'What can they say about a man who sells toys?' Gerhardt had told Giovanni. 'It ends a conversation.'

'Toys,' the officer said dismissively. 'Where do you sell toys?'

'In Locarno.'

'Your accent isn't Swiss.'

'It's Italian, I know. My father is Swiss, my mother is Italian. They moved to Locarno from Trieste when I was a teenager. I think I'll talk like this always.'

'And you have reservations at this place, the Hotel Seven Arches in Jerusalem?'

'Yes, I have a reservation. For one week.'

'You didn't check any luggage. This bag you have? It's enough clothes for one week?'

He'd been selected for an additional security check in Barcelona. His bag had been thoroughly searched.

'I like to travel light. I'll probably use the hotel laundry.'

The passport was returned. The trial was over. 'Enjoy your biblical tourism, Mr Egger.'

As instructed by Gerhardt, he took a Nesher Tours taxi to Jerusalem, a highway ride that took just over an hour. He pretended to nap to avoid conversing with the driver.

As the taxi climbed the Mount of Olives toward the hotel, the Old City of Jerusalem revealed itself in all its glory. He could see the city walls, the Dome of the Rock, and to its rear, the Church of the Holy Sepulchre. These were landmarks he had always dreamed of visiting and now that he was here, rather than feeling joy and excitement, he was consumed with dread. His family was being held and he'd been told their fate rested in his hands. He had one simple task to accomplish, like Gerhardt had said, almost trivial in its execution. Once done they would be released and his travails would end.

One clear photograph. That was all.

Then he would be free to return to his life as a priest and would never hear from these men again.

He had asked, why couldn't they do it themselves, why force him?

Gerhardt had explained it to Giovanni this way: he and his accomplices were known to the authorities for reasons he would not elaborate upon. They were on no-fly lists and even with fake papers they were liable to be picked up with facial recognition software or other means.

And before Gerhardt let him out of the car at the Barcelona airport, he had warned him that any attempt to contact the authorities, call a friend, a priest, a family relation, would be detected and his mother and the others would have their throats cut. We have ways of monitoring you, Gerhardt had said. Doubt this at your family's peril.

Had he believed all of this? Any of it? He didn't even know. He was too tired, too worried, too scared to process the instructions and the threats. All he felt able to do was robotically follow their demands. And pray. He would place himself in the cradling hands of God.

The front-desk clerk at the hotel, a young man with a close-shaved head and small skullcap, welcomed Giovanni and took his passport.

'I see you requested a specific room,' he said.

'Is that a problem?'

'No it's not a problem at all. Have you been here before? I don't find you in our system.'

'It's my first time.'

'How did you know about the room?'

'From a friend. He told me it had a view.'

'I think you'll be happy you took the advice of your friend,' the clerk said giving him his room key.

'Oh, Mr Egger,' the clerk called out as he was heading for the elevator. 'It seems you have a FedEx waiting for you.'

When Giovanni entered the room, he dropped his bag and almost floated toward the picture window. The high, panoramic vista over the Old City was stunning and there, in the foreground, was the golden dome, the Dome of the Rock.

The FedEx was still in his hand. He pulled the tab. A sealed letter was inside bearing the typed name of Hugo Egger. He opened it and removed a folded piece of stiff cardboard, taped on one end. He had been told in advance what was going to be inside but seeing it, gently holding it between thumb and fore-finger, was a surprisingly moving experience.

A thorn.

A Holy Thorn that had painfully adorned the head of his savior, Jesus Christ.

Suddenly he felt a sharp, stabbing sensation in his scalp and he winced in pain. He put his forefinger against the painful area and felt warm liquid bathing his fingertip. The rivulet of blood coursed down his forehead to his cheek and onto the collar of his shirt.

Then he saw the face, that wonderful face and he stood immobile until the vision was gone.

He put the thorn back in its cardboard holder, sat on the bed and intently stared out the window at the holy city, looking in the direction of Golgotha, the place of the crucifixion.

They were in the sitting room of the flat on Via Veneto when the vision hit, catching them in the middle of a conversation and cutting off the flow of words.

It was vivid and bright and full of color and light. It didn't seem to last a very long while, though they would both say that the passage of time was hard to gauge.

Then Irene said, 'Ow,' and rubbed at her hairline while Cal did the same thing.

The vision winked out as abruptly as it had come.

Irene looked over at Cal and asked, 'Did you . . .?'

'Yes,' was all he needed to say before she urgently asked for paper and a pen.

He hurried for his bag and stood over her while she furiously sketched. He didn't bother trying to make his own drawing. Within a minute he saw that she was faithfully reproducing what he had seen himself.

While she was still adding the detail of a window frame and draperies, he shocked her by saying, 'I know where that is.'

'Where?'

'Jerusalem.'

'Are you sure?'

'I'm absolutely sure. I've been there many, many times. That's the Dome of the Rock. The dome is golden.'

'Yes, golden,' she said breathlessly. 'And the building is blue and white. I need colored pencils or paint to do it justice.'

When she was done she got up and stood by him to inspect the drawing from a distance.

'It's perfect,' he said.

'Giovanni's in Jerusalem?' she said. Her voice was shaky.

'He's got to be,' Cal said. 'Look, I know the city like the back of my hand. I know it from every angle, every quarter. The view out this window is from the Mount of Olives. There's only one place to stay up there. I stayed there myself when I spoke at a meeting of biblical archaeologists. It's called the Hotel Seven Arches. And Irene . . .'

'Yes?'

'You felt it too, just here,' he said pointing to a spot on his scalp.

'That's where a crown would rest on a man's head. A crown of thorns.'

Cecchi arrived within an hour of Cal's call.

He studied the drawing and compared it to the scenic photos Cal had bookmarked from the hotel's website.

'So your brother is communicating with you again,' Cecchi said.

'I don't know if he's consciously trying to reach out to us,' she said, 'but he is.'

'So someone's taken him from Spain to Israel,' Cecchi said.

'I thought you said there was an international alert out for him,' Cal said. 'Wouldn't he have been spotted at an airport?'

'If he had used his own passport, probably yes.'

'Do you think the people behind this are that sophisticated?' Irene asked.

'They are certainly not ordinary criminals,' Cecchi said. 'What is their goal? Only God knows, but they're quite sophisticated. May I take your drawing?'

She gave it to him.

'My mother. My aunt. My nephew. You said you'd call.'

'I will. I need a little more time. I have my work cut out for me.'

Comandante Caral parked his official car outside Terminal One at the Barcelona Airport and went straight to the security operations center. The security director was an ex-Civil Guard officer he knew quite well. They exchanged pleasantries and got down to the business at hand. The fellow had the photo of Giovanni that Caral had emailed earlier.

'Acting on your request, Comandante, we searched for a Giovanni Berardino on all reservation and check-in systems and flight manifests. No one by that name passed through this airport during the days I searched.'

'It's possible he was traveling on fake identity papers.'

'Always a possibility, sure. So we had to review security camera footage for the last three days at the check-in desks for all the flights to Israel. By the way, did you know how difficult this was?'

'Difficult, why? How many airlines could fly this route?'

'Non-stop, not many, only Iberia, El-Al and Arkia. One-stop – you don't even want to know. Over a dozen.'

'Look, I appreciate your efforts. This is a high-profile case. I owe you, Pau.'

'Well, we had no luck at the check-in desks. There were too many poor images to conclude that your man was or wasn't here.'

'Shit.'

'But since you say you owe me, you should be prepared to pay. I found him, at least I think I did.'

'Show me.'

'I found this man at the security checkpoint passing through the magnetometer. You tell me if you think he's the same guy.'

Caral held the two photos next to one another. The photo in his left hand was a clear shot of a hatless Giovanni in his black shirt and clerical collar. The other photo was less clear, of a man in civilian clothes and a cap.

He studied the pictures and asked, 'Any other views?'

'That was the best.'

'There doesn't seem to be anyone with him,' Caral said.

'There's a family with kids that's gone through and two old ladies behind him.'

'I agree. It looks like he's traveling on his own.'

Caral looked at the photos again and said, 'You know, I think it's our man. I think it's definitely him.'

Armed with the information from Caral, Cecchi contacted his counterpart at the SISMI, the Italian Military Intelligence and Security Service, and laid out his case for getting the cooperation of the Israelis.

'Is this some kind of joke?' the deputy director asked.

'You're where I was on this a few days ago,' Cecchi said. 'But a picture like this one led to finding the gang's hideout in Spain. The DNA evidence from there confirmed that the priest was kept there.'

'You believe this shit.'

'I absolutely do.'

'And you want me to contact the people at Mossad, the most humorless sons-of-bitches in the intelligence community and tell them we've got a psychic lead that there's a missing, kidnapped Italian citizen at a hotel in Jerusalem.'

'That's right, I do.'

The intelligence man shook his head and said, 'Christ almighty.'

It was dark when Cecchi returned to the VIP flat on the Via Veneto.

Cal could tell immediately that something was wrong. He saw Cecchi eyeing the glass of wine in his hand and offered him one.

Cecchi tasted it. 'Was this here?'

'It was,' Cal said.

'Not bad for a government guest house,' Cecchi said.

Irene was impatient and wanted to know what he had to say.

'I'm afraid I don't have good news,' the officer said. 'Our intelligence services talked to Mossad. They didn't take our request for assistance seriously. In fact, I'm told the Israelis were quite rude. Something along the lines of having too many important security issues on their plate to divert resources to chase after clues from a so-called psychic source.'

Irene looked despondent. 'So they won't help,' she said.

'They will absolutely not help.'

'And you can't go there yourself?' she asked.

'The Carabinieri have no jurisdiction in Israel,' he replied. 'I'm sorry.'

'Then guess what?' Cal said.

Both Cecchi and Irene said 'what?' at the same time.

Cal finished his wine. 'Then we're going.'

TWENTY-NINE

Giovanni had taken all his meals in his room, as instructed. His only contact with people had been telling the maid through the door that he did not want to have cleaning done and asking the room-service waiter to leave the cart in the hall.

He ate his breakfast staring out the window at the Old City, wishing in the midst of his misery that he could at least get a measure of solace from visiting the sacred sites. But he'd been warned. Any deviation from the plan and his family would be butchered like farm animals.

The hotel phone rang sending his heart into overdrive. It was the first call he had received.

He recognized Schneider's voice. 'Good morning, father. Have you enjoyed your breakfast?'

Was he really being watched? Or was this an educated guess to keep him under control?

'How is my family?'

'They are well. They have been told they will soon be released if you complete your assignment. You received the thorn yesterday.'

'It came.'

'Keep it safe. The fate of your family is in play. You will receive the next delivery this morning. It will be one of several items packaged together. This was done to confound Israeli customs. You will know the true relic. Please repeat the key instruction.'

'Why?'

The tone was stern and impatient. 'Because I need to know you will do the task properly, that's why.'

'I'm supposed to keep the relics as far away from each other as possible until the last moment. I am to take a photo of myself with each relic with Jerusalem in the background, with the phone you gave me. I am to text the photos back to you.'

'That's correct. And don't forget to keep one relic by the window, one in the bathroom, one in the hotel safe.'

'Will you tell me why?'

'There are certain things I am not at liberty to explain. You must simply accept my orders and act accordingly. Do you like the room we chose? Isn't the view quite stunning?'

Giovanni didn't want to normalize the situation with pleasant banter. He stayed quiet.

'Well, all right then,' Schneider said curtly. 'I will be in touch with you soon regarding the second package. Remember to remain in your room, out of sight.'

Schneider hung up the phone. The only other person in his Berlin office was Gerhardt, his feet resting on the coffee table. No one else would have acted so casually in front of the bank chairman, but Gerhardt was always a special case – a son, neither biological nor officially adopted, but nevertheless the closest thing Schneider would ever have to a child. Gerhardt was now a full decade older than his father, Oskar, had been the day he was killed in Antarctica, but in Gerhardt, Schneider could vividly see his old friend. The same irreverence, the same individuality, yes, even the same kind of coarseness. Schneider's wife didn't know it, but a quarter of his fortune would go to Gerhardt upon his death, a quarter to his wife, and the rest to the Knights of Longinus to further the cause. He almost shuddered to think what Gerhardt would do with the riches. How many whores, how many auto-mobiles could a man buy? But he wouldn't be around to see it, would he? All he cared about was that his promise to Oskar would be fulfilled.

Gerhardt stretched his arms and yawned. 'Are you sure there'll be an explosion when they touch?'

Schneider placed his fingertips together pensively. 'We know from Rahn's letters to Himmler and our own personal experience that if they get close to one another, heat is generated. Rahn speculated that somehow the relics in Vienna came into direct contact while he was at lunch. That blast involved only a tiny piece of metal from a nail. This one will involve the entire relic. There should be quite the explosion, far more powerful than the one that rocked the Imperial Treasury back in 1935. We can only wait and hope. If fate is kind, the explosion will be massive and Jerusalem will be destroyed. If extraordinarily kind, then we will wipe out the whole of Israel and then some. This will go a long way to finishing the job that Hitler started.'

'Not only Jews live there,' Gerhardt said.

'Killing Arabs is icing on the cake.'

'Then what?' the big man asked.

'Once it's happened, we'll release a communiqué from the Knights of Longinus detailing what we've done and how we've done it. We'll release the photos of the priest with the relics. How delicious! The relics of Christ in the hands of a revered and holy priest as the instrument of Israel's destruction. There will be condemnation, of course, from all the usual quarters. But also, there will be a call to action, a rallying cry from nationalists and patriots across Germany and Europe who will see this for what it is; the first volley fired in the new war that some will call a holy war, that will usher in the beginning of the Fourth Reich. Out of the chaos of a fractured Middle East and the turmoil of Jews and Arabs and Christians at each other's throats, we will rise to fill the bloody void.'

Gerhardt got up and declared his intention to have a second breakfast.

'Doesn't the ideology mean anything to you?' Schneider asked.

'If you're happy, Lambret, I'm happy. I'll leave the ideology to you.'

Giovanni's phone rang again. He felt his gut knot up as he went to answer it. He couldn't bear speaking to the disembodied Germanic voice a second time in the day. But it was only the hotel front desk informing him that he'd received another FedEx. The package was left at his door per his instruction and he retrieved it shortly after the clerk departed.

The box was heavy. The postage was over one hundred euros.

The customs declaration read: Decorative Items – Interior Design. Value – 250 euros.

He peeled the flap open and reached in.

His hand settled on something flat and angled. When he pulled it out he saw it was a filigreed brass bookend. Then, its matching pair. The next item was wrapped in bubble wrap, an ornamental magnifying glass with a carved bone handle. The last item, the largest, was also done up in bubble wrap.

He knew what it was before he began to remove the tape. The shiny gold sleeve showed through the plastic bubbles. He'd never seen the artifact in Vienna and he wasn't even sure if he'd even seen photos of it. But he'd been told what to expect. Again, he found the anticipation overwhelming. In his humble hands, he'd be holding another relic of Christ.

When the bubble wrap fell away onto the floor, he felt the heft of the Holy Lance. He allowed his finger to dance along its sharp, black edge to the tip of the spear. The very tip that had pierced Jesus's flesh.

The pain hit him hard and fast.

At first he thought it was a cramp or a pulled muscle affecting one of the muscles between his ribs.

But it was worse than that, far worse.

The vision also came hard and fast. The face was so serene that it distracted him from the agonizing pain.

When the vision passed, he put the lance down on the bed and went to the bathroom mirror where he lifted his shirt.

There was blood.

Blood dripping from a wound on the right side of his chest.

He dropped to his knees on the bath mat and began to pray as fervently as he had ever prayed.

By the time they landed at Ben Gurion Airport, Cal and Irene were exhausted. They had spent another fitful night in Rome and on the El Al flight both of them had their naps interrupted by the same stabbing pain in their ribs. They hadn't been able to sit together but Cal had half-stood to seek Irene's attention at the height of the pain. He had seen her, three rows back, holding her right side, her face contorted. Later, when the pain had subsided, he had met her for a brief exchange by the galley.

'Did something happen to him?' she had asked desperately.

'I don't know. Maybe.'

'Do you think someone hurt him?'

'Not necessarily. It might be . . .'

'Might be what?' she had asked.

He had wished he'd kept quiet but her pleading eyes had forced him to continue.

'The next stigmata,' he had said. 'Jesus was pierced on the right side of his chest. Giovanni may have just taken possession of the lance. He's getting the relics one at a time. Someone's probably bringing them to him. You saw the way our bags were checked when we left Italy. He couldn't have been carrying them himself. Israeli security is too tough. Once he gets the Holy Nail the game's over.'

When they landed and cleared passport control and customs, Cal picked up his hire car. Soon they were speeding along the same route to Jerusalem that Giovanni had traveled. Arriving at the hotel forecourt they left the car with the valet and hurried inside.

At the reception desk the clerk, a prim middle-aged woman began to ask for their names and passports, when Cal thrust a photo of Giovanni in her face.

'This man is staying at the hotel,' he said. He looked at the clerk's name badge. 'Do you recognize him, Magda?'

'A priest,' she said. 'I haven't seen any priests here recently. When they come they come in groups. We have no groups.'

'He might not be dressed like as a priest,' Irene said.

'What's the name?'

Cal said, 'Giovanni Berardino, but we don't think he's traveling under that name.'

'To check in you need a passport. Are you saying someone checked into our hotel on a false passport?'

'Possibly, yes.'

'Then you should talk to the police.'

More people arrived at reception and began queuing behind them.

'Could we speak to the manager?' Cal asked.

The clerk shot him a sour look. 'Maybe you can come back a little later. I've got guests to check in.'

'We've got reservations,' Cal said.

'Why didn't you say so? Passports, please.'

The hotel manager wasn't much more accommodating. She told them she didn't recognize the man and questioned why they were so sure he was a guest.

Cal lied. 'He said he was going to stay here.'

'But there was no one by that name in our register.'

'He may have other identity papers.'

'That would be a crime. As Magda told you when you checked in, if you have reason to think a criminal act has been committed you should see the police. I can give you their address.'

Irene's eyes were filling with tears. Cal and she had talked about contacting the police but it was impossible. Their story was too bizarre. If the Italian security services hadn't been able to gin up Mossad's interest in the case, what chance would they have? He squeezed her hand.

This act of tenderness coupled with Irene's apparent distress must have touched the manager because she said, 'My dear, what's the matter?'

'Giovanni is my brother. He's gone missing and we're very worried about him.'

'And you really think he's here.'

'We do,' Cal said.

'But not under his real name.'

'Like I said, we don't think so.'

The manager looked at her watch in an obvious show of impatience.

'Tell you what. Let me make copies of the photo. I'll leave them at the front desk, at housekeeping, in the restaurant kitchen. That's all I can do.'

THIRTY

Cal and Irene repeatedly walked every inch of the hotel public spaces until they had to return to their rooms out of weariness. Their windows were facing north, overlooking the hills of Bethlehem; the wrong direction to see the

Old City. But the view from the hotel restaurant was identical to the one in their visions. In the middle of the night, after an intractable bout of tossing and turning, Irene got dressed and walked the halls again. There were two hundred guest rooms, all of them occupied according to the manager, and she lingered before each door, straining to hear Giovanni's voice, perhaps in prayer, perhaps in despair.

What would happen, she thought, if she were to knock on doors, swiftly apologizing for waking up guests? She and Cal had discussed the option and had concluded that the hotel would have thrown them out in short order. Then where would they be? In any event, she lacked the courage to confront angry guests.

In the morning, they met as planned at six a.m. outside the restaurant and sat there, nursing coffees, until breakfast service ended four hours later. Every time new people entered their heads jerked up, but Giovanni was not among them.

'What now?' Irene asked.

'One of us can hang out in the lobby and the other can walk around and try to get a look into the rooms getting serviced,' Cal said.

She told him about her night prowl and volunteered for lobby duty.

'Be on the lookout for anyone coming in with a parcel for a hotel guest or a package from a courier or a delivery company.'

She nodded but first she said she wanted to call Cecchi.

He answered straight away on his mobile. The reception was poor.

'Is there any news?' she asked.

'I told you I would call if there were any developments,' he said.

'So there's nothing?'

'Nothing that I can speak about, I'm afraid.'

'I have to tell you, I'm frantic,' she said.

'I can appreciate that. Did you arrive in Israel?'

'We're here.'

'And?'

'We haven't found him yet. It would be much easier if we had the support of their police or their government.'

'I tried,' Cecchi said. 'The Italian government tried. There

were too few facts, too many soft speculations to get the attention of the Israelis.'

'Even though we think their country is in danger.'

'What can I say?'

'But you believe us, don't you?'

'I'm a good Catholic, signorina. I believe in the miracles of
the Church. My mind was always going to be open once sleight
of hand or fabrication was excluded.'

'Thank you for that.'

'Now I must get back to work to find your family. Please try
to stay safe.'

Cecchi pocketed his phone. Bathed in sweat he rapped on
the partition between the rear of the surveillance van and the
driver's cab.

'For God's sake, turn up the air conditioning,' he said.

At mid-afternoon, Giovanni's phone rang while he was rewrapping
his oozing wrists. The wastebasket in the bathroom was already
half-filled with bloody dressings. He ran to the phone, leaving a
trail of blood spots on the carpet.

It was the Germanic voice.

'Do you have it?'

'Have what?'

'The third package, man. The third package!'

'It hasn't arrived.'

'But it has. We've received the delivery confirmation from
FedEx.'

'Then the hotel hasn't delivered it yet.'

'Call down immediately. I will call you back in five minutes.'

'You'll release my family soon?'

'Five minutes.' The phone went dead.

Giovanni called the front desk and asked if a package had
arrived for Mr Egger.

'Yes, sir,' he was told. 'Would you like to come down for it?'

'Could you please bring it up?'

Cal had been sitting across the lobby. He'd relieved Irene and
let her return to her room for a rest. After a few hours of pretending
to read the newspaper he felt a need to stretch his legs and get
a few minutes of sun. He stepped outside into the heat of the

Jerusalem summer just as the front desk clerk called over a bellman and handed him a FedEx box for Room 208.

Giovanni collected the box outside his door and the moment he picked it up his wrists began to ache terribly.

He left it on the dresser and sat on the bed, staring at it, afraid.

The phone rang.

He let it ring until it stopped.

What if he never answered it again? Would they simply leave him alone? Would they send someone to his room? He assumed they had people nearby. He'd been warned time again that they knew his every move. But if he went incommunicado, would they make good on their threat and hurt his family? He couldn't risk that, could he?

Slowly and hesitantly, he approached the box, enduring a crescendo of wrist pain. Like the previous delivery, the box was heavy and had a declaration form describing Iron Decorative Items – Interior Design. With the package on his lap his hands seemed to fail him. He struggled mightily with the gummed flap until it was free.

All he could do was turn the box upside down and let the contents slide out onto the bed, each item in bubble wrap. He didn't need to unwrap them to know which one was precious and which ones were worthless pieces of metal. He fought through the pain to pick up one of the tubes of bubbles, ripping the tape with his teeth and slowly unwrapping it.

The warm, rough metal was heavy in his hands for only a moment or two, before the pain became so great he cried out loudly enough so that if any guests had been in the adjoining rooms, they surely would have sought help.

Then it happened.

His wrists erupted and like a spray of volcanic magma, blood shot up, splashing the ceiling.

The phone was ringing again but it seemed like the sound was coming from a great distance. The ringing persisted as Giovanni slipped into unconsciousness.

The only light came from a single, naked bulb and Giovanni was scared he would lose his footing on the narrow, stone steps.

The old monk, Brother Augustin, was having no problem

navigating the run of stairs even with his cataract eyes and flop-
ping sandals.

'Follow me, young man, follow me.'

The crypt was smaller than Giovanni had expected. It was also
quite dark since the light from the staircase bulb didn't penetrate
into the whole of the chamber. He was about to use the flashlight
on his mobile phone, when the monk hit a wall switch and two
wall fixtures winked on, casting a sickly yellow glow.

'What was your name, again?' the monk asked.

'Giovanni.'

'Giovanni,' the monk repeated. His grin showed the black gaps
between his teeth. 'I have a gift, young man. Do you want to know
what it is?'

Giovanni swallowed hard and he wondered if it had been a
good idea to accept the monk's invitation. He wanted to run up
the stairs or call out for his friend, Antonio, to come down.

'I have the gift of reading a man,' Augustin said. 'I can tell what
a man holds in his heart. Do you know what you hold in yours?'

'I'm not sure I do.'

'Why did you decide to become a priest?'

'I'm not a priest yet.'

'So you said, but soon you will take your Holy Orders.'

Giovanni had been asked the question countless times. His
responses had typically ranged from, 'I want to devote myself
to serving God,' to 'I would like to help my fellow man.' But
now, under the withering gaze of this old man he couldn't seem
to come up with a response.

'Do you know why you are hesitating?' the monk asked. Before
he could reply, Augustin supplied his own explanation. 'It is
because the answer is in your heart rather than your head. That
is true spirituality. I saw it in your eyes. I saw it in the way you
carry yourself. You have great humility. You have a gentleness
of spirit. I was that way too when I was your age. That is why
I was chosen.'

'Chosen for what?'

'Come.'

They walked across the smooth stones. Although Augustin
trod right over the stone markers of medieval burials, Giovanni
couldn't bring himself to step on them. So he zigzagged his way

to the nook that was located directly below the stone altar of the church. The nook had a stone shelf and on it was a small bronze box, green with oxidation.

The monk took the box down from the shelf and said, 'I was chosen a long time ago and now I choose you. You see, Giovanni, this monastery has a very ancient tradition, perhaps one of the most ancient traditions in all of Christendom. There is no written or oral history of how St Athanasius came to possess what is in this box, but possess it we did. It came to us from the Holy Land in the early times of the Church. The tradition is this: one monk and one monk alone, was chosen to be its keeper. One monk and one monk alone, was chosen to be devoted to its care – with all the attendant pleasure and pain of that responsibility. I am now a very old man and I will not live much longer. When I dine, I turn to my left and I turn to my right. I see no novices, no young monks. I see only my dear Brother Ivan who is not much younger than me. I always knew, no, I always hoped that this day would come when a young priest would arrive as a tourist and leave as the keeper of what is inside this box.'

Giovanni felt a lump form in his throat. Was it from fear or some vague sense of pride at having been singled out?

'What's inside?'

'This.'

The monk lifted the lid. There was just enough light from the nearest wall fixture for Giovanni to make it out.

It was a rough black spike with a broken flat head.

'A nail?' he said.

'Not just a nail, Giovanni, but a Holy Nail, one of the Roman spikes used to nail the wrists of our Lord, Jesus Christ, to his cross.'

'But how do you know it's real?' the young man asked.

The monk grinned again and reached for it.

And when it was firmly in his palm his face changed showing an expression that Giovanni couldn't fathom, but would come to understand all too well. It was a perfect mixture of horrible pain and exquisite pleasure.

Then something else happened.

Blood began streaming down the monk's hands, not in a trickle. A torrent.

* * *

Cal was by the hotel parking lot, admiring the views when his face convulsed in pain and his hands balled up in some kind of a reflex. The pain in both wrists was so intense he thought he might black out. It seemed almost incredible that his skin remained smooth and unblemished.

'You ok, mister?' the attendant asked.

Cal had only one thought – Irene – and he began to run back to the lobby. Inside, he bounded up the stairs to the first floor and banged on her door.

'Irene? It's Cal. Open up!'

He heard moaning through the door and would have put his shoulder to it if she had taken longer to answer.

She held up her hands and said, 'The pain, it's terrible. Something's happened to him, something bad.'

'He's got the nail,' Cal said. 'We're out of time.'

It was as if their thoughts were twinned. They both ran from her first-floor room and sped down the corridor, pausing at each guest room to shout out his name and to kick at the bottom of the door because their hands were too painful to knock.

'Giovanni! Giovanni!'

Soon some guests were opening doors, others, scared of a terror incident were cowering in place, calling the operator to report a disturbance.

'What?' an elderly man said, calling after them. 'What do you want?'

'Sorry,' Cal called back. 'We're looking for someone.'

'Yes, yes,' the guest said. 'Giovanni. I heard your shouting. I'm not deaf.'

They had banged on half the doors on the level when the manager stepped off the elevator and approached with a warning finger.

'You two! Stop what you are doing! You are bothering my guests.'

'It's an emergency,' Cal shouted, kicking another door. 'Giovanni!'

'No. No! Stop it now!' the manager yelled.

They ignored her, keeping up their frantic pace, going door-to-door, while the manager spoke in Hebrew into her walkie-talkie.

'Did you get all of them on your side?' Cal shouted to Irene.

'This is the last one,' she cried after kicking the door.

'Upstairs!' Cal said, running alongside and steering her to the stairwell.

'Hey! Stop!' the manager said, getting back on her walkie-talkie.

The second floor corridor was empty.

Room 200 was opposite the stairwell and that's where Cal started, repeating the routine while Irene started across from him at Room 201.

He moved quickly, ignoring a woman who poked her head from room 202 and quickly retreated, slamming and bolting her door.

204.

206.

208.

The pain in Cal's hands was waning and he used his knuckles to hit the door.

'Giovanni! Giovanni!'

Inside, the priest was laying on his side, unresponsive, his bed a bloody mess.

Cal moved on.

The manager appeared on the floor and this time she was not alone. Two armed security guards, tough young men, were beside her and one called out in English.

'You, mister! You, lady! Stop what you're doing and come here!'

Cal ignored them until he heard the other one say, 'Believe me, we will shoot you!'

'Irene, stop,' Cal said. 'They've got guns.'

'But Cal,' she protested.

The guards ran up to them demanding they raise their hands.

In frustration, Irene kicked one more door and crumpled to the floor, crying her eyes out.

Cal ignored the guards and went to her, sliding his back against the wall until he was sitting beside her.

Then he cradled her in his arms and said, 'We tried, we tried our best.'

The guards were standing over them, semi-automatic pistols pointed down at their heads.

'Get up now and come with us! This is your last warning.'

'Irene, it's over,' Cal said gently. 'We've got to go.'

*   *   *

Cecchi was complaining to his men, 'The thing I always hated about surveillance was when you had to go to the bathroom.'

'When was the last time you sat in one of these vans?' he was asked.

'You were probably sucking at the teat, that's how long. I'll be back in a few minutes.'

'Can you bring back coffee?'

Cecchi made a rude gesture and said, 'Get your own coffee. I'm your boss, not your secretary.'

Cecchi, dressed in civilian clothes, climbed out the van doors and trotted across the street to a café.

Simple forensics had led Cecchi to this street in Ostia Antica, thirty kilometers from Rome. Knuckleheads will always screw up, he had reminded his men and sure enough, the fingerprints of a known criminal, Gianni Crestani, had been pulled off the flush lever in a toilet in Domenica Berardino's flat. The raid at Crestani's apartment had yielded his bank statement and Cecchi got a judge to compel the bank to release the records of his financial transactions to the Carabinieri. And there they found it: four smallish withdrawals from the same cashpoint on Viale Vasco da Gama in four days. Cecchi's men had fanned out, showing a picture of Crestani to merchants in the neighborhood. The owner of a pizzeria a few doors from the cashpoint had identified the man as a recent and repeated patron of his store and based on the lead, Cecchi had ordered the surveillance for Ostia.

Cecchi left the café and was looking for a gap in the traffic to cross the street when he froze.

A man walked by him on the sidewalk. He was ninety-nine percent certain it was Gianni Crestani.

In a split second Crestani's back was to him. He watched as he casually sauntered into the pizzeria and then Cecchi sprinted across the street and climbed into the van as his mobile started ringing in his pocket.

'That's me calling,' one of his men said. 'It's Crestani.'

'I saw him,' Cecchi said, settling into his seat by the video monitor. The camera was trained on the front of the pizzeria.

'What do we do now?' the officer asked.

Cecchi thought about it and said, 'We wait for the pizza to come out of the oven.'

THIRTY-ONE

The sound was pleasant but it was very far away.

It sounded like a bird, a happy, chirping bird, but as it got louder it became less melodic and angrier.

Giovanni's eyes blinked open. The first thing he saw was a bloody wrist. Then the sound registered.

The telephone.

He reached for it and had to use all of his strength to make his hand grasp the handset.

'Hello?' he asked, his voice quavering, his confusion on full display.

The voice.

It all came flooding back. He knew where he was. He remembered his sorry state.

'Where the hell were you?' Schneider demanded.

'I was . . . I think I fell asleep.'

'You didn't hear the phone? I called five times.'

'I . . .'

'What's the matter with you?'

'Nothing. Are you going to let my mother go?'

'Yes, yes, soon, as I've said countless times. Did you get the third package?'

'Yes.'

'So you've got the nail?'

'It's here.'

'Then it's time. I have the photos of you with the thorn and the lance. Take the photo, the one with the nail and send it.'

'I will.'

'Then it will be time for the last steps.'

'I see.'

'Do you? Do you see? Do you remember exactly what I've asked of you?'

'I think so.'

'You think so? That isn't good enough, my friend. You must

do exactly as you've been instructed. For the final time, here are the steps. One: Place a table in front of the window and make sure the curtains are open. Two: Get the lance and place it on the table. Three: Get the thorn. Take it from the cardboard holder and place it so that it touches the tip of the lance. Finally: Get the nail. Place it on the table beside the lance. One end of the nail must touch the thorn, the other end must touch the lance. Then take the last photo of yourself with the relics in the foreground and the city of Jerusalem in the background. One last selfie.'

Giovanni was weak from blood loss.

'And text that photo to you also?'

'Yes,' Schneider said impatiently.

'Why the photos?' he asked groggily.

Schneider's voice was thick with anger.

'Now look,' he said, 'this has already been explained to you. The photographs are of immense value to us. Propaganda value. These are the holiest relics in the Christian world and my organization possesses them. We lacked the nail and now it is ours. We will make a tremendous announcement when we release the photos. It will be a political announcement of great importance to us. You will see and you will understand, but by then your work for us will be over. When you have taken the last photo, leave the phone in the room and go to the airport. Go home. Your family will be waiting for you. My people, the ones who have been watching you will collect the relics and the phone.'

Giovanni's voice was slurred. He felt sleepy. 'I still don't understand why you had to make me do this for you. If you have people here, they could have taken the pictures.'

'But they are not the famous priest with the stigmata of Christ. They are not Padre Gio. People will see you and it will strengthen our message. Now enough of this. It is time to finish your job. It is time for you to return home. Does your room phone have a speakerphone?'

'Yes.'

'Then put the phone onto the speaker and get the nail. Send me a photo of you holding it. I want to see it. Can you do that?'

'It's very painful.'

'Do it anyway.'

Schneider made sure that the priest had shifted to speaker mode then hit his own mute button. He turned to Gerhardt who was lounging on a nearby chair.

'What the hell is wrong with him?' Schneider asked.

'He's a strange one, didn't you notice?'

'It's more than that. He doesn't sound well.'

'At this point, a trained monkey can finish the job,' Gerhardt said. 'The idiot doesn't know that he's never going to take the last photo. A selfie! Good one, Lambret. As soon as the nail touches the other pieces – BOOM!' He spread his fingers in the universal sign of detonation.

'Hopefully, a very large boom,' Schneider said.

Schneider received a text of Giovanni holding up the nail with the Dome of the Rock clearly visible over his shoulder. He took the phone off mute.

'The photo is good. I can see you've been bleeding,' Schneider said.

'Yes, I've been bleeding a lot.'

'Well, you'll be able to get your health back soon, I think. Put the nail back where you were keeping it and go bring the lance to the table.'

He heard a weak voice say, 'I'm getting it.'

Cal argued with the security guards and the hotel manager, while he and Irene were taken down the elevator. When they reached the lobby he was still arguing.

'You're making a big mistake,' Cal said. 'This woman's brother is somewhere in the hotel and he's in danger. Your hotel is in danger. The entire city might be in danger.'

One of the guards pointed a finger at him and said, 'Mister, you're making terroristic threats and we don't tolerate this.'

The other guard asked the manager if she wanted them to call the police.

'It's not necessary,' she sighed. 'I just want them to go. We're getting their things from their rooms and then they can leave us. Some peace and quiet would be nice.'

A young man with a shaved head and skullcap appeared behind the reception desk and greeted the other clerk in Hebrew. 'Hello, Magda, how've you been?'

'Good, Ori, how was the army?'

'Like always. A boring weekend. What's going on here?'

'This guy and this lady have been causing a big disturbance. They're getting kicked out.'

'What's bugging them?'

'I've no idea.'

The clerk logged onto his terminal and while waiting for it to boot up his eye wandered to the piece of paper taped to the backstop of the counter. He pulled it off and headed for the door.

'Hey, where are you going?' Magda said.

He ignored her and went around to the lobby where he approached the manager.

'What?' she said. 'Can't you see I'm busy, Ori?'

Cal stopped arguing when he saw the clerk hold up their photo. Irene saw it too.

'Have you seen my brother, Giovanni Berardino?' she asked.

'I checked him in but he didn't go by that name,' the clerk said. 'It's Hugo Egger.'

Cal shouted, 'What room? What room is he in?'

The young man thought for a moment and said, 'Room 208 if he hasn't checked out already. I can look on the computer.'

But Cal and Irene weren't going to wait. They bolted toward the staircase, the security guards shouting for them to stop.

Gianni Crestani emerged from the shop holding four boxes of pizza. Two of Cecchi's ROS officers were on the street, one smoking, the other casually reading a newspaper.

'Hold back,' Cecchi said into their earpieces. 'Don't crowd him.'

Crestani moved fluidly down the sidewalk and was soon out of view of the van's cameras.

Cecchi sounded tense. 'Don't lose him.'

'We've got him, boss. Take it easy.'

'You're out of your mind,' Cecchi said to the technician beside him in the van. 'Taking it easy is the last thing I'm going to do.'

Cecchi couldn't seem to contain himself any longer. He exited the van, letting his street men know that he was coming up behind them.

One of the men spoke into his cufflink microphone, 'Should we mobilize the hostage rescue team, boss?'

'Feeling a bit insecure?' Cecchi replied some fifty paces away.

'When was the last time you fired your pistol?' the officer asked.

'Two months ago at the range, but I had a very nice grouping.'

The three ROS officers kept walking until the one closest to the target alerted the others that Crestani had put the pizza boxes down to open the door of a five-story apartment building, the one above an auto dealer.

'Get in there,' Cecchi ordered. 'Don't lose him but don't get made. We're coming.'

The lead officer saw Crestani disappear into the building. He let the others know and silently counted to ten before slipping inside as quietly as he could. The hallway was empty but he heard footsteps to his right, going up the staircase. He whispered his position into his cuff, pulled his gun from its paddle holster and pulled the slide back to chamber a round, holding the slide firmly as it went forward, to prevent a loud snapback.

He tiptoed up the stairs, straining to hear Crestani's footfalls. He continued for one more flight before hearing a door open and close.

'Third floor,' he whispered to the others. 'What's your position?'

'I'm in the building,' his colleague said. 'The boss is right behind me. Which apartment?'

'Stand by.'

The lead officer took the last flight of stairs two at a time and slowly opened the third-floor landing door. Peeking down the hall he saw Crestani entering one of the flats. He ducked back into the stairwell.

'Third door on the right, third floor.'

'Wait for us,' Cecchi said. 'We're almost there.'

He didn't have to wait long for his two comrades to arrive. Cecchi put his hand on his shoulder and asked in a whisper if he was ready.

'Ready, boss.'

'Then let's go.'

They crept up to the door and inspected it before backing away.

'You think you can kick it in?' Cecchi asked.

The lead officer whispered back, 'It's made of wood, I'm made of steel.'

Cecchi drew his Beretta and disengaged the safety.

He inhaled deeply and said, 'When you're ready, do it.'

The officer reared back and crashed his boot into the door jamb. The jamb held.

'Again!' Cecchi shouted. The officer replanted his feet and delivered another blow. This time wood splintered and the door crashed open.

'Armed police! Show yourself with your hands up!'

The two officers in the lead blocked Cecchi's view, but he heard the shouts.

A man, 'Gianni! The police!'

Another man, 'Grab the kid!'

A child, 'Mama!'

A woman, 'Take your hands off him!'

Then a gunshot, a deafening gunshot and the lead officer fell, clutching his chest.

The second officer fired off three quick rounds then he too staggered and slumped against a wall.

Crestani was five meters away down the hall. The thug was taking aim at him with a silver handgun and Cecchi felt the trigger of his Beretta yielding to the crook of his finger.

'Where is the lance? Talk to me, father,' Schneider said through the speakerphone.

Giovanni had it in his hand. 'I've got it,' he said weakly. The stabbing pain in the right side of his chest was once again making it hard to breathe.

'Louder, please, I can hardly hear you.'

'I've got it.'

'And what are you doing with it?'

'I'm putting it on the table.'

'It must touch the thorn.'

As the lance came closer to the thorn, Giovanni cried out. The lance fell from his hand and hit the table with a loud thud.

'What happened?' Schneider shouted.

'It burned my hand!' Giovanni said.

'Where is it? Where's the lance?'

'It's on the table. It's orange! The thorn is orange! The table is smoking!'

'Calm yourself, father. This is just some kind of chemical reaction. It's completely expected. Are they touching?'

'No.'

'You must make them touch.'

'I can't. It's too hot.'

'Then take your shoe and use it to push the lance until it touches. Do this now, please.'

'You'll release my family?'

'Any minute now, as long as you finish the job.'

'How will I know?'

'I will put your mother on the phone.'

'She's there?'

'Very close, yes. She is waiting for you to finish.'

Giovanni removed one of his shoes and poked at the orange-hot lance. The rubber sole of the shoe hissed and melted. He pushed some more until the tip made contact with the slender thorn.

In an instant, both relics turned from orange to red. Flames began to leap from the surface of the wooden table.

'There's a fire!' Giovanni shouted.

Schneider hit the mute button and said to Gerhardt, 'We should have thought of this. A glass or metal top would have been better.'

'He just needs to hurry, I think,' Gerhardt said matter-of-factly.

Off mute, Schneider said, 'You need to move quickly to get the photos before the room catches fire. We know for sure that the temperature will decrease when the nail will come in contact. Hurry! I have just told my people to prepare to release your mother, your aunt and your nephew.'

Giovanni was scared to touch the nail. He'd already lost so much blood. If he lost too much more, he'd pass out again or maybe worse. And the pain would be terrible.

He got a wash towel from the bathroom and used it to pluck the nail from the open hotel safe where he'd left it. His wrists began to throb more heavily, but at least the pain was tolerable.

He turned towards the window and began walking towards the wooden table just as a flame rose higher and caught a gauze curtain.

It would soon be over. He wanted to go home so badly, back to his family, back to his church in Monte Sulla, back to the life of a humble priest.

'Giovanni!'

It was coming from the hall.

It got louder. 'Giovanni!'

He recognized the voice.

'Irene?' he said softly.

The speakerphone came to life. Schneider sounded alarmed. 'What did you say? Is someone there?'

There was a pounding on his door.

'Giovanni! It's me, it's Irene! Open the door!'

Schneider heard the calls and seething, he pounced on the mute button. 'I thought you killed her!'

Gerhardt shrugged and said, 'I thought I did too. Maybe I should have checked the news from Munich.'

Schneider shot him a vicious glance and got back on the line shouting at the priest. 'Under no circumstances are you to open the door before you place the nail. Do you understand me?'

Cal was beside Irene at the door when the security guards and the manager caught up with them.

'Giovanni!' Cal shouted. 'This is Calvin Donovan. I'm here with your sister. Please let us know you're in there.'

They all heard it. Faintly, but they heard it. 'Yes, I'm here but I can't open the door.'

The security guards were about to pull Cal away when the manager told them to stop.

She sniffed and whispered, 'Smoke,' and hurriedly took out her passkey.

Cal was first in.

He stopped in the entry and drank in the scene through the smoky haze. Giovanni had one shoe on, one shoe off. Blood was streaming down his hands. He was holding the Holy Nail in a terry washcloth. There was a burning table near the window on the verge of collapse and on it was the Holy Lance.

A disembodied Germanic voice was calling out in English.

'Who's there? Tell me what's happening!'

Giovanni looked at Cal and then he looked at the speakerphone. Then he saw Irene and began to weep.

'Giovanni, we've found you,' she cried in Italian.

'Where's mama?' he asked in a daze.

Cal too spoke in Italian. 'The police are looking for her. She and your aunt and your nephew are going to be found.'

Schneider couldn't understand what they were saying but he seemed to grasp the situation. 'I'm the only one who knows where Giovanni's family is located. I'm the only one who can save them. I'm the only one who can kill them. Giovanni, finish the job and I will release them immediately.'

Cal took a step forward and when he did, Giovanni took a small step backwards towards the burning table.

Cal stopped dead and addressed him as calmly as he could. 'What do they want you to do?'

'I'm to place the nail so that it touches the lance and the thorn.'

Cal wheeled around and said to the manager and security guards, who were at the threshold of the room, and spoke quietly but urgently in English, 'Don't come in, there's a bomb. You need to evacuate the hotel.'

'My God,' the manager said, fleeing with the guards. Cal could hear her screaming in Hebrew into her walkie-talkie as she ran down the hall.

Schneider filled the brief silence. 'This is a lie. There's no bomb. Don't believe this rubbish, Giovanni. Finish the job and you can speak to your mother immediately. She's in the next room.'

'Can I speak to her now?' Giovanni asked.

'That is not possible. Finish it.'

Giovanni took another baby step toward the table and the nail began to glow. The terry cloth fibers of the towel began to smoke and singe.

'No, don't, Giovanni,' Irene said. 'Please don't.'

Schneider sounded desperate. 'Your nephew is here too. I am told he is a fine young boy. Federico is his name, I believe. He has a long, white neck. My man has a sharp knife against the skin. He will be a sacrificial lamb if you don't immediately finish.'

'Irene . . .' Giovanni said robotically moving closer to the table, his arm outstretched.

The nail was orange, the washcloth was smoking.

Irene's phone rang. She instinctively pulled it from her bag but she didn't look at, let alone answer it.

'Cut the boy's throat in ten seconds!' Schneider yelled. 'He's got ten seconds to live, Giovanni.'

The priest's hand hovered over the table, centimeters away from the lance and thorn. The cloth was flaming now and the pain made Giovanni's eyes water.

The phone was still ringing in her hand.

Cal yelled at her, 'Who is it, Irene? Maybe it's Cecchi.'

She looked at the caller ID and said, 'My God, yes,' but dropped it on the floor.

Cal dove for it and caught it on the last ring.

'It's Donovan,' he said.

'We've got them!' Cecchi said. 'They're safe.'

THIRTY-TWO

'Professor Donovan, how may I be of assistance?'

The long-bearded bishop, the Patriarch of Jerusalem, was dressed in a heavy black robe adorned with the chunky regalia of his station. He seemed supernaturally cool and collected inside his sweltering, humid office in the Armenian quarter of the city.

'Your Beatitude,' Cal said, 'I must thank you for granting me an audience on incredibly short notice.'

'I know of your work, professor,' he said in a thick Greek accent. 'I may even have some of your books in my library.'

Cal simply thanked him. One didn't engage in small talk with a laconic prelate like Nectarius II so he got to the point.

'The reason I'm here today is that I have something to donate to the Church, specifically to the Church of the Holy Sepulchre which you administer with the other custodians.'

'A monetary donation?'

'No, an object, Your Beatitude. A relic to be precise.'

A bushy gray eyebrow arched.

'What sort of a relic?'

'Objectively, I can characterize it as an important one, perhaps one of the most significant relics in Christianity. It's a relic with a clear provenance directly to Christ.'

'Are you speaking of a Holy Relic?'

'I am.'

'Do you have a photograph of this relic?'

'No, but you can see it with your own eyes.'

The patriarch, a man wholly unaccustomed to games, was clearly enjoying this one. He watched Cal don a pair of gloves and dip his hand into his bag. He held up the lance.

'The Holy Lance,' the prelate said. 'The Spear of Destiny. I have seen it with my own eyes when I visited Vienna. Surely this is a facsimile.'

Cal laid it on the desk. The patriarch couldn't peel his eyes away.

'The one in Vienna is a fake, commissioned by Heinrich Himmler. The Nazis kept the real one in a hiding place.'

'What hiding place?'

'That I don't know.' He'd already decided he wasn't going to talk about the potential destructive power of the relic or the cataclysmic plans of the Knights of Longinus. There was no need for that. 'But it recently surfaced,' Cal said. 'A neo-Nazi group was going to use it for propaganda purposes. I was involved with an effort to stop them and I'm pleased to say, we were successful.'

'I do not understand. Is the relic stolen?'

'The Nazis stole it from Austria. The Austrians stole it from the Germans in the eighteenth century. Ever since it was used on Calvary it was stolen over and over. I haven't had the time yet, but I'll be preparing a written document for you that will explain what I know about the provenance of the lance and how I came to possess it. Your Beatitude, I'm sure there will be controversy. If you choose to accept the relic, I'm sure there will be loud denials from the Austrian government concerning its authenticity, perhaps followed by demands for its return if they come to accept the truth. You will put forward counterclaims.

It will be a messy legal process but a worthy one, in my opinion. This is an immense treasure of Christianity and my colleagues and I believe it belongs in the traditional place of Christ's crucifixion and his tomb, the Church of the Holy Sepulchre.'

'May I examine it?' the patriarch asked.

'Of course. But you should use these gloves.'

'Why is that?'

'I'm told that holding it in one's bare hands can cause a certain discomfort.'

The patriarch ignored the warning, donning his spectacles and reaching across his desk. He cradled it in both hands and inspected one side, then the other.

Suddenly he gasped in pain. But then his face melted into a puddle of pleasure.

Cal decided to say nothing, but to bear silent witness.

The patriarch gently returned the lance to his desktop and slowly reached with his left hand to touch the right side of his chest. It was hard to see the wet spot against the blackness of his robe. He hesitantly looked at the tip of his pointer finger then held it up for Cal to see. It was red with blood.

'My dear God!' the patriarch said. 'This truly is the Holy Lance.'

When Cal returned to the Hotel Seven Arches, Giovanni was finishing the last of his many interviews with the police and the Italian ambassador was leaving for his office in Tel Aviv.

Armed with fire extinguishers, the hotel security guards had put out the small blaze in Giovanni's room. The hotel manager summoned the police but before they arrived, Cal and Irene had hastily prepared themselves for the inquiries that were bound to follow. Giovanni and his family had been victims of a plot, that much was evident. The explanation for why they'd been taken hostage was going to be tricky.

They quickly rejected the idea of handing the relics over to the police. The thorn was a moot point. It was so brittle from heat that it had disintegrated into dust when Giovanni tried to save it from the charred table. But the lance and the nail, if placed next to one another, were potentially dangerous and they had no desire to tell the authorities the truth. It would be like letting the genie out of the bottle. What if another Holy Thorn were found? There was more than one extremist group in the world that might try to finish what the Knights of Longinus had started.

Cal proposed an alternative fate for the relics and Irene and Giovanni endorsed the plan. As the authorities arrived, Irene was spiriting the nail and the lance, wrapped in bath towels, to her room.

Cal had insisted on being present during Giovanni's initial interview with the police, arguing that the young priest was in no shape to endure questioning on his own. He was bleeding and in shock – that much was clear – and while the medics were bandaging his wrists and giving him oxygen, Cal had answered the first wave of questions, spinning a tale on the fly and giving Giovanni a roadmap for subsequent statements.

Cal had presented himself as a consultant to the Vatican, commissioned to investigate the priest's stigmata. He had become friendly with the family and had volunteered to help find Giovanni when he'd been abducted. He had told the police inspectors that a neo-Nazi group had been responsible, kidnapping his family to pressurize him into acting as their agent. Cal had said that they were trying to force the revered stigmatic to detonate a suicide vest at a holy site in Jerusalem, as a high-profile act of provocation and terror aimed at Israel. When Cal saw the fire in the room, he had warned the hotel staff about a bomb without knowing if the vest had already been delivered. A man on the speakerphone had been giving orders. After the hotel staff had left the room to evacuate the building, Cal said that he heard the man telling Giovanni to go to the Via Dolorosa, where someone would pass him the vest and give him instructions where to set it off. When he'd accomplished his suicide mission, his family would be released.

Why had there been a room fire? Cal had furiously racked his brain for an explanation, then blurted out that he thought Giovanni might be silently trying to draw attention to get help. And from his bed, Giovanni, who had been listening carefully to Cal's inventions, had removed his oxygen mask and had said, yes, that was so.

*   *   *

On his return from seeing the patriarch, Cal found Giovanni in his new room on a different hotel floor. Irene was sitting at his bedside.

'How did it go?' she asked.

'Mission accomplished. The lance has a new home. Any problems with the police?'

'They asked the same questions many times,' Giovanni said weakly. 'I gave the answers you gave. The Italian ambassador was very nice and very helpful. He gave me a temporary passport in my real name. He was able to connect us to mama at the hospital in Rome where they took her with Carla and Federico. They're shaken but in good health. They witnessed bloodshed, I'm afraid. Two policemen were shot. One died. Both the men who held them were killed by the police.'

'Lieutenant Colonel Cecchi was the hero,' Irene said.

'I'm sending that guy a case of good wine,' Cal said.

'They wanted to take Giovanni to the hospital but he wouldn't go,' Irene said. 'I'm very cross at him. They say he needs a transfusion.'

'I'll go to the hospital after I see mama. I just want to go home.'

'I'll go see the manager, take care of the bill and book us on a flight to Rome,' Cal said. 'But we've got one more thing to do before we get on a plane.'

The sand was hot to their bare feet but the waves were dancing in the evening light and the water was beckoning. The three of them walked straight to the shoreline and into the surf. The beachgoers who saw them could only come to one conclusion as they moved from the promenade to the sea. The tall, well-built man was wearing swimming trunks and carrying a small metal box in his bandaged hand. The dark-haired woman in a T-shirt and shorts walked between the other two. The shorter, rotund young man was the least beach-ready with khaki trousers, a long-sleeved button-down shirt and baseball cap. His right hand too was heavily bandaged and he walked unsteadily, helped along by the woman. The inescapable impression was that this was some sort of family unit, or friends perhaps, on a somber mission to scatter a loved one's ashes into the sea.

With the water lapping their ankles they stopped and

contemplated the setting sun. Behind them was the city of Tel Aviv, modern and vibrant. From the promenade, the music of a dozen bars carried down to the water.

'It seems like a pity,' Irene said. 'Something so precious.'

'It's more than a pity,' Cal said, stripping off his polo shirt. 'The archaeologist in me is crying like a baby.'

Giovanni was the only one who didn't waver. 'It has to be done. When something good can become perverted into something so evil then the path is clear.'

'This will be our secret,' Cal said. 'There's not a single person beyond the three of us who needs to know about this.'

Cal was a strong, athletic swimmer, even with a box in one hand. He alternated between a side and breaststroke. Soon, Irene and Giovanni were but small figures on the shore, amidst waders, beach-tennis players, families and lovers. The sun got lower and redder and began to quench at the watery horizon. He stopped, treaded water and looked around to make sure he was the only one so far out. At first, he had an urge to gauge his distance from the shore and his relative position to the tallest buildings on the skyline, but then he stopped himself from attempting to triangulate. He would never try to come back to this spot.

He didn't engage in a special set of thoughts. He didn't say a prayer. He opened the hinged lid of the ten-shekel pencil box and tipped it upside down.

The Holy Nail, one of the two carpentry spikes the Romans had used to impale Christ's wrists to a wooden cross, splashed into the sea and began its plunge to the ocean floor, never to be seen again.

THIRTY-THREE

The papal gardens were in full summer bloom and the fragrant perfume of the linden trees filled Cal's nostrils. Under the watchful eyes of men from the Swiss guards and the Vatican Gendarmerie, Pope Celestine and Cal were taking in the sun, walking and talking.

'So that's what I know,' Cal said. 'Our contact at the Carabinieri tells me that the man, who was trying to get Giovanni to do this terrible thing, hasn't been identified. He was using a disposable phone.'

'A burner,' the pope said, his lips curling upwards. When Cal expressed surprise that he knew the expression, he replied, 'Even the pope watches Hollywood movies sometimes.'

'I hope the ringleader is found and found soon,' Cal said. 'I know first-hand that he and his men are ruthless killers.'

The pope's smile was gone. 'There is much evil in the world, so much evil,' he said shaking his head. 'We can only truly combat the forces of darkness with the forces of light. Faith, love and charity: these are our weapons.'

'What will happen with Giovanni?' Cal asked.

'Happen? He will continue on with his good work. We will let him remain with his flock in Monte Sulla. If more people wish to attend mass in his church than in my Basilica of Saint Peter then so be it. This does not upset me. I feel I can talk to God and that God can hear my prayers. But the connection between the Lord and Padre Gio, well, this is something truly special. You may invoke the mysteries of quantum mechanics. I invoke the mysteries of faith. Perhaps we are referring to the same phenomenon.'

'Perhaps we are.'

The pope stopped walking and turned to face Cal. 'Now professor, you have suffered and endured much in your quest to save this priest and to serve the Church. The pope would like to do something for you. Some token of our friendship and admiration.'

'There's really nothing I require,' Cal said. 'It's been my honor to have been at your service.'

'Please, there must be something.'

Cal thought for a moment and said, 'Well, there is something I would truly treasure.'

'Tell me, please.'

'I'd like to be able to do something that I don't believe has ever been granted to an outside academic. I'd like to have unrestricted access to browse the Vatican Library and the Vatican Secret Archives.'

'Consider it done, professor. I will issue a decree to the cardinal librarian and the cardinal archivist. I hope that as a result of this special privilege that you will come and visit us often. My door will always be open to you.'

'Thank you, Holy Father. I'm humbled and grateful.'

Their walk complete, the pope told Cal there was one more thing he wished to say.

'You know, professor,' he said with a twinkle in his eye, 'if you had offered the Holy Lance to the Vatican, we would likely have accepted it.'

Cal had only one more full day in Rome before his flight home, but he was too dog-tired to do anything that night but hang out in his hotel room and order dinner in. He'd heard from Irene that Giovanni was recovering in the hospital, fortified by blood transfusions and mama's food. If all went well, he'd be discharged in the morning and taken straight back to Monte Sulla to celebrate Sunday Mass. It would be a media circus but he was determined to get on with life as a parish priest.

Irene was staying with her mother, aunt and nephew in the Carabinieri flat on the Via Veneto. At noon, they'd be driven back to Francavilla but before they left, he'd see her for coffee. He was anxiously still trying to work out what he'd say. He wanted to see her again, he wanted her in his life but how was that going to work? And what did she want? He poured all three of the minibar vodkas into a glass and gulped them down. Within seconds the clear medicine took effect and he felt his anxieties melting away. He'd wing it with Irene in the morning. He was good at winging it with women.

There was a knock on the door and a muffled announcement of room service. He was sunk so low into his chair that he had to work to push himself free of it.

If he weren't tipsy, he might have thought more of the waiter's ill-fitting jacket, his tortured rendition of '*buonasera signore*' and his leaving the door ajar after he wheeled in the cart. And he might have reacted more aggressively when the waiter lifted the cloche to reveal not a plate of rigatoni, but a semi-automatic pistol quickly pointed at his chest.

Cal backed up a few paces, suddenly more attentive to the

waiter's face. It belonged to an older, distinguished man, a gentleman with an unmistakable air of privilege. The white service jacket was an absurdity, not just because of its fit but because this man didn't seem to have a servile bone in his body.

'Professor Donovan,' Schneider said. 'Finally.'

He recognized it as the disembodied Germanic voice from Jerusalem.

The room door opened and closed again.

Gerhardt he recognized from sight. The big blonde man, wearing the clothes of a hotel worker, was holding the same pistol and suppressor Cal had seen him wielding in Munich.

His sense of revulsion was overwhelming.

This was the man who had stripped and humiliated Irene.

This was the man who had left them to die by fire.

And this was the man who was probably going to kill him tonight with a bullet he wouldn't hear.

'Please don't move, Professor,' Schneider said.

Gerhardt took a few long strides to get behind Cal. Immediately he felt a sharp then a burning pain from the needle Gerhardt had stabbed into his buttock.

'Now you may sit,' Schneider said.

The effect of the injection was swift. Cal wobbled onto the sofa while Gerhardt adjusted the drapes. Schneider removed his white jacket and substituted it for a fine cashmere sports coat neatly folded in the warming tray of the food cart. He sat opposite Cal, casually resting his pistol on his lap.

Cal felt a need to try and count the wavy lines forming and dissolving in front of his face. When he lost count he started again. He tried to say the count out loud but if anything came out he couldn't hear it.

There was another cart in the room. He tried to stand up to announce that there was no need for all these carts, but he only managed to get halfway up. Gerhardt was there to prevent his body from striking the corner of the wrought iron coffee table. In one athletic move, the muscular fellow had Cal up on a big shoulder and tipped into a hotel laundry cart.

THIRTY-FOUR

He figured it out quickly enough.

Whatever had been in the syringe had worn off. He was no longer in his hotel room. He swiveled his neck from side to side getting the lay of the land. This was a private home. He was in a large bedroom with modern paintings on the wall. A plug-in security camera was pointed at him from a chest of drawers.

Cal was expecting to find himself tethered to the bed but surprisingly he wasn't. He put his feet down and tentatively took a few steps, but his head felt like a water balloon stretched to the breaking point. He sat back down and tried to find an effective place to rub away his throbbing headache.

Two sets of footsteps were coming up the stairs. Apparently he'd been the video entertainment for the Germans.

'Where are we?' Cal asked Schneider.

'Not so far from the city center. A quiet villa on the Via Appia Antica.'

'Nice place to live. Yours?'

'It belongs to a colleague.'

'Also a nice place to die,' Gerhardt said, playfully waving his gun. 'We're not far from the catacombs.'

'So why am I still alive?'

Schneider pulled up a chair.

'This doesn't require a lot of fuss and it doesn't require a long, drawn out interrogation,' he said. 'You will tell us what we need to know and there will be no pain. If you refuse, there will be unbelievable pain and then it will still come to the same conclusion. And this is quite important for you to know; if you give us bad information we will interrogate and we will hurt Irene Berardino and Giovanni Berardino. One or both of them will probably tell us what we need to know before they are killed. Today, the police are watching them. Tomorrow they will no longer be under protection. Do you understand your situation?'

Cal nodded. He understood perfectly.

'Good. You already know what I am going to ask. Tell me what happened to the relics. They belong to us and we want them back.'

Cal massaged his eyes. A wave of nausea rippled his gut. *Typical*, he thought. *I'm going to die with a hangover.*

'What's the plan?' Cal asked. 'You want to have another crack at Israel?'

Schneider sighed. 'Curious to the last. The mark of an academic. We followed your curious wanderings around Italy and Germany to see what you'd find about our mutual interests. You did well. Too well. We tried to kill you twice. The third time won't be lucky. So, it will be Israel or New York or Los Angeles or any place with a large number of Jews. We'll finish what Hitler started and take it from there.'

'Teutonic knights, riding into the sunset.'

'No. The sunrise. Dawn of a new day and all that. Now come, I'm not here to talk about the past or the future. Only the present should concern us. Where are the relics?'

Cal was thinking fast about how he was going to play this out. At this stunningly depressing moment all he really cared about was protecting Irene. His story had to be convincing and the best way to persuade someone of the truth was to tell the truth. Mostly.

'The thorn was burned to ash. We tried to pick it up but it was dust.'

'Pity,' Schneider said.

'You believe him?' Gerhardt said.

Schneider shrugged. 'So far, yes. The other relics?'

'They're at the bottom of the deep blue sea.'

That elicited a deep frown from the older man. 'Oh yes? How did this happen?'

'We went to Tel Aviv the next day. I rented a jet ski and went out a long way into the Mediterranean. First I tossed the lance, then I rode some more and I tossed the nail. No landmarks, no GPS coordinates. I couldn't find them if my life depended on it, which I guess it does.'

'And why did you do this?'

'Didn't want you assholes or any assholes in the future to blow up Jews, or Christians, or Muslims, or people of any stripes. It didn't take a lot of thought.'

'An historian who destroys precious historical artifacts,' Schneider said, standing up. 'How very disappointing.'

'You're just going to accept what he says?' Gerhardt asked. 'Let me ask him my way.'

'I think he's telling the truth. In any event he is unlikely to change his story, even with your methods. When we have the girl and the priest, we will see if they tell the same story. Then we'll know for sure.'

Cal stood too, prompting Gerhardt to raise his gun and slide in between Schneider and the professor.

'I've told you everything,' Cal said, his voice rising and his head pounding. 'Leave them alone.'

'It's no longer your concern,' Schneider said. 'Give me the gun, Gerhardt.'

'Why?' the big man asked.

'Despite a long and interesting life, there's something I've never done. I've never killed a man. I think this would be a good time to rectify this. Is the safety off?'

'Yes.'

'Give it to me.'

The handoff between the two men took no more than two seconds and in that time, Cal made one last desperate attempt to stay alive.

As Schneider was raising the gun to waist level, Cal threw himself forward, chopping at his gun arm with his left hand and swinging his right fist into Schneider's forehead.

Before Gerhardt landed the first blow to his midsection, Cal heard three sounds in rapid succession: Schneider's low grunt as the man tumbled to the floor, the clattering of the gun against the tiles and the low, pneumatic percussion of a silenced round discharged into a wall.

Gerhardt was an enraged bull, pounding Cal with heavy fists and jackhammer knees. Cal tried to fight back but his fists seemed to be hitting concrete. Nothing he could do was slowing down the hailstorm of blows.

The big man also did some kicking and Cal got hammered with a boot to the abdomen that sent him falling backwards against the dresser. He hit it hard and fell to his knees. There was something horribly vulnerable being doubled over like this.

Gerhardt was closing the short distance and if Cal stayed down he was going to get kicked in the head and that would be it. Reaching for something, his hand caught against the handle of a dresser drawer. He tried to pull himself up but he pitched forward, the drawer flying out of the dresser, scattering matronly underwear around the room.

Gerhardt stood over him measuring him for an incapacitating blow. Maybe a boot slammed down on his neck or maybe a two-handed ax-chop to the back of his head.

The ax it was.

Gerhardt started to lower the boom like an executioner, when Cal blindly swung the drawer by its handle with every last bit of his strength.

There was a crunching sound of wood or skull or both.

Gerhardt was on the floor next to him surrounded by pieces of wood. He was still moving. His arms and legs were pushing against the ground, attempting to right his big, toppled body.

Cal was on all fours. His hand was empty. He wanted to stand and he used the dresser like a ladder to get to his feet. There was a crystal lamp on the dresser, a fancy, feminine fixture, lying on its side next to fallen picture frames and shattered glass. The lamp found its way into Cal's hands and when he lifted it over his head, the cord unplugged itself and the lamp went dark.

He heard himself shouting, 'You're not going to hurt her again, you're not going to hurt her again,' and he saw blood, so much blood. The crystal lamp buried itself over and over inside Gerhardt's skull.

Schneider moaned and woke to see a battered, mangled head.

At first he seemed to smile, thinking perhaps that it was Donovan's, but the truth hit him and he began to wail, 'Gerhardt! No!'

Cal was panting for breath. The room was a slowly spinning top.

Both men saw Gerhardt's pistol at the same time but Cal made the first move.

He lunged for it, felt the rough grip in his fist and wheeled around, looking for his target.

Schneider was lurching down the hall, his shoulders hitting one wall, then the other until there was a door in front of him.

Another bedroom.

He closed the door behind him and locked it.

Cal followed, raging at him, screaming, 'You're not going to hurt her again, you bastard!'

Schneider frantically searched the desk, then the nightstands to the left then the right of his bed. He'd been told it was there, in case he ever needed it. There he found a small revolver, its cylinder full. Cal was putting his shoulder to the bedroom door.

Schneider ran into the bathroom, locked that door too and faced the mirror over the sink.

He was a little boy again.

He was his father.

He was himself.

He stared at his reflection. 'Don't look away!' he screamed as the gun pressed to his temple went off, showering his brains against the pretty wallpaper.

THIRTY-FIVE

'No, I insist,' Cal told Irene over the phone. 'I'm doing well. They're discharging me this afternoon. You need to stay with your mother. I'm pushing off my flight. I'll come to you in Francavilla. You just have to promise one thing.'

'Yes?'

'That you won't make fun of my face. It looks remarkably like an aubergine.'

He was at a private clinic in Rome, under the care of the pope's personal physician, but he hadn't required much in the way of treatment. He was bruised and battered, but there were no broken bones beyond a hairline fracture to a couple of ribs. But he was sick of hospitals and wanted out. He'd been a patient three times this summer, three more times than the past thirty years combined.

His physician came by after lunch and did a final cursory exam before declaring him fit to travel with a rib binder.

'You don't know Umberto Tellini, do you?' Cal asked the doctor.

'Of course. Everyone knows Tellini.'

'Do you know if he's on duty today? I'd like to say goodbye.'

'In fact, I'm sure he is not at the clinic. I'm personally covering his patients. He's taken the day off.'

'When you see him, tell him I'm sorry I missed him.'

'It was good of you to come and visit me,' Giovanni said.

He was in the garden of his parish house in Monte Sulla, taking in the sunshine and using the quietness of the afternoon to think, meditate and, most of all, pray.

'What kind of a doctor would I be, if I didn't come to check on my most esteemed patient?' Tellini said. He was carrying a small medical bag.

'I didn't know I was your patient,' Giovanni said, looking up from his bench. He caught himself. 'I'm sorry. That was rude.'

'Don't apologize. The Vatican is concerned about your health. I will personally communicate with the pope when I return to Rome.'

'I'm feeling stronger. The bleeding has stopped, you know.'

'Has it?'

'Ever since the nail was . . .'

Tellini took a few steps forward, looming over the priest. 'Was what?'

'Lost.'

'Lost where?'

'I couldn't say. You'd have to speak with Professor Donovan about that.'

'But here I am, speaking to you.'

Giovanni didn't like the new, hard edge to Tellini's voice.

'As I've said, doctor, thank you for coming to visit. Please tell the pope I am well. I'm afraid I must resume my prayers now.'

Tellini's face changed from solicitous to menacing. 'Where is it?' he said.

Giovanni stood. 'You must go now.'

'Tell me.'

'I will have to call out if you don't leave.'

A knife appeared in Tellini's fist. 'For the last time, will you tell me where we can find the nail?'

'We?' Giovanni asked.

'This is bigger than one man. I've lost compatriots. Killed in my own house. It doesn't matter. We endure. And we must have it.'

Giovanni sighed heavily. 'I believe that men like you must never possess it. And you won't. You must believe me. The nail will never be found. It's but a sliver of iron at the bottom of a vast and deep ocean.'

The doctor let out a shuddering sigh and raised his hand. 'Then there's this.'

The sun glinted off the polished steel as Tellini thrust the knife fast and deep into the priest's chest.

Cal knew he'd be making a detour well before he saw the sign for Monte Sulla. He was in Abruzzo, on his way to see Irene in Francavilla, when an overwhelming feeling of serenity washed through him and with it came the urge to say a final goodbye to Giovanni.

In Francavilla, Irene had been food shopping for her mother, when she too was struck by a sense of tremendous peacefulness that made her feel light and airy.

Pulling into the high, medieval town, Cal parked his hire car in the piazza of the Church of Sante Croce. The last time he'd been there, Padre Gio had been celebrating mass and it had been a madhouse. He had no doubt that Sunday would be a riotous occasion, the first Sunday since their priest rejoined his church. But today, all was quiet.

He knocked on the door to Giovanni's parish house and was greeted by both the nuns, Sister Vera and Sister Theresa. They were wearing aprons powdered with baking flour and both seemed happy.

'Professor Donovan,' Sister Vera said. 'I don't think we were expecting you but you must stay for supper. Padre Gio will be so pleased to see you. He told us how you saved him and his family.'

'I hope I won't be disturbing him.'

'Oh no,' Sister Theresa said. 'He's in the garden praying. You missed the doctor by the better part of an hour. He said he couldn't stay for supper.'

'Which doctor?'

'Dr Tellini. He came by to see how Padre Gio was doing.'

Cal went through the lounge to the back garden.

At first he didn't see anything, but then his eye fell upon a stone bench and a dark shape on the ground behind it.

'Oh Jesus.'

He walked to the bench slowly, trying to postpone the inevitable for a few moments.

Giovanni, dressed in clerical black, was splayed out upon the green grass, his body forming a cross.

Four shiny steel spikes pinned his wrists and his ankles to the turf. A knife, its handle wet with blood, was sticking out of the right side of his chest.

But Cal didn't want to look at the pieces of steel piercing his body.

He wanted to look at his face, an open-eyed face, seemingly searching the sky, fixed into an expression of pure, unadulterated joy.

At the mouth of the Tiber at Ostia, where the great river empties into the Tyrrhenian Sea, two boys were fishing. The waters were murky brown, a swirling torrent and the boys were frustrated that their buckets were still empty.

In Berlin on the Potsdamer Platz, the German Federal Police were drilling open Lambret Schneider's office safe, discovering a small leather-bound notebook containing the particulars of all the men who called themselves the Knights of Longinus.

At the chapel of the Domus Sanctae Marthae, Pope Celestine was celebrating morning mass with his household staff and wiping away bitter tears as he dedicated his homily toward the memory of Padre Gio, a young priest who was touched by God and taken too soon.

On the Viale Nettuno in Francavilla, the trunk of his hire car open, Cal was holding Irene and letting her cry her eyes out into his shoulder. He knew at that moment they would never see each other again for Cal would always remind her of the saddest time in her life.

'I could stay a few more days.'

She shook her head and looked away. A tear slowly made its way down her cheek.

'Two people who've been through so much together are never going to be separated,' he said.

'Quantum entanglement?' she said.

'Yeah. Quantum entanglement.'

And on the riverbank one boy turned to the other and said,

'One more cast. I'm getting hungry.'

'No, three more.'

'All right, three more,' the first one said.

He cast his lure low and long, one of the best of the day and began jigging the lure back to the shore.

Disappointment set in when the line was almost reeled all the way in but then he hit a resistance, a big one, and he jerked his rod up to set the hook.

'Reel harder! Harder!' the other boy cried.

'It's huge, it's a monster,' the first boy said straining with exertion.

Something huge indeed broke the water but it was no fish.

First there was a bare arm with black ink. Black as night. The tattoo of the Holy Lance with SS lightning bolts.

Then the rest of him, a shirtless man with a plastic identification badge looped around his neck.

The badge read: *Agostino Gemelli University Polyclinic, Dr U. Tellini.*